For Love or Money

Born in Preston, Lancashire, **Penny Jordan** now lives with her husband in a beautiful fourteenth-century home in rural Cheshire, England. Hers is a success almost as breathtaking as the exploits of the characters she so skillfully and knowingly portrays. Penny has over seventy-five novels published, including the *New York Times* bestseller *Power Play*. With over fifty million copies of her books in print and translations in nineteen languages, she is a leading author of extraordinary scope.

PENNY JORDAN

JORDAN

For Love or Money

SANDRA MARTON

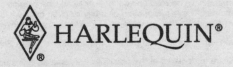

HARLEQUIN®

TORONTO • NEW YORK • LONDON
AMSTERDAM • PARIS • SYDNEY • HAMBURG
STOCKHOLM • ATHENS • TOKYO • MILAN • MADRID
PRAGUE • WARSAW • BUDAPEST • AUCKLAND

FOR LOVE OR MONEY

Copyright © 2003 by Harlequin Books S.A.

ISBN 0-373-83560-4

The publisher acknowledges the copyright holders of the individual works as follows:

UNWANTED WEDDING
Copyright © 1996 by Penny Jordan

THE BORGHESE BRIDE
Copyright © 2003 by Sandra Myles

CONTENTS

UNWANTED WEDDING

Penny Jordan

CHAPTER ONE

'GUARD, will you marry me?'

Rosy paced the floor of her bedroom, a fixed, strained expression on her face, her hands gripped into two small fists at her side and her normally clear, guileless dark blue eyes shadowed as she repeated the same four words over and over again under her breath. Even now she still wasn't sure she was actually going to be able to say them out loud.

'Will you marry me? Will you marry me? Will you marry me? Will you marry me?' There, she *had* said it and, even if the words hadn't sounded quite as firm and assured as she would have liked, at least they had been spoken. She was over the first hurdle, she told herself bravely, and if she could manage that one, then she could surely manage the other.

She swallowed hard and looked at the telephone beside her bed. There was no point in shilly-shallying; she might as well get the whole thing over and done with.

But not up here. Not sitting here on her bed in the privacy of her bedroom while she...

Quickly, she averted her eyes from the pretty girlishness of her flower-sprigged bedcover, virginal white with a scattering of flower posies. She had been fourteen the year she had chosen it; she was almost twenty-two now.

Twenty-two, but as naïve and unworldly as a girl still—or so she had been told.

Her throat closed nervously. She didn't need to remind herself exactly who it was who had said those words to her.

Quickly, she opened her bedroom door and hurried downstairs. She would use the phone in the room which had been her father's study and, before that, her grandfather's. To say those words in that room would be appropriate somehow, would lend them weight and dignity.

She picked up the receiver and punched in the numbers jerkily, her body tensing as she heard the ringing tone.

'Guard Jamieson, please,' she told the girl on the other end of the line. 'It's Rosy Wyndham.'

As she waited to be connected to Guard she nibbled nervously at her bottom lip—a childhood habit she had thought she had outgrown.

'Only children do that,' Guard had warned her the year she was eighteen. 'Women...'

He had paused then and looked at her mockingly, causing her to ask him unthinkingly, 'Women do what?'

'Don't you really know?' he had quizzed her mockingly. 'Women, my dear, innocent Rosy, only carry these kind of scars—' he had leaned forward then and slowly run the tip of his finger along her swollen bottom lip, with its two small tooth indentations, pausing to touch them in such a way that the sharp *frisson* of sensation that had run through her had actually become an open physical convulsion of her whole body '—when they've been left there by a lover... A very ardent lover...'

Of course he had laughed at the scorching colour that had stained her skin. Guard was like that. In the old days he would have been a freebooter, a pirate—a man who cared for no one and made his own laws, his own rules, so her grandfather had always claimed. Her grandfather, although he would never admit it, had always had something of a soft spot for Guard, Rosy suspected.

'Rosy, what is it? What's wrong?'

The sound of his voice reverberating roughly in her ear caused her to tighten her grip on the receiver as her body rebelled against the knowledge of how unsettling she still sometimes found him—even though, with maturity, she had learned to ignore the taunting, loaded comments with which he still sometimes liked to torment her.

He wasn't like that with other women; with other women he was all sensual charm and warmth, but then, of course, he didn't see her as a woman, only as—

'Rosy are you still there?'

The irritation in his voice jerked her back to reality.

She took a deep breath. 'Yes, I'm still here, Guard... Guard, there's something I want to ask you. I...'

'I can't talk now, Rosy. I've got an important call waiting. Look, I'll call round tonight and we can discuss whatever it is then.'

'No.' Rosy started to panic. What she had to ask him was something it would be far easier for her to say at a safe distance; she thought of asking him to marry her, of proposing to him face to face— She gave a small, worried gulp, but Guard had already replaced the receiver and it was too late for her to tell him now that she didn't want to see him.

As she replaced her own receiver she stared sadly around the room.

Four hundred years of history were encapsulated in this room, this house. It had stood here since Elizabeth

I had bestowed the land on Piers Wyndham, a gift, so the official story ran, for courtly services; a gift, so the unofficial one went, for something far more personal and intimate.

Piers had called the house he had built Queen's Meadow, in acknowledgement of Elizabeth's generosity. It wasn't a very grand house, nor even a generously large one, but in Rosy's view it was certainly far too extravagantly large for one person or even one family—especially when she knew from her work at the shelter how many people were homeless and in desperate need of a roof over their heads.

'So what would you do, given free choice?' Guard had taunted her the last time she had raised the subject. 'Turn the place over to them? Watch them tear out the panelling and use it for firewood; watch them…?'

'That's unfair,' she had protested angrily. 'You're being unfair…'

But even Ralph, who was in charge of the shelter, had commented on more than one occasion that she wasn't streetwise enough; that she was too soft-hearted, too idealistic, her expectations and beliefs in others far too high. She suspected that Ralph was inclined to despise her, and at first he had certainly been antagonistic towards her, deriding her background and her accent, condemning her comparative wealth and lifestyle and comparing it to those of the people who used the shelter.

'Makes you feel better, does it,' he had jeered, 'spending your time doing good works?'

'No, it doesn't,' Rosy had told him honestly. 'But my money—my wealth, as you call it—is in trust and I can't touch the capital even if I wanted to. If I found a "proper" job, paid work, I'd be taking that job away from someone who needs to earn their living.'

She and Ralph got on much better these days, although he and Guard loathed one another. Or rather Ralph loathed Guard; Guard wasn't human enough to allow himself to feel that kind of emotion about anyone. In fact, she sometimes doubted that Guard had ever felt a human emotion in his entire life.

She knew how much Ralph resented having to go cap in hand to Guard for money towards running the shelter, but Guard was the wealthiest man in the area, his business the most profitable.

'He's a very rare combination,' her father had once told her. 'An entrepreneur—successfully so—and an honest man as well, highly principled.'

'An arrogant bastard,' was what Ralph called him.

'Sexy,' was what one of Rosy's old school-friends had breathed enthusiastically when she had come down to pay Rosy a visit. Married, and bored with her husband already, apparently, she had eyed Guard with an open, hungry greed that Rosy had found not just embarrassing, but somehow humiliating as well. It was as though Sara, with the hot, burning looks she was constantly throwing Guard's way, the none-too-subtle hints and sexual innuendoes, the physical contact of deliberately contrived touches, was somehow underlining her own sexual immaturity, and reinforcing all the taunts that Guard had ever made about her.

She was well aware that Guard thought her naïve and unawakened—but so what? All right, so his comments and taunts might fluster and sometimes even hurt her, but she had made a vow to herself a long time ago that she was not going to rush into a sexual relationship before she was ready for it; that she was not going to experiment with sex for sex's sake; that when she finally explored the world of her own sexuality it would be with a partner who felt as she did, a man who loved her and who was not ashamed to acknowledge that fact and with whom she could let down her guard and reveal the vulnerable, romantic, loving side of her nature.

So far she had not met that man, but when she did, she would know him, and she was not, after all, in any hurry. She was only twenty-one. Twenty-one and still a virgin. Twenty-one and about to propose marriage to Guard, who was most definitely not anything of the kind and who—

She glanced at her watch. Four o'clock. She knew that Guard often didn't leave his office until well after everyone else had gone, which meant it could be seven o'clock or even eight before he came round. All those hours to wait. All those hours nerving herself to deliver her proposal.

What would he say? Laugh himself silly, no doubt. Her face burned hotly with chagrin at the thought.

It was all her solicitor's fault, she decided crossly. If Peter hadn't suggested—

She walked over to the window, remembering Peter's last words to her before he left: 'Promise me that you'll at least ask him, Rosy.'

'Sacrifice myself to save this place? Why should I?' she had demanded angrily. 'It isn't even as though I *want* the house. You know how I feel...'

'You know what will happen if Edward inherits it,' Peter had countered. 'He'll destroy this place simply for the pleasure it will give him.'

'And to get back at Gramps. Yes, I know that,' Rosy had agreed.

Edward was her father's cousin; he and her grandfather had quarrelled long before Rosy was born—a bad quarrel over money and morals which had resulted in her grandfather's banning Edward from ever setting foot inside the house again.

Every family had its black sheep; theirs was no exception. Even now, in middle age, despite his outward air of respectability, his marriage and his two sons at prep school, there was something unpleasant about Edward.

He might never have actually broken the law in his financial dealings, but he had certainly crossed over the line under cover of darkness on one or more occasions, her father had often stated.

Her father.

Rosy turned her attention away from the window and looked towards the desk. Her father's photograph was still on it. The one he had had taken in uniform shortly before his older brother's death.

He had left the army then and come home to be with his father—he had been no stranger to death himself since the death of Rosy's mother.

Queen's Meadow had meant everything to them, her father and her grandfather. She loved the house, of course—who could not do?—but she felt no sense of possessiveness towards it, far from it.

It wasn't pride she felt as she walked through its rooms, but guilt.

If only things had been different. If only Edward had been different, she could have so happily and easily have walked away from here and bought or rented herself a small place in town and given all her time and attention to working at the shelter.

But how could she do that now?

'Edward will destroy this place,' Peter had warned her. 'He'll tear the heart out of it, sell off everything that's worth selling, and then he'll tear it down brick by brick and sell off the land to one of his cronies who'll—'

'No, he can't do that,' she had protested. 'The house is listed and—'

'And, knowing Edward, he won't find it at all difficult to find someone who's willing to claim that they misunderstood the instructions they were given. Just how long do you think this place could stay standing once it was assaulted by half a dozen determined men with bulldozers? And of course Edward would make sure that nothing could be connected with him. He hated your grandfather, Rosy, and he knew how much Queen's Meadow meant to him and to your father.'

'Too much,' Rosy had sighed. 'No, this place is an anachronism, Peter. No matter how beautiful it is, for one family to live in a house this size... Oh, why couldn't Gramps have listened to me and deeded it to a charity? Why couldn't he?'

'So you don't care what happens to the house? You don't mind Edward inheriting it and destroying it, destroying four hundred years of history?'

'Of course I mind,' Rosy told him fretfully. 'But what can I do? You know the terms of that idiotic will Gramps made as well as I do. In the event of both his sons predeceasing him, the house and his estate go to the closest of his blood relatives to be married within three months of his death and capable of producing an heir. He made that will years ago after Uncle Tom died, and if Dad hadn't—'

She had broken off then, her throat choked with tears. Her father's death so unexpectedly from a heart attack just weeks before her grandfather had slid from a coma and into death was something she still hadn't fully come to terms with.

'Edward fulfils all the terms of that will and he—'

'*You* are your grandfather's closest blood relative,' Peter had reminded her quietly.

'Yes, but I'm not married. And not likely to be, at least not within the next three months,' Rosy had told him drily.

'You could be,' Peter had told her slowly, 'with an arranged marriage. A marriage entered into specifically so that you could fulfil the terms of your grandfather's will. A marriage which could be brought to an end very easily and quickly.'

'An arranged marriage?' Rosy had stared blankly at him. It sounded like something out of one of her favourite Georgette Heyer novels; fine as the theme for a piece of romantic froth, but totally implausible in reality.

'No,' she had told him impatiently, shaking her head so hard that her dark curls had bounced against her shoulders. Irritably she had pushed them off her face. Her hair was the bane of her life—thick, so dark it was almost black, and possessing of a life of its own.

A little gypsy, her grandfather had often fondly called her. But whenever she had tried to have her wild mane tamed, it had rebelled, and reverted to its tumbling mass of curls almost as soon as she had closed the hairdresser's door behind her, so that eventually she had given up trying to control it.

'It's out of the question and, besides, it takes two to make a marriage—even an arranged one—and I can't think of anyone who—'

'I can.' Peter had anticipated her quietly.

Was she imagining it, or did his words have a slightly ominous ring to them? She paused, shifting her gaze from the Grinling Gibbons carving on the staircase to her solicitor's face, eyeing him suspiciously.

'Who?' she demanded warily.

'Guard Jamieson,' Peter told her. Rosy sat down abruptly on the stairs.

'Oh, no,' she announced firmly. 'No, no, never.'

'He would be the ideal person,' Peter continued enthusiastically, as though she hadn't spoken. 'After all, he's never made any secret of how much he wants this place.'

'Never,' Rosy agreed drily, remembering how often Guard had bombarded her grandfather with requests—demands, almost—that he sell Queen's Meadow to him. 'If Guard wants the house that badly, he can always try to persuade Edward to sell it to him,' she pointed out.

Peter's eyebrows rose. 'Come on, Rosy. You know that Edward hates Guard almost as much as he did your grandfather.'

Rosy sighed.

'Yes,' she agreed. It was true. Guard and Edward were old business adversaries and, as her father had stated on more than one occasion, there hadn't been a confrontation between the two men yet out of which Guard had not come the winner. 'The mere fact that he knows how much Guard loves this place would only add to his pleasure in destroying it.'

'We're only talking about a business arrangement between the two of you, you know, some simple basic formalities which would enable you to fulfil the terms of the will. In time the marriage could be dissolved. You could sell the house to Guard and—'

'In time? How much time?' she had asked him suspiciously.

'A year—a couple of years...' Peter had shrugged, ignoring her dismayed gasp. 'After all, it isn't as though you want to marry someone else, is it? If you did, there wouldn't be any problem, any need to involve Guard.'

'I can't do it,' she told Peter positively. 'The whole idea is completely ridiculous, repulsive.'

'Well, then, I'm afraid you'll have to resign yourself to the fact that Edward will inherit. Your grandfather's already been dead for almost a month.'

'I can't do it,' Rosy repeated, ignoring Peter's comment. 'I could never ask *any* man to marry me, but especially not Guard...'

Peter had laughed at her.

'It's a business proposal, that's all. Think about it, Rosy. I know how ambivalent your feelings towards Queen's Meadow are, but I can't believe that you actually want to see Edward destroy it.'

'No, of course I don't,' Rosy had agreed.

'Then what have you got to lose?'

'My freedom?' she had suggested hollowly.

Peter had laughed again. 'Oh, I doubt that Guard would interfere with that,' he had assured her. 'He's much too busy to have time to worry about what you'll be doing. Promise me that you'll at least think about it, Rosy. It's for your sake that I'm doing this,' he had added. 'If you let Edward destroy this place, you're bound to feel guilty.'

'The way you do for putting all this moral blackmail on me?' Rosy had asked him drily.

He had had the grace to look slightly uncomfortable.

'All right, I'll think about it,' she had agreed.

And ultimately she had done more than just think about it, Rosy acknowledged, as she dragged her thoughts back to the present.

'The trouble with you is that you're far too soft-hearted.' How often had she heard that accusation over the years?

Too often.

But Peter was right. She couldn't let Edward destroy Queen's Meadow without at least making some attempt to save it. By sacrificing herself. A wicked smile curled her mouth, her eyes suddenly dancing with bright humour. Oh, how chagrined Guard would be if he could read her mind. How many women were there who would look upon marriage to him in that light? Not many. Not *any*, she admitted, at least not from what she heard.

Well, all right, so she was peculiar—an oddity who for some reason could not see anything attractive in that magnetic sexuality of his which seemed to obsess virtually every other female who set eyes on him. So she was immune to whatever it was about him that made other women go weak at the knees, their eyes glazing with awe as they started babbling about his sexy looks, his smouldering eyes, his mouth and its full, sensual bottom lip, his shoulders, his body, his awesome charismatic personality, his single state and the subtle aura not just of sexual experience, but of sexual expertise which clung to him like perfume to a woman's body.

Oddly, the last thing that most of them mentioned about him was his wealth.

Well, she could see nothing remotely sexually attractive about him, Rosy decided crossly, and she never had. As far as she was concerned, he was an arrogant, sarcastic pig who enjoyed nothing more than making fun of her.

Only last month at a dinner party, when the hostess had been remarking to her that the male cousin she had had visiting her had begged her to seat him next to Rosy at dinner, Guard, who had overheard their hostess's remark, had leaned over and said sardonically, 'Well, if he's hoping to find a woman somewhere under that mass of hair and that very unflattering outfit you're wearing, Rosy, he's going to be very disappointed, isn't he?'

Since the 'unflattering outfit' he referred to had been a very carefully chosen collection of several different layers of softly toning shades of grey, all determinedly hunted down in a variety of charity shops, carried home triumphantly and repaired and laundered, Rosy had shot him an extremely bitter look.

'Not all men judge a woman on how she performs in bed, Guard,' she had told him through gritted teeth.

'Luckily for you,' he had responded, not in the least bit fazed by her retaliation. 'Because, according to all the gossip, you wouldn't have the faintest idea what to do there.'

She had flushed, of course, the hot colour crawling betrayingly over her skin, not so much because of what he had said—after all, she was not ashamed of the fact that she was not prepared to jump into bed with every man who asked her—but because of the way Guard was watching her, because of the amusement and mockery in his eyes, because, oh, so shamingly and appallingly, just for a second, she could actually almost *see* him in bed with some anonymous woman, his body bare and brown, his hands stroking the woman's paler, softer skin while she clung to him with small, pleading sounds of need...

She had blinked away the vision immediately, of course, telling herself that it must have had something to do with the sexy film she and a friend had been discussing earlier in the day.

She and Guard had continued their argument later in the evening, just before Guard had left with the extremely glamorous and elegant-looking blonde who was accompanying him.

'Anyway,' Rosy had told him, her small chin jutting out defiantly as she felt herself losing ground, 'it makes sense these days *not* to have too many sexual partners.'

'The present climate is certainly a convenient hedge to hide behind,' Guard had agreed suavely. 'Especially when...'

'Especially when what?' Rosy had challenged him.

'Especially for you,' he had told her blandly.

The return of his companion had prevented Rosy from saying anything else.

An arranged marriage with Guard. She *must* have been mad to let Peter talk her into such a crazy idea. But he *had* talked her into it and she couldn't back out now. Did Guard want Queen's Meadow enough to agree? Half of her hoped not. And the other half...

'All right, Rosy, what's this all about? And if you're after another donation to that charity of yours, I'm warning you that right now I'm not feeling in the most generous of moods...'

Dumbly Rosy watched Guard walk into the hall. Her heart was beating so heavily it felt as though it was going to force its way through her chest wall.

She couldn't remember ever, ever feeling so nervous before—not even when Gramps had found out about her sneaking out at night to go poaching with Clem Angers. She had had Guard to thank for that, of course, and—

Firmly, she brought her thoughts back to the present.

Guard was slightly earlier than she had expected, and if the sight of him wearing the expensively tailored dark suit with its equally expensive, crisp white cotton shirt had not been one that was already familiar to her, she suspected she would have found it extremely daunting.

But then Guard *could* be daunting, even when he was casually dressed, she acknowledged, and it wasn't just because of his height, nor even because of those broad shoulders and that tautly muscular physique over which her female friends cooed and sighed so stupidly, either.

There was something about Guard himself—an air, a manner, a certain intangible something—that set him slightly apart from other men, made him stand out from other men, an aura of power and control, of...of sheer maleness, so potent that even she was acutely aware of it, she admitted. Aware of it, but not attracted by it, she reminded herself sharply. *She* could never be attracted by Guard; he was not her kind of man. She liked men who were softer, warmer—more approachable, more... more human, less...less sexual?

Nervously, she cleared her throat.

'What's wrong?' Guard asked her drily. 'You're staring at me like a rabbit at a dog.'

'I'm not afraid of you,' Rosy retorted, stung.

'I'm extremely glad to hear it. Look, I'm due to fly out to Brussels in the morning, Rosy, and I've got a briefcase full of documents to read before I do. Just tell me what you want, there's a good girl, and don't start backtracking now and telling me it isn't important. We both know that there's no way you'd get in touch with me if it weren't.'

The irony in his voice made her frown slightly but he was watching her impatiently, unfastening his jacket, reaching up to loosen the knot in his tie.

As she focused on the movement of his hands, she could feel the knot in her stomach tightening.

'Come on, Rosy, don't start playing games. I'm not in the mood for it.'

The verbal warning was accompanied by a forbidding, hooded look that reminded her of former peccadilloes and his merciless punishment of them.

She swallowed nervously. It was too late to back out now.

Screwing up her courage, she took a deep breath.

'Guard, I want you to marry me...'

CHAPTER TWO

Rosy had automatically closed her eyes as she spoke, but in the silence that followed her stammered request she was forced to open them again.

'What did you say?'

The words, evenly spaced out and ominously soft, were snapped out between Guard's strong white teeth, and he was looking at her as though it was her bones, her body, he would really like to inflict that punishment on, she recognised nervously as she cleared her throat a second time.

'I—I asked you if you'd marry me,' she repeated quickly, suppressing her body's physical instinct for flight.

'Is this some kind of joke?'

He sounded very angry, Rosy recognised, which rather surprised her. She had spent most of the last few hours trying to envisage exactly what his reaction to her request was going to be. That he might be angry had never even entered her head. Amusement, mockery, contempt, disdain, an outright refusal—all of these things she had expected, but anger...

'No, it isn't a joke,' she told him, adding grimly under her breath, 'I only wish it were.

'It was Peter's idea,' she continued doggedly. 'I told him it was crazy, but he says it's the only way we can stop Edward from inheriting the house and destroying it. You know the terms of Gramps' will.'

'I know them,' Guard agreed, 'but I hadn't realised this place meant so much to you that you'd be prepared to fulfil them. What happened to all that insistence that you weren't going to marry until you fell in love, until you were sure that your love was returned? Or was that just a girlish fantasy that faded in the reality of losing this place?'

'No, it wasn't,' Rosy told him angrily, 'but...'

He had taken off his jacket and gone to stand in front of the huge, open fireplace which, along with the Grinling Gibbons carving on the stairs, dominated the hallway.

Guard suited the house, Rosy recognised, before hurriedly looking away from him. With his height and the aura of power and authority which he wore with much the same swagger and flair with which her original ancestor must have worn his cloak, he looked much more at home here than she did herself.

The large rooms, the dark panelling, overshadowed her. In looks and build she took more after her mother's family than her father's. Whereas most of the portraits of her ancestors showed stocky, sturdy-looking individuals, she was small and slender—thin, Guard had once disparagingly called her.

It was still *her* home, though, and a part of her, much as she was reluctant to admit it, would hate to see it destroyed. She was honest enough to recognise that, despite her own feelings towards Guard, the house would be safe in his hands.

'But what...?' he demanded. 'But you love this place so much that you can't bear to give it up? But you love me so much that...?'

He threw the last question mockingly at her, already knowing the answer, but Rosy still gave it to him.

'No, of course not,' she denied vehemently.

Why was he looking at her like that? Watching her with those hooded, eagle-sharp eyes that made her feel so uncomfortable.

'So, you don't love either the house or me, but you're prepared to marry me to keep it.'

'To *save* it,' Rosy corrected him quickly, 'from Edward and… And it would be an arranged marriage,' she added carefully, turning her back slightly towards him. For some reason, she found it easier to talk to him like that. She felt safer knowing that he couldn't see her face, and that she didn't have to see his.

'An arranged marriage. And it needn't last very long. Peter said we could probably even get an annulment and that we need not— That we wouldn't be—' She broke off awkwardly, so anxiously conscious of the uncomfortable quality of his silence that unwarily she turned round to look at him.

'We wouldn't be what?' he encouraged her mockingly. 'Cohabiting…intimate…having sex…making love…?'

Rosy hated the way he almost caressed the words, rolling them over his tongue, purring over them almost, enjoying every second of her own discomfort, she was sure.

'If that's supposed to encourage me to agree, you don't know very much about the male sex and its ego, Rosy. Do you really think that a man—*any* man—wants to stand up in court and tell the world that he isn't man enough to take his wife to bed? Do you honestly believe that anyone, but most especially that repulsive cousin of yours, is going to believe the fiction that you and I are

genuinely husband and wife when the very mention of
the word sex is enough to turn you into a physical em-
bodiment of the traditional, trembling, untouched virgin?
Oh, no, my dear. If I were crazy enough to agree to this
fraudulent marriage of yours—and it's a very big ''if''—
in the eyes of the rest of the world it would have to look
as though it was very much the real thing, even if that
did mean that ultimately, you'd have to undergo the indignity of going through a divorce.'

Rosy's heart had started thumping heavily as he
spoke, but when she realised that he wasn't, as she had
expected, going to refuse her proposal outright, she
stared uncertainly at him, her face still flushed from her
earlier embarrassment. It was only Guard who made her
react like that when he talked about sex, she admitted
crossly. Not even when the teenage boys who used the
shelter made what were sometimes extremely blunt and
often crude comments did she get as embarrassed or self-
conscious as she did with Guard.

'But it wouldn't *be* a real marriage,' she insisted, turning round to focus watchfully on his face. You were
supposed to be able to tell what was really in a person's
mind from their eyes, but that rule didn't apply to Guard.
She could *never* tell what he was thinking. 'I mean, we
wouldn't be...'

'Lovers,' he supplied for her. 'It would certainly be
very hard to imagine. The only time I've ever held you
in my arms, you damned near scratched my eyes out,'
Guard reminded her grimly.

'You terrified me,' Rosy defended herself. 'Picking
me up like that. It was dark and I...'

'You were out clandestinely with Clem Angers,
poaching your grandfather's salmon.'

'Clem had been promising to take me out for ages to

show me the badgers' sett. And then *you* had to interfere
and spoil everything,' Rosy remembered indignantly.
'He had been promising me that he'd take me just as
soon as I was sixteen.'

'Really? I do hope you didn't use that unfortunate turn
of phrase when you were explaining what you were doing to your father. Sweet sixteen,' he continued, ignoring
the angry flush darkening Rosy's face. 'Sweet sixteen
and never been kissed. Just refresh my memory for me,
will you, Rosy? *How* old are you now?'

'Twenty-two almost,' she told him impatiently.

'Mmm…and presumably now well-experienced in the
art of kissing, if nothing else. You certainly ought to be
after the practice session I witnessed last New Year's
Eve at the Lewishams' ball.'

Rosy's flush deepened as she remembered the incident
he referred to. One of the Lewisham cousins, a rather
intoxicated, impressionable young man, who had been
gazing adoringly at her from the other side of the dance
floor all evening, had caught up with her just as she tried
to make her escape, grabbing hold of her in the semi-
darkness of the passageway that led to the cloakroom,
imprisoning her in his arms for a few brief seconds while
he pressed impassioned kisses against her determinedly
closed mouth. It had been a harmless enough episode.
He had presented himself rather sheepishly and shame-
facedly at Queen's Meadow the following afternoon, full
of remorse and apologies, and begging for a chance to
make a fresh start, which Rosy had tactfully refused. But
up until now she had had no idea that Guard had even
witnessed the small incident.

She turned away from him, pacing the room edgily.

'Why on earth don't you buy yourself some decent
clothes? After all, it's not as though you can't afford it.

Your father left you very well provided for. Or wouldn't it impress dear, sanctimonious Ralph if you turned up looking like a woman rather than a half-grown child?'

'Ralph is not sanctimonious,' Rosy denied angrily as she turned to face him. 'And as for my clothes...' She frowned as she glanced down at her well-worn leggings and the thick, bulky sweater which had originally belonged to her father.

'I dress to please myself, in what feels comfortable. Just because *you're* the kind of man who likes to see a woman humiliating herself by dressing up in something so skin-tight she can barely walk in it, never mind run, teetering around in high heels... Mind you, I suppose at your age that *would* be your idea of style,' she added disparagingly.

'I'm thirty-five, Rosy,' Guard reminded her grimly, 'not some ageing fifty-year-old desperately fighting off middle-age, and as for my ideas of style, personally I think there's nothing quite so alluring as a woman who has enough confidence in herself to dress neither to conceal her sexuality nor to reveal it—a woman who wears silk or cashmere, wool or cotton, clothes cut in plain, simple styles—but then *you* aren't a woman yet, are you, Rosy?'

For some reason Rosy couldn't define, his comments, his criticism had hurt her, making her leap immediately to her own defence, her voice husky with emotion as she told him fiercely, 'I *am* a woman, but *you* can't see that. You only think of women in terms of sex—the more sexual experience a woman has had, the more of a woman it makes her. Well, for your information—'

She stopped abruptly. Why was she letting him get to her like this? Why did they always end up quarrelling, arguing, antagonists?

'For my information, what?' Guard challenged her.

'Oh, nothing.' Rosy retreated. She had been a fool to listen to Peter. If, as he said, the only way to save the house was via an arranged marriage, then it would have to be with someone else. *Anyone* else, she decided savagely. Anyone at all just so long as it wasn't the arrogant, hateful, horrid man standing in front of her, watching her with those mesmeric, all-seeing, all-watchful golden eyes.

'All right, I know,' she told him bitterly. 'It was a stupid idea, and I was a fool to think you'd agree, no matter how much you might want Queen's Meadow. I'd be better off advertising in the personal columns for a husband...'

Something flickered briefly in Guard's eyes, a tiny movement so swiftly controlled that Rosy felt she must have imagined it.

'I haven't given you my answer yet.'

Rosy looked up at him.

'You're talking about taking a potentially very dangerous course,' he continued warningly, as Rosy remained silent. 'Edward is bound to be suspicious.'

'But he can't *do* anything. Not so long as I've fulfilled the terms of my grandfather's will.'

'Mmm... Edward is a very tricky character. It wouldn't be wise to underestimate him. There's an element of fraud in this whole plan of yours.'

'Fraud?' Rosy interrupted him anxiously. 'But...'

'I'll be back from Brussels the day after tomorrow. I'll give you my answer then. And, Rosy,' he told her as he turned to leave, 'in the meantime, no ads in the personal columns, hmm?'

It wasn't fair, Rosy reflected indignantly when he had

gone. *Why* did he always have to make her feel like a child? And a particularly stupid child at that.

'You've forgotten to put sugar in my coffee again,' Ralph reproved Rosy. He frowned slightly, his sandy eyebrows lifting almost into his hairline as he added, 'In fact you've seemed very preoccupied altogether these last couple of days. Is something wrong?'

'No…no, nothing,' Rosy denied untruthfully.

'Mm. You know, Rosy, it's a pity you didn't work a bit harder at persuading your grandfather to leave Queen's Meadow to us. Hallows, the engineering place, is closing down next month and that's bound to put more pressure on us. God knows how many more it's going to make homeless. We haven't got anything like enough beds here as it is. When I think of that damned big house and all those rooms…'

'Yes, yes I know,' Rosy agreed guiltily. She hadn't discussed with Ralph the terms of her grandfather's will and, since Edward had already made it plain that he expected to inherit the house, Rosy had simply allowed Ralph to believe that as well.

When she had first announced that she was going to do voluntary work at the shelter, she knew her father had been a little concerned but, needless to say, it had been Guard who had taken it upon himself to warn her that, in view of her family connections and her comparative wealth, Ralph might put pressure on her to help fund the shelter.

'Ralph would never do anything like that,' she had protested then, indignantly. And she had believed it… *Had* believed it… *Still* believed it, and if Ralph was cross with her because he felt she ought to have persuaded her grandfather to leave Queen's Meadow to their charity, well, she could understand why.

She could never walk into the old, run-down shabby building on the outskirts of the town without a small pang.

They all did their best to make it as homely as possible, but the rooms still had that air about them that reminded her of the boarding-school she had attended when she and her father had first returned to England from his army posting in Germany. She hadn't stayed there long, but it had left a lasting impression on her.

The first spring she had worked at the shelter she had arrived one morning with the boot of her small car filled with vases she had 'borrowed' from home and the back seat covered in a mass of daffodils.

Ralph had found her just as she was placing the last vase in position.

She winced even now when she remembered how angry he had been.

'You waste money on flowers when we barely have enough to buy them food,' he had shouted at her.

She had never made the same mistake again, but sometimes the sheer austerity of the shelter weighed her down, her own feelings adding to the compassion and anguish she already felt at the plight of the young people they took in.

Today, though, she was guiltily aware that her mind was more on her own problems than those of the homeless. Guard was due back this afternoon. What would his decision be? What did she *want* his decision to be?

She knew quite well what Ralph would say were she to ask him for his advice, and the modern, aware part of her agreed with him: there were far more important things to worry about than a house; there were people,

her fellow human beings, in far more need than a building and yet, when she walked round the house, something she had found herself doing increasingly frequently
recently, she was also emotionally aware of the love, the
care, the human effort that had gone into making it what
it was. It wasn't the material value of the Grinling
Gibbons carving on the staircase that smote her with
guilt at the thought of its destruction, it was her knowledge of the work, the craftsmanship which had gone into
its carving. If she closed her eyes she could almost instantly be there, smell the fresh, pungent odour of the
new wood, feel the concentrated silence of the busy ap-
prentices as they watched their master, see the delight
and pride in their faces when they were finally allowed
to make their contribution, when their work was finally
inspected and passed, the experienced hands of the master running critically over their carving while they held
their breath and waited for his verdict.

The plasterwork on the ceilings, the furniture in the
rooms—all of it had been created with human endeav-
our, with human pride.

Ralph would no doubt see another side of it, of ap-
prentices injured and maimed, thrown out of work to
starve, of workmen paid a pittance by their rich patrons.

'What's up, boyfriend giving you a hard time?'

Rosy turned her head to force a smile in the direction
of the thin, pimply boy watching her, ignoring his companion's snigger and clearly audible, 'I'll bet if he was
she wouldn't be looking so miserable,' without even a
hint of the betraying colour that Guard could conjure so
easily with a comment only a tenth as sexual.

'Have you heard anything about that job you went for
yet, Alan?' she asked, ignoring both comments.

'Nah... Don't 'spose I'll hear owt, either.'

'You could try getting some qualifications,' Rosy suggested, 'going to night school.'

She already knew what the answer would be and wasn't surprised when the boy shook his head in denial of her comment. When a system had failed you as badly as it had failed these youngsters, it must be hard to have any faith in it, Rosy acknowledged as she watched the two of them swagger off in the direction of the television lounge.

An hour later, as she drove home, her stomach was already cramping at the thought of hearing Guard's decision. To her surprise, as she pulled up at the rear of the house in what had originally been the stable yard, she saw that an unfamiliar car was already parked there.

As she got out of her own car she eyed the bright red Rolls-Royce uncertainly. She went into the house through the back entrance, through a maze of passages, past a cluster of small, dark rooms.

She could hear voices in the front hall and she tensed as she recognised one of them. Edward, her father's cousin. What was he doing here and, more important, how had he got in?

Taking a deep breath, she pushed open the door into the hall.

Edward was standing with his back to her, his bald head shining in the light from the overhead chandelier which he had switched on.

Both he and the man with him were looking up at it.

'Mmm...I suppose it could fetch a tidy bit, although there's not so much call for that sort of thing now. Too big and too expensive. We'd probably be better shipping it abroad, finding an agent—' He broke off as he turned round and saw Rosy, and touched Edward's arm, drawing his attention to her.

'Ah, Rosy…'

Edward's genial manner didn't deceive Rosy. It never had. She shared her grandfather's and her father's dislike and distrust of him.

'What are you doing here, Edward?' Rosy demanded, ignoring his pseudo-friendly overtures.

The man with him had moved slightly out of earshot and Edward's expression changed as he glanced over to where his companion was studying the carved staircase, his eyes hardening as he recognised Rosy's hostility.

'Just checking out my inheritance,' he told Rosy smoothly.

'It isn't yours yet,' Rosy reminded him fiercely.

Edward gave a dismissive shrug. Unlike her father and her grandfather, Edward had run to fat in middle-age and the angry flush now mantling his face emphasised his heavy jowliness.

Her father had once remarked that Edward had a very nasty temper. On the few occasions when Rosy had met him, the tension that emanated from Edward's wife seemed to confirm her father's comment, but this was the first time she had witnessed any evidence of Edward's temper at first hand.

'Not yet, maybe, but it soon will be,' he told her angrily. 'And there's not a damn thing you or anyone else can do about it. For once in his life, the old man was too clever for his own good. How much do you reckon the staircase will fetch, Charlie?' he called out to the other man, smirking when he saw Rosy's expression.

As she watched and listened to him, any ideas Rosy might have had about appealing to his better nature died. He simply didn't have one, she recognised. He would *enjoy* destroying the house.

She heard the heavy wooden front door creak as

someone pushed it open, and turned round warily, but it wasn't another of Edward's 'business associates' who had walked in, it was Guard.

He walked over to the fireplace just inside the doorway, frowning as he studied the scene in front of him.

Rosy saw the antagonism and, along with it, the apprehension flare briefly in Edward's eyes as he glared across at him, but Guard wasn't even looking at Edward, he was looking at her—looking at her, Rosy recognised in sudden, dizzy confusion, in a way she had never envisaged seeing him look at any woman, but most especially not her.

She blinked a little, her own eyes darkening as they were caught and held in a gaze of such smouldering sensuality that it actually made her physically shiver. When had Guard's eyes developed that ability to turn from cool, distant gold into hot, smouldering amber? Where had he learned to look at a woman in such a way that she and every other person in the room with her was instantly conscious of Guard's desire for her? Only Guard didn't desire her; he didn't even like her, he—

'Guard.' Rosy exclaimed weakly, her hand going automatically to her throat to protect the small pulse beating so frantically there. 'I…I didn't think you'd be back until much later.'

'I shouldn't have been,' Guard told her, 'but I couldn't bear to be away from you any longer.'

Rosy gaped at him. She could feel her skin burning. What was Guard trying to do to her? He must know as well as she did that—

She froze in shock as he crossed the hallway, dropping the briefcase he had been carrying with a small, heavy thud as he took hold of her, holding her so tightly against his body that she could feel the strong bite of his fingers

against her flesh; her face was buried against his chest,
any verbal response she might have wanted to make
smothered, as he murmured throatily, 'God, I've missed
you.'

Rosy gulped in air nervously.

'Have you told Edward our good news yet, my love?'

Their good news? What good news? Rosy jerked protestingly against Guard's strong hold, lifting her head,
the impulsive words clamouring for utterance.

But she never got to say them. Instead, the swift descent of Guard's head and the hard, totally unexpected
warning pressure of his mouth on hers stopped her.

Guard holding her. Guard kissing her. Kissing her?
Was that what he was doing? It didn't feel much like a
kiss. She opened her eyes and looked anxiously into his.
They were still that unfamiliar, heart-thumping, pulse-
racing amber colour, and the mouth that had clamped so
firmly on hers, silencing her, somehow didn't feel anything like she might have imagined Guard's mouth
might feel if she had ever actually allowed herself to
wander into the pitfall of such dangerous imaginings,
which she hadn't... It felt...it felt...

A dizzying wave of sensation hit her as Guard's
mouth moved slowly over hers.

Her eyes were still open and so were his, almost hyp-
notising her into obeying the silent commands he was
giving her. She could feel her mouth softening beneath
the sensual impact of his, her whole body relaxing, melt-
ing into his, relaxing and yet at the same time being
invaded by a peculiar and unfamiliar *frisson* of sensation.

To her horror, Rosy could actually feel her nipples
hardening and peaking. With a small cry of protest she
tore her mouth away from Guard's.

'You're right,' he agreed, as though she had spoken. 'This isn't the time or place.'

His voice sounded soft, a husky purr that made small shivers of sensation run up and down her spine. He reached out and touched her mouth with his thumb.

'What the hell's going on?'

Dizzily, Rosy dragged her gaze away from Guard's face and turned to look at Edward.

'Hasn't Rosy told you?' Guard asked politely. 'She and I are getting married. I've sorted out the special licence,' he told Rosy softly, turning away from Edward, ignoring the anger emanating from him, the questions he was asking, behaving, Rosy recognised enviously, as though Edward simply wasn't even there, as though the two of them were completely on their own, as though...

'The wedding will be just the way you wanted it to be. Very small, very quiet. In church...'

In church! Rosy tensed, but this time she managed to hold back her shocked words.

'You can't do this,' Edward was blustering angrily beside them. 'Don't think I don't know what the pair of you are up to. Don't think I won't—'

'Edward...' Without raising either his voice or his head, and still looking directly at her, Rosy marvelled, Guard had managed to silence Edward's outpourings and to get his attention. 'I think it's time you left,' Guard continued evenly. 'I'll show you out.'

Now Guard did move away from her and at another time Rosy might almost have been amused by the chagrin in Edward's expression and the confusion of his friend, who was demanding to know exactly what was going on and why Edward had brought him out on such a wild-goose chase.

'You haven't heard the last of this,' Edward warned

Guard threateningly, before turning to leave. 'You aren't married yet, and besides—'

'Goodbye, Edward,' Guard interrupted him suavely, firmly closing the front door.

'Did—did you mean that?' Rosy asked him, dry-mouthed in the heavy silence that followed Edward's departure. 'About our getting married?'

'Yes,' Guard told her calmly. 'What is it, Rosy?' he asked with an abrupt return to his normal, mocking manner towards her. 'Having second thoughts?'

Rosy glanced towards the staircase and then up at the chandelier and shook her head numbly, not daring to trust her voice to make any vocal reply.

CHAPTER THREE

'DOES it have to be a church ceremony?' Rosy asked Guard uncomfortably, uncrossing her leggings-clad legs and getting up from her chair to go and stand in front of the library window.

She had been caught off-guard when he had arrived half an hour ago; nine o'clock on a Saturday morning was not exactly a time she was used to having visitors.

'Visitors?' Guard had drawled, as she had told him as much, hastily running the fingers of one hand through her tangled hair, while she surreptitiously tried to lick the small smear of jam from her toast off the fingers of the other.

In her grandfather's day, breakfast, especially at weekends, had always been a semi-formal affair, served in the breakfast-room. But, since she had been on her own, Rosy had taken to eating in the large, comfortable kitchen. Mrs Frinton, who used to come in daily to clean and cook, was now only coming in once a week. Rosy felt guilty about allowing someone to cook and clean for her when she was perfectly capable of doing both herself.

'My dear Rosy, you and I are about to be married, supposed in the eyes of the rest of the world to be desperately in love. What would seem odd to them is not so much my calling so early in the day, but the fact that I haven't stayed here all night.'

Predictably and irritatingly, Rosy had felt herself starting to flush.

'I have an extremely busy schedule, and there are certain things we need to discuss before the rest of the world learns our news.'

'Why should anyone else be remotely interested in what we're doing?' Rosy had demanded crossly, as Guard followed her into the library. 'Or by the rest of the world do you really mean all your girlfriends?'

The look Guard had given her had scorched her into wary silence.

Like her, Guard was dressed casually, but whereas her leggings and top shrouded the feminine shape of her body, Guard's jeans, surprisingly well-worn with telltale patches of lighter colour on them, clung snugly to his body, outlining the hard, taut muscles of his thighs, revealing their maleness in a way which was normally mercifully concealed by his more formal business suits.

There was, Rosy was discovering, also something almost hypnotic about the way Guard walked—about the way the denim revealed the movement of those muscles. She had been relieved when he had finally seated himself in one of the deep library chairs.

'Yes, it does,' Guard answered her original question now. 'Why the objection?'

'Well, it's just…' Rosy shrugged uncomfortably, unwilling to betray herself to his further mockery by admitting that, while she was no regular churchgoer, she felt that it was somehow wrong to marry him in church when she knew—when they *both* knew—that their marriage was simply a convenient expediency.

'Just what?' Guard pressed her.

'It's just…just that a church wedding is so much more fuss,' she fibbed lamely. 'And…'

She could feel her skin colouring under the look Guard was giving her. This morning, in the sharp, clear daylight, it seemed impossible that those clear, cold eyes could ever really have burned with that heat, that desire...that intensity she had seen last night. Nervously she looked quickly away from him. She had told herself last night, after he had gone, that that interlude—that incident—was something she was simply not going to think about. Guard had done it for Edward's benefit, and she supposed she ought to be grateful to him for going to so much trouble, but...

But it was something that most definitely must not happen again.

'Stop hedging, Rosy,' Guard told her sharply. 'You don't want to get married in church because it isn't a "real" marriage. That's typical of you and your muddled, ideological outlook on life. Try thinking things through from a more logical viewpoint. Like it or not, you and I in our different ways both have a certain standing in the local community. Edward isn't going to be happy about what we're doing, we both know that. There's no point in adding fuel to the flames of his suspicions. A small, quiet ceremony is something we can get away with—just—particularly in view of the recent deaths of your father and grandfather. Not to have a church ceremony isn't. And as for the fuss, you can leave all the arrangements to me. Which reminds me, you'd better have a word with Mrs Frinton and ask her if she's free to come back here to work full-time.'

'What for?' Rosy asked him. 'I'm only using a few of the rooms and—'

'*You* may be, but after we're married we're bound to have to do a certain amount of entertaining. I have business associates who'll want to be introduced to my new

wife, and unless you're proposing to give up your work
at the shelter to be here full time—'

Give up her work at the shelter? 'Certainly not,' Rosy
told him vehemently.

'Good. So it's agreed then. You'll contact Mrs
Frinton, tell her that we're getting married and that I'll
be moving in here and ask her—'

'You're moving in here?'

'Well, it is the normal thing for a married couple to
live under the same roof,' Guard pointed out to her sardonically. 'Unless of course you want to move into my
apartment. Although…'

His apartment? Rosy stared at him. When Peter had
first mooted the idea of her asking Guard to marry her,
she hadn't been able to think very far past the ordeal of
actually having to propose to him.

'But we can't live together,' she began, panic suddenly beginning to infiltrate her voice. 'We don't…'

'We don't what? Oh, come on, Rosy…how old are
you? You can't be that naïve. You *must* have realised
when you came up with this plan of yours to stop
Edward inheriting this place that you could hardly convince the world that this is a genuine marriage if we're
living at separate addresses. Have some sense.'

Rosy could hear the exasperation creeping into his
voice.

'I hadn't really thought that far ahead,' she admitted
weakly. 'I just wanted—'

'You just wanted to save the house from Edward. I
know,' Guard finished for her. 'You're twenty-two years
old, Rosy. Isn't it time you started to grow up?' he asked
her scathingly.

'I *am* grown-up,' Rosy responded indignantly. 'I'm an
adult now, Guard, a…'

'A what?' he asked her softly. 'A woman?'

'Yes,' she told him fiercely, her eyes darkening with anger as she saw the look he was giving her as he crossed the room.

'Turn round,' he commanded, 'and look at yourself in that mirror and tell me what you see.'

She was tempted to refuse, but the memory of how quickly and easily he had overpowered her the previous evening stopped her.

Reluctantly, instead, she did as he had demanded, staring defiantly not at her own reflection in the huge Venetian mirror over the fireplace, but at him.

How tall he looked in comparison to her own meagre height and how broad, the powerful, muscular structure of his torso clearly evident beneath the soft, checked woollen shirt he was wearing.

Her own top, in contrast, wide-necked and baggy, revealed all too clearly the vulnerable delicacy of her own bone-structure, the soft black wool somehow highlighting the translucency of her pale skin, the feminine curves of her breasts.

'A woman! You look more like a child,' Guard mocked her. 'In years you may be a woman, Rosy, but you're still hiding behind the attitude and looks of a child.' He moved in front of her, his thumb-tip rubbing briefly against her mouth, its touch gone as she instinctively lifted her hand to his wrist to push him away, her eyes dark with shock and anger.

'No lipstick,' he told her. 'No make-up of any kind.'

'It's Saturday morning,' Rosy protested. What she didn't tell him—what she couldn't tell him—was that she had overslept, that last night she had been unable to sleep because…because…

She could feel the flesh of her bottom lip prickling

sensitively where he had touched it; instinctively she
went to catch it between her teeth and then stopped
abruptly, remembering.

'No make-up,' Guard continued remorselessly,
'clothes that hide your body, deliberately de-sexing it.
Has *any* man ever seen your body, Rosy? Touched it?
Touched you here?'

The fleeting touch of his hand against her breast made
her tense in outraged protest, even while her body registered that there was nothing remotely sexual in his
touch.

'I don't have to apologise to you or anyone else for
not wanting to indulge in casual sex,' Rosy defended
herself angrily. 'And just because I don't jump into bed
with every male who asks me, that doesn't make me
immature, or less of a woman!'

'No, it doesn't,' Guard agreed. 'But the way you blush
whenever I say anything with even the remotest sexual
connotations, the way you back off from me, the way
you so openly betray your inexperience sexually, *they*
all say that you're not a woman, Rosy, and they'll certainly say that you're not a married woman.'

'Well, there's nothing I can do about that, is there?'
Rosy snapped at him, turning away from him so that he
wouldn't see either that she was blushing or that his
comments had, for some odd reason, actually hurt her.
'Unless you're suggesting that I go out and find a man
to go to bed with just so that I don't embarrass you with
my—my lack of womanliness...'

'My God, if I thought...'

Rosy gasped as she felt Guard take hold of her, shaking her almost, and then releasing her just as abruptly,
so that she didn't even have time to open her mouth to
protest at his rough treatment of her. She could hear

anger in his voice as he told her, 'This isn't some game we're playing, Rosy. It's reality—and a damn dangerous reality at that. Have you actually thought of what could happen to both of us if Edward takes it into his head to bring a case against us for fraud?'

'He wouldn't…he *couldn't* do that,' Rosy protested.

'You saw the look on his face as well as I did when he learned that he wasn't going to inherit this place,' Guard reminded her. 'One hint—just one hint that this marriage of ours is a put-up job, and he'll have his lawyers on to us so fast…'

'But he *can't* find out. He *can't* prove anything,' Rosy protested shakily.

'Not as long as we're both careful,' Guard agreed, 'and as long as you remember that you and I are now a couple. A couple who, as far as the rest of the world are concerned, are desperately in love—so desperately in love that they can't wait to be together, to be married.'

Rosy gulped nervously. She had a good imagination—a very good imagination—but trying to imagine herself desperately in love with Guard…and trying to imagine *him* reciprocating that love!

'Any more criticisms?' Rosy challenged him, fighting off the feeling of panic and despair flooding her.

The look Guard gave her made her stomach muscles cramp nervously.

'Don't tempt me,' he advised her warningly.

Suddenly Rosy had had enough.

'You don't *have* to do this, you know,' she reminded him. 'No one's forcing you to marry me, and I certainly don't want to marry you. Look, why don't we just forget the whole thing, Guard?' she exploded angrily. 'Why don't we—?'

'Why don't *you* try thinking before you open that

pretty little mouth of yours?' Guard interrupted her savagely.

For some reason he looked even more angry now than he had done before, Rosy realised.

'Haven't you forgotten something? Edward knows we're supposed to be getting married.'

'So... We can pretend we've had a lovers' quarrel. It happens all the time; you should know that,' she told him with daring flippancy.

Oddly enough, her jibe seemed to have less effect on him than her earlier one about their not marrying.

'Lovers invariably make up those quarrels, at least until they aren't lovers any longer,' Guard told her drily. 'No, Rosy, we're committed now. It's too late for any second thoughts.'

'At least Peter was right about one thing,' Rosy told him with forced bravado. 'You must want this place one hell of a lot. You'd *have* to want something one hell of a lot to go through *this* to get it.'

She gave him a small, defeated shrug as she turned her back on him, trying to ignore the sinking, miserable sensation in the pit of her stomach as she tried not to contemplate her immediate future.

'Yes,' she heard Guard agreeing somberly. 'I would.

'I've already had a word with the vicar, by the way,' he informed her, changing the subject. 'He agreed with me that a quiet, mid-week ceremony would seem best...'

Rosy spun round.

'You've already done *what*? But...'

'*You* were the one who proposed to *me*,' Guard reminded her.

Rosy snapped her teeth together, suppressing the urge to scream. No matter what she said or did, Guard always managed to outmanoeuvre her—to outwit her.

Well, one day... One day very soon *she'd* be the one to outwit him, she promised herself and, as far as she was concerned, that day could not come fast enough.

'Did you and the vicar fix an actual date, or am I allowed to have some say in that?' Rosy asked with acid sweetness.

'Yes, a week on Wednesday,' Guard told her, ignoring her sarcasm.

'So soon? But...' Rosy gulped back her protest as she felt the cold sensation of apprehension spreading through her body.

'There's no point in delaying things,' Guard told her. 'We've only got two months to fulfil the terms of your grandfather's will. I've got several business trips coming up; in fact I'm due in Brussels again the day after the wedding, which unfortunately means that we shan't be able to have a traditional honeymoon.' When he saw Rosy's expression, he laughed sardonically. 'Yes, I thought that might appeal to you.

'The fact that we're getting married so quickly will mean that we won't need to invite many people. Neither of us has any family to speak of, and I thought we'd smooth any ruffled feathers by giving a formal reception-cum-party here later in the year. As I said, you can leave all the arrangements to me, apart from one thing. Your dress...'

'My dress?' Rosy looked at him suspiciously, guessing what was coming. 'I'm not going out and wasting money on a wedding-dress,' she warned him.

'No. So what *are* you going to wear? Not, I trust, the outfit you have on now?'

Rosy glowered at him. 'Don't be ridiculous. I'll—'

'Look, Rosy, I'm not going to waste my breath arguing with you. Your family had, and still has, a certain standing locally, which meant an awful lot to your grandfather. I appreciate that you're a modern young woman, that inherited wealth and everything that goes with it runs counter to your own beliefs, but sometimes, for the sake of other people's feelings, we have to compromise on our own principles.'

'You mean *you* want me to wear a traditional wedding-dress so that I don't let *you* down?' Rosy suggested dangerously.

'No, that is *not* what I mean.'

The anger in Guard's voice made her look directly at him. She really had annoyed him, Rosy recognised. There was a dark stain of colour angrily flushing his cheekbones and his mouth had tightened ominously. Even the way he moved, pacing restlessly from the fireplace to come and stand directly in front of her, revealed his loss of patience with her.

'*I* don't give a damn if you go to the altar wearing sackcloth and ashes, which is quite plainly what you want to wear. What is it, Rosy? Afraid that some people—someone—might not fully understand the motivation behind this marriage, that *he*—this someone—might not realise the great sacrifice you're making? Well, let me warn you now, Rosy, if you even think of telling Ralph Southern the real reason for this marriage...'

Ralph? What on earth was Guard talking about? Why should she tell Ralph anything of the sort? She already knew just how he would react if she did, just how contemptuous he would be of her desire to protect and preserve the house...

'If you think,' Guard continued grimly, 'that I—'

Rosy shook her head. Suddenly all the fight had gone out of her.

'All right, Guard. I'll wear a proper wedding-dress,'

she told him woodenly, but she knew that her eyes had filled with tears and, although she tried to turn away, she wasn't quite quick enough and Guard had seen them too.

She heard him swear under his breath and then say roughly, 'All right. I'm sorry if anything I've said hurt you—but you must realise that—'

'No, it's not—it isn't anything you've said,' she said fiercely, blinking back her tears. 'I already know exactly what you think of me, Guard. It's just…' She lifted her head, unaware of how vulnerable the bravado of her stance and the resolution in her voice actually made her as she told him, 'I always imagined that when I got married…when I chose my wedding-dress…it would be—' she swallowed back the tears forming a hard lump of emotion clogging her throat '—that I'd be choosing it, *wearing* it, for a man who loved me…for a man I loved.'

She could see a small muscle beating tensely in Guard's jaw. Perhaps he was not, after all, as she had previously imagined, she recognised. Perhaps he, too, somewhere deep down inside him, had once imagined marrying for love.

'Still,' she told him, trying to appear more light-hearted than she felt, 'I suppose I can always do that the —'

'The next time,' Guard supplied harshly for her.

Rosy couldn't understand what she had said to make him so openly and furiously angry.

'I suppose you think I'm being stupid—over-idealistic, naïvely romantic,' she flung at him defiantly, ignoring the instinct that told her that what she was doing was somehow dangerous. 'But I *am* romantic, Guard, and I *am* idealistic. Perhaps by the time I get to your age I might feel as you do, that loving someone and being loved by them isn't important, that it's something to sneer at and mock, but I can't help the way I feel,' she told him challengingly, lifting her head and forcing herself to make eye-contact with him, despite the nervous flutterings in her stomach. 'And just because you don't feel the same—'

'You know nothing about what I might or might not feel,' he interrupted her bitingly. 'What I may or may not have already felt or experienced...'

Rosy could feel the wave of heat burning up over her skin as she recognised the truth of what he was saying and, with it, all that he was not saying.

Guard was an experienced, highly attractive, highly sensual man; there must have been women—or a woman—in his life to whom he had been emotionally as well as physically attracted and somehow, subtly, with his response to her own outburst, he had made her unwantedly aware of that fact.

For as long as she had known him she had felt compelled to battle and react against the air of control and authority that he exuded but now, for some reason, instead of challenging his remark, instead of asking him why if he had experienced such feelings he was still single, as she would once have done, she swallowed back that challenge.

'Let me warn you, Rosy,' she heard him saying as she turned her head away from him. 'This quest of yours to find this romantic, idealistic love isn't one that's going to be carried out whilst you're married to me. Your search for love's holy grail is one that will have to wait, I'm afraid.'

Rosy looked uncertainly at him. His comment was the kind that was normally accompanied by the mockery which always got so easily under her skin, but there was no glint of taunting humour in his eyes on this occasion, no familiar irritatingly knowing curl to his mouth.

In fact, she had rarely seen him looking so grimly serious, she recognised warily.

'For the duration of this marriage, as far as the outside world is concerned, *I* am your lover…your beloved…in every sense of those words.'

The cold flatness of his voice robbed his words of any hint of sensuality, but nevertheless Rosy could feel her skin flushing as her imagination, always her worst enemy where her run-ins with Guard were concerned, reacted to the evocative words he had used: lover, beloved. She shivered suddenly, trying to banish the images conjured up by her overactive imagination—images of two people, two lovers, their bodies entwined in an embrace of such intimacy, such compulsive desire and need for one another, that there could be no mistaking the nature of their relationship, either physically or emotionally.

Hastily, Rosy tried to banish her mental pictures, rushing into protective speech as she told Guard fiercely, 'You needn't worry. I shan't do anything to spoil your image. I mean, it just wouldn't do, would it? Guard— the fabled, famous lover—married to a woman who doesn't want him…'

'It isn't *my image*, as you call it, that concerns me,' Guard returned grimly. 'It's my professional reputation, and yours. You do realise, don't you, that technically what you and I are doing is fraudulent?' He took advantage of her wary silence to continue more easily, 'And as far as being married to a woman who doesn't want me is concerned… You aren't a woman, Rosy, you're a girl, and I doubt that I should have much trouble finding solace elsewhere, do you…?'

For sheer arrogance there was no one like him, Rosy

decided rebelliously as he turned away from her, reaching into the inside pocket of his jacket as he did so.

'You're going to need these,' he told her matter-of-factly as he handed her a small jeweller's box.

Rosy's fingers trembled slightly as she opened it, a small, totally involuntary awed gasp escaping her lips as she saw the rings inside it. The wedding-ring was plain and simple, heavy yellow gold; the engagement ring that went with it… She stared at the sapphire with its surround of dazzling, square-cut diamonds.

'It…it's beautiful,' she told Guard shakily.

The sapphire was a dense, dark blue, virtually the same colour as her own eyes, she recognised in surprise as she studied it.

'I can't wear it, Guard,' she protested huskily. 'It's… it's far too valuable.'

'You must wear it,' Guard contradicted her firmly. 'It's what people will expect—look for.'

Had he chosen the sapphire deliberately? Rosy found herself wondering. Or had it simply been a random decision, made in haste and irritation, the connection between the colour of the stone and her eyes unnoticed by him?

'Here…give me your hand.'

Reluctantly, Rosy did so, tensing slightly as he removed the ring from its box and slid it firmly down over her ring finger.

'It's…it's very beautiful,' she told Guard politely. 'Thank you.'

'Is that the best you can do? You sound like a child thanking an adult for some extra pocket money. It *is* customary to thank one's prospective bridegroom in a rather more intimate fashion for such a gift.'

His glance dropped to her mouth as he spoke, and

Rosy was irritated by the wave of self-consciousness that swept over her. He was doing it deliberately, of course. Well, she'd show him. Gritting her teeth, she lifted her face obediently towards his, instinctively closing her eyes as she waited…and waited.

When nothing happened, she opened her eyes and glared angrily at Guard.

'If that's the best you can do, then the more of this marriage of ours that's conducted out of public view, the better,' Guard told her cynically. 'For your information, my dear Rosy, a newly engaged, supposedly ecstatically in love woman does not screw up her face and react to the thought of being kissed by her fiancé as though she's been told she has to take a dose of medicine.'

'But we aren't ecstatically in love,' Rosy reminded him crossly.

'And for all the reasons I've already been through with you, it is extremely important that no one else other than us knows that,' Guard pointed out. 'Edward isn't a fool, Rosy,' he warned her. 'If he thinks he's got the slightest chance of disputing your claim to this place, he's going to take it.'

'So what am I supposed to do?' Rosy demanded defensively. 'Take lessons in how to kiss a man as though I love him when I don't? No, thanks, I don't need them,' she snapped.

'No? That's not the impression I got. A kiss between two committed lovers is nothing like the jumbled, bungled efforts you've obviously experienced,' Guard told her.

Rosy glared furiously back at him, caught between anger and embarrassment. She wanted to tell Guard that she knew exactly what it felt like to exchange wildly passionate kisses with a man she wanted, but she was uncomfortably aware that it simply wasn't true.

The kisses and the men she had known so far had all left her depressingly unmoved.

'I'm not an actress, Guard,' she told him more cautiously instead. 'I can't manufacture passion to order...'

'No?' Guard commented softly. 'Then perhaps it's time you learned.'

He was still holding her hand; holding her hand and standing so close to her that all he had to do to close the gap between them was simply to take a single step towards her.

Rosy tensed as she waited for him to imprison her in his arms, knowing he was far too strong for her to be able to break free; but instead he slowly lifted his free hand and gently brushed her hair back off her face.

'This is how a man deeply in love touches a woman, Rosy,' he told her quietly. 'She seems so vulnerable, so delicate, so precious to him that he's half afraid to touch her, half afraid that the merest sensation of her skin against his fingertips will ignite a passion within him that he simply cannot control. He wants her...her wants her desperately and overpoweringly, and yet at the same time he wants to go oh, so slowly with her, to savour and hold on to every millisecond of contact with her.

'He is caught between those twin needs—his hunger for her, his urgent desire to possess and devour her, and his desire to worship her, to give her all the pleasure he can...all the pleasure there is. And so he touches her skin, gently and perhaps even a little unsteadily and, as he does so, he looks into her eyes, wanting to see in them that his passion, his need, his *love* are reciprocated, wanting to see that she *knows* and understands how great the strain of his self-imposed self-control is.

'If she does return his feelings, she, too, will reach out and touch him.'

Mesmerised by the soft timbre of Guard's words, Rosy didn't even blink as he lifted her left hand to his jaw.

Freed momentarily from the hypnotism of his eyes, she flinched a little beneath the sharp quiver of unexpected sensation that ran through her body as her fingertips touched the slight roughness of Guard's jaw.

He had turned his head away from her and she gasped out aloud as she felt his lips caressing the soft centre of her palm and then the inside of her wrist where her pulse was beating so fast that its frantic race was making her feel quite dizzy.

'A man in love will take his time in reaching his ultimate target,' Guard was telling her softly. 'He'll kiss her throat, her ears...'

Rosy trembled as she felt the soft brush of Guard's mouth against her skin.

'But all the time what he really wants...'

Rosy tensed as she felt the warmth of Guard's breath moving across her face. Her mouth had gone apprehensively dry, her lips parting a little in her need to draw extra air into her lungs.

'Her mouth will draw him like a magnet...lure him, make him ache from head to foot in his need to taste its velvet softness—to taste *her*, to possess her in what is in reality a sensual preparation and stimulant, a taste of what is to come when they enjoy a far more intimate exploration of one another.

'When a man in love kisses a woman's mouth and explores the taste of her already, in his mind, in his *body*, he is imagining—anticipating—the far more intimate taste of her.'

Rosy shivered. She was drowning in a flood of consuming heat caused by what she told herself was fury and embarrassment at what Guard was doing…saying to her.

She could feel the warmth of his breath against her lips, the heat of his palm against her scalp beneath her hair as he supported her head with one hand; the other was slowly caressing her back, stroking dangerously along her spine.

'He kisses her gently at first,' Guard told her. 'Like this…'

The pressure of his mouth against hers, so light that it was barely there at all, should surely not be having such a traumatic effect on her, Rosy fretted anxiously. It was sheer instinct, her desire to get what was, after all, an extremely uncomfortable and embarrassing episode well and truly behind her, that was making her want to press her mouth more urgently against Guard's.

'And then, as his need for her overwhelms him, like this…'

Rosy gasped in protest as the pressure of Guard's mouth on hers changed and hardened so quickly and devastatingly that shock paralysed her.

So this, then, was the way a man kissed, the way his mouth moved with hard urgency on yours, Rosy thought dizzily, the way the embrace involved not just the pressure of his mouth on your own but the whole of his body…and the whole of yours as well.

She was trembling, Rosy recognised, trembling helplessly, overwhelmed by her awareness of the vast gulf which lay between Guard's sexual experience and her own.

And the shock of that knowledge was somehow like

a physical pain, aching through her body, making her eyes sting with sharp tears.

When the pressure of Guard's mouth against her own eased, she felt almost sick with relief, until she realised that he wasn't going to release her at all—that he was—

'Open your mouth, Rosy,' he instructed her. 'Only children kiss with their mouths closed, or didn't you know that?'

'Of course I know,' she snapped indignantly, stiffening in outrage as Guard refused to let her continue, covering her mouth with his own, drawing the breath from her as he demonstrated what he had just been telling her.

Rosy had exchanged such kisses with boys before, exchanged them and felt mildly saddened because she was not feeling the almost mystical intense passion and sense of intimacy she had expected to feel.

But with Guard it was different... With Guard...

She could feel herself starting to tremble convulsively as her body registered its awareness of what was happening.

Confused, bewildered thoughts tumbled headlong through her brain as she tried to comprehend why it was that Guard's mouth...Guard's kiss...Guard's manufactured and totally fictitious passion should have the power to deceive her senses into believing...wanting...

With a small, frantic cry, she jerked back from him. She had never seen Guard's eyes look so...so...

She flinched as he reached out and touched her bottom lip with his thumb, demanding raggedly, 'Don't...'

'Turn round,' Guard told her.

Unwillingly she did so.

'Now look in the mirror.'

Guard was standing behind her, his hands resting

lightly on her shoulders, his face unreadable as Rosy focused unwillingly on their reflections.

'When a woman's been thoroughly kissed...*properly* kissed,' Guard told her quietly, 'it shows here...'

Rosy tensed as he reached out and touched the swollen fullness of her mouth, her eyes immediately darkening in response to his touch.

'And if she's particularly sensitive and responsive,' Guard continued calmly, 'it even shows here as well.'

The clinical detachment with which he so accurately traced a circle around the areola of her nipple took Rosy's breath away so completely that she was unable to utter any kind of protest.

Because of her thick sweater it was impossible for him to see—to *know*—how her nipples had swelled and hardened when he kissed her. Totally and completely impossible.

And there was certainly nothing in his clinical detachment to suggest that he did know, Rosy reflected with feverish relief as he released her and stood back from her.

Even so, she could still feel the hot, self-conscious colour sweeping up over her body despite her efforts to suppress it.

She struggled to think of something to say—some throw-away, casual remark to make—but her brain refused to supply one, her thought processes reduced to a thick, immobilising, treacle-like sludge.

As Guard turned away from her to walk towards the door, she found herself wondering silently how many women there had been in his life who had generated the reality of the passion he had manufactured to show her.

As he reached the door, he turned back towards her, warning her, 'It's too late to change your mind now, Rosy.'

CHAPTER FOUR

'YOU'RE doing what?'

There was no mistaking the shock nor the anger in Ralph's voice, Rosy recognised unhappily.

It had taken her over a week to bring herself to the point of telling Ralph about her marriage. Not because she had anticipated his reaction—she hadn't—but because she had been afraid that he would guess the truth.

Peter, as well as Guard, had warned her of the dangerous position she could put herself in if people started suspecting that her marriage was simply a ploy to keep the house.

'You and I may know how altruistic your motives are,' Peter had told her, 'but others may not.'

'Guard says that Edward could bring a case for fraud against us,' Rosy had told him. 'Is that true?'

'It's a possibility,' Peter had agreed cautiously. 'But he would have to have strong, almost irrefutable proof that the marriage was sham in order to do that. To be able to prove, for instance, that there was quite definitely no possibility of the marriage producing a child...'

'But there isn't,' Rosy had told him quickly. 'You know—'

'*I* know, *you* know and *Guard* knows,' Peter had anticipated her, 'but no one else knows—nor must anyone else know.'

And so Rosy had put off telling Ralph about her marriage, afraid that she might not be able to play her role of deliriously-in-love bride-to-be adequately enough to deceive him.

In the end, though, it wasn't her lack of love for Guard he had questioned, but Guard's for her.

'For God's sake, Rosy, don't you *see* what he's after?' Ralph demanded. 'He wants the one thing that he knows his money has never and will never be able to buy.'

'You mean me?' Rosy quipped.

'No, I don't. I mean Queen's Meadow,' Ralph told her grimly. 'It's no secret that he's always wanted the house. Your grandfather refused to sell it to him.'

'Guard and I love each other, Ralph,' Rosy interrupted him, superstitiously crossing her fingers in the folds of her skirt as she did so, glad that Ralph was looking directly at her as she told the lie.

'Oh, Rosy…can't you see? Men like Guard don't fall in love with—'

He broke off, his thin, slightly foxy face flushing slightly. 'Look, I don't want to hurt you, Rosy. You're an attractive girl—a very attractive girl—but in terms of…of experience, you and Guard might almost have come from different planets.

'You've seen here at the shelter the havoc that unbalanced relationships can cause, the pain that comes from an unequal relationship. Can you honestly tell me that you and Guard are equals in every way; that you and he…?'

'We're in love, Ralph,' Rosy repeated. 'And—'

'And he'll teach you everything you need to know. Both in bed and out of it. Rubbish,' Ralph told her. 'If you really, honestly believe that, then you're not the person I took you for. Sure, he'll enjoy playing with you for a few weeks—a few months possibly—but after that… Don't go through with it, Rosy. You don't need to marry him. You—'

'Yes, I do.'

The quiet, sad admission was made before Rosy could help herself, the words spoken so softly under her breath that Ralph couldn't hear them.

She looked up as the office door burst open and a woman, accompanied by two small children, came rushing in demanding to speak to Ralph.

Liz Phillips was one of their regulars at the shelter, periodically leaving her violent husband, announcing that there was no power on earth that could ever make her go back again, only to do exactly that within weeks of having left him.

'She must love him so much,' Rosy had commented innocently when she had first started working at the shelter.

'Yeah, like an alcoholic loves his drink, an addict his next fix; she's addicted to him, to the violence of their relationship,' Ralph had told her grimly. 'A part of her needs and craves what she sees as the excitement and uncertainty of their relationship. But for every Liz Phillips we get here, we get a hundred women who do genuinely want to break away from their relationship and start again, who need us to help them to make that break.'

'How do you recognise the difference?' Rosy had asked in bewilderment.

'With experience,' Ralph had told her shortly. 'Like everything else.'

Then, she had thought that Ralph was being unfairly hard. Now she knew better but, for once, as she finished her work, it was not the concerns of the shelter and its inmates that were absorbing her, but her own worries.

Guard had not looked too pleased when she had told him she wanted to invite Ralph to their wedding, but Rosy had remained adamant that she wanted him there.

Peter was giving her away. Guard had drafted a notice to be put in the Press, announcing their marriage; only a handful of people had been invited to the actual ceremony.

The ceremony. In two days' time she and Guard would be married. Husband and wife. It was a situation her imagination could still not encompass. She and Guard...husband and wife...Mr and Mrs... She and Guard participating in a deception which, if it was ever discovered...

Did all brides feel like this? Rosy wondered nervously as the car stopped outside the church and Peter got out. Or were her hands icy-cold, her mind and emotions frozen and numb simply because of the circumstances surrounding her particular marriage?

This morning, putting on her wedding-dress, standing stiffly in front of the mirror while Mrs Frinton fussed over her, fastening the hundred and one tiny satin-covered buttons that ran from the nape of her neck right down under the bustle and bow that ornamented the back of her dress, she had felt such anguish and guilt, such pain, that she had been tempted to tear off the dress and simply walk away...disappear. But then Peter had arrived and with him the flowers Guard had sent her, and events had developed a momentum it was impossible for her to resist.

And now here she was, walking into the lofty parish church, past the stained-glass window donated by one of her ancestors. The ivory satin of the wedding-dress, which had been her mother's and was a Dior original into which she had still had to squeeze herself—despite the weight she had lost this last week—so tiny had been her mother's waist, still had, clinging to its folds, a faint hint of the perfume Rosy could remember her mother wearing. Wearing it made her feel as though she was carrying a little of her mother with her.

That knowledge brought hot tears to her eyes which she fiercely blinked back.

The veil, once white but now ivory with age, had been her great-grandmother's. In wearing garments which had originally been worn with love, she felt as though she were somehow compensating for the lack of emotion in her own marriage.

Marriage. It *wasn't* a marriage, she reminded herself starkly. It was a business arrangement, that was all. A contract...

The church felt cold, the stone slabs beneath her feet striking icy-cold through the thin soles of her shoes.

The church was bleakly empty, only the first two pews filled. Someone, Guard presumably, had arranged for the hugely extravagant cream and white floral decorations which warmed the cold, austere dimness of the building.

As she saw Guard for the first time Rosy's footsteps faltered slightly and, even though he could not possibly have heard the soft, distressed sound she suppressed, he turned round.

He looked so remote and distant. It seemed impossible to imagine that she was actually marrying him. Rosy shivered, glad of the protection of her veil to hide her expression from him.

'Edward's watching you,' Peter warned her. 'Smile.'

Edward. Rosy hadn't even realised he was in church, but now she could see him, and with him his wife and his sons—two pale, subdued copies of their mother, hair slicked back, school uniforms on. Rosy flinched slightly as she looked hurriedly away from the taller of the pair.

By her marriage to Guard she was depriving him of his opportunity to inherit Queen's Meadow. Only, if Edward inherited, there would no longer be a Queen's Meadow for him to inherit.

She clung to that knowledge for comfort as she finally reached Guard's side.

The raucous, inappropriately joyful peal of the bells was making her feel sick, Rosy acknowledged as she blinked in the sharp clarity of the sunlight. Or was it the shock of that moment when Guard had thrown back her veil and looked so deeply into her eyes as the vicar pronounced them husband and wife that, for a fraction of time, even she had almost been deceived that the emotion, the intensity, the passion which had darkened his eyes as he looked into hers had been real.

There were people milling all around her. Where had they come from? Dizzily she recognised some of the women from the shelter, people who had known her father and grandfather, all of them smiling, laughing, making teasing comments about the suddenness of her marriage. All of them apart from Edward.

Rosy tensed as she saw the malevolence in his eyes.

She had always known he didn't like her, but it had never worried her. *She* did not like *him*, but now she recognised his dislike was different. Now she was standing between him and what he coveted, what he had assumed would be his.

A small shiver ran over her.

'What is it, what's wrong?'

Rosy tensed in surprise at Guard's question. She hadn't expected him to notice her small, betraying *fris-*

son of apprehension. He had appeared to be deep in conversation with Peter, too deeply involved to be aware of her.

'Nothing,' she told him guardedly, aware that Edward was still watching her, watching them both.

'That's a beautiful dress,' someone commented to her.

'Thank you. It was my mother's,' she responded absently.

'I thought I recognised it.'

That was Guard, catching her unaware for a second time, making her mouth open in a small 'O' of astonishment as she turned to face him.

'Your father had a photograph of her wearing it on his desk,' Guard reminded her. 'It suits you. The colour complements your skin. It has the same warm tint…'

He reached out and brushed his fingers lightly against her throat as he spoke.

'Edward's watching us,' Rosy warned him in a small, stifled voice.

'Yes. I know.'

'Do you think he suspects?' Rosy asked him nervously.

'If he does, this should stop him,' Guard assured her.

'This…?' Rosy looked up at him questioningly and then went still as she recognised the slow accomplished movements of his body, performed like some magical sleight of hand so that, to their onlookers, it must seem as though the way he took her in his arms, the way he held and kissed her, were the actions of a man so deeply in love with his bride that not even their discreetly curious observation could prevent him from exhibiting his feelings.

Unexpectedly, behind her closed eyelids, she could feel the hot burn of tears.

This was no time to go stupidly sentimental, she warned herself shakily. No time to compare the emotions her mother must have felt when she wore this dress to her own—

'Oh, I think it's all so romantic,' Edward's wife sighed enviously, as Guard released Rosy. 'It's just such a shame that your father...'

'John knew how I feel about Rosy,' Rosy heard Guard saying calmly.

He certainly had, Rosy acknowledged, but not in the way that Guard was implying. She could well remember her father once making an idle and half-envious comment about Guard being able to have any woman he wanted.

Rosy had been just seventeen then and she had reacted accordingly.

'He couldn't have me,' she had told her father challengingly.

Her father had laughed.

'You aren't a woman yet, poppet, and I doubt very much that Guard would *want* you anyway. He knows you far too well...what a little shrew you can be at times...'

'Where are you going for your honeymoon? Or aren't we allowed to ask?' Rosy heard Edward enquiring.

'We aren't,' Guard replied for her. 'At least not yet. I have a meeting in Brussels in two days' time which I couldn't put off. Rosy and I fly out there tomorrow morning.'

They flew out there? Rosy stared at him, but Guard was looking in the opposite direction, answering some comment that the vicar's wife had made to him, and Rosy had to wait until they were alone in the bridal car to ask him uneasily, 'Why did you tell Edward that we're both going to Brussels? He's bound to suspect something if he discovers that I haven't gone.'

She whispered the question, even though the glass panel between them and the driver was closed. That was what deceit did to you, she recognised mournfully. It made you cautious…wary…*guilty*.

'There won't be anything for him to discover,' Guard told her promptly. 'I meant what I said.'

'You mean you're expecting me to go to Brussels with you—without even asking me?' Rosy demanded indignantly. 'But I can't—I'm supposed to be working at the shelter…'

'Don't be ridiculous, Rosy,' Guard told her dampeningly. 'Dedicated though he is, Ralph is hardly likely to expect you to go back to work quite so quickly.'

'But I want to,' Rosy told him aggressively.

'If you do, you'll be putting us both at risk,' Guard warned her. 'It takes more than a church service to make a marriage, Rosy.'

Angrily, Rosy turned her head away from him. She knew full well what it took to make a marriage, but their marriage wasn't going to include *that* particular ingredient, and Guard knew it.

'It takes,' Guard continued calmly, 'a degree of intimacy which *most* couples develop in bed, but which you and I will have to find another way to manufacture. We need some time on our own to establish ourselves in our new roles, Rosy…'

When she didn't respond, he continued inexorably, '*You* were the one who wanted this marriage—'

'To save the house,' Rosy interrupted him angrily. 'Not because…'

In her heart of hearts she knew that Guard was right that the awkwardness she felt when she was with him

was bound to betray her, but the last thing she wanted
to do was to spend time on her own with him. In her
view, that would only exacerbate the problem, not solve
it.

'I don't want to go away with you, Guard,' she told
him dangerously now. 'I don't want to come back and
have people looking at us…speculating…imagining…
believing…'

'What?' he challenged her, his eyebrows lifting.

'You know what,' Rosy muttered, avoiding looking
directly at him.

'Thinking that we've been to bed together? Most of
them assume that we've already done that. Imagining
that we've spent the whole of the time we've been away
making love…that my supposed business meeting is just
a fiction and that in reality the hours I should have spent
seated behind some boardroom table have been spent
exploring every inch of your body, stroking and caressing it until I know every contour of it, every hollow and
curve.'

Out of the corner of her eye Rosy could see the way
his glance was lingering on her breasts and immediately
the hot, agitated colour flared in her face.

'Such embarrassment,' Guard mocked her. 'You'd
burn with that colour from the tip of your toes to the
top of your head if I told you exactly what I'd expect
and want the woman I loved to do to my body the first
time we went to bed together,' Guard told her outrageously. 'Have you ever even *seen* a naked man, Rosy?
Never mind—'

'Of course I have,' she lied hotly, interrupting him.
'I realise how much you like making fun of me,
Guard,' she added with angry dignity. 'Yes, I do
get…embarrassed when you talk about such—such in-

timate things. And no, my experience doesn't come any-where near matching yours but, contrary to what you seem to believe, I *prefer* to be the way I am. *Anyone* can get sexual experience,' she added, gathering confidence when he didn't make any attempt to interrupt her or mock her. 'And just because I choose *not* to do so—'

'Just as a matter of interest, Rosy, *why* have you chosen not to do so?'

'You *know* why,' Rosy told him huskily.

'Because you're saving yourself for the man of your dreams,' Guard mocked her. 'What happens if you never meet him, Rosy? Have you ever asked yourself that?' Guard demanded with such unexpected savagery in his voice that his anger shocked her.

CHAPTER FIVE

'BUT this isn't a hotel,' Rosy protested as Guard swung their hired car up the drive and stopped in front of the entrance to an impressive, stone-built château.

Ever since Guard had made his announcement that she was going to Brussels with him Rosy had protested and argued that she didn't want to, but it hadn't made any difference.

'And what am I supposed to do,' she had exploded angrily, 'while you're in your meetings?'

'You've never struck me as a person so uninterested in her fellow human beings that she suffers from boredom, Rosy, far from it...'

Rosy had glared suspiciously at him. Compliments from Guard? He must have some ulterior motive, and she suspected she knew quite well what it was. She wasn't a complete fool.

'I'm not going with you, Guard,' she had told him. 'I don't *want* to go with you.'

But, somehow or other, all her protests had been overruled and now here she was, glaring frustratedly at Guard's profile, thoroughly incensed by his ability to remain calm when all her emotions were a seething mass of churning chaos.

She wasn't used to being married; she wasn't used to having a husband, to being part of a pair...a couple, and she resented Guard's apparent assumption that *he* should be the one to decide what they should and should not do—what she should and should not do.

'No, it isn't a hotel,' he responded calmly now. 'It's a private home. Madame, the châtelaine, is French and, rather than sell the property after her husband's death, she decided to supplement her income by taking in paying guests. Like most Frenchwomen, she is not just an excellent cook, but a first-rate hostess and extremely skilled in the art of making one comfortable.'

Rosy frowned. Something in Guard's voice when he spoke about the owner of the château irked her a little. Without his having described her in any detail, Rosy immediately had a mental image of one of those elegant, ageless Frenchwomen whom she, personally, had always found particularly intimidating.

'But you said you had business in *Brussels*,' she objected. 'This place is miles away.'

'A little over two hours' drive,' Guard told her. 'That's all. And staying here gives me an excuse not to get involved in the Brussels political scene, which can be as pedantic as the people involved in it. I thought you'd like it here. You've always said you prefer the country to the city.'

Rosy looked away from him. It was true that she *did* prefer the country, and normally she would probably have enjoyed such a trip, but normally she would not have been making it with Guard—as his wife.

Guard was already climbing out of the car and going round to open her door.

Unwillingly, she had exchanged her normal favourite wear of leggings and a comfortable top for a long jersey skirt with a matching waistcoat. Beneath it she was wearing a soft, cream shirt. The outfit had a matching knitted jacket which she had brought with her just in case she felt cold.

She had worn the outfit knowing that it wasn't likely to crease, a fact of which she was uncharacteristically glad as the door of the château opened and Guard's Frenchwoman appeared.

Predictably, she was dressed in black—a wool, crêpe skirt which Rosy suspected must have come from one of the couture houses, teamed with a plain satin shirt and a cashmere knit draped flatteringly round her shoulders. The pearls gleaming at her throat—all three rich ropes of them—had to be real, just like the diamonds on her fingers and in her ears, but it wasn't her elegance that struck Rosy as she reluctantly fell into step beside Guard, it was her age, or rather her lack of it.

The woman was not, as she had expected, somewhere in her late fifties or early sixties, but far closer to forty—closer, in fact, to Guard in age than she was herself, Rosy recognised.

Quite why that knowledge should cause her to feel so hostile towards Madame, she had no idea, but that she was not alone in that feeling became quite clear.

Madame turned to Guard, totally ignoring Rosy, to say coolly to him, 'Oh, I hadn't realised that you would be bringing a…friend with you.'

'Rosy is my wife,' Guard explained firmly, drawing Rosy forward and introducing her.

Friend or wife, it plainly made no difference as far as Madame was concerned; she was obviously not pleased about Rosy's presence.

'I had put you in your normal suite,' she told Guard, somehow or other managing to stand in between them so that she was facing Guard but had her back to *her*,

Rosy observed, as she listened to the Frenchwoman speaking to Guard in her own tongue.

Rosy's own French was extremely fluent. She had a gift for languages which had been fostered during the years her father had been stationed in Germany. Her French was, in fact, far more fluent than Guard's.

'However, if you should prefer another room...' Madame was saying.

Another room. Rosy's heart thumped uncomfortably.

She had assumed that they would be staying in Brussels in a large, anonymous hotel and that they would, as a matter of course, have separate rooms. After all, Guard could have as little desire to share the intimacy of a bedroom as she did.

'No, my usual suite will be fine,' Guard was assuring their hostess.

The large, draughty hallway of the château made Rosy glad of her long skirt.

Queen's Meadow was kept relatively warm by its low ceilings and thick panelling, but this place, with its lofty rooms and bare stone walls, must be a nightmare to heat, Rosy reflected as Madame preceded them up the stone staircase.

Its carpet, although well-worn, was decorated with what Rosy presumed were the arms of her late husband's family. Rosy paused to examine them more closely, wondering if she was correct in interpreting that the bend sinister in one quarter of it with the fleur-de-lys meant that at some point in history one of the château's châtelaines had been a Royal mistress and had borne her lover a son.

Up ahead of her, Madame was walking side by side with Guard, saying something in French about regretting the fact that his wife's presence meant that they would not have their normal tête-à-tête dinner together.

Guard's urbane and English, 'No, I'm afraid not, but I'm sure that Rosy will thoroughly enjoy sampling your wonderful culinary skills,' made Rosy glower at him. There was surely no need for him to practise his role of supposedly loving husband *here*.

It was on the tip of her tongue to say that, as far as she was concerned, he and Madame could enjoy as many tête-à-têtes as they wished, but instead she suppressed the impulse, contenting herself with a less-than-warm smile in Madame's direction and telling her in her own fluent French that she was indeed thoroughly looking forward to such a treat.

Apart from a narrow-eyed look and a faint pursing of her artfully carmined mouth, Madame made no comment. But she was no longer talking to Guard in French, Rosy noticed, as the older woman walked them along a corridor, stopping outside a heavy, wooden door.

'I trust everything will be to your liking,' she told Rosy formally and without conviction.

This time it was Rosy's turn to be distantly unresponsive.

As the woman left them the thought crossed her mind that the relationship between her and Guard could have been far more intimate than that of hostess and guest but, oddly for her, it was a suspicion that she didn't voice.

Her impetuosity had always been something of a joke in the family, and she was ruefully aware that she did have a tendency to speak before she thought, but when it came to Guard's personal life, and his sexual experience, it wasn't just reticence that held her back.

Just thinking about Guard and sex made her stomach

clench nervously and her body grow hot and wary. There was, she admitted, something simply far too dangerous about the whole subject for her to risk making any kind of unguarded comment about it, to risk giving Guard the opportunity to taunt her about her own comparative innocence and ignorance.

And yet with other men she felt no such discomfort—quite the opposite. As she walked past Guard and into the suite's sitting-room she was immediately aware of the scent of Madame's perfume, lingering on the air. Silently, she studied her surroundings—the giltwood furniture, the hugely ornate gilded mirror above the fireplace, the rococo work and the silk wall-hangings in a pale green moire that seemed to shimmer with a life of its own.

Vases of white, waxy lilies added to the room's elegance; it would have been easy to find such a setting quite intimidating, Rosy recognised as she frowned down at the faded Aubusson rug on the floor.

'I normally use this bedroom,' she heard Guard saying from behind her as he opened one of the two doors leading out of the room. 'It has an adjoining bathroom; the other one does not, but if you'd prefer...'

What she'd prefer would be to be at home, on her own, Rosy recognised grimly, as Guard well knew.

'I don't care,' she told him dismissively and then couldn't resist adding, 'Hadn't you better have the one with the bathroom? After all, I'm sure Madame will expect you to be properly groomed before you join her for your usual tête-à-tête.'

'Jealous?'

The soft taunt, so unexpected and so impossible, shocked her into silence.

Jealous... How could she be? Guard meant nothing to

her. The only emotions that existed between them were a dismissive contempt for her on his part, and an impotent antagonism towards him on hers.

Jealous... It was impossible, unthinkable, and Guard knew it. So why had he said it?

She shook her head, unable to bring herself to make the denial. Why should she when there was nothing to deny?

Instead, she turned her head away from him and reminded him fiercely, 'I didn't want to come here, Guard.'

'Maybe not, but you are here. *We* are here, and while we're here—'

As she started to walk away from him, he moved towards her, barring her way to the bedroom door.

'Look at me, Rosy,' he commanded. 'You aren't a child any more, to be indulged by being allowed to walk away from an argument to save face when you know you can't win it.'

'An argument?' Rosy gave him a bitter look. 'When has anyone ever been *allowed* to argue with you, Guard? I thought you were omnipotent—all-seeing, all-knowing. So...go on... While we're here, what? I can sit like an obedient child playing gooseberry whilst you and Madame—'

'There is nothing between Madame la Comtesse and me,' Guard told her grimly, emphasising the older woman's title.

'Maybe not, but *she* would like there to be,' Rosy guessed intuitively.

'I repeat, there is nothing between us,' Guard continued, ignoring Rosy's comment. 'But even if there were...'

'It would be none of my business,' Rosy supplied sarcastically.

'Perhaps not,' Guard agreed levelly. 'But that was not what I was going to say. What I was going to say, Rosy, was that you should at least try to put your antagonism towards me to one side occasionally and apply the laws of logic and rationality, instead of giving way to those over-imaginative emotions of yours.

'The reason I insisted that you come with me on this trip was to give us both time to adjust to our new... status. To have done that and then brought you into the presence of my lover would hardly make much sense, would it?

'The time to worry, my dear, is not when I insist on your accompanying me on business trips, but when I start making excuses *not* to take you.'

For some reason he was smiling, a fact which infuriated Rosy so much that she could feel her face starting to burn with angry colour.

'So much passion and so little outlet for it,' Guard mocked her, touching one hot cheek with a cool fingertip.

'Stop patronising me, Guard,' Rosy demanded heatedly. 'I'm not a child.'

'No?' The smile disappeared, to be replaced by an assessingly level look. 'If only that were true.'

'No, thank you. No more wine for me,' Rosy refused, shaking her head and valiantly trying to suppress a yawn.

Guard had not exaggerated Madame's culinary talents, but Rosy had not really enjoyed the meal. The way Madame had deliberately excluded her from the conversation and concentrated exclusively on Guard had at first amused and then later irked her.

To be fair, she had to admit that Guard had done his best to reverse Madame's bad manners, making a point of bringing Rosy into their discussions, but Rosy had grown tired of the game and longed to make her excuses and escape to her bed.

'In fact, if you don't mind, I think I'll go to bed,' she added quietly, standing up before Guard could say anything and formally thanking their hostess, and complimenting her on thc meal.

Guard's quiet and totally unexpected, 'I think I'll come with you,' shocked her into protesting.

'No, you stay here.' But Guard was already slipping his hand under her elbow and adding his thanks to hers as he walked with her to the door.

'You didn't have to do that,' Rosy snapped once they were in the hallway. 'You could have stayed.'

'What, and leave my new bride on her own?' Guard drawled mockingly.

Rosy glowered at him, compressing her lips.

'There's no need to be so sarcastic,' she told him crossly. 'I'm not a complete fool, Guard. I know quite well that you—'

When she stopped, he prompted, 'That I what?' But Rosy refused to be drawn, shaking her head. What was the point in saying what they both knew? That she was the last person that Guard would want to marry—and the last person to want to marry *him*?

'I don't know why you brought me here,' she repeated untruthfully, her temper suddenly exploding. 'What am *I* supposed to do with myself while you're in Brussels. Ask Madame to give me some cooking tips?'

'You won't be staying here,' Guard told her promptly. 'You're coming with me.'

'What?' Rosy stared at him.

'I think you'll find Monsieur Dubois rather interesting and, since he doesn't speak English and my French is rather on the pedestrian side, I'd certainly appreciate your assistance.'

What did Guard mean? She'd find Monsieur Dubois interesting? Guard's business involved providing extremely detailed and complex computer programs, a subject about which Rosy knew very little, as Guard well knew.

'Monsieur Dubois is a keen environmentalist,' Guard continued, correctly reading her mind. 'He is the spokesperson for a very influential group lobbying the EEC for better and tighter controls over the destruction of the natural vegetation of the countryside and, since that's something I know you take a keen interest in, you should have a lot in common.'

It was so unlike Guard to make a comment to her that did not include mockery of one sort or another that for once Rosy could think of nothing to say.

'And, of course, having you to translate for me will save me the cost of hiring an interpreter,' Guard added.

Rosy flashed him an indignant look. Just for a second she had almost been deceived into thinking that for once he was treating her as an equal, an adult. She was so irritated that she was almost tempted to refuse to go with him, but the alternative of staying at the château was not an appealing one.

'I've got some notes I need to read up,' Guard told her as he unlocked their suite door, 'so if you want to use the bathroom first…'

Rosy knew she ought to feel grateful to him for his

tact, but instead she felt ruffled and awkward, like a child sent to bed to be out of the way of the adults. Was Guard's claim that he wanted to do some work simply a ruse to get rid of her so that he could go back downstairs to rejoin Madame?

If Guard wanted to be with the Frenchwoman, then he had no need to lie to her, Rosy decided angrily. He was a perfectly free agent in *that* respect; they both were.

So why did the thought of Guard and Madame, their dark heads close together while Madame's scarlet, pouting mouth whispered in Guard's ear, cause her such an uncomfortable and unpleasant sensation in the pit of her stomach?

Its cause, Rosy decided, thoroughly disgruntled, was surely not so much an emotional reaction to the thought of Madame's overpainted, full red mouth against Guard's ear, but rather a physical reaction to the reality of Madame's over-rich food in her stomach!

When she had first agreed with Peter to try to save the house she had not fully realised exactly what she was letting herself in for, she admitted bleakly as she undressed and stepped into the huge, claw-footed bath. The last couple of weeks had been far more stressful than she had expected—than she wanted to admit.

There had been a moment at the wedding breakfast when she had looked at the familiar faces around her and suddenly and sharply ached for the comforting and familiar presence of her father and grandfather.

Mortified by her own weakness and the tears which had filled her eyes and choked her throat, she had quickly bent her head over her plate, hoping that no one had noticed. Guard had been safely engaged in conversation with Edward's wife, or so she had thought, which had made it even more humiliating when he had pushed a large, clean handkerchief into her hand and told her quietly, 'I miss them too, Rosy. That at least is something that we do share.'

Unexpectedly, tears filled her eyes now. Crossly she blinked them away. What was the matter with her these days? She had never been the crying type.

Madame might be generous with her food, but she was mean with her hot water, Rosy decided as she washed herself quickly and jumped out of the bath, wrapping herself in a thick, white towel and then rubbing her body briskly with it—as much to banish her too-intrusive memories as to dry her skin.

As she pulled on her cotton T-shirt, with its cartoon drawings on the front, she grimaced at her reflection in the bathroom mirror.

No one seeing her now would ever be deceived into believing she was a rapturously happy bride, she acknowledged.

When and if Guard did marry, she doubted that it would be to a woman—a *girl*—who wore cotton T-shirts to bed and plain white underwear. She doubted that Madame, for instance, even possessed such garments.

Picking up her discarded clothes, she headed for the bedroom, calling out as she entered it, 'Guard, I've finished in the bathroom now.'

Silence. Had he heard her? She frowned, nibbling at her bottom lip as she stared at the closed bedroom door, glancing uncertainly from it to the bed and then back again. The last thing she wanted was to be woken up by Guard rapping on the door to find out where she was.

Sighing under her breath, she walked over to the door and opened it.

Guard was seated at the desk in front of the window, his head bent over the papers spread over it. Rosy watched him for a few, brief seconds. It was a very rare experience for her to have the opportunity to study him unobserved. He was a very handsome man, a very charismatic man, she acknowledged with a tiny thud of her heart. A man most women would love to be married to. But she was not one of them, she told herself hastily. When she married…

'What's wrong, Rosy?'

The calm question, asked without Guard's lifting his head or looking at her, made it plain that he was not, as she had imagined, oblivious to her presence at all.

'If you're going to tell me that you can't sleep without your favourite teddy bear,' he added grimly, 'then I'm afraid…'

Anger darkened Rosy's eyes. She hadn't slept with her teddy bear for years. Well, not until these last few weeks, when she had felt so devastated by the double loss of her grandfather and father.

'I came to tell you that the bathroom's free,' she informed him with awful dignity.

'Would you like a nightcap before you go to bed?'

His question took her by surprise, her eyes widening slightly and her skin flushing as he put down the papers he had been studying and turned towards her.

She would like a drink, Rosy recognised, but she was acutely conscious of the fact that she was in her nightshirt.

'I—I'd better go and get my dressing-gown,' she told him uncomfortably. 'I—'

She tensed as he stood up, the dark eyebrows lifting sardonically as he came towards her.

'That's very considerate of you, Rosy,' he told her sardonically. 'But hardly necessary. I think I have enough control over my manly passions not to succumb to a fit of lust at the sight of you in your nightwear. After all, it's hardly the most seductive of garments, is it? Not exactly bridal…'

'I suppose when *you* go to bed you wear silk pyjamas,' Rosy defended herself wildly, remembering reading a book in which the hero had been thus clad. 'But for your information—'

She stopped abruptly as Guard started laughing. She had rarely seen him laugh before and for some reason the sight and sound of him doing so now caused a hard, sharp pain to pierce the middle of her chest.

'What is it? Why are you laughing?' she demanded suspiciously.

'No, Rosy,' Guard told her, shaking his head, mirth lightening his eyes so that they seemed more amber than their normal formidable eagle-gold, 'I do not wear silk pyjamas. In fact,' he added dulcetly, watching her closely, 'I don't wear anything at all.'

Rosy couldn't help it; she could feel herself blushing, a betraying wave of scarlet colour washing up over her body and engulfing her in humiliating, self-conscious embarrassment… Not just because of what Guard had said, nor even because of his laughter, but because, unbelievably, unwantedly and untenably, she had just had the most appallingly clear mental image of Guard's naked body—a body which, in that brief, illuminatory vision, had been both arrogantly male and erotically aroused…

She swallowed hard, too caught up in her own emotional shock to be aware of the way Guard's amusement had turned to frowning scrutiny of her suddenly over-pale face and harrowed expression.

'Go to bed, Rosy,' she heard Guard telling her

abruptly. 'You've been under a lot of strain recently, and a good night's sleep—'

Suddenly it was all too much for Rosy.

'I'm not a child, Guard,' she told him chokingly. 'I'm a woman, an adult, and it's time you recognised that fact and treated me as one.'

Angrily she blinked away the temper-tears blurring her vision, only to hear Guard saying warningly to her, 'Don't tempt me, Rosy. Don't tempt me.'

CHAPTER SIX

'*MADAME*... So Guard has married at last. I cannot say I blame him,' Monsieur Dubois told Rosy with warm appreciation in his eyes as he shook her hand in response to Guard's introductions.

'And so, how long have you been married, my friend?' he asked Guard in his careful English.

'Not very long,' Guard told him. 'Not very long at all.'

'How angry you must be with me, *madame*,' Monsieur Dubois apologised to Rosy. 'But not so angry as Guard, I suspect. But he is the only person I could trust to do this all-important work for us. It is vital that when we present our case to the authorities we have all the information at our fingertips. These days one doesn't just need knowledge and eloquence, one must have facts, figures, graphs. One must be computer litcrate or risk the consequences.

'Guard has told you something of our work?' he asked Rosy, as he guided them into his large office overlooking the business centre of the city.

'Something,' Rosy agreed, reluctantly admitting to herself that she was rather enjoying herself. It felt good to be using her brain, her linguistic abilities, and it felt even better knowing she had a skill that Guard could not quite match, she acknowledged ruefully.

As Guard had said, Monsieur Dubois's English was

very limited and many of the technical terms he used when he started enthusiastically to explain to her the needs of his organisation were unfamiliar even to her, although she was quickly able to interpret their meaning.

While Guard was following their conversation, she could see from his frowns that he was having difficulties. Without really knowing why, she found herself gently stopping Monsieur Dubois and then turning to Guard, quickly explaining to him what was being said, unaware as she did so of the quiet air of authority and self-assurance in her manner and voice or the maturity it gave her.

When Monsieur Dubois eventually glanced at his watch and exclaimed over the length of time he had kept them, Rosy was surprised to discover how quickly the hours had flown and how much she had enjoyed what she was doing, despite the fact that she had always claimed to her father and to Guard that computers and all that went with them were just not her thing and she was more than happy to keep matters that way.

As they got up to go, Monsieur Dubois turned to Guard and told him, 'My wife and I are giving a small family party this evening. Nothing of any great merit, a simple affair to celebrate our elder daughter's attainment of her degree. I should be delighted if you could both join us, but perhaps you have other plans…?'

'None,' Guard responded promptly. 'What time would you like us to arrive?'

As soon as they were alone, Rosy turned to Guard and protested, 'I can't go to a party, Guard. I haven't brought anything suitable with me to wear.'

'So? Brussels is not on another planet,' he told her drily. 'It does have shops, some very good ones too, I believe. Although I must warn you, Rosy, Monsieur

Dubois is the rather old-fashioned sort and I suspect that
his obviously very high opinion of you would suffer
somewhat were you to dress in something you have lib-
erated from disinterment. He would, I suspect, take it
rather as an insult if you turned up at his daughter's party
wearing something from a charity shop.'

Rosy turned on him angrily.

'I don't need any lectures from you, Guard, on what
I should and should not wear,' she snapped. At home in
her wardrobe she had two formal 'little black dresses'
bought specifically to wear when she went out with her
father or grandfather to various social events. *She* might
prefer the comfort of her leggings or the sumptuous feel
of the velvets and silks she snapped up from sales and
markets, but she would not for the world have upset or
embarrassed either of them by wearing something she
knew would make them feel uncomfortable.

Guard, though, was a very different matter.

However, she had liked Monsieur Dubois and had recognised for herself, without having to be told by Guard,
that he was the old-fashioned sort.

'Unfortunately, I have another meeting this afternoon,' Guard told her, glancing at his watch. 'Otherwise
I'd come with you.'

'No, thanks,' Rosy told him curtly. The last thing she
wanted was to have Guard standing over her in some
dress shop telling her what she should buy.

'What about lunch?' Guard asked her.

'I'm not hungry,' Rosy lied. The euphoria and pleasure she had felt earlier had now gone. Guard hadn't just
made her angry with his comments about her clothes, he
had— He had what? Offended her? Hurt her?
Impossible. Nothing Guard could say could ever do that.
He simply didn't have that kind of power over her.

'If you need some money, Rosy...' Guard offered, but Rosy shook her head.

'I can afford to pay for my own clothes, Guard,' she told him fiercely.

'Yes, I know. You know, Rosy, when you eventually find this perfect, wonderful man of yours, I hope you'll try to remember what prehistoric creatures we males still are in many ways.'

'What do you mean?' Rosy asked him suspiciously.

'I mean that, despite the fact that I cannot think of anything more abhorrent than the kind of clinging woman who wraps herself around you with all the stranglehold of a piece of ivy, we men still enjoy the pleasure of feeling that we can spoil and indulge our woman.'

'By rewarding them for good behaviour by buying them something in the same way that you'd throw a dog a biscuit,' Rosy challenged him, her eyes flashing with contempt and anger. 'The man *I* love will treat me as his equal, Guard—in every way. The last thing he'd want would be for me to feel beholden to him for anything. What we give each other will be given freely.' She broke off, frowning as she saw the way Guard was looking at her.

'What is it? What's wrong?' she asked him uncertainly.

She had never seen him looking at her like that before, never seen him watching her with such intense concentration.

'Nothing's wrong,' he denied harshly. 'But one day, Rosy, you're going to have to grow up and to learn the pain that comes with such idealism. I hope for your sake that, when you do, there's someone around to pick up the pieces...'

'Just so long as it isn't you,' Rosy muttered defiantly

under her breath. Trust Guard to want to have the last word, to want to put her down.

It was almost an hour now since Guard had dropped her off in the shopping quarter of the city, but so far she had seen nothing she wanted to buy, Rosy admitted as she passed in front of a small boutique to study the dress in the window. Of black velvet and silk taffeta, it had a black velvet bodice with a slightly off-the-shoulder neckline and long, tight sleeves; the bodice fitted tightly, snugly over the waist and the taffeta skirt flared out from just above the hips.

The expensive fabric and the colour gave the dress sophistication, but the skirt made it a younger woman's dress, not the kind of thing which could be worn by Madame la Comtesse, for instance.

Determinedly, Rosy walked into the shop.

'It's a very small size, a couture model,' the saleswoman began doubtfully when Rosy enquired about the dress. But once Rosy had removed her coat, she added more warmly, 'But, yes, it will probably fit you.'

It did...just... She had had to remove her bra to try it on, otherwise the straps of her underwear would have shown, but the bodice of the dress was stitched in such a way that it gave her just as much shape as though she had been wearing a bra, Rosy admitted as she studied her reflection in the mirror.

The richness of the velvet seemed to emphasise the creamy texture of her skin, the way her curls caressed the unfamiliar bareness of her exposed shoulders giving her a slightly vulnerable look that made her frown slightly.

'It might have been made for you,' the saleswoman enthused.

'It's very expensive.' Rosy hesitated—and she would have to buy new evening shoes to go with it. In the end it was the memory of Guard's contemptuous dismissal of her clothes and her taste that made up her mind for her.

'You won't regret buying it,' the saleswoman assured her, as she packed the dress for her. 'A dress such as this is an investment, a classic. It will never date.'

No, but I shall, Rosy reflected wryly as she made her way back to a shoe shop she had passed earlier.

'You managed to find something, then?' was Guard's only comment when he picked Rosy up later at their appointed meeting place.

In addition to the dress, she had several other packages: shoes, a small evening bag to go with them, a soft cashmere wrap to wear over the dress and a pretty seventeenth-century enamelled box she had noticed in the window of an antiques shop and which she had bought as a small gift for Monsieur Dubois's daughter.

Something more anonymous and safer might have been a wiser choice, she acknowledged as Guard drove out of the city, but the box had been so pretty.

'Damn,' Guard cursed softly, suddenly causing Rosy to glance questioningly at him. 'I meant to ask you to buy something for Gerard's daughter. It's too late to turn back now and—'

'I've got her something,' Rosy told him, turning in her seat to retrieve the parcels she had put on the back seat of the car.

She unwrapped the small box, carefully balancing it on the palm of her hand to show him.

When he said nothing, her heart sank slightly. Obviously he didn't approve. Well, that was just too bad, she decided crossly. She liked it and—

'You know, Rosy, there are still times when you can surprise me. You affect to be uninterested in tradition, you state that you think it's almost a crime for somewhere like Queen's Meadow still to be a private home, and then you go and buy something like this…'

'If you don't like it—' Rosy began challengingly, but Guard was already shaking his head in denial of her statement.

'I think it's perfect,' he told her simply. 'Perfect.'

His compliment was so unexpected that Rosy had no idea what to say. She raised her eyes to his and then tensed slightly as she saw the way he was looking at her. It was as if…as if… A funny, unfamiliar, achey sensation filled her chest, radiating out from just where her heart was.

'Rosy…'

Why, when she had, after all, heard him say her name so many times before, was the sound of his voice suddenly making tiny quicksilver shivers dart up her spine? Why did the sound of it suddenly remind her of a tiger's purr, of soft velvet on smooth skin, of the seductive whisper of a man to his lover…?

Hurriedly, she rushed into speech, desperately pushing away such dangerously contentious thoughts.

'I even managed to remember to buy wrapping-paper, Guard, and a card. Do you know her name? I should have asked Monsieur Dubois. I hope she doesn't think that we're intruding. After all, it is her party and she doesn't know us.'

'Her name, I believe, is Héloïse,' Guard responded, his voice suddenly oddly flat. 'As to whether or not she'll resent our presence, I should imagine that is extremely unlikely.'

He didn't speak again until they were driving into the

château, and then it was only to remark that, since they had both missed lunch, she must be hungry and he would ask Madame if it was possible for them to have a light meal in their suite.

'Ah, good, you're ready. We should be all right for time, but—'

Rosy tensed as Guard suddenly fell silent as he caught sight of her. She watched him uncertainly from the open bedroom door.

In the shop she had been so confident that the dress was the right choice, but now suddenly she wasn't so sure.

Guard's silence, the way he was looking at her… She swallowed nervously.

'What's wrong? If it isn't suitable…'

'No…' Guard was shaking his head as he turned away from her to pick up the jacket he had placed on the back of a chair and put it on. 'It's fine…'

His voice sounded oddly strained, almost slightly hoarse, Rosy recognised, her attention distracted from her own appearance as she watched the way the movement of Guard's body stretched the white fabric of his shirt against the long, sinewy muscles of his back.

She could see the movement of them beneath his skin through his shirt. Her mouth had gone slightly dry.

She felt breathless and slightly on edge, her senses abruptly and unfamiliarly heightened so that, across the space that separated them, she was suddenly sharply aware of the clean male scent of Guard's body. She gave a small shudder, her pulse suddenly racing, the bodice of her dress tightening slightly against her breasts as though— She glanced down at her body and gave a small, stifled gasp as she saw the raised outline of her nipples pushing against the velvet fabric, embarrassment flushing her skin as she turned round quickly and hurried back into the bedroom, calling out quickly to Guard, 'My wrap…I almost forgot… It's quite chilly and—'

Could Guard hear the agonised, embarrassed confusion in her voice as clearly as she could? She was not cold at all, but what other explanation could there be for that quite unmistakable physical reaction?

'You're cold?'

Guard was frowning as he followed her into the bedroom.

'I—I was. I'm all right now,' Rosy fibbed as she hugged the wrap protectively around her body. 'I—I thought you wanted to leave,' she reminded him. 'We don't want to be late.'

'Nor do we want to be too early,' Guard told her drily, and then reminded her, 'We are, after all, very newly married…'

When she continued to look blankly at him, he explained grimly. 'Use your intelligence, Rosy. We're newly married and supposedly very much in love. Do you really imagine if that was actually true that there's any way I'd be letting you walk out of here so easily, or that you'd want me to?

'Oh, no—' His voice had dropped to a soft whisper that was almost a hypnotic caress, Rosy acknowledged, as she felt another feverish shudder run through her.

'If we were really what we're supposed to be, right now that stunningly fetching little number you're wearing would be lying on the bedroom floor and you, my dear, would be lying in my arms.'

'Stop it, Guard, stop it,' Rosy protested shakily.

'We're not in love. We're not... It isn't like that...
and...'

'No, it certainly isn't,' Guard agreed drily. 'Are you
sure you need that wrap?' he added as he walked to the
door and opened it for her. 'You look quite flushed...'

Rosy glared at him as she swept past him. He knew
quite well what had caused her skin to colour up like
that, damn him.

Did he also know that all she had on under her dress
was a tiny pair of briefs and a pair of silky, hold-up
stockings?

Of course not, how could he? And yet there had been
something about the way he had looked at her when he
made that comment about the dress lying on the floor
and her lying in his arms which, for some reason, had
immediately conjured up in her imagination an image of
herself almost completely naked, her breasts pressed flat
against his chest, while he ran his hands up over her
back and told her what he wanted to do to her and what
he wanted her to do to him, how he wanted to touch her
and how he wanted her to touch him.

As she hurried downstairs another shudder racked
Rosy's body, a sharper one this time, saw-edged and
painful, making her bite down sharply on her bottom lip
in suppression of it.

Her fears that she might feel awkward and uncomfortable among people that she did not know, or that
Monsieur Dubois's daughter might resent her father's
having invited them, were very quickly dispelled—not
only by Monsieur Dubois's and his wife's warm welcome of them, but additionally by the enthusiastic reception they received from Héloise herself, and Rosy
was very quickly drawn into the circle of younger people

surrounding her while Guard remained talking with their host and hostess.

Héloise and her friends were a lively, intelligent crowd, very vocal in expressing their ideals and beliefs, teasing Rosy a little—but not unkindly—over what they saw as her nation's reluctance to accept the concept of European citizenship. But Rosy soon discovered that, like her, they too were very concerned about the plight of those less fortunate than themselves, and she was soon absorbed in a discussion with one of Héloise's male friends about the growing problem of the city's homeless.

Renauld, although physically nothing like Ralph—he was much more sturdily built, with thick, curling brown hair and hazel eyes that, Rosy couldn't help but notice, warmed with very open male appreciation when he looked at her— shared very many of Ralph's ideals, leavened with a sense of humour that Ralph tended to lack.

'It seems to me that this is a problem that is common to all nations,' Renauld enthused, as he detached Rosy from the others so that he could talk exclusively to her. 'It occurs to me that we would all have much to gain from exchanging our experiences—sharing what we have learned with one another.'

'Hold a conference, you mean?' Rosy teased him.

'Perhaps something a little less formal than that. I go to Britain occasionally on business, and I should be very interested in visiting your shelter, if that could be arranged.'

'I'm sure it could,' Rosy responded enthusiastically. 'I know Ralph would be very interested to meet you.'

'You are some way out of London, though, from what you tell me,' Renauld began. 'Is there a hotel…?'

'Oh, there'd be no need for that,' Rosy assured him quickly, impulsively. 'You could stay with us.'

'Now that I shall look forward to,' Renauld told her softly.

'Don't take Renauld too seriously,' Héloise warned her teasingly ten minutes later when she came over to join them. 'He is a terrible flirt...'

'You are being very unfair, Héloise,' Renauld protested, unabashed by her comment. 'I am very good at it.'

The three of them were still laughing when Guard came to join them several minutes later.

'I'm afraid it's time for us to leave,' he told Rosy, explaining to the others, 'We have an early flight to catch in the morning.'

'So soon?' Rosy protested, unable to conceal her surprise when Guard told her drily what time it was.

'No need to ask if you enjoyed yourself,' Guard commented once they were in the car heading back to the château.

There was a note in his voice that Rosy couldn't quite place. Not anger or irritation exactly, but something...

'You and young Renauld Bressée certainly seemed to find plenty to talk about.'

Young Renauld...? Rosy's forehead creased in a small frown. During their conversation, Renauld had told her that he had just passed his twenty-fifth birthday, which might make him younger than Guard, but it certainly didn't merit that odd note of dismissive contempt in Guard's voice.

'He was telling me about a scheme he's involved with that's similar to our shelter,' Rosy responded defensively. 'He seemed very interested in the work we're doing. I—I invited him to come down and meet Ralph the next time he's in London on business,' Rosy added, rushing through the sentence and avoiding looking at Guard as she spoke.

Although why she should feel she had somehow done something wrong—that she had somehow angered Guard—she really had no idea, she told herself firmly.

'And that would be the sole purpose of his visit, would it?' Guard challenged her. 'To meet Ralph?'

Rosy was glad of the darkness of the interior of the car as she felt herself starting to blush slightly.

There was an edge to Guard's voice which underlined her earlier discomfort.

'Of course. Why else would he come?' she demanded.

'Oh, come on, Rosy, even *you* aren't *that* naïve,' Guard told her bitingly. 'It was pretty obvious that Bressée was far more interested in inspecting your bed than those at the shelter.'

'That's not true,' Rosy protested. 'And even if it were—'

She stopped abruptly, suddenly realising that the claim she had been about to make that it was no business of Guard's was no longer wholly true. She had, she recognised, almost forgotten their new relationship.

'Even if it were what?' Guard demanded in a hard voice. 'You aren't interested in him? That wasn't the impression I was getting.'

'We were *talking*, that was all,' Rosy objected. What was wrong with Guard? It was almost as though… As though what? As though he was jealous? Impossible. But even though Rosy assured herself that she had done nothing to merit Guard's attitude towards her, she could already feel the happiness she had experienced at the party starting to drain away. She turned away from Guard and looked bleakly out of the window into the darkness.

She gave a small shiver, remembering what Peter had told her when she had asked him how she and Guard would end their 'marriage'.

'You will have to stay together at least a year,' Peter had warned her. 'Anything less than that and it would be bound to cause suspicion. Initially, you could publicly opt for a "trial separation" and then slowly move from that towards divorce.'

At least a year. Suddenly it seemed a very, very long time.

'There's no point in sulking, Rosy,' she heard Guard telling her tersely. 'You knew what the situation was going to be; the part you'd agreed—chosen, in fact—to play. You're a very new bride, and very new brides do not ignore their husbands and flirt with another man.'

'If you mean Renauld, I was *not* flirting with him,' Rosy protested angrily. 'We were simply talking.' She paused, her eyes flashing as she turned to look at him. He was concentrating on his driving, his gaze fixed firmly ahead of him, his jaw warningly taut.

'*You* may not be able to have a conversation with a woman without flirting with her, Guard,' she told him recklessly, ignoring the message her senses were relaying to her, 'but not *all* men are like you. Thank God,' she muttered under her breath.

'No, they're not,' Guard agreed harshly. 'I doubt your precious Ralph, for instance, or Renauld Bressée, would be prepared to put their reputation at risk in a fraudulent marriage just because—'

'Just because what?' Rosy pressed, when Guard stopped speaking. 'Because I asked you? You're not being fair, Guard. We both know exactly why you agreed to this marriage. You married me because you want Queen's Meadow.'

As she said the words, Rosy felt her throat starting to close up as a wave of intense desolation swept over her.

She hadn't wanted any of this—a fictitious marriage, a husband who didn't even particularly like her, never mind love her. The last thing she had ever wanted was to live a life filled with lies and deceit, to live with a man who felt nothing but irritated contempt for her, who constantly criticised her.

Everything she was having to do went so totally against her deepest principles that it was no wonder she was feeling so uncomfortable with herself, so on edge and miserable.

She had been a fool ever to listen to Peter, to think that—

'And of course the Ralphs and the Renaulds of this world are far too perfect, far too high-minded even to consider doing such a thing, is that what you think?' Guard demanded tautly. 'Don't kid yourself, Rosy,' he warned her. 'If you'd dangled the deeds of Queen's Meadow in front of Ralph for bait, he wouldn't even have thought twice about the moral implications of such a marriage.

'And as for Renauld, did he think to tell you, I wonder, while he was flirting so assiduously with you, that both his and Héloise's family have assumed for years that the two of them will eventually marry? They're distant cousins with complex property and business connections—a marriage between them would tie things up very nicely as far as the families are concerned. Not that that would have stopped him bedding you, of course.'

'Stop it…stop it…' Rosy protested shakily, lifting her hands to cover her ears as she turned her face towards him.

'Why do you always have to be so critical, so cynical?' she demanded passionately. 'Why do you always have to spoil everything for me? I'm not a complete fool, Guard, whatever you might think. Just because I choose—because I *prefer*—to see the best in people, that doesn't mean that I'm not aware.'

As she blinked back the angry tears threatening to flood her eyes she turned away from him, her voice low and slightly rough with pain as she told him, 'All right, so maybe Ralph would have agreed to marry me if I'd offered him Queen's Meadow, but at least *he* wouldn't have wanted the house for himself. He would—'

'He would have destroyed it just as surely as Edward,' Guard interrupted her flatly. 'Grow up, Rosy. Do you honestly, truly believe that Ralph would have cared a single jot for the house or its history? That he wouldn't have quite happily torn out the panelling and boarded up the staircase if that was what it would have taken to get the place passed as an institution?

'Do you know what would have happened to Queen's Meadow in those circumstances?' Guard demanded harshly. 'It would have had to comply with fire regulations, with safety regulations and with God alone knows what else as well. And if you think that *anything*—anything at all—of the original house would have been recognisable to your father or grandfather by the time Ralph and his cohorts had finished with it, then you're a fool.'

'You've never liked Ralph, have you?' Rosy accused furiously. 'You've always made fun of him, sneered at him. Well, don't think I don't know why, Guard—' Rosy stopped abruptly as she half turned towards Guard to see how he was receiving her furious tirade.

He didn't look as she had expected—neither furiously angry nor mockingly contemptuous.

His jaw was clenched as though he was holding himself under immense control and, as she watched him, Rosy saw a small muscle jerk slightly, pulsing against his skin, and the look in his eyes when he turned his head...

An involuntary shudder seized her as Rosy heard him invite her softly, 'Go on, Rosy...'

Oh, how she wished she'd never started this conversation, but it was too late to back down now... Much too late.

'You resent the fact that he isn't like you, that he doesn't care about money or material things,' Rosy challenged him bravely. 'Because he's—'

She tensed as Guard started to laugh, so confused by his unexpected reaction that it actually alarmed and upset her more than if he had actually raged furiously at her in denial of her assertion.

'Ralph, not care about money? Then how come he's constantly bombarding *me* with requests for donations for his precious shelter?' Guard taunted her.

'That's different,' Rosy objected. 'He doesn't want it for *himself*. He—'

'No? Is that what you really think, Rosy? All right, I agree he doesn't want money to spend on himself, on *possessions* for himself, but he certainly wants the glory he knows damn well he can get by lifting that pathetically amateur outfit of his into something much more high-profile and professional.'

Rosy bit her bottom lip and looked away from him. Cruel though Guard's comments were, they held a certain hard, gritty core of truth which she herself was far too honest to be able to deny.

To her relief, she realised that they had reached the entrance to the chateau. With any luck, Madame would be lurking in the hallway awaiting their return—or rather Guard's return.

'What—nothing to say for yourself, no passionate defence of your precious Ralph? And why is that, I wonder?' Guard observed cynically as he brought the car to a smooth halt in front of the château.

Rosy did not deign to answer him. What, after all, was the point?

Tiredly, Rosy reached for the zip of her dress. Madame had not, after all, been waiting for them but, once they had reached their suite, Guard had announced that he had some work to catch up on, and had promptly seated himself at the desk, totally ignoring her.

Which, of course, was exactly what she wanted. So quite why it should have made her feel so bad-tempered and irritable, she had no idea. It couldn't be because she had lost an argument to him, nor even because she was beginning to feel so oppressed by the burden of her unfamiliar and unwanted role.

She frowned as the zip on her dress ran smoothly for a couple of inches and then jammed. Irritably, she tried to work it free.

Ten minutes later, with her arms aching and the zip still well and truly jammed, she admitted defeat, acknowledging that she now had only two options open to her: either she would have to go to bed in the dress, or she would have to ask Guard for help.

Reluctantly, she walked towards the bedroom door and opened it, standing uncertainly just inside the doorway whilst she studied Guard's downbent head.

He was seated with his back towards her, making notes on whatever it was he was reading, his concentration so intense that Rosy hesitated to interrupt him.

Perhaps if she tried the zip one more time…

'Yes, Rosy, what is it?'

Rosy's startled gaze flew to meet Guard's as he put down his pen and turned towards her.

'It's the zip on my dress,' she told him awkwardly. 'It's stuck and…'

'You'd better come over here and stand in the light where I can see what I'm doing properly,' Guard informed her, motioning her to the centre of the room as he correctly anticipated her request. 'Perhaps you are growing up after all,' he added wryly, as he took hold of her shoulders and turned her round so that he could examine the back of her dress.

'What do you mean?' Rosy demanded stiffly, sensing a fresh taunt and trying to turn round, but Guard was holding her shoulders too firmly for her to move.

It was an odd sensation to feel his fingertips on her bare skin, to see in the mirror over the fireplace the pair of them standing together in a pose which could almost have been one of intimacy…of lovers…

A tiny *frisson* of sensation ran over her skin, an odd and unfamiliar awareness of Guard, not as she always thought of him, but as a man. If it had been Guard whom she had met at the party tonight, for instance, Guard who had flattered her, flirted with her…

Mortified by the extraordinary direction of her own thoughts, she looked down at the floor.

'When did it happen, Rosy?' Guard asked her softly. 'When did preserving a dress become more important to you than preserving your hostility towards me?'

'I don't know what you mean,' Rosy fibbed. Was that a sign of maturity, to decide it was preferable to ask Guard to help rather than tear her dress?

If so, she was beginning to wish that she had made a

more immature decision, she acknowledged; she could feel the tension crawling along her spine as she felt the warmth of Guard's breath on the skin of the nape of her neck, as he pushed the weight of her hair out of the way so that he could investigate the jammed zip.

She had read books in which the heroine virtually swooned in ecstasy as the hero pressed impassioned kisses against her nape, but had scornfully dismissed such descriptions as being wildly exaggerated.

Now… She swallowed hard, curling her fingers into two small, shocked fists while the warmth of Guard's breath against her skin, as nebulous as mist floating across a meadow, nevertheless had an effect on her senses that was so potent that she—

It was Guard's irritated, 'Keep still, Rosy,' that made her realise what she was doing; she was moving her body back into his as though…as though she actually *wanted*…as though she was actively seeking to intensify that soft *frisson* of sensual warmth which had bathed her skin in such unexpected sensation.

'Oh, leave it, Guard,' she protested, trying to pull away from him, frantically aware that something had gone wrong, that somehow her body had got its messages all tangled up and that, for some inexplicable reason, it had suddenly decided to react to Guard, to respond to Guard as though—

'Keep still. I can see what the problem is now. There's a small piece of cotton caught in the zip. I think I can work it free, though.'

'Where? Let me see it—I can probably do it myself,' Rosy protested, trying both to pull away from Guard and to swivel round so that she could see over her shoulder but, as she moved forward, Guard managed to free the zip, leaving the soft, supple velvet to slither free of her shoulders and her upper body.

Frantically, Rosy grabbed hold of the velvet, her face flushing as deep a pink as the exposed peaks of her nipples as she stood in mesmerised shock while Guard made a slow and very thorough visual inspection of her half-exposed body.

'Stop it, Guard. Stop looking at me like that,' she blurted out huskily, her voice trembling as much as her body. She wanted to turn and run but for some reason she couldn't move. She could only stand there while Guard's gaze slid lingeringly over her body.

'Like what?' he asked her softly. 'I am, after all, your husband, Rosy, and in reality…'

As he took a step towards her Rosy stared at him with huge, shocked eyes, her nakedness—the original reason for the feeling of excited, nervous sensation crawling slowly through her stomach—forgotten as she felt herself trembling in the golden heat of Guard's gaze, unable to look away from him.

'In reality,' he continued softly, 'have you any idea what it would be doing to me right now, seeing you like this, if we really were man and wife? If you'd deliberately wanted to do so, you couldn't have chosen a more sensually provocative pose, do you know that? The injured innocent clutching her clothes to her body, and yet at the same time exposing—'

Rosy shivered as his gaze dropped to her breasts, hot colour scorching her face as she felt her nipples start to ache.

'If I really were your husband, Rosy, I wouldn't be standing here talking to you,' Guard told her roughly, 'and it wouldn't just be your mouth that would be left swollen and sensitive from my kisses…

'What's wrong?' he taunted her, when he heard the small, shocked gasps she gave. 'Surely you're not so innocent, so naïve, that you didn't *know* that it isn't just the feel of a woman's breasts and nipples in his hands that turns a man on; that the sensation of caressing and suckling a woman's breasts, the sound of her soft cries of pleasure, the—'

'No... No...' Rosy moaned in protest, finally tearing herself free of her imprisonment and turning round to run almost headlong into her bedroom, slamming the door closed behind her and leaning on it while her body shook as though she had a fever and her heart pounded so hard that it made her feel sick.

The hot tears of anguish that crawled silently down her flushed face from behind her closed eyelids had nothing to do with outrage or embarrassment, or anger against Guard for what he had done.

Just for a moment, while she had listened to the hypnotic softness of his voice, she had actually seen his dark head bent over *her* body, his mouth caressing *her*—

Her stifled denial left her throat raw and aching. Shock, bewilderment, guilt, fear—all of them formed a lump of incomprehensible pain and panic that hurt physically as well as emotionally. She had not just mentally visualised Guard's dark head bent over her body, she had also felt...

Trembling from head to foot, her face white with shock, Rosy slowly levered herself away from the door.

What was happening to her? What had happened to her?

She showered quickly.

She walked slowly from the bathroom and got ready for bed, refusing to meet her own reflection in the mirror, conscious of the way the fabric of her nightshirt seemed to rub against the suddenly sensitive peaks of her nipples.

Her face burned with renewed colour.

There was something wrong with her, there had to be, imagining Guard caressing her like that... Imagining herself wanting him to, her body aching for him... needing him...

It was just a trick of her imagination, she assured herself; tomorrow she would feel differently, be back to her normal self...

CHAPTER SEVEN

'WHAT'S wrong, Rosy? Not still sulking because I broke up your flirtation with Bressée, are you?' Guard asked drily.

Cautiously, Rosy turned her head to look at him, reaching for her seatbelt as she did so, when the stewardess announced that they would shortly be landing.

Had Guard really forgotten what had happened last night? The way he'd looked at her, the things he had *said* to her?

He was frowning slightly as he fastened his own seatbelt, a hint of impatience tightening his mouth.

It seemed almost impossible this morning to believe that he was actually the same man who had made her so shockingly, so sensuously—aware of him, and of herself, of her sexuality, her vulnerability.

Had she perhaps overreacted to the whole incident, built it up in her own shock and embarrassment into something much more than it had actually been? Had she been lying awake half the night, dreading having to face Guard in the morning, dreading what he might say, unnecessarily?

It had almost been something of a let-down when he had made no reference at all to the incident, calmly behaving towards her just as he had always behaved, treating her more like an irritating child than a—

Than a what? A woman? A nervous skein of hair-fine

sensations tightened ominously in her stomach, her face and body suddenly uncomfortably hot.

'Come on, Rosy,' Guard instructed her as the plane bumped down on to the tarmac. 'The last thing we need now is to arrive back looking as though we aren't speaking.'

'I'm *not* sulking,' Rosy told him stiltedly. 'I'm just…tired, that's all.'

'Tired—after a two-day business trip? That will raise a few eyebrows,' Guard derided tauntingly, ignoring her self-conscious flush to continue, 'Once we've picked up the car, I'll drop you off at Queen's Meadow, and then I want to go on to my office to go through a few things, and to the apartment. Did you sort out a room with Mrs Frinton?'

Rosy shook her head. She was behaving a bit like an ostrich, she knew, but so far she had not been able to bring herself to deal with the practicalities thrown up by their marriage.

On the night of their wedding she had slept in the room she had occupied since childhood, while Guard had slept in one of the guest-rooms, but she knew that there was no way they could continue to preserve the fiction that their marriage was a love match if they continued to sleep in separate rooms with almost half a mile of corridor between them.

'I—I thought— There are two guest-rooms with an interconnecting door and, if I made up the beds myself, then Mrs Frinton won't—'

'Mrs Frinton won't what?' Guard interrupted her. 'Mrs Frinton won't guess that we're sleeping in separate beds? That's fine, Rosy, just as long as she doesn't. If it ever gets out that you and I *are* sleeping separately,

you can depend upon it that Edward will have his lawyers on to us so fast…'

Rosy shivered.

'Aren't there any rooms with twin beds?' Guard asked
her.

'Only in the attic bedrooms,' Rosy told him, 'and it
would look odd if we slept up there.'

'Indeed,' Guard drawled.

'Cheer up,' Guard mocked her later, once they were on
their way home. 'Remember, it's only for a year and—
who knows?—you might even get to like it.'

'Never,' Rosy told him vehemently, and then immediately flushed a bright and betraying red as she remembered how last night, just for a second, she had experienced that dismaying and extraordinary flood of physical
desire.

'Be careful, Rosy,' Guard warned her, adding
obliquely, 'Some men might be tempted to take that as
a challenge, to prove to you that—'

As Rosy stiffened automatically in rejection of his
taunt, Guard turned into the drive, breaking off to ask
her, 'Isn't that Edward's car?'

'Yes,' Rosy agreed flatly.

'Mm… I wonder what *he's* doing here. Staging a wel-
come-home party, do you think? How very thoughtful
of him.'

'Edward never does anything thoughtful,' Rosy told
him grimly. 'He always has an ulterior motive.'

'Mmm… Well, there are no prizes for guessing what
it is this time, are there?'

When Rosy looked questioningly at him, Guard explained.

'The house, Rosy, the house.'

'But it's too late for that. He *knows* we're married.'

What was Edward doing at Queen's Meadow? she wondered, worried, as Guard opened the car door for her and she got out. He knew how much she disliked him, how unwelcome his presence would be.

'Smile, Rosy,' Guard reminded her as he opened the heavy front door. 'Smile.'

As he held the door open for her she had to walk so close to him that it looked almost as though his arm was actually draped possessively across her shoulders and, as she turned towards him to tell him that the last thing she felt like doing was smiling, he looked down at her and murmured dulcetly, 'That's better. Now, if you move a bit closer towards me and open your mouth a little, who knows? It *might* almost appear to an onlooker that you're waiting for me to kiss you.'

To kiss her!

Indignation flashed in Rosy's eyes but, before she could say anything, Mrs Frinton came hurrying into the hallway, looking very upset and anxious.

'Oh, Rosy...I mean Mrs...'

'Rosy is still fine, Mrs Frinton,' Rosy assured the older woman. 'You look upset. Is something wrong?'

Before Mrs Frinton could answer, Rosy heard someone coming downstairs. As she look upwards, she realised that it was Edward, smiling his fake, crocodile smile at them.

'Ah, Rosy—and Guard!' he exclaimed, his smile disappearing as he shook his head and told them dolorously, 'Bad news, I'm afraid. We discovered last week that the subsidence at home which we thought was only a minor problem is far, far more serious. In fact, we've had no option but to move out of the house while the surveyors and lawyers get to work sorting everything out.

'Margaret was worried about our moving in here without being able to let you know, but I told her she was being silly. After all, what else are families for if not to help one another out in an emergency? Where else *could* we go? With all my confidential papers and the work I do at home, it would be impossible for us to move into some hotel. The noise alone would play havoc with Margaret's migraines, and then when the boys come home for half-term... No—I said immediately that we should come here.

'Margaret is still at home, supervising the last of the packing, but she should be here soon. I've taken the liberty of instructing Mrs Frinton to prepare Grandfather's suite for us, although of course we'll have to have a couple of beds brought down from the attic floor. We prefer them these days, you know. Margaret doesn't sleep well and...'

Dumbstruck, Rosy stared at him, hardly able to believe what she was hearing.

'Of course I know that you two young people are only just newly married, but I promise you you'll hardly know we're here and you'll find Margaret a big help, Rosy, my dear. She's used to running a large household—organising dinner parties, that kind of thing.'

Rosy drew in a shaky breath, opened her mouth and then closed it again, not trusting herself to speak. Instead, she gave Guard an imploring look. Thank goodness he was here with her. He would know how to deal with Edward, how to make him leave.

But, to her shock, instead of instantly demanding that Edward *did* leave, Guard said almost conversationally to him, 'Rosy's grandfather's suite—that would be the master suite, I take it?'

'Yes, that's right,' Edward agreed affably, and then added with what, to Rosy, was sickeningly fake concern, 'Oh, I did check with Mrs Frinton that you and Rosy weren't using it, of course. She didn't actually seem to know where you'd be sleeping…'

A look Rosy didn't like flickered in the sharp, foxy eyes as he glanced from Guard to her and then back to Guard again.

'Of course, the bathroom attached to the master suite leaves a lot to be desired and—'

'Which is why, I'm afraid, you'll have to pick another room,' Guard interrupted him calmly, whilst Rosy's eyes widened in disbelieving shock. What was Guard saying? Why hadn't he told Edward that he couldn't stay—that he must leave!

She tensed as Guard reached out and placed his arm around her, drawing her closer, her body stiffening in outraged rejection as she glowered at him.

'Rosy and I were just discussing our plans for reno-vating that part of the house on the flight home,' Guard continued. 'In fact I intend to get in touch with the ar-chitect tomorrow. To be honest with you, Edward, I should have thought you'd have found the upper storey bedrooms more appropriate. Especially, as you say, with half-term coming up. And, of course, as you remarked yourself, Rosy and I are still rather protective of our privacy…as newly-weds…'

As he spoke, he turned towards Rosy and added ten-derly, 'Isn't that so, my love?'

Fortunately, he didn't wait for her to make any reply and neither did Edward.

'By the upper storey, I take it you are referring to the

attic bedrooms,' Edward demanded warily, 'the servants' quarters…'

'That's right,' Guard agreed evenly. 'And now if you'll excuse us, Edward, we have one or two things we need to attend to. Since you aren't here as a guest, I know you won't expect us to stand on ceremony with you. Oh, and I'm afraid you won't be able to call on Mrs Frinton for any assistance. I'm afraid I've behaved in what Rosy insists is a rather chauvinistic fashion and left it to them to organise the removal of my own possessions from my apartment and find new homes for them here. Which reminds me, Edward…I know you won't take offence but, since we are to be sharing the same roof, I know you'll understand if I say that the library and study will both be off-limits to you and your family. As a newly married man, I shall want to spend as much time as I can with my wife, which means that I shall be working, as far as possible, from home.

'You don't have to worry about anything on that side of things, darling,' Guard added, smiling lovingly down into Rosy's indignant eyes. 'I'll make all the arrangements with the technicians and so forth about installing the telex and the computer stuff.

'Mrs Frinton—Rosy and I have both had a tiring few days. Do you think it would be possible for us to have a little light lunch in the winter parlour? I won't ask you to join us, Edward,' Guard continued smoothly. 'I appreciate how busy you must be… Bad luck—about the subsidence, I mean,' Guard added, as Edward watched him warily.

It was only the almost painful pressure of Guard's fingers round her arm that prevented Rosy from exploding into angry speech before they reached the sanctuary of the small, panelled winter parlour, but once they were there and the door was safely closed behind them, she pulled herself out of Guard's restraining hold and demanded tearfully, 'Why didn't you tell Edward to leave? Why did you let him think it was all right for him to stay here? He *can't* stay here, you know that. I don't *want* him here. I don't believe he really doesn't have anywhere else to go. He's just doing this because... because...'

'Go on,' Guard told her grimly. 'Because what?'

'Because he wants to spy on us,' Rosy flashed fiercely. 'Because...'

'Because he's obviously suspicious?' Guard suggested grimly.

Woodenly, Rosy looked away from him.

She was only just beginning to realise the import of Edward's presence at Queen's Meadow and what it really meant. At first she had simply assumed that he had moved in to annoy them, out of spite and malice, but now Guard was making her acknowledge that he could have a far more sinister and dangerous purpose.

As the seriousness of what Guard was saying sank in the colour seeped from Rosy's face, leaving it pale and strained.

'You're saying that he suspects that we're not...that we don't...that our marriage... But he's only guessing,' she protested as she paced the floor nervously and then swung round to look pleadingly at Guard, willing him to agree with her.

'At this stage, yes,' Guard acknowledged. 'But don't underestimate him, Rosy. He's a very dangerous man.'

'If you really think that, then why are you letting him stay here?' Rosy demanded. 'You should have told him to leave.'

'And risk making him even more suspicious? No, I couldn't do that. I warned you that something like this might happen, right at the outset, Rosy.'

'No, you didn't,' Rosy denied passionately. 'You never said anything about Edward's moving in with us or—'

'Not specifically,' Guard agreed. 'But I did point out to you the risks we were taking, and I did warn you, as well, that there was no way I was going to allow my reputation—professional or personal—to be jeopardised by this marriage.

'Don't delude yourself, Rosy. It won't just be Queen's Meadow that we stand to lose. If Edward suspects that he might be able to make a case against us—' He paused, shaking his head. 'People have faced prison sentences for less.'

'Prison…' Rosy's face went white with shock. 'No,' she whispered. 'No… You're just trying to frighten me.'

She tensed and Guard frowned warningly at her as someone knocked on the parlour door.

When Guard opened it to admit Mrs Frinton carrying a large tray, she relaxed slightly, but her tension soon returned when the housekeeper looked uncomfortably at them both and then burst out, 'I don't want to say anything out of place, only I did work for your grandfather for a long time, and it was obvious that he and Mr Edward— Well, it's just that Mr Edward has been asking an awful lot of questions.'

'What kinds of questions, Mrs Frinton?' Guard asked her calmly.

How could he be so calm after what he had just said to her, the fright he had just given her? she wondered miserably.

Prison. It was impossible. Wasn't it?

'Well, he wanted to know what room you and Rosy would be using, for instance,' she replied. 'He said it was because he didn't want to upset anyone by taking the room you wanted, and he said that he'd noticed how Miss Rosy's things were still in her old room…'

Rosy gasped in outrage. How dared Edward go into her room? If her grandfather were still alive, he would never—

If her grandfather were still alive, none of this would ever have happened. She would have had no need to marry Guard. She would have had no need to lie and deceive.

She could feel the hot, anguished tears burning the backs of her eyes.

'I said as how I didn't know which room you'd be using, but he kept going on about it. Asked which one you'd used after the wedding…' Mrs Frinton flushed uncomfortably as he looked at them both.

'It's all right, Mrs Frinton,' Guard assured her quickly. 'As a matter of fact we were going to discuss with you which room we shall be using. As I'm sure you'll understand, there are certain rooms which, for emotional reasons, Rosy doesn't want to use. Her father's bedroom, for instance, and her grandfather's. I've already explained to her that I can hardly share the bed in her present room,' Guard added softly, causing Rosy to give him a flushed and indignant glare. They had discussed no such thing, and if he thought he was being funny… Obviously Mrs Frinton knew they wouldn't be using that room. It only had a single bed in it, for one thing.

'We had thought we'd walk round the house together and make our choice that way, although I suspect whichever room we choose will only be a temporary arrangement, since most of the bathrooms need modernising. I personally rather like large Edwardian baths—for a variety of reasons,' Guard added wickedly, with a look at Rosy that made both her and Mrs Frinton blush, 'but Rosy insists that she would prefer something a little more modern and I must admit that I'm going to miss the high-powered shower in my apartment…'

Rosy waited until Mrs Frinton had gone, angrily shaking her head when Guard asked her if she wanted something to eat, wondering how on earth he could so calmly tuck into the sandwiches Mrs Frinton had made, for all the world as though nothing was wrong.

'You *know* we've already decided which rooms we were going to use,' she burst out.

'*Were* being the operative word,' Guard interrupted her quietly, putting his plate to one side and getting up. 'Things are different now, Rosy, which is why, for the duration of Edward's and his family's stay here, you'll be sleeping in my bedroom.'

'*Your* bedroom?' Rosy questioned uncertainly. 'But where will you sleep?'

She had already guessed the answer, and the look he gave her confirmed her worst suspicions.

'Oh, no,' she protested quickly. 'No… Not that. I'm not sharing a room with you, Guard—sleeping in the same… No… We can't.'

'We don't have any alternative,' Guard informed her grimly. 'It's either sharing a room *and* a bed with me, Rosy, or potentially sharing one in one of Her Majesty's prisons with someone else.'

'No,' Rosy denied. 'No. You're just trying to frighten me.'

'What? Do you really think I'm so desperate for a woman that I need to frighten *you* into sleeping with me? Grow up, Rosy,' Guard told her sardonically. 'It isn't sex that's worrying me right now. It's fraud.'

Rosy chewed worriedly on her bottom lip.

'You really mean it, don't you?' she asked him slowly. 'You really do think that Edward suspects.' She gave a small shiver, her eyes registering her fear. 'We wouldn't really go to prison, would we, Guard? I mean, it isn't as though—'

'As though what? As though we've done anything wrong in conniving together to deprive Edward of his inheritance? I doubt that the courts would take such a lenient view.' He gave her a wintry look. 'Of course, if you prefer to ignore my advice and take the risk of—'

'No,' Rosy denied quickly. She was really beginning to feel afraid now.

'I'm no more happy about the situation than you are,' Guard told her. 'I agreed to marry you, Rosy, not sleep with you and, believe me, if there'd been any way I could have got Edward to leave without adding fuel to the fire of his suspicions, I would have done so.'

Guard didn't want to sleep with her, to share his bed with her? Rosy frowned as she recognised that she was not finding this information quite as reassuring as she ought.

Those odd feelings that floated, haze-like, just beyond her grasp—were they really chagrin, pique and the hurt of rejection? Surely not!

'So…this room would seem to be the most suitable. Unless you'd prefer one of the others?'

Silently, Rosy shook her head.

She and Guard had just spent an hour inspecting the bedrooms.

Rosy had paused briefly outside the door to the two

adjoining rooms which she had originally believed they
would occupy, but Guard had firmly taken hold of her
arm and drawn her away, murmuring grimly to her,
'Think yourself lucky that I've managed to insist that
Edward isn't sleeping on the same floor as us, otherwise
I suspect we'd have him in the room next to us eagerly
monitoring every sound—or lack of them.'

When he saw the revulsion darken her eyes, Guard
had grimaced cynically.

'You find that offensive. Well, I promise you, it's
nothing to what could be dragged up in Court...'

Now they were standing in a large, corner room at the
opposite end of the house from the rooms she and her
father and grandfather had occupied.

Rosy stood in silent contemplation of the huge, four-
poster bed.

Perhaps at one time this room, with its large, comfortable bed, its warm panelling, its fireplace, and even
its deep window-seat, had represented sanctuary to another woman—had even, perhaps, been somewhere
where she had known love and pleasure—but *she* could
not see it like that. She bit down hard on her bottom lip,
trying to keep her anguish at bay.

She was afraid, she recognised shakily, afraid for almost the first time in her life. Not of Guard, no matter
how much she might balk at having to share a room—
and a bed—with him. No, what she feared was the danger he had revealed so trenchantly to her.

'We couldn't...we wouldn't really go to prison, would
we?' she asked him in a small voice through dry lips.

'What do you want me to tell you, Rosy? A comforting lie to make you feel better? *You're* the one who
keeps telling me that you're a woman and not a child,'
he reminded her.

'But if Edward believes that we're sleeping together, that we're really married, then you think that he'll stop being suspicious?' she persisted stubbornly.

'It would certainly give him less grounds for his suspicions,' Guard agreed. 'But don't underestimate Edward, Rosy. He's a liar and a cheat and, like all liars and cheats, he knows very well how to recognise those traits in others.'

'I don't think anyone's slept in this room since Gramps's seventieth birthday party,' Rosy told Guard in a strained voice as she ignored his comment and walked over to the larger of the room's two windows.

The velvet covering the window-seat was old and faded, like the curtains and the bed-hangings, but it still had a richness, a softness, an air of luxury about it that no modern fabric could match.

'This velvet came from Venice,' Rosy told Guard stiltedly. 'My grandmother bought it when she and Gramps were there on their honeymoon…'

'Yes, I know,' Guard responded quietly.

There was a note in his voice that Rosy had never heard before. He sounded almost as though he felt compassion for her…pity…

'Rosy, I know that this isn't easy for you…'

Rosy stiffened as she recognised that he had left the bed and was coming up behind her.

If he touched her now— Her spine tensed as she turned away from the window, rushing into hurried speech.

'We'll need fresh bedding and…and towels. There are some linen sheets, I think, that should be large enough— Irish ones that were a part of my great-grandmother's trousseau. It's a very big bed…'

'A very big bed,' Guard agreed. 'With more than

enough room in it for both of us and a couple of bolsters.'

'Bolsters?'

Puzzled, Rosy turned round.

'Yes, bolsters,' Guard agreed. 'You put them down
the middle of the bed to split it into two. At one time,
no romantic novel worthy of its name would have been
without them, or so I've heard,' Guard told her drolly.

Rosy gave him a wan smile.

'We couldn't use them even if we had any,' she told
him. 'Edward might see them…' Her voice cracked suddenly, hot tears flooding her eyes. 'I never dreamed it
would be like this,' she cried miserably. 'I just wanted
to protect the house, that's all.'

'Yes, I know. Come on, have a good cry. It will make
you feel better,' Guard told her, crossing the floor and
drawing her into his arms with surprising gentleness.

She had no time to reject him or to protest; this was
a Guard she had not previously known, she recognised
as she succumbed to the comfort of being held firmly in
his arms, of having the warm solidity of his body to lean
on.

Being held like this by him brought home to her how
alone she now was—her father and her grandfather both
gone, no loving, paternalistic figure for her to turn to
with her troubles any more.

This knowledge made her tears flow faster, soaking
through the fine white cotton of Guard's shirt.

'It wasn't supposed to be like this,' she protested, half
hiccuping the words.

'I know.'

How comforting Guard's voice sounded, as comforting as the protective way he was holding her.

'Guard, I'm so afraid. What are we going to do?'

The whispered admission made his arms tighten slightly around her. Guard must be afraid as well, Rosy acknowledged, otherwise he would never have stressed the danger of their situation to her so strongly.

'Well, there *is* one way we could get Edward off our backs—permanently.'

Rosy tensed and lifted her head from his shoulder, staring up at him in shocked disbelief.

'Tell the truth, you mean? Admit that we deliberately set out to deceive him? No… We couldn't do that.'

Rosy shivered as Guard suddenly released her, stepping back from her and turning his back on her, his voice familiarly harsh, his whole manner towards her hurtfully distancing.

'No, you're right, we couldn't,' he told her. 'Look, I've got to go into my office, Rosy,' he said crisply, glancing at his watch. 'I'll get back just as soon as I can. With any luck, Edward will be too busy transporting his confidential papers to hound you too much while I'm gone.'

What had happened to the closeness, the warmth which had seemed to exist between them only moments ago? Rosy wondered, shivering slightly. Where had it gone?

What she ought to be asking herself was where it had come from in the first place, she told herself tiredly when Guard had gone. And if it had actually existed at all, or if she had simply imagined it.

There was quite definitely no history of any emotional rapport between them—far from it—and yet she could have sworn, when Guard had taken hold of her, that he had genuinely wanted to comfort her, to reassure her, to be close to her.

Guard wanting to be close to her? Now she *was* letting her imagination run away with her.

No doubt in reality he was cursing the day he had ever been foolish enough to agree to marry her.

'I just hope you appreciate what we're doing for you,' she whispered to the house, gently touching the panelling as she opened the bedroom door.

'There's something about a proper bed made up with proper bed-linen,' Mrs Frinton exclaimed in satisfaction as she stepped back to admire both her own and Rosy's handiwork.

The four-poster bed, along with every piece of furniture in the room, including the panelling, had been polished; the windows had been cleaned; the brass taps on the huge Edwardian bath and basin rubbed to a shine and, finally, the bed made up with linen sheets, blankets and a traditional hand-embroidered bedspread.

Because of the bed's width, it had taken both of them to make it up, and Rosy grimaced inwardly at Mrs Frinton's comment, remarking that modern duvets certainly made life a lot easier.

'You'd have a hard time getting a duvet for a bed this size,' Mrs Frinton responded. 'Big enough for a whole family, it is.'

A family. A small shadow touched Rosy's eyes as she glanced down at the bed.

There was a hollow, empty feeling inside her, a hard, painful sense of being very alone, of not having anyone close to her for her to share her life with. It was a feeling she had never experienced before, a feeling of which, she recognised on a small *frisson* of disquiet, she had first become aware this afternoon, just after Guard had removed the protection of his arms from around her body.

When her grandfather had made his will, he had wanted the house to stay in the family, to be lived in, to be loved by his descendants.

Guard would love it and live in it, Rosy told herself firmly. Guard would protect the house and eventually his children would grow up here.

Guard's children, but not hers. Hers would only know of the house through her memory of it.

The intensity of the desolation that swept over her frightened her all the more because she wasn't entirely sure what was causing her misery—the thought of her children not growing up at Queen's Meadow, as she had done, or the thought that Guard's children would.

And yet she had never previously felt possessive about the house, far from it. About the house, or about Guard?

The small *frisson* became a deep shudder, a small, painful flowering of knowledge unfurling inside her, which she quickly and fearfully tried to smother with a flurry of small-talk to Mrs Frinton.

It was just Edward's presence in the house that was making her so anxious and unhappy, she told herself. That was all.

CHAPTER EIGHT

'WELL, now, I expect you two will want to be left on your own.'

The only smile Edward gave Rosy made her stomach heave with loathing.

'Well, don't hang about, then, Margaret,' he ordered his wife, his pseudo good humour quickly disappearing as he turned away from Rosy and glared across the dinner table at his wife.

'There's still a lot of stuff to be sorted out. How on earth you manage to be so useless I really don't know.'

Rosy tensed with angry resentment on Margaret's behalf as the older woman's thin, sallow face flushed and she immediately and awkwardly stood up, hurrying to obey her husband's demands.

Automatically, Rosy tried to help her, pushing her own chair back and saying quickly to her, 'Why don't you leave it until tomorrow, Margaret? I'm not due to go down to the shelter until the afternoon, so I could give you a hand, and I'm sure Mrs Frinton wouldn't mind helping us out as well—'

'The shelter...' Edward's eyebrows rose as he rudely interrupted Rosy. 'Dear me, I should have thought Guard would have put a stop to your going down there. With all the riff-raff who use the place, there's no knowing what you could—'

'They are *not* riff-raff.' Rosy cut him off angrily.

'None of them wanted to be made homeless, Edward; none of them wanted to have to depend on others, on the State for charity and...'

She tensed as Guard reached for her hand, wanting to snatch her fingers out of his grasp but not quite daring to do so. Her work at the shelter had always been a slightly sensitive issue, especially with her grandfather, who had been inclined to be old-fashioned in his views, and Rosy suspected that Guard shared both his and Edward's opinion that what they were trying to achieve with the shelter was a waste of time and money.

Defensively, she tried to pull her hand out of Guard's, unwilling to hear him adding his criticism to Edward's, but instead of supporting Edward as she had anticipated, he said firmly, 'Rosy is quite right, Edward, and these people deserve not just our sympathy but our practical support as well. But quite apart from that, even if I did not share Rosy's belief in what she does, I would hardly have the right to interfere. Rosy is my wife—an equal partner in our relationship. I respect her right to make up her own mind about what she does and does not do. After all, if there isn't mutual respect and trust between a man and a woman, how can there be love?'

Rosy turned round to look at Guard in astonishment. She had never expected to hear him express such views. They were so completely alien to the Guard she thought she knew; the Guard she had always dismissed as domineering and arrogant.

Out of the corner of her eye, she just caught sight of Margaret's face with its wistful, unhappy expression.

Poor Margaret. How tragic to be married to a man like Edward, and how even more tragic if she had actually once loved him.

The small incident stayed in her mind and when she

and Guard were eventually on their own she turned impulsively to him and asked him uncertainly, 'Did you mean what you said earlier? About...about believing that...that loving someone means respecting and trusting them?'

The thoughtful look he gave her made Rosy wish she had not raised the issue.

'That's a first for you, isn't it?' Guard asked her drily. 'Actually acknowledging that *I* might have thoughts and feelings instead of...?'

'Instead of what?' Rosy pressed.

He simply shook his head and told her calmly, 'Yes. I do believe that respect and trust go hand in hand with love—with *genuine* love, that is, not the far more common and ephemeral lust that so many people confuse it with.

'Loving someone means loving them as they are, accepting them as themselves, *wanting* them to be themselves instead of trying to change them to fit into our own preconceived image of what the person we love must be. It means loving them *because* of the person they are, not in spite of it...'

He frowned as Rosy gave a small shiver and asked her softly, 'What is it, what's wrong?'

'Nothing,' Rosy lied, knowing that she dared not allow herself to look directly at him just in case he saw the emotion in her eyes and guessed how much his words had affected her.

Would anyone ever love her like that, so completely and so honestly?

It shocked her that it should be Guard of all people who had described love to her in exactly the same terms as she would have chosen herself; Guard who, had she been asked, she would have insisted quite unequivocally could not possibly have understood—never mind shared—such ideals.

'You look tired,' she heard Guard telling her. 'Why don't you go to bed before Edward decides to inflict his company on us? He's probably had enough of bullying Margaret.'

'Do you think she once loved him?' Rosy couldn't resist asking quietly.

'Him? No,' Guard told her decisively, shaking his head. 'The man she might have been deceived into thinking he was? I suspect, unhappily for her, yes. Poor woman...'

'I wonder why she stays with him when he's so horrible to her.'

'He's probably damaged her sense of self-esteem and self-worth to such an extent that she can't leave. And then, of course, there are her sons.'

'He's such a horrible person. He *likes* hurting her, bullying her...'

'Yes,' Guard agreed, adding warningly, 'And that is nothing compared with what he's likely to want to do to us if he ever discovers the truth about our marriage.'

Rosy gave a small shiver.

'Don't, Guard,' she begged, her apprehension showing in her eyes.

'It's all right,' Guard reassured her. 'There's no reason why he should find out, not if we're both...careful...'

'I never thought he'd do anything like this,' Rosy whispered. 'Move in here and—'

'Stop worrying about it,' Guard told her. 'You're supposed to be a deliriously happy bride, remember?'

Rosy gave him a wan smile.

'I suppose it could be worse,' she agreed, forcing another smile. 'After all, if we were really in love, having

Edward or anyone else here would be the last thing we'd want…'

'The very last thing,' Guard agreed softly.

For some reason that Rosy couldn't quite define, something in the way he was looking at her and the tone of his voice suddenly made her heart skip a beat and her face flush slightly.

'You're right,' she told him huskily, 'I should go to bed. I *am* tired…'

'I'll be an hour or so yet,' Guard responded. 'I've got one or two things I need to do.'

'Good—goodnight then,' Rosy mumbled awkwardly, avoiding looking at him as he held the door open for her.

She was halfway down the upper corridor when she heard Edward calling her name. Immediately she tensed, taking a deep breath before turning round.

'Having an early night?' Edward asked her mockingly as he reached her.

Somehow or other, Rosy managed to stop herself from responding in the way she would have liked, saying quietly instead, 'I thought Margaret looked very tired at dinner tonight, Edward. It must be quite a strain for her, having to move over here at such short notice.'

'Oh, she likes to make a fuss about nothing,' Edward responded dismissively. 'She's like that. Where's Guard?' he asked inquisitively.

'He had one or two things to do downstairs,' Rosy answered.

The way Edward was looking at her made her feel both uncomfortable and angry at the same time.

'Not getting tired of you already, is he?' he taunted.

'You'll have to watch him, you know, Rosy. A man with his reputation…'

'Guard chose to marry *me*,' Rosy responded fiercely. 'Any past relationships he might have had are exactly that, Edward—past.'

She felt rather proud of her response and it certainly seemed to rattle Edward.

'What are you doing here on this floor anyway?' she demanded, seizing her advantage.

'I was just on my way down to collect some of the stuff we unloaded into the garages earlier,' Edward told her. 'I want to get everything inside as soon as I can. It will take me at least a couple of hours yet to move it all. You know, Rosy, you really should have thought a little harder before you rushed into marriage with Guard. You're taking a very big risk, you know.'

Rosy could feel her heart starting to pound anxiously.

'What—what do you mean?' she challenged Edward, hoping that he wouldn't see the nervous guilt in her eyes.

What was she going to do—to say—if he told her that he knew why she had married Guard? *Why* had she let him corner her like this when Guard wasn't here? Why had she…?

'You *know* what I mean,' Edward told her softly. 'Oh, I can understand why you fell for him. Guard certainly knows how to handle a woman, but then of course he's had a lot of practice… But have you asked yourself this, Rosy—*why* has he married you?'

'Because he loves me,' Rosy replied instantly.

Just for a moment she had thought that Edward had actually guessed the truth.

But even if he hadn't, it was obvious that he suspected something, Rosy acknowledged as she turned on her heel and left him.

*   *   *

With only the lamps on in the bedroom, the large room looked surprisingly intimate and cosy.

It was the bed that did it, Rosy decided. It looked… It looked…

Hastily she averted her gaze from it. Well, what it *didn't* look was as though it had been designed for one solitary celibate sleeper. Very, very much the opposite…

Reluctantly, Rosy stepped out of the bath and reached for a towel. She had felt so luxuriously relaxed lying there, lapped by the soft, warm water, that she could almost have fallen asleep.

Still smiling, she walked into the bedroom to collect her nightshirt, and then stopped, her smile disappearing abruptly as she remembered that her nightshirt, along with the rest of her clothes—and her underclothes—was still in her old bedroom.

In all the fuss of getting this room ready, the anxiety of Edward's unexpected and unwanted descent on them, she had completely forgotten about moving her things.

She looked uncertainly at the bedroom door, nibbling at her bottom lip. Dared she take the risk of running down the corridor, dressed just as she was with a towel wrapped about herself, to retrieve her clothes, or should she get dressed just in case Edward saw her?

She was still debating the matter when the bedroom door opened and Guard walked in.

Rosy stared at him.

'I thought you said you'd be a couple of hours,' she reminded him, making sure that the towel was completely secure.

'I did, but Edward was sniffing around making pointed comments about bridegrooms and neglected brides.'

'Is he still there?' Rosy asked him anxiously.

'Yes. Apparently he's got some stuff he wants to get upstairs tonight. Why?'

Rosy grimaced uncomfortably.

'I forgot to move my things from my old room.'

Guard gave a small, dismissive shrug.

'So you can move them in the morning. If he says anything, you can just tell him that there wasn't time to move them before the wedding.'

Rosy wriggled uncomfortably within the confines of her towel. 'No,' she contradicted him, 'you don't understand. I—I haven't got anything. *Anything*,' she repeated insistently. 'My—my underwear, my nightshirt, they're all still in my old room, and so is the bag I brought back from Brussels,' she added unhappily.

She winced as she saw the look Guard was giving her.

'I just forgot all about it,' she defended herself. 'What with finding Edward here and then having to get this room organised. I'll have to go and get them.'

'No,' Guard told her sharply.

'But I've *got* to have my nightshirt,' Rosy protested, panicking. 'I haven't got anything to sleep in. It's all right for you, you've got your things.'

She and Mrs Frinton had unpacked the bag Guard had brought over from his apartment with some of his clothes in it, even though he had told them both wryly that he didn't expect them to do so.

'A new bride, Rosy,' Guard informed her now, 'does not leave her husband's bed to go in search of a nightshirt, and to do so would be especially unwise in our present situation, with Edward still prowling about. No…I'm afraid that for tonight at least you'll just have to sleep as you are—in your skin.'

Rosy stared at him.

'No,' she choked. 'I can't…'

'Of course you can,' Guard contradicted her. 'I do it all the time.'

Aghast, Rosy glanced from him to the huge bed and then back again.

'I am not sleeping with you in that bed without either of us having… With both of us… Without either of us having any clothes on,' she told him primly.

'Why not?' Guard asked her calmly.

Rosy stared at him in baffled confusion.

What did he mean, why not? Wasn't it obvious?

'Well, because it just isn't done,' she floundered unhappily.

Guard's eyebrows rose.

'Is that so? It seems to me that you have some very odd views on marriage, Rosy. *That*, I can assure you, is *exactly* how it's done.'

He paused, watching her while she curled her toes protestingly into the carpet and the blush she could feel warming her body swept over her from head to toe.

'There is nothing—nothing,' Guard repeated softly, 'which is quite so sensual, so pleasurable as the feel of skin against skin, body against body.'

An odd, dizzying sensation seemed to have infiltrated her body and, along with it, a sort of aching, yearning need spiked with a bitter-sweet, sharp spiral of dangerous excitement. Skin against skin, Guard had said, body against body. He had not been speaking personally at all, so why did she suddenly feel hot all over, her imagination shocking her with mental images of *their* skin, *their* bodies…?

As fresh heat filled her face, Rosy retreated to the far side of the bed.

'What is it, Rosy?' he teased her. 'Afraid your unbridled desire for me might get totally out of control at the thought of my vulnerable, naked body in bed next to you, and that you might…'

Rosy knew that he was only joking, laughing at her, but, for some extraordinary reason, instead of being relieved by his attempt to lighten things, she actually felt—

She swallowed hard, too distressed by her emotions to allow herself to give them a name.

Not trusting herself to speak, she reverted instead to childhood, picking up a pillow from the bed and hurling it angrily at Guard.

He caught it with derisive ease, openly laughing at her.

'Baby,' he taunted her. 'Well, if that's the way you want to behave, Rosy…'

He moved so quickly she had no chance to evade him as he scooped her up off the floor and held her at arm's length, still laughing at her as she kicked out protestingly, demanding to be set free.

Still laughing, Guard started to comply with her request but, as he released her waist, and her toes touched the floor, Rosy felt the towel start to slide from her body.

It was like that moment in the château bedroom all over again, only this time… This time…

As she struggled frantically with numb fingers to resecure the towel, she heard Guard saying quietly, 'Maybe you're right, Rosy. Maybe sleeping together isn't such a good idea after all, but I'm afraid we just don't have any choice,' he added, his voice suddenly unfamiliarly harsh. '*Neither* of us has any choice, so we'll just have to make the best of things. At least the damn bed's big enough to allow us both some degree of privacy…'

No wonder Guard looked so angry with her, Rosy acknowledged, as he disappeared into the bathroom, leaving her to crawl miserably beneath the bedclothes. If she hadn't been such an idiot and forgotten to move her clothes…

Her throat felt tight with suppressed tears and her feet were cold, she decided miserably. Why on earth had she been such an unsophisticated idiot and made all that fuss about not having her nightshirt? It was obvious from the way Guard had acted, the way his manner had changed after he had seen her naked body, that he didn't have the smallest degree of sexual desire for her.

Which, of course, was just as it should be—and just how she wanted it to be, wasn't it…? Of course it was, she told herself firmly as she lay as close as she could to the cold edge of the bed and closed her eyes, trying to ignore the sounds coming from the bathroom.

Unlike her, Guard obviously preferred to shower. She gave a small, unhappy shiver as she was unexpectedly tormented by a mental image of his naked body, his skin gleaming wetly like heavy, rich satin.

She didn't want him. Of course she didn't… She didn't even like him, never mind love…

With a small, defensive sob, Rosy reached for one of the spare pillows and held it down firmly over her ears, blotting out the tormenting sounds from the bathroom.

CHAPTER NINE

ROSY woke up with a start. Someone was knocking on the bedroom door. She tensed as she recognised Edward's voice calling Guard's name and her own.

Guard. Her tension increased as she recognised that the reason she felt so deliciously warm and had no doubt been so reluctant to wake up was that, somehow or other, she had relinquished her hold on the edge of the bed and was now lying virtually in the centre of it, curled up next to Guard.

'It's all right, Rosy, you stay there. I'll go and find out what he wants,' she heard Guard telling her as he sat up and switched on the bedside lamp, swinging his legs on to the floor at the same time. Rosy hastily averted her gaze from his naked body.

A warm glow suffused her skin as she didn't look away quite quickly enough and was left with a vivid image of the awesome perfection of his body.

Out of the corner of her eye, she saw him pick up his robe from the end of the bed and shrug it on, and expelled a small sigh of relief.

'Yes, Edward, what it it?' she heard Guard asking grimly, as he half opened the door, positioning his body, she noticed gratefully, so that Edward couldn't see past him into the room. But Edward, it seemed either couldn't interpret Guard's body language or preferred not to do so, and virtually pushed past him, exclaiming, 'It's Margaret! Is Rosy...?'

He seemed more disappointed than relieved to see her there, Rosy recognised as Edward came to an abrupt halt at the foot of the bed.

Uncomfortably conscious of her nudity, Rosy clutched the bedclothes protectively to her body as Guard demanded curtly, 'What is it, Edward? What's wrong with Margaret?'

'Er...she's got a headache, and I was wondering if Rosy had some aspirin or something. We can't seem to find ours.'

'Headache?' Guard's eyebrows snapped sharply together in anger. 'You wake us up at two o'clock in the morning because your wife's got a headache?'

'Well, it's more of a migraine than a headache,' Edward defended himself.

'If Margaret suffers from migraines, I doubt very much that mere aspirin would do anything for them,' Guard told him.

Rosy struggled to sit up slightly, and keep her body covered up at the same time as she told him quickly, 'I'm sorry, Edward, but I don't have anything like that up here. You should find some downstairs in the medicine cupboard in the kitchen. Poor Margaret,' she added sympathetically. 'She must be in dreadful pain...'

'Yes, well, I'll go down and see if I can find something for her,' Edward told them. 'I'm sorry if I disturbed you...'

He didn't look sorry at all, Rosy reflected uneasily as Guard walked with Edward to the door and very pointedly opened it for him.

'Poor Margaret,' Rosy repeated nervously as Guard walked back towards the bed.

'Poor Margaret indeed—if in fact she *does* have a migraine,' Guard responded grimly. 'Personally, I doubt it, and in fact—'

'What do you mean?' Rosy asked him anxiously, her body suddenly tense with apprehension. 'Are you trying to say that Edward woke us up deliberately so that he could check—?'

'That we were actually sleeping together? I think there's a strong possibility,' Guard confirmed grimly.

The severity of Guard's expression made Rosy's heart miss an anxious beat.

Looking away from him, she nibbled worriedly at her bottom lip.

The bed dipped slightly beneath Guard's weight as he got in beside her and switched off the bedside lamp.

'Guard,' Rosy asked him in a small voice, 'how suspicious do you think Edward really is? I mean, he must have guessed something, mustn't he, to come down here…?'

'It looks like it,' Guard agreed after a small pause but, as Rosy made a small distressed sound, he added, 'But there's no point in jumping to conclusions, or in worrying, and after all, nothing he saw in here tonight could possibly have given him the confirmation he was looking for—far from it.'

Rosy knew that Guard was speaking the truth, but she still felt disturbed and on edge.

'Edward's gone now. Go back to sleep,' Guard told her.

'I can't,' Rosy admitted shakily. 'I'm afraid, Guard,' she added. 'What if Edward does find out and…?'

She heard the rustle of the bedclothes as Guard turned over and switched on the lamp.

'There's nothing for you to be afraid of,' he told her quietly as he looked down at her.

He was half sitting up, the bedclothes round his waist, the upper half of his body exposed as he leaned over her.

'What is it, Rosy? You're not crying, are you?' he asked her softly.

Quickly Rosy shook her head, but she knew he must have seen the suspicious shine in her eyes.

'You said we'd go to prison,' she told him in a stifled voice, by way of explanation.

'I said we *could*,' Guard corrected her.

Rosy saw his chest expand as he drew in a deep breath. An odd *frisson* of sensation ran across her skin, as delicate as the velvet touch of a cat's sheathed paw and yet, at the same time, so powerful that she rushed into speech to try to stifle it.

'I never thought I could ever be so afraid of someone like Edward,' she told Guard huskily.

'And I never thought I'd see the day when you admitted that you were afraid of anything—especially to me,' Guard responded. 'It's all right, Rosy. I promise you that everything's going to be all right. Come here…'

When he reached out and took her in his arms, Rosy was too surprised to speak.

How long was it since anyone had held her like this, comforted her like this? she wondered shakily as Guard reached up and smoothed her hair back off her face.

'I still can't believe that Edward would actually do something like that,' she whispered. 'That he would actually come here in the middle of the night to check…'

'Stop thinking about it. He's gone now,' Guard soothed her.

'Yes, I know,' Rosy responded, lifting her head from

his shoulder to look anxiously into his eyes. 'But, Guard, if we hadn't been sharing the bed... If you'd been sleeping in the chair or if I'd been—'

'Wearing your nightshirt,' Guard interrupted her wryly. 'As I said, Rosy, forget it.'

'I can't,' Rosy protested, shivering suddenly and burying her face against Guard's shoulder. 'I can't.'

'Rosy.'

Rosy tensed as she heard the harsh tension in Guard's voice, but she didn't respond to the pressure of his hand on her shoulder urging her away from his body. She didn't *want* to move away from him, she recognised; she didn't want to go back to her own cold and lonely side of the bed. She didn't want...

'Rosy.'

Her body quivered as the warm gust of Guard's fiercely expelled breath touched her skin.

'Rosy...'

His voice sounded different now—thicker, slower, less determined, more—

Her heartbeat had become dangerously unsteady. The warmth of Guard's breath against her skin told her just how close his mouth was to her throat, so close that if she just moved the tiniest little bit...

She shivered in sharp pleasure, her pulse-rate accelerating frantically as she felt Guard's mouth brush her skin.

'Rosy...you know what's going to happen if you don't let go of me, don't you?' she heard Guard warn her softly.

Let go of him? Her eyes widened in shock as she realised what he meant. Somehow, without knowing she had done so, she had curled one hand possessively around the hard muscles of his forearm, or at least as far round them as her slender fingers could stretch. Let go of him? But she didn't *want* to let go of him, she recognised with a shiver of intense sensual awareness. She wanted to stay exactly where she was with his body next to hers, his hands...his mouth...

'Guard.'

Could *he* hear the shocked confusion in her voice, the need...the desire...?

Her eyes widened as his hand slid beneath her hair to cup her face and she saw that he had. His own eyes looked darker, brighter, the pupils enlarged.

Nervously, Rosy caught her bottom lip between her teeth.

'Don't do that,' she heard Guard protest in a thick, slurred voice.

And then it was his mouth, his teeth, that released her tortured lip from its bondage, explored and caressed it, driving her to such an unimagined frenzy of need that Guard had to hold her down against the pillow while he satisfied her frantically whispered pleas to be kissed properly and not so cruelly teased.

'Properly... Like this do you mean, Rosy?' she heard him demanding rawly before his mouth covered hers.

No one had ever kissed her so intensely, so demandingly before, but it was the strength of her own passion that shocked her, not Guard's. It was as though her untutored body had somehow developed a wilful sensuality of its own.

Without any conscious effort on her part her body arched, her arms clung, her lips parted and, if she could have done so, a stunned, shocked part of her recognised, she would have wrapped herself so intimately and erotically around Guard that—

If she *could* have done so? She trembled as Guard

dragged his mouth away from hers and muttered roughly, 'My God, Rosy, you witch. If I didn't know better I'd—'

He didn't finish his sentence; the hand which had been caressing the smooth skin of her back had come to rest against the side of her breast and, without even having to think about it, Rosy had moved just enough for the warmth of his palm to cover the hard point of her nipple. The urge to move against that warmth, deliberately create an erotic friction that could only intensify the sharp, deep yearning flooding her body, was so intense that she had to stifle the vocal expression of it in her throat.

But Guard must have heard it, or knew without having to hear it, because his fingers were already caressing her nipple, his mouth moving downwards over her body.

As she felt his mouth carefully take the place of his fingers, drawing her nipple with agonising slowness into a moist caress, Rosy shivered helplessly, her eyes betraying her sensual vulnerability when Guard slowly released her nipple and then told her rawly as he circled the damp areola with one fingertip, 'That's nothing, Rosy. But this...'

As his mouth recaptured her nipple and he started to suckle rhythmically, the feeling that poured through her was so intense that her whole body twisted frenziedly, her nails digging into Guard's skin.

In response, Guard's suckling became deeper and more urgent; he pushed the bedclothes away from her body, his hand caressing the curve of her hip, sliding round to press firmly against the lower half of her stomach, just as though he knew that the ache he was causing in her breast had its beginning right there, deep inside her body where his hand rested, as though he knew that somehow, its warmth, its pressure did something to ease a little of the almost painful sharpness out of the ache that possessed her.

There had never been a time when she had ever felt anything like this, she acknowledged dizzily, when she had felt so—so driven, so—so in need, so helplessly out of control.

She shivered as Guard released her nipple and the air struck coolly against her hot, damp flesh.

In the soft light, she looked down at Guard's dark head, still bent over her body as he kissed the hollow between her breasts and then moved lower.

Her own flesh looked so alien to her. Her breasts swollen...flushed—the one Guard had caressed still engorged, still aching...

She tensed as his tongue circled her navel, her body clenching.

Guard's hand had left her stomach and was resting on her outer thigh, sliding beneath her to lift her so that—

Now she did protest, her eyes wild with shock at the sight of Guard's dark head between her thighs, his fingers dark against her so much paler skin as he lifted her body effortlessly, arranging it, imprisoning it in a position of such intimacy that Rosy could feel herself flushing. But she still couldn't drag her gaze away from the sight of his dark head bent over the most vulnerable, sacred part of her body.

When his lips brushed the soft flesh of her inner thigh, Rosy shivered uncontrollably, self-consciousness forgotten in the tide of sensation that flooded through her.

Guard was still kissing and caressing her skin, moving closer to the most sensitive part of her.

Even before he got there, her body was responding to him, aware of him, wanting him, ignoring the shocked demands of her mind that it abandon such wantonness.

Heat poured through her as she heard the thick, pleasured sound Guard gave when he discovered how femalely responsive she was to him—how welcome was the delicate touch of his tongue against the small nub of flesh so sensitive to his caress that Rosy's whole body was gripped by the paroxysm of aching pleasure that shot through her.

She knew Guard must have felt it too, because his hands suddenly tensed on her body and he raised his head to look at her, the skin along his cheekbones drawn taut and burning darkly with heat.

The look he gave her made her heart slowly somersault.

'No,' she protested huskily, as Guard bent his head back to her body.

'Yes,' he insisted thickly, telling her, 'Have you any idea what doing this feels like? How addictive the taste of you is, how much I've wanted you like this? You're right, Rosy,' he said roughly. 'You're a woman-- wholly, completely and utterly so.'

Rosy shuddered in silent ecstasy as his mouth refound her.

This time the pleasure was different because this time her body and her senses were prepared…knew. She held her breath as she felt the exquisite agony of anticipation build up inside her, releasing it on a sharp, aching cry of release as the pleasure engulfed her, sweeping her up in its roaring, leaping, flooding tide.

'Guard, now, now…please… I want you inside me now.'

She cried out the words almost without knowing she was saying them, knowing only that there was a small part of her that still ached…that still needed, that felt empty and unfulfilled, and that the only thing that could satisfy it was the feel of Guard's body within her, the sensation of him moving deep inside her. She felt him slowly release her, separating himself from her, smoothing away the bedclothes from her body and then kneeling back from her.

As he moved her breath caught in her throat. In the dim light she had seen the full power of his body—how aroused he was, how male.

'Say that again,' he demanded. 'Tell me again that you want me.'

She should have been intimidated into desire-stifling, shy self-consciousness by the way he was looking at her, by the roughly aroused tone of his voice, but instead...

Instead she felt a power, a knowledge she had never known she could possess and, instead of flinching coyly beneath his regard, Rosy held his gaze, stretching her body with languorous sensuality, parting her legs, her spine arching slightly in subtle, sensual invitation as she told him huskily, 'I want you, Guard. I want you now... please, now...now.'

She moaned in eager excitement as his hands slid up over her body, his touch, his gaze, his arousal showing his response to her.

As his hands cupped her breasts he leaned over her and kissed her mouth slowly, with gentle precision, and then she reached up to him and wound her arms round him, pulling him down against her with fierce, demanding desire.

'Is this what you want, Rosy...? This...?' he demanded urgently as he held her, touched her, filled her with the full power of his body.

'Yes. Yes. Yes...' Rosy told him compulsively as she clung to him and urged him physically and vocally to thrust even deeper within her.

'You're so small,' Guard protested unsteadily. 'So—'

'I want you,' Rosy repeated. 'Please, Guard, please…
I want all of you…'

She felt his body shudder as he tried to resist her and
failed.

The sensation of his moving so gently and so deeply
within her filled her with female joy and triumph. Her
body, unlike his, might be untutored in such intimacy
but it had its own power, its own strength, the strength
to sustain the fierce maleness of Guard's release and to
match it.

Against her body she could feel the intense drumbeat
of Guard's heart starting to slow down slightly. His arms
were wrapped around her as he held her tightly against
him, his skin damp with sweat, like her own.

Now that the need, the desire which had driven her
was sated, she suddenly felt very shy and unsure of herself.

Held fast in thrall to her physical and emotional yearn-
ings, she had known only that she loved Guard and that
she wanted him. And that he had wanted her. But now,
suddenly, the enormity of those emotions evoked a sharp
fear within her. Loving Guard was such a new concept
for her. Wanting him—needing him—with so much passion and intensity made her feel very vulnerable.

She felt his lips brush her cheek in a light caress, his
breath warm against her mouth. Panic overwhelmed her.
Quickly she turned her head away, aware of the tension
in his body as he withdrew slightly from her to look
down at her.

'Rosy! What…'

Rosy rushed nervously into speech, unsure if she
wanted to hear what Guard might be going to say.

'Well, at least now Edward isn't going to be able to claim that our marriage isn't legal.'

She felt Guard's body stiffen.

'Is that what all this was about?' he demanded curtly, withdrawing completely from her. 'Is that why—?' As he swore under his breath, Rosy flinched. 'My God... and I actually thought—'

'Guard?' Rosy questioned uncertainly, but he wasn't listening to her, he wasn't even looking at her, she recognised unhappily as he moved over to the empty side of the bed and snapped off the light.

Keeping his back towards her, he told her grimly. 'Go to sleep, Rosy. Just go to sleep...'

Miserably, Rosy curled her body into a small, tight ball. Her body ached slightly in unfamiliar places, her throat felt tight with tears and, ridiculously, after the wanton way in which she had begged Guard to make love to her, much as she longed to do so, she couldn't bring herself to tell him how much, how very much she needed now to be held and reassured by him, to be told that he understood how she felt, that he knew how difficult it was for her to come to terms with the reality of her feelings for him... her love.

The words trembled on her lips and were suppressed as her eyes burned with hot tears.

Perhaps Guard wasn't holding her... reassuring her... because what had happened between them didn't mean the same to him. Because he *didn't* feel the same way about her as she did about him.

Men *were* like that about sex, weren't they? They could enjoy it without feeling any emotional involvement with the woman concerned.

But he *must* know how she felt. He must have recognised what had happened to her. After all, he knew

her views on casual sex, he knew she would never—
could never—give herself so completely to a man without…without loving him.

As the tears started to roll down her face, she bit down
hard on her bottom lip to stop herself from making any
noise.

Cautiously, Rosy opened her eyes, but it was all right.
She was alone in the bed, alone in the room, apparently.

She sat up slowly, hugging the bedclothes protectively
round her body, her face flushing as she recognised the
cause of the slight ache deep within her body.

'You're so small,' Guard had said, but the deep, compulsive thrusting of his body within her own hadn't hurt
her at all—in fact, the ache she felt now…

Caution was replaced by wistful longing as she looked
at the empty space in the bed next to her.

Last night she had been silly to let Guard turn away
from her without telling him how she felt; today things
would be different, she told herself optimistically. But
where was Guard?

She pushed back the bedclothes and then frowned as
she remembered that she didn't have any clean clothes.
She would have to put on her worn ones and go down
to her bedroom. Her frown deepened as her gaze focused
on a neat pile of white underclothes on one of the bedroom chairs. Her underclothes.

Someone, and it could only have been Guard, had
anticipated her need. A small smile started to curl her
mouth.

Guard was quite right, she decided half an hour later
as she emerged from the bathroom, showered and
dressed. Her girlish nightshirts were not really the thing

for a married woman, and oh, so totally unnecessary when she had Guard next to her in bed to keep her warm.

A nightshirt, or indeed any other kind of nightwear, was not only unnecessary but unwelcome as well when it came between her and the sensual warmth of Guard's skin, the touch of his hands and mouth, when—

Shakily Rosy tried to banish her wantonly erotic thoughts, but as she glanced in the mirror she suspected that her flushed face and shining eyes gave her away.

When Guard saw her, would he immediately be reminded of last night? Would he perhaps suggest that they come back upstairs and—?

Dizzily, Rosy opened the bedroom door and hurried towards the stairs. She had never imagined that loving someone would make her so physically aroused or so responsive, but then Guard was so very, very special. She drew in a small, ecstatically happy breath, her whole body glowing with pleasure and love.

As Rosy got to the bottom of the stairs, Mrs Frinton came out of the library.

'Where's Guard?' Rosy asked her eagerly, a happy anticipatory smile already curling her mouth.

Mrs Frinton looked slightly perplexed by Rosy's question, as though it had surprised her.

'He's gone out, Miss Rosy,' she told her. 'He said to let you sleep in as you'd had a disturbed night and to tell you that he wouldn't be back until late this evening. Something about having dinner with an important client in London.'

Rosy's face fell, her earlier joy turning to bewilderment.

Why hadn't Guard woken her, said something? How could he leave her like that after last night, without a word? Without any kind of acknowledgement of what had happened? The day suddenly yawned emptily ahead of her, full of hours which would drag slowly past while she waited for Guard's return.

'Can I get you some breakfast?' Mrs Frinton offered.

Silently, Rosy shook her head, swallowing back the hard lump blocking her throat.

Ten minutes later she was on her own in the library, standing staring disconsolately out of the window when the door opened. For a moment, she thought it was Guard, her spirits lifting, a welcoming smile warming her mouth as she turned round. But it wasn't Guard who was walking into the room, it was Edward.

'No Guard?' Edward commented. 'Well, don't say I didn't try to warn you. You do realise why he married you, don't you, Rosy?'

Go away, Edward, Rosy wanted to tell him, but the words were stuck in her throat. Instead, she turned her head away from him, trying to silence him by ignoring him, but Edward simply laughed unkindly.

'Don't want to hear the truth, is that it? Can't face up to it? Well, my dear Rosy, I'm afraid we all have to face up to unpleasant things from time to time. I found it extremely unpleasant, for instance, learning that I wasn't going to inherit this place.'

'You knew the terms of Grandfather's will,' Rosy told him unsteadily.

'Oh, yes, indeed,' Edward agreed nastily. 'And I wasn't the only person who knew then, was I, Rosy? Weren't you the *least* little bit suspicious when Guard proposed to you? He's known you long enough, after all. If he'd really wanted you he'd have—'

'I don't have to listen to any of this, Edward,' Rosy protested angrily. 'Guard's and my feelings, our marriage, are private. They don't have anything to do with you.'

'Oh, yes, they do,' Edward contradicted her bitterly. 'Grow up, Rosy, and face facts. He married you for one reason and one reason only. He married you for Queen's Meadow, but he won't really be secure here until he's got you pregnant, will he? Until he's sure that his child will inherit. What's wrong, Rosy?' Edward taunted her. 'Surely you didn't really think that the reason he's so keen to take you to bed is because he wants *you*? Grow up. If he'd wanted you that badly, he'd have had you years ago,' he told her crudely, while Rosy gasped in shocked, distraught protest, all the colour leaving her face, and Edward reinforced his cruelty by adding, 'Why should a man like him want you? He could have any woman he wanted—any woman…

'I don't want to hurt you, Rosy,' Edward lied, abruptly changing tack, his voice becoming nauseatingly soft and wheedling. 'I'm just trying to help you, protect you. You could leave him now, before it's too late. Show him that you've seen through him. How can you stay with him, after all, knowing that he doesn't really want you? You *know* that he doesn't want you, don't you, Rosy? If he did, he'd be here with you, wouldn't he? Do you even know where he is or who he's with?'

Rosy daren't turn round and confront Edward. If she did he would see the hurt in her eyes.

Guard *had* married her for Queen's Meadow. Of course he had… She knew that—had known it all along. How on earth could she have been so stupid to believe otherwise?

'Edward, have you got a minute? I can't seem to find my car keys.'

Rosy's body sagged with relief as she heard Margaret's timid voice from the doorway.

She could hear Edward's irritable, carping voice as he followed his wife out into the hallway. Was it really only last night that she had been pitying Margaret for being married to a man who so obviously didn't love her, wondering how on earth she could bear to stay married to him? How blindly and foolishly she had tempted fate. What was it the Greeks had called fate's swift reprisal for such temerity? Nemesis, that was it... Nemesis.

Well, Guard was most definitely her nemesis. Guard and her helpless, pathetic, unwanted love for him.

Guard *didn't* love her and she had been a fool ever to think he did—or that he could.

Just because *her* feelings for him had changed so dramatically, that didn't mean that his for her had undergone a similar metamorphosis.

But he *had* made love to her, held her, touched her, caressed her and taken her to the heights of ecstasy and held her there...

A small sob forced its way past her lips.

Because she had begged him to, pleaded with him to. He was a man, after all, with a very potent male sex drive.

How could she have been so stupid? And how could she ever face him again now, knowing...? Thank God Edward had inadvertently made her realise the truth before she had actually told Guard that she loved him.

She gulped painfully. At least her pride would still be intact, even if her heart wasn't.

If Guard said anything to her about what had happened, she would simply have to pretend that it had been the result of her fear, her panic that Edward might discover the truth.

CHAPTER TEN

'ROSY.'

Rosy tensed as she heard Guard calling her name. She had almost reached the front door; could she possibly open it and escape? He was back early anyway. In the month they had been married he had worked late virtually every evening. She herself had planned to be out when he came in, just as she had been every evening this last week.

It had been a godsend when Ralph had asked her if she could possibly switch shifts with one of the other voluntary workers. She had not only agreed, she had opted to work several extra evenings as well.

She had seen the way Ralph frowned as he asked her, 'Are you sure? Won't Guard object?'

'Guard's very busy himself,' Rosy had told him truthfully. Very busy with his work, or very busy avoiding her?

Her mouth curled in a small, bitterly painful smile. It seemed like a lifetime ago now since she had so naïvely worried about having to share a bed with Guard.

Then, when he had teased her about the effects of his proximity on her libido, it had never occurred to her just how prophetic his words might turn out to be. Why should it? She had been so unaware then, so unknowing.

Now...with Edward and Margaret still in the house

they had no option but to continue to share a bedroom and a bed, but Guard always took care to make sure he stayed downstairs until she was asleep, or until he thought she was asleep and, out of pride, Rosy obligingly went along with the deceit. Lying there with her eyes closed while he moved about the bedroom and the bathroom, trying desperately to hold at bay the feelings, the needs, the emotions that were causing her so much pain.

Not even when she was sure that Guard himself was asleep did she allow herself the luxury of tears. She dared not. If Guard should wake up and find her crying…

Once or twice in the week after that night, she had been aware of him watching her and, on several occasions, she had sensed that he was going to say something about what had happened, but each time her own fear of what he might actually be going to say caused her to evade the subject.

The worst time had been the night after they had made love.

Rosy had gone to bed early, knowing that there was no way she could possibly sleep, and knowing as well that there was no way that she could stay downstairs with Guard.

She had been pretending to be asleep when he came into the bedroom, but she had obviously not deceived him, because he came over to her and told her softly, 'I know you're awake, Rosy. We have to talk.'

'No,' she had denied in panic, guessing what it was he wanted to say. He wanted to tell her that he had guessed how much she loved him but that he did not love her. He wanted to remind her of the terms of their marriage, to shatter the illusion of their lovemaking that she was clinging on to so desperately by telling her that, to him, it had been nothing other than a mere sexual encounter, that the emotion, the intensity, the closeness and commitment she had felt had all been fabricated by her own imagination and need.

'No... I don't want to talk,' she had told him fiercely, adding childishly, 'There isn't anything to talk about.'

She had tensed a little as she saw the muscle beating angrily in his jaw, but he hadn't argued with her or pressed the matter, simply saying heavily, 'Very well, Rosy, if that's what you really want.'

She hadn't responded. How could she? Instead, she had turned her face away from him as he walked away from her, curling herself into a small, miserable ball. What she really wanted was *him*—his love, his loving. What she really wanted was for him to take her in his arms and tell her that he loved her, that he wanted her, that he couldn't and wouldn't live without her.

'Rosy,' Guard called again, his voice ominously sharp.

It was too late for her to take flight now, Rosy recognised; he was already in the hall.

'What is it, Guard?' she asked him, without looking directly at him. 'I was just on my way out. I'm working at the shelter this evening. I must go, otherwise I'm going to be late.'

'No,' Guard told her softly. 'Tonight you're not working *anywhere*, Rosy. Tonight you and I are going to talk.'

'But I can't let Ralph down.' Rosy panicked. 'He's expecting me and they're already short-staffed because of all these meetings Ralph's been having about renewing the lease.'

Their landlord at the shelter had recently announced that he intended to sell the building when the lease ran out. Ralph was trying to find a way of raising enough money for them to buy the building themselves, but so far he had not had much luck. He had even asked to suggest to Guard that he buy the building for them.

'No. I can't do that, Ralph,' Rosy had told him uncomfortably.

And nor could she provide the money herself, since her capital was all tied up in various trusts.

'We can talk tomorrow,' she suggested now.

'Can we?' Guard asked her sardonically. 'Are you sure that by the time tomorrow comes you won't have found something far more important to do? No, Rosy. I'm not the most patient of men at the best of times but, given the situation, I accept that things aren't easy for you. But running away never solved anything, you know.

'When you and I married, we made a bargain and that bargain was that, as far as anyone else was concerned, our marriage would appear perfectly normal. It isn't normal, Rosy, for a couple who've only been married a month to spend so little time together, especially when one of that couple makes it plain that she—'

'*You're* the one who's always working late,' Rosy interrupted him dangerously.

'Am I? And how would you know what time I come home, Rosy, since you're never here?'

Rosy stared at him. She knew because Edward had taken good care to make sure that she did, never missing an opportunity to comment pointedly on the fact that

Guard had not arrived home until gone eight or nine and, certainly when Rosy returned home from her shift at the shelter after eleven, he was invariably shut in the library still working.

'We made a bargain,' Guard repeated grimly. 'But *you* aren't making any attempt to keep your side of it, are you? You'd rather spend all your time at the shelter.'

'It seemed the best thing to do,' Rosy told him woodenly.

'What? Best? Best for whom?' Guard demanded savagely. 'People are starting to talk,' he warned her. 'They're starting to wonder what kind of marriage we have, what kind of relationship when we're spending so much time apart. My God, I've even had Edward offering me commiseration and advice, warning me that people are beginning to comment about the amount of time you're spending with Ralph. Edward also seems to think that Ralph might have tried to persuade you to help finance the shelter.'

'Is that—is that what you wanted to talk to me about?' Rosy asked jerkily, warily.

'One of the things,' Guard agreed.

One of them? What were the others? Rosy wondered miserably. Only yesterday Edward had commented on how unhappy she looked; 'lovelorn' was the word he had used to describe her, pseudo-sympathetically pretending to feel sorry for her because Guard was neglecting her.

'You mustn't wear your heart on your sleeve so obviously,' he had advised her. 'Men like Guard enjoy the chase, the hunt. You've made it all far too easy for him, Rosy, and now he's bored.'

'*Has* Ralph asked you for money, Rosy?' Guard asked her sternly.

'He's worried about the lease, about losing the premises,' Rosy responded indirectly. 'The shelter needs—'

'The shelter needs...' Guard interrupted her angrily. 'Tell me something, Rosy, do you ever think about any other needs? Anyone else's needs? Or are you really so blind that—?'

He broke off as the door opened and Edward walked into the hall.

'Sorry,' he apologised insincerely, his foxy eyes flicking from Rosy's pale face to Guard's angry one and back again. 'Have I interrupted a bad moment?'

'Did you want something, Edward?' Guard asked him irritably, without taking his eyes off Rosy's face, ignoring his question.

'Yes, if you don't mind, Guard, I wanted to have a word with you. The boys will be home from school soon and Margaret's fussing about the lack of proper fire-escape facilities on the upper floor and I must say I have to agree with her. For safety's sake, I really think we ought to move down a floor while they're here...'

Quickly, Rosy headed for the door, ignoring Guard's sharply commanding, 'Rosy...wait...'

Half expecting that he would come after her, she almost ran to her car, her hands shaking as she unlocked the door and got in.

'We have to talk', he had said, but she couldn't. She was far too afraid of what he might say, of hearing him tell her that he had had enough, that he was leaving.

And yet, really, wouldn't that be for the best? How long could she go on living so close to him, knowing how much she loved him, knowing that Edward was watching their every movement, knowing that her time with him was steadily trickling away, living in dread of betraying her feelings and having to bear the pain of hearing him say that he didn't want her love...?

All evening at the shelter, she was anxious and on edge, unable to concentrate properly on what she was doing, and it was a relief when her shift finally came to an end and she was free to go home.

The first thing she noticed as she parked her car outside the house was that Guard's car was missing.

Her heart took a forlorn dive into misery, even though she tried to tell herself that it was just as well that he wasn't there.

Her head had been aching all evening, and she was in the kitchen taking a couple of aspirin when Edward walked in.

'Not feeling very well?' he asked her sharply.

'I've got a headache,' Rosy responded listlessly. She hated the habit he had of always appearing when she least wanted him to, it was almost eerie, intimidating, as though he was secretly spying on her.

'Guard's gone out,' he told her, watching her.

'Yes, I realise that,' Rosy agreed tonelessly.

She wanted to leave the kitchen but Edward was standing right in front of her, almost physically barring her way.

'He had a telephone call—from a woman,' Edward told her with relish. 'He said to tell you that he'd be away all night.'

Rosy felt the blood drain from her face, and knew that Edward had witnessed her body's reaction to her emotions.

'Oh, poor Rosy, you have got it badly, haven't you?'

Edward sympathised insincerely. 'But you can't win, you know. Sooner or later he's going to leave you. Oh, he'll stay long enough to make sure of this place, but he's already getting bored with you, isn't he? A young woman of your age, he probably expected to get you pregnant straight away... *Are* you pregnant, Rosy? You've been looking very pale recently...'

Rosy gasped in outraged anger.

'That's none of your business,' she told him fiercely.

'Oh, yes, it is,' Edward responded softly. 'It's very much my business. Just as this house is very much my business. I hope you aren't pregnant, Rosy, because if you are... Well, let's just say that in a house like this there are all kinds of hazards for a woman in a delicate condition, if you take my meaning. Guard wouldn't be very pleased if you lost his baby, would he, Rosy? All that time wasted. The boring job of having to do it all again to be faced, when he would obviously so much rather spend his time with someone else... You've only been married a month and already he's bored with you, Rosy. Leave him now, while there's still time. He only wants the house. He doesn't want you. He's never wanted you.'

With a small sob, Rosy managed to push her way past her tormentor, almost running out of the kitchen as she headed for the stairs and the security of her bedroom.

The security? How could she feel secure here now, after what Edward had just said, the threats he had just made?

He must be mad, deranged—but Rosy knew that he wasn't. She shivered violently as she curled up in the middle of the bed.

How would she feel right now if she had actually been

carrying Guard's child? The cold sickness, the fear, the anguish, the protective way her hand instinctively covered her stomach told her the answer.

She couldn't go on like this, loving Guard, wanting him, knowing he didn't love her, living in fear of Edward and his threats.

But where else could she go? The shelter? A wryly bitter smile curled her mouth at the thought... Hardly.

'You're not eating your breakfast.'

'I'm not hungry,' Rosy responded wanly to Guard's terse comment. It was Saturday morning and for once he had no serious business to take him out of the house.

Nothing had been said about her refusal to agree to talk to him, and no explanation given to her for his absence all night earlier in the week.

Guard was just pushing his chair back from the table and standing up when Edward walked into the breakfast-room.

'I've got to go out later,' Guard told her distantly. 'I don't know how long I'll be away. What are your plans?'

'I've—I've got some shopping to do later,' Rosy fibbed, avoiding looking at him, her whole body tensing as she felt him looking at her.

'Ah, these modern marriages,' Edward quipped, smiling at them.

He wasn't smiling an hour later as he caught up with Rosy on the stairs, just after Guard had gone out.

'Stop making it hard for yourself, Rosy,' he advised her. 'Leave him. He's making it very obvious how little he thinks of you—and how much he thinks of her.'

'Her?'

The betraying, agonised word had escaped before Rosy could silence it.

'Oh, come on.' Edward smirked. 'You can't be that naïve. Your husband stays away all night; there can only be one reason, can't there? There's got to be someone else, hasn't there, Rosy? Several someone elses if Guard's reputation is anything to go by.'

Suddenly, Rosy had had enough. She could feel the tears filling her eyes and threatening to spill down her face. All Edward's barbed pinpricks, all his cruelty, all his threats, all the pain and misery of loving Guard and knowing she wasn't loved in return suddenly became too much for her.

Head down, she turned and fled to the sanctuary of the bedroom.

The bedroom—*their* bedroom—the room and the bed she shared with Guard.

Shared with him. She squeezed her eyes tightly closed against the hot, betraying flood of her tears.

As the scalding tears burned their way down her face, she reached out helplessly for Guard's pillow, wrapping her arms round it and burying her face in it, trying to absorb the faintly lingering scent of him into her own body, as though it were a drug which could ease her pain.

'Rosy…Rosy, what is it? What are you doing up here?'

Guard. But he had gone out. Rosy tensed as she heard his voice, not daring to turn round.

'What's wrong?' Guard asked. 'Aren't you feeling well? Rosy, answer me…'

He was standing next to the bed now, leaning over

her, his hand reaching out towards her. Miserably, Rosy
lifted her face out of his pillow.

'You're crying?'

He sat down on the bed next to her. Next to her, but
still apart from her, Rosy noticed.

'What is it? What's wrong?'

'Nothing,' Rosy lied.

'Is it Ralph? The shelter? Have you…?'

Ralph? Rosy stared at him. Why should she be crying
over Ralph?

'Ralph! Of course it isn't,' she denied fretfully.

There was a look in Guard's eyes which made her
heart suddenly start to thud unsteadily.

'Well, if it's not Ralph then what, or rather who, is
it?' Guard persisted quietly.

Edgily, Rosy sat up and moved slightly away from
him.

'I thought you had to go out,' she told him.

'That can wait,' Guard responded flatly. 'This can't.
What is it, Rosy? And don't tell me nothing. The day
''nothing'' makes *you* cry…'

To Rosy's consternation, he suddenly reached out and
touched her hot, damp face in a gesture which could
almost be mistaken for tenderness, just as the look in his
eyes could almost be mistaken for real, genuine concern.
But that would be a fatal mistake for her to make, she
warned herself, another fatal mistake.

She couldn't tell him the truth. How could she,
when——? She tensed abruptly as she heard someone
walking down the corridor.

'It's Edward, Guard,' she exclaimed in panic. 'Don't
let him come in. Don't——'

'Edward?'

As she heard the sharp query in Guard's voice, Rosy's face flooded with betraying colour.

'Is it *Edward* who's the cause of this…these?' Guard demanded, his fingers brushing gently against her face.

Rosy bit down on her bottom lip, not trusting herself to answer, but she couldn't stop the hot, sad flow of tears that gave away her real feelings.

'Tell me,' Guard commanded her. 'All of it, Rosy,' he warned her. 'I want to know what the hell's been going on. What the hell he's done to cause this.'

'I can't,' Rosy protested miserably. 'Please don't make me, Guard. I just wish he would go away,' she wept. 'I hate having him watching me, spying on me. He knows, Guard. I know he does and he —'

'He knows what?'

'That this isn't a real marriage…a proper marriage,' Rosy told him. 'He keeps telling me—threatening me—'

'Threatening you?' Guard interrupted her sharply. 'Rosy, there's nothing he can do to either of us now,' he told her. 'Surely you must have realised that. No matter what the reasons were for our marrying, what our intentions were concerning the reality of that marriage, Edward's power to damage us was totally destroyed the night you and I turned our marriage from a fiction to a reality. There's nothing he can do now, no legal recourse open to him.'

'No—no legal one,' Rosy agreed tiredly.

Guard frowned at her.

'Rosy, what is it…? What are you trying to say?'

She was shivering now, her body suddenly very cold; she felt ill almost, like someone suffering from a very bad virus.

'Rosy!' Guard warned her.

Wearily, Rosy shook her head.

'He keeps saying I should end our marriage,' she told him quietly. 'He thinks you're trying to… He thinks…' Flushing, she ducked her head, unable to bring herself to look at him as she told him unsteadily, 'He thinks that if you and I have a child that your claim to the house will be more secure. He's guessed that that's why you married me, Guard. He even threatened—' She swallowed hard and gave a small, hard laugh. 'He told me that—that in a house like this it would be very easy for a woman to lose her baby…'

'*What*?'

Rosy winced as she heard the fury in Guard's voice.

'Stay here,' he told her.

He was gone less than half an hour and when he came back, the controlled, totally blanked-off expression in his eyes made Rosy feel afraid.

What had he said to Edward and, even more important, what had Edward said to him? Had he told Guard about her feelings? Had he—?

'Edward's gone, Rosy,' Guard told her flatly. 'And he won't be coming back.'

Rosy stared at him. How on earth had Guard managed to make him leave so easily and so quickly? Edward had been like a limpet in his determination to stay, and Guard had told her that there was too much risk involved in insisting that he left.

'He's gone? Just like that?'

Fresh tears rolled down her face, but this time they were tears of relief.

'Oh, God, Rosy. Rosy, don't cry…'

Rosy tensed as Guard moved towards her, obviously

intending to take hold of her and comfort her, flinching back from him, her eyes wide and dark with distress.

'There's no need to back away from me as though I'm some kind of— I'm not going to touch you.'

'No, I know you aren't,' Rosy agreed woodenly, looking hurriedly away from him as she felt fresh tears starting to fall.

'Well, if you know that, then why on earth—?' she heard Guard saying. 'Rosy,' he demanded softly, his voice suddenly changing. 'Rosy, look at me.'

'I can't,' Rosy whispered. 'I can't.'

'Yes, you can.'

She trembled as Guard's hand cupped her face, gently tilting it upwards so that he could look into her tear-drenched eyes.

'Now,' he told her quietly, 'if you *know* I'm not going to touch you, then why flinch away from me like that?'

Rosy blinked hard, trying to suppress her tears, her lips trembling as she failed and the full force of her emotions stormed through her, shattering her defences.

'It's because I *want* you to touch me,' she told him in a tormented, husky voice. 'Because I love you and I want you and I can't bear— Guard...Guard...'

Her protest was smothered beneath his mouth as he reached out for her, holding her so tightly that she could feel the fierce beat of his heart as though it were her own.

'Rosy...Rosy.'

She scarcely recognised the stifled, intense voice as Guard's, the fiercely whispered endearments, the hungry, passionate kisses. Surely she must be imagining them, she thought dizzily.

Surely this *couldn't* really be Guard, holding her like

this, kissing her mouth, her face, her throat... Telling
her how much he loved her, how much he had always
loved her, telling her he had waited for what felt like
half his life, her lifetime, to hear her say what she had
just said.

'But you can't love me,' Rosy protested shakily, pushing him slightly away from her and looking up into his
eyes, her own shy and bewildered. 'You've always disliked me—hated me.'

'Oh, Rosy,' Guard groaned. 'Only *you* could think
that. Only you *do* think that. Why the hell do you think
I married you?'

Rosy frowned.

'Because I asked you to. Because you wanted the
house.'

'No, Rosy,' Guard corrected her thickly. 'I wanted
you. Did want, have wanted, do want, will want,' he
stressed, ticking each assertion off on her fingers, pausing to kiss each one of them tenderly and then less tenderly as he saw the expression in her eyes.

Rosy felt her whole body jerk in shocked reaction to
the sensation of his sucking on her fingertips.

She could feel what he was doing to her right down
to her toes. And everywhere else as well.

'But you didn't *want* to marry me. I had to ask you,'
she reminded him in a small voice. 'And you said you
needed time...'

'Time to get myself under control and work out just
how capable I was of going along with what you were
asking. You were damn lucky I didn't snatch you up
there and then and take you to bed, just to show you
exactly what I thought of your plans for our business

marriage. Perhaps that's what I should have done,' he added, lifting his head to look at her.

Rosy couldn't conceal the sharp *frisson* of excitement that ran through her, or the hot colour burning her skin.

'*Would* you have liked that, Rosy?' Guard asked her thickly, letting her see just how much her reaction was affecting him, exciting him, Rosy recognised, on a small wobble of uncertain delight. 'Would you have liked it if I'd carried you off to bed and made love to you?'

'I… Oh, Guard, how can you possibly have loved me without my knowing?' Rosy demanded giddily.

'With extreme frustration,' Guard told her drily, 'and a hell of a lot of jealousy.'

'You, jealous? Of whom?'

'Ralph, for one,' Guard told her quietly. 'And Bressée for another. My God, when I saw the way you were letting him flirt with you…I've always considered myself a very logical and cautious human being, but that night… I wanted to take you to bed and stamp the seal of my possession on you so clearly that no man—no man—would ever doubt that you were mine.'

'Edward said you didn't love me. That you just wanted the house,' Rosy told him painfully. 'He said— he said you had someone else and I thought… Why, if you love me, Guard, did you…? Didn't you…?' She stopped and looked pleadingly at him. 'Why didn't you say something that night, the night…?'

'Oh, Rosy. How little you know,' Guard told her, but his derisive look was, Rosy recognised, more for himself than for her. 'I was angry with myself for—for letting things get out of hand, for letting my feelings, my needs, destroy my self-control. You'd turned to me for comfort—in fear and panic. I never intended…I thought you must have guessed how I felt and that was why you refused to talk about what had happened.'

'I thought you were angry with me,' Rosy whispered. 'In the morning when I woke up and you weren't there…'

'I thought you wouldn't want me to be there.'

Rosy gave him an uncertain look.

'But you must have known. You must have guessed that I—'

'That you what? Responded passionately to me? Yes, I knew that, but then you've always been passionately intense about everything you've done.'

'But I begged you to make love to me,' Rosy reminded him, half-ashamed. 'I…'

'You told me you wanted me, but I dared not let myself believe that that was anything more than the impulse of the moment, a reaction brought on by the trauma of what you were enduring. And then, of course, I also had my guilt to deal with.'

'Your guilt? For making love to me?' Rosy asked him, frowning.

'Among other things,' he agreed.

'What other things,' Rosy demanded, perplexed.

'Agreeing to marry you instead of trying to help you find some other way round the problem,' he told her, watching her face carefully. 'Taking advantage of Edward's decision to move in here…'

'Taking advantage? In what way?'

Guard looked at her and then at the bed.

'In the way that led to your and my becoming lovers. Do you honestly think I couldn't have gone and got your clothes for you if I'd really wanted to, Rosy?'

'But you didn't want to sleep with me. You said so,' Rosy protested.

'Oh, Rosy,' Guard groaned. 'Of course I wanted to sleep with you. I wanted to sleep with you, touch and kiss you, love you. I wanted it all and more—much, much more. I wanted you to hold me, to touch me, to want me. To love me,' he told her huskily.

He cupped her face and looked down into her eyes.

'Do you really believe I couldn't have found some way of getting rid of Edward, some way of ensuring that we didn't have to share a room, if that was really what I'd wanted? Have I shocked you?'

Rosy shook her head.

'Surprised me,' she admitted. 'I had no idea.'

'I think I fell in love with you the night I found you poaching,' Guard told her softly. 'Grubby, undersized, very angry—a little girl, still, in so many ways and yet in so many others very, very much a woman. Or at least that was what my emotions and my body told me. My mind...' He shook his head.

'I knew it was too soon. You were too young. You didn't even like me. But then you went on not liking me—not liking me but reacting so emotionally to me that I couldn't stop myself from clinging to the hope that maybe...just maybe—'

'I'd fall in love with you,' Rosy broke in softly.

'Is that what's happened, Rosy?' he asked her quietly.

Rosy shook her head. 'No, I haven't fallen in love with you, Guard,' she told him firmly, lifting her hand to his face in an instinctive gesture of comfort as she saw his pain. 'Falling in love is for teenagers, girls. I'm a woman. I love you, Guard,' she told him emotionally.

'I love you as a woman loves a man—wholly, completely, for ever.'

She trembled as she saw the moisture in his eyes, reaching up to pull him down against her, whispering to him, 'Oh, Guard… Guard…'

Some time later, lying naked in his arms, watching as he reached out his hand to cup her breast, reluctant, it seemed, even now to release her, she smiled lovingly at him.

His thumb stroked the tip of her nipple, swollen still from their earlier lovemaking.

'Were you really jealous of Ralph?' she marvelled.

'Extremely,' Guard responded wryly. 'A fact which Edward played on to very good effect.'

'He manipulated us both,' Rosy acknowledged. 'What did you say to him to make him leave, Guard?' she asked him.

Guard's head paused in its descent towards her breast. 'I told him that if he ever, ever said or did anything to upset you again, I'd make him regret it for the rest of his life. I also told him that if he wasn't out of the house and out of our lives within half an hour he'd find his financial and business affairs under the kind of scrutiny that would make the Fraud Squad look tame.'

His mouth opened gently over her nipple.

'Mmm…' Rosy closed her eyes, stretching her body luxuriously beneath his caress. 'I thought you'd—'

'What?' Guard asked her throatily, releasing her nipple to smile into her arousal-darkened eyes. His hand stroked the satin-soft skin of her thigh, his own eyes darkening as she made a small, soft sound of pleasure.

'Is there something else you'd rather be doing?' he suggested.

'No…nothing,' Rosy denied, unsteadily.

Guard's mouth returned to her nipple, caressing it with such slow deliberation that it was almost a torment.

'How would you like it if I did that to you?' she protested as her body started to tremble with arousal.

'Try me,' Guard invited her.

For a moment she thought he was joking, but then she realised that he meant it.

Shyly and a little uncertainly at first, she touched the soft-haired flesh of his chest with her lips, slowly moving closer to his flat male nipple.

The sensation of taking it into her mouth was unexpectedly erotic, so much more so than she had anticipated that it made her tense slightly and hesitate.

'No, Rosy… Don't stop…don't stop,' she heard Guard groan thickly as his hands came up and held her head against his body. She could feel his fingers trembling slightly against her scalp, feel the fierce, fast beat of his heart, the arousal of his body as it responded to her hesitant suckling.

If touching him like this gave him so much pleasure, then how much more pleasure could she give him by caressing him with the same kind of intimacy he had shown her?

She almost started to ask him, but then stopped. There were some things, she decided quietly, that a woman needed to discover for herself.

He didn't say anything when she touched his thigh, nor when she placed some light butterfly kisses over his belly, but she could feel his tension, feel it in his sudden almost painful grip on her wrist as she moved down his body.

He didn't try to restrain her, but he didn't encourage

her either, and for a moment Rosy almost changed her mind.

What if he didn't want her to…? Didn't like…? But *she* wanted to, she recognised, on a sudden sharp ache of desire. She wanted to touch him, taste him, know him with the same intimacy with which he knew her.

The musky, male scent of his body made her own ache sharply. She could feel his tension as she slowly slid her mouth down over him, touching him with her tongue, delicately exploring him, startled by the surge of pleasure that what she was doing gave her, the immediate and now easily recognised reaction of her flesh to what she had always naïvely assumed was a caress that sexually pleased only the recipient and not the giver.

Guard's hand fell away from her wrist as a deep shudder racked his body. Beneath her fingertips the muscles in his thigh were tense.

'Rosy… Oh, God, Rosy… No more. No more,' she heard him protest in a stifled voice as she continued to caress him. His hands gripped her shoulders and his body writhed fiercely as he almost dragged her up the bed.

'Didn't you like it?' Rosy asked him uncertainly as he buried his mouth in her throat.

'Like it…?' His body shook as he rolled her on to her side and his hand stroked her thigh, lifting it. 'Like it? Yes, I liked it,' he told her roughly as he started to move against her.

'But you didn't show it. You didn't hold me against you the way you did when I sucked you here,' she told him, touching his nipple.

Her voice had become breathy and soft as she felt him enter her.

'That wasn't because I didn't want to. It was because I dared not,' Guard told her rawly. 'Did you want me to?'

'Yes,' Rosy admitted. 'Yes, Guard, it made me want you so much.'

'That's good,' Guard told her, 'because it certainly made me want you.'

As he moved inside her, Rosy wrapped herself blissfully around him.

'Oh, Guard, that feels so good…so good…so good.'

'Still love me…?'

Sleepily, Rosy opened her eyes. She was lying curled up against Guard's body where she had fallen asleep after the last time they had made love.

'Mmm… More than ever,' she told him. 'Do you love me?'

'Yes,' Guard told her quietly. 'Above and beyond anything else there ever has been in my life or ever will be. You *are* my life, Rosy. My life and my love. Today, tomorrow, always and for ever. I love you.'

Sandra Marton used to tell her stories to her dolls when she was a little girl. Today, readers around the world have fallen in love with her sexy, dynamic heroes and outspoken, independent heroines. Her books have topped bestseller lists and won many awards. Sandra loves dressing up for a night out with her husband as much as she loves putting on her hiking boots for a walk in a desert or a forest. To write to Sandra, send a SASE to P.O. Box 295, Storrs, Connecticut, U.S.A., or e-mail her at www.sandramarton.com.

THE BORGHESE BRIDE

Sandra Marton

CHAPTER ONE

ITALY was in the midst of the hottest summer anyone could recall. This last week in July, people said, would go down in the records.

For Dominic Borghese, the last week in July was already memorable. It had been for the last five years.

Dominic took a pair of dark glasses from the visor in his cherry-red Ferrari and slipped them on as he sped along a narrow road in the Tuscan hills.

He'd made errors in his life. He'd never been too proud to admit that. A man didn't rise from the gutter as Dominic had without making an occasional misjudgment, but the memory and the scale of the errors he'd made that last week in July five long years ago stayed with him.

One involved a loan he never should have made.

The other involved a woman.

Of the two mistakes, the loan was easiest to write off. In fact, he was on his way to do that this morning. It had bothered him for years that he'd agreed to the loan in the first place. Not the money, but the terms he'd accepted.

Dominic had no wish whatsoever to acquire ownership of the company the *Marchesa* del Vecchio had put up as collateral. She was an old woman; he'd accepted her offer rather than simply given her the amount she'd requested because he'd known her pride would not let her take the money otherwise.

Now, thanks to his accountants and some discreet inquiries, he knew she would not be able to pay the debt. Well, he'd find a way to tell her he was wiping the slate clean when he saw her in less than an hour. If that wounded her precious, blue-blooded pride, so be it.

Dominic stepped down on the gas pedal.

The other mistake, which he'd made at the start of that same week five years before, was impossible to rectify.

He'd been in New York on business, attended a charity function that bored him out of his skull, gone out on the terrace to get away from the idle chatter, the flashbulbs, the women coming on to him with faces made perfect by injections and nips and tucks and God only knew what...

And found himself in his apartment less than an hour later, making love to a nameless woman with a beautiful face, a soft voice and a desire as quick and hot as his...a woman who'd slipped from his bed while he slept.

He'd never seen her again.

And he'd never forgotten her.

Dominic's jaw tightened.

It was stupid to still think about her, but he knew the reason. She'd been a mystery that night, a blond, blue-eyed vision in a white silk suit, refusing to give him her name, saying as he took her in his arms that this was all a dream and that it must stay that way.

How could a man forget a mystery?

He could still remember the taste of her mouth, the scent of her skin, the feel of her body under his hands.

Stupid, indeed. If only he could expunge the memory

of the woman as easily as he was going to expunge the debt of the *marchesa*…

Dominic sighed.

For a man who'd begun life with the deck stacked against him, these odds really weren't bad. One out of two. Surely, he could live with that.

He relaxed a little, shifting his long legs under the dashboard, loosening his grip on the leather-covered steering wheel. There was no point in even thinking about the woman. Thinking about the *marchesa* was different. He'd be at her *palazzo* in half an hour and he still hadn't come up with an easy way to tell her he didn't want her money; not the principal, not the interest, and most assuredly not the company she'd put up as collateral.

Thinking about it made him smile. If those he did business with knew what he was planning, they'd never believe it.

At thirty-four, Dominic owned the world, or so people said. Men who'd come up the hard way, as he had, admired him. Men who had inherited their wealth instead of wresting their first million from a sweltering emerald pit in a Brazilian jungle, smiled to his face and slandered him behind his back. Dominic knew it but didn't give a damn. Only a fool would judge a man by the blueness of his blood.

So what if they could trace their ancestry back through the centuries? He could trace his to an alcoholic mother who'd chosen his surname because she guessed he'd been conceived one dark night near the walls of the Villa Borghese.

At twelve, the sordid little story had been painful to hear. By thirty, just about the time he realized he'd already earned more money than most of his detractors would make in a lifetime, it had lost its bite.

The most recent rumor said that he was descended from an illicit liaison between a sixteenth-century Roman prince and a housemaid.

Dominic found it amusing.

Gossip couldn't touch his wealth or his power, and it certainly didn't keep women from his bed.

They were always stunning, their faces often familiar to readers of society and celebrity columns. They were women with good minds—dull ones bored him—and invariably they had careers and pursuits of their own. Dominic preferred it that way because he had no wish for commitment. Not yet. Thirty-five had always seemed the right age to find a wife who would look good on his arm, make sure his home was a quiet, comfortable haven, and give him an heir.

A son would truly make the name Borghese legitimate.

Wealth, power, legitimacy. What more could one ask from the bastard son of a street-walker?

But not just yet.

He had a year to go before he turned thirty-five. Until then, he was going to go on enjoying his freedom…and occasionally toy with the idea of having his people locate the woman from that hot July night in New York. He'd almost done it five years ago, but why give a simple sexual encounter more importance than it deserved? Just because he couldn't get her out of his mind…

"Hell," Dominic muttered, and floored the gas pedal.

Concentrate, he told himself. Concentrate on the task that lay ahead. Perhaps if he reviewed that first encounter with the *marchesa*, he'd find a hint in it of how he could tell her to keep the three million American dollars he'd lent her and keep her pride as well.

It was a significant sum of money and he wasn't a bank, which was precisely what he'd told the lady the day she'd come to see him at his office.

Come to see him? That was putting a spin on it. The *marchesa* had invaded his office. She was eighty years old and frail-looking, but she'd managed to bully her way past the information desk in the lobby, past the receptionist on the floor that belonged only to him, and almost past his secretary.

Nobody, not even the *Marchesa* del Vecchio, could get by Celia.

"There's a woman insisting on seeing you," Celia had told him and when Dominic sighed, she'd put her hands on her hips and said no, not *that* woman—he'd been in the process of politely easing himself out of a relationship that had gone stale. This woman, Celia had said, was elderly. She had a sharp tongue and a short temper.

Dominic had lifted one dark eyebrow. "Do I know her?"

"She says you met at the opera. She is the *Marchesa* del Vecchio."

"I don't recall."

Celia told him the rest, that the *marchesa* had somehow talked her way past both the desk and the reception area.

"Really." Dominic's green eyes narrowed. "Tell the people at both desks that if such a thing happens again, they're fired. And tell the *marchesa* I'll see her. Five minutes, Celia. That's all. After that—"

"Ring your private line. Yes. I know."

He stood in the doorway to greet his uninvited guest.

She was a slender, white-haired woman with a ramrod-straight posture that had probably been bred into her elegant bones, though now she needed an ebony walking stick to maintain it.

"*Marchesa.* What a delightful surprise."

"Nonsense. I am sure that my visit is a surprise, Signore Borghese, but I am not so foolish to think it is a delightful one. Why would a handsome young man like you be happy to see an old woman like me?"

She was forthright. Dominic liked that. Few people were when dealing with him. He helped her to a chair across from his desk and sat down.

"May I offer you some tea?"

"It is four in the afternoon, *signore.* Do you generally take tea at this hour?"

"Well, no. To be honest—"

"I have heard you are always honest. It is the reason I am here." The *marchesa* rapped her stick sharply against the terrazzo floor. "Sherry," she barked at Celia, hovering in the doorway. "Very dry."

Dominic glanced at his secretary. "For both of us, *prego,*" he said smoothly and tried to make small talk with his visitor, who clearly had no interest in accommodating him. He breathed a small sigh of relief when, at last, they were alone with a silver tray bearing two small glasses and a decanter on the table between then. "*Marchesa,*" he said, lifting his glass.

The *marchesa* nodded, took a delicate sip of sherry and got down to business.

She told him something all Italy had known for some four hundred years. The del Vecchio money came from land holdings outside Florence and from a family-owned business called *La Farfalla di Seta.* The business had been started in the fifteenth century by the third *Mar-*

chesa del Vecchio, whose husband had gambled away his fortune and left her penniless. That *marchesa* and her daughters, schooled in the delicate arts of sewing and embroidery as ladies were in those days, fed herself and her household by making lingerie of fine silk and lace. It was hand-stitched, hand-embroidered, and handsomely priced.

It was very expensive still. Dominic knew from personal experience. Lingerie from *La Farfalla di Seta* was a gift much appreciated by beautiful women.

"I have heard of it," he said politely.

"The Silk Butterfly," the *marchesa* said with distaste. "That is how it is known in America, where our business is now located. I do not like that name. We are an old and honorable family enterprise with our roots, our heart, in *Firenze*. In Florence," she'd added, as if Dominic might not understand the language of his birth. "But I am not a fool, *signore*. I know that it is American taste that leads the way. Like it or not, those who expect to succeed must follow."

"Please, call me Dominic. And tell me why you've come here, *Marchesa*."

The old woman didn't bother offering courtesy for courtesy by suggesting he dispose with her title. Instead, she put down her glass and folded both gnarled hands around the silver head of her walking stick.

"The Silk Butterfly is my most prized possession."

"And?"

"And, I need six billion *lire*."

"Three million U.S. dollars?" Dominic blinked. "I beg your pardon?"

"My granddaughter is in charge of our operation. She tells me we face competition. She tells me we are in desperate need of modernizing, that we must move from where we have been for fifty years to a different location. She tells me—"

"She tells you a great deal," Dominic said with some amusement, "this granddaughter of yours. Are you sure she is right?"

"I am not here for advice, *signore*."

"Dominic."

"Nor am I here so you can question my granddaughter's decisions. She has been in charge of *La Farfalla* for several years. More importantly, I raised her after the death of her parents. She is Italian enough to understand the importance of the company to our *famiglia*, but American enough to understand the importance of staying in business, which we will not do without an infusion of capital. That is why I have come to you, *signore*, as I said. I need six billion *lire*."

Dominic's private telephone line rang. Celia, he thought, and not a moment too soon.

"I see," he said, reaching for the phone. He put his palm over the mouthpiece and smiled politely. "Well, I wish I could help you, *Marchesa*, but I am not a bank. And, as I'm sure you realize, my time—"

"—is valuable," the old woman snapped. "As is mine."

"Of course. Forgive me, but this call—"

"The call is from the watchdog who guards your door. Tell her I am not yet done, *signore*, and I shall do my best to take no more than five more minutes of your precious morning."

Dominic couldn't recall the last time someone had spoken to him that way. Those who came to him for a favor shuffled their feet, at least metaphorically. The *marchesa* was an irritant, an annoyance…and a breath of fresh air.

He put the phone to his ear, told Celia to hold his calls, then steepled his hands under his chin.

"Why would you come to me for money, *Marchesa?* As I said, I am not a bank."

Her answer was blunt. "I have been to the banks. They turned me down."

"Because?"

"Because they are foolish enough to think a small company cannot succeed, because they think the days when women were willing to spend hundreds of dollars for a frivolous garment are over, because they believe my granddaughter should not bear the entire responsibility for The Silk Butterfly."

"And you think they're wrong?"

"I know they are," the *marchesa* said impatiently. "Women will always covet expensive nonsense and if they don't buy it themselves, men will buy it for them."

"What about your granddaughter? Are you so sure she's capable of running The Silk Butterfly?"

If a woman like the *marchesa* could be said to snort, that was what she did.

"My granddaughter has a degree in business from an American university. She is smart, determined, and capable of doing anything she sets her mind to. She is like me."

Dominic nodded. He had no doubt that was true. He could easily envision a middle-aged duplicate of the old woman seated opposite him, a sharp-tongued spinster with a stern expression and a no-nonsense attitude.

"All right," he said. "You want me to lend you money. Tell me why I should."

"Borghese International recently acquired a French fashion group."

Dominic was impressed. The news of the financial coup had not yet become public knowledge.

"And?"

"And," the *marchesa* said impatiently, "surely you can see the benefits of incorporating our name and clientele under the one umbrella."

Dominic sat back. There might be some benefit, yes. He could get an answer from his research team, but he doubted it would be worth three million dollars. And why would the *marchesa* tell him the importance of *La Farfalla* to her family and then offer to sell it to him?

"Let me understand this, *Marchesa*. You are asking me to buy—"

"I am asking you to lend me money, young man. How many times must I repeat myself? You will make the loan, I will agree to repay it in five years at a rate of interest upon which we will agree."

"So, you don't wish to sell to me?"

"Are you deaf? No. I do not wish to sell to you or anyone else. I speak of a loan. Only a loan."

Puzzled, Dominic shook his head. "I repeat, *Marchesa,* I am not a bank."

For the first time since she'd entered his office, the *marchesa* seemed to hesitate.

"I am willing to admit there is some small risk in what I ask."

"And?"

"And, for the courtesy of making me the loan, I will give you a five percent interest in The Silk Butterfly."

Dominic said nothing. Five percent of a failing company was a pathetic offer, but he was too polite to tell her that.

"Should I not be able to repay you…" The *marchesa* drew a deep breath. "Should such an unlikely thing happen, you will become the sole owner of *La Farfalla di Seta*. And your French fashion group will be able to make their own garments using that name."

The old woman sat back, hands still folded around the walking stick, but now Dominic saw that her hands trembled. For the first time he realized what it had taken to bring her here. She had to be in desperate financial straits. She'd probably pledged all her assets to keep the company going, but what she was putting on the line now were her family's name and heritage—her most valuable possessions.

His people would confirm tomorrow what he was sure he knew today. The *marchesa* was broke and in debt up to her eyeballs, and what she was offering in return for three million dollars was probably not worth half that amount to him. He knew he should tell her that but for a man who was reputed to have no heart, he couldn't bring himself to do it quite so directly.

"I have heard that you are a man willing to gamble," she'd said, while he searched for words. "Is that not the way you began your fortune, Signore Borghese? By risking everything, including your very life, on a project that was dangerous and even foolhardy?" She smiled and he glimpsed the girl she must once have been. "You stand to lose nothing, Dominic. It is I who must take the risk this time, not you."

At that, Dominic had risen from his chair and gently drawn the old woman to her feet.

"Done," he'd said. "Three million American dollars, five years to repay at two percent."

"Eight and a half."

He'd laughed. "Does a bargain offend you, *Marchesa?*"

"Charity offends me when it is not needed. Eight and

a half percent, *signore*. That is, as they say, the going rate.''

''Four.''

''Six and a half, and that is my final offer.''

Dominic thought about reminding her that it wasn't the borrower who made offers, it was the lender. Instead, he'd lifted her hand to his lips.

''You drive a hard bargain, *Marchesa*. Very well. Six and a half percent, repayable in five years.''

''And five percent of The Silk Butterfly will be yours as soon as the papers are drawn up.''

''*Marchesa*, that really isn't…'' The look on her face had stopped him. ''Fine. Let your attorney send me the papers to sign and I… What's the matter?''

''I prefer not to have my attorney do this, *signore*. If you could deal with the legal aspects…?''

He knew what that meant. Her attorney would tell her she was making a bad deal. Dominic sighed. His would tell him the same thing.

''*Marchesa*,'' he'd said gently, ''perhaps we could simply pledge our honor on our deal, yes?''

The old woman had smiled and placed her hand in his, and he had not seen or heard from her until yesterday when she'd called his office and invited him to lunch at her *palazzo*. He'd almost declined, but then he'd recalled the report that had confirmed his suspicion that she couldn't possibly pay off the loan that was now due in less than three days, and he'd said he'd be delighted.

Ahead, tall iron gates stretched across the narrow road. He'd reached the *palazzo* and he still hadn't come up with a way to leave the *marchesa* her pride while telling her he was writing off the loan.

Dominic slowed the Ferrari, looked up at a camera

GET 2

HOW TO GET YOUR 2 FREE BOOKS AND FREE GIFT!

1. Peel off the MIRA® sticker on the front cover. Place it in the space provided at right. This automatically entitles you to receive two free books and an exciting surprise gift.

2. Send back this card and you'll get 2 "The Best of the Best™" books. These books have a combined cover price of $11.98 or more in the U.S. and $13.98 or more in Canada, but they are yours to keep absolutely FREE!

3. There's <u>no</u> catch. You're under <u>no</u> obligation to buy anything. We charge nothing – ZERO – for your first shipment. And you don't have to make any minimum number of purchases – not even one!

4. We call this line "The Best of the Best" because each month you'll receive the best books by some of today's most popular authors. These authors show up time and time again on all the major bestseller lists and their books sell out as soon as they hit the stores. You'll like the convenience of getting them delivered to your home at our special discount prices . . . and you'll love your *Heart to Heart* subscriber newsletter featuring author news, horoscopes, recipes, book reviews and much more!

5. We hope that after receiving your free books you'll want to remain a subscriber. But the choice is yours – to continue or cancel, anytime at all! So why not take us up on our invitation, with no risk of any kind. You'll be glad you did!

6. And remember...we'll send you a surprise gift ABSOLUTELY FREE just for giving THE BEST OF THE BEST a try.

SPECIAL FREE GIFT!
We'll send you a fabulous surprise gift, absolutely FREE, simply for accepting our no-risk offer!

Visit us online at
www.mirabooks.com

BOOKS FREE!

Hurry!

Return this card promptly to GET 2 FREE BOOKS & A FREE GIFT!

| Affix peel-off MIRA sticker here |

YES! Please send me the 2 FREE "The Best of the Best" books and FREE gift for which I qualify. I understand that I am under no obligation to purchase anything further, as explained on the back and on the opposite page.

385 MDL DRTA   185 MDL DR59

FIRST NAME	LAST NAME

ADDRESS

APT.#	CITY

STATE/PROV.	ZIP/POSTAL CODE

THE BEST OF THE BEST™ — Here's How it Works:

Accepting your 2 free books and gift places you under no obligation to buy anything. You may keep the books and gift and return the shipping statement marked "cancel." If you do not cancel, about a month later we will send you 4 additional books and bill you just $4.74 each in the U.S., or $5.24 each in Canada, plus 25¢ shipping & handling per book and applicable taxes if any.* That's the complete price and — compared to cover prices starting from $5.99 each in the U.S. and $6.99 each in Canada — it's quite a bargain! You may cancel at any time, but if you choose to continue, every month we'll send you 4 more books, which you may either purchase at the discount price or return to us and cancel your subscription.
*Terms and prices subject to change without notice. Sales tax applicable in N.Y. Canadian residents will be charged applicable provincial taxes and GST. Credit or Debit balances in a customer's account(s) may be offset by any other outstanding balance owed by or to the customer.

mounted in a tall cypress and waited as the gate slid open.

Perhaps he could tell her a complex tale of taxes, of the benefits to her and to him if she would permit him to declare the money he'd lent her a bad debt.

It just might work.

An hour later, over *espresso* served in sixteenth-century *cristallo* cups, he knew that his scheme was doomed. The *marchesa* had politely avoided talk of business until they'd finished eating. Now, at the first reference to taxes, profits and losses, she waved her hand in dismissal.

"Let us spare each other polite chitchat and get to the truth, *signore*. As you probably already suspect, I cannot repay the money I owe you."

Dominic nodded. "I did suspect that, yes. But it's not a problem."

"No, it is not. We have an agreement. The Silk Butterfly is yours."

Her head was high but the quaver in her voice gave her away. Dominic sighed in exasperation.

"*Marchesa*. Please listen to me. I cannot—"

"You can. You must. That was our agreement."

Dominic ran a hand through his hair. "Agreements can be changed."

"Not for people of honor," she said coldly, "which we both are."

"We are, yes, but…I wish to forgive you the money, *Marchesa*. Truly, I don't need it. I give more to charity each—" A mistake. He knew it as soon as he said it. "I didn't mean—"

"The del Vecchios do not accept charity."

"No. Certainly not. I simply wanted to—"

"You wanted to renege on the terms of our arrangement."

"No. Yes. Dammit, *Marchesa*..."

"It is not necessary to resort to profanity, Signore Borghese."

Dominic shot to his feet. "I am not resorting to anything but logic. Surely you can see that."

The *marchesa* lifted her head. Her eyes, still a vibrant blue, pinned him mercilessly to the spot. Such a vibrant blue, Dominic thought, frowning. Where had he seen that color before?

"What I see," she said, "is that I misjudged you. I thought you were a person of honor."

Dominic stiffened. "If you were a man," he said softly, "you would never get away with saying something like that to me."

"Then do not try to avoid complying with our agreement."

Dominic stared at the haughty old face, mumbled a word learned on the streets in his childhood under his breath, and paced across the dining room. He covered the distance from one wall to the other three times before turning toward the *marchesa* again.

"I would not be a man of honor if I took The Silk Butterfly from you. You may not see it that way, but that's how it is."

The *marchesa* sighed. "I suppose I can see your point."

Later, Dominic would realize she'd agreed far too quickly but at that moment, all he felt was relief.

"I will agree to a change in terms."

"Excellent." Dominic reached for the old woman's hand. "And now, if you will forgive me, it's a long drive back to—"

"You must admit," the *marchesa* said softly, "The Silk Butterfly would make an excellent addition to your French fashion group."

Something in her tone gave him pause, but he knew her pride made it necessary for her to hear him say she was right.

"Yes. Yes, I agree, it probably would have. But—"

The old woman rapped her cane against the floor, as she had in Dominic's office five years before. A maid appeared, so quickly it was apparent she'd been waiting in the hall, hurried toward them and handed the *marchesa* a silver picture frame.

"During this entire time," the *marchesa* said, as she waved the maid out, "did you never think to meet my granddaughter?"

"Why would I? You told me she was more than capable of running The Silk Butterfly."

"She is." The *marchesa* looked at the photo she held in her hands and smiled. "Still, I'd hoped you and Arianna would have become acquainted." Her eyes lifted to his. "She is a woman you would find appealing, I am sure."

Dio, was that where this was leading? Was this the price of the old woman's pride? Dominic had spent more than any man's fair share of evenings listening politely to what could only be described as sales pitches on the fine qualities of young women whose families found his money sufficient reason to overcome any qualms they might have about his lineage. Was he going to have to endure an hour's worth of paeans about the *marchesa's* spinster granddaughter? Her unattractive, overaged, undersexed…

The *marchesa* turned the picture toward him. Dominic felt the blood drain from his head. He was looking at a face he'd seen before, a face that still haunted his dreams after five years. Hair the color of sunlight. Elegant cheekbones. A soft pink mouth and eyes a shade of blue he suddenly recognized, for he'd seen them in the face of the *marchesa*.

Somehow, he managed to draw air into his lungs.

"Who is this?"

"My granddaughter, of course. Arianna."

Arianna. The name suited the woman. Dominic's head was spinning. He needed air.

"*Marchesa*. I think—I really think…" He cleared his throat. "I must leave. It's getting late and the drive back to Rome is—"

"Long. Of course. But surely you want to hear the way in which I propose to settle our debt."

"Not now. Another time. Tomorrow, or the next day, but—"

"But what? My Arianna is beautiful. Surely you can see that."

"She is, yes. But—"

"She is bright and healthy and of child-bearing age."

"What?" Dominic barked out a laugh. "*Marchesa*. For heaven's sake—"

"You are not getting any younger. Neither is she. Don't you want to breed sons? Don't you want to found a dynasty?" The *marchesa* raised her chin. "Or continue one as old as mine and Arianna's?"

Dominic dragged in another breath. "Surely you aren't suggesting—"

"Surely I am. Marry my granddaughter, Signore Borghese. Merge our two houses. You will gain The Silk Butterfly and I will not lose it. Then we will both know that the del Vecchio debt is fully paid."

CHAPTER TWO

IT WAS a perfect summer morning in New York. Not too hot, not too humid. Just perfect.

Perfect, except for The Silk Butterfly.

Arianna del Vecchio Cabot, seated in an eighteenth-century chair that was her legacy through her father's family, the Mayflower Cabots, her elbows resting on a fifteenth-century desk that was her legacy through her mother's family, the del Vecchios of Florence, sighed and looked out the window of her office.

In a city of offices filled with computers, Arianna's place of work appeared to be an anachronism.

It was an expensive, deliberate illusion.

The Silk Butterfly was housed in a modern building on a busy street, but once you stepped past the front door, you found yourself in a replica of a Florentine *palazzo*. High ceilings, frescoed walls, travertine marble floors and soft lighting all combined to suggest an earlier, more gracious time.

The *New York Times* had done a piece on the Butterfly's new look and location four years earlier and dubbed it "elegant." *A LA MODE* magazine had shown less restraint by pronouncing the place sexy and exciting. It was, said a TV entertainment program, the ultimate in romantic settings.

Yes! Arianna had thought when she'd heard those descriptions. Moving had been a big, incredibly expensive gamble but hearing such accolades had convinced her she'd done the right thing. Until then, the Butterfly's primary customers had been old-line society matrons who'd bought their trousseaus at the shop half a century before. Arianna wanted to hold on to them but she also wanted to appeal to young women with the taste and money to indulge in the sexy lingerie her new design team created.

The Silk Butterfly had been a diamond mounted in a Victorian setting instead of a Tiffany solitaire, its beauty recognized by only a select few.

The action, as the fashion magazines called it, had all moved out of the old neighborhood. Arianna had known they had to move with it, but first she'd had to convince her grandmother. Then she'd had to wait for the necessary capital, find the right location, the right architect and builder.

The result was breathtaking. Young women with high-powered jobs flocked to the Butterfly. So did the men who were their lovers.

There was only one catch. By the time Arianna opened the new shop, it was too late. Dot-coms failed. Technology stocks crumpled. Men who'd thought nothing of buying a few thousand dollars worth of silk for the women they wanted to impress were jobless. Women who'd splurged on sexy lace to wear under their serious wool suits went back to wearing garments bought off the rack.

The Silk Butterfly was still beautiful, still a place that made people ooh and aah. Unfortunately, they oohed and aahed without spending money. The old clients, ladies with white hair and financial managers far too conservative to have succumbed to the allure of the internet, could still afford the Butterfly's luxuries, but they didn't buy the outrageously expensive new designs. And when the tenor of the times made people turn away from frivolity, the eventual default of the loan her grandmother had taken became a certainty. The Butterfly was doomed. A family-owned business that had flourished for centuries was about to die. Arianna lived each day knowing it was she who'd delivered the fatal wound.

How much longer until her small kingdom was gone? The loan was due tomorrow, but the dissolution of a complex business took time. Bankers, accountants, attorneys would gather to pick over the corpse. Like the captain of a ship, she'd be expected to remain on board until it went under.

Arianna gave another deep sigh. It was one hell of a badly mixed metaphor, but it summed things up. The Butterfly was dying and she would have to watch it happen.

The worst part had been telling her grandmother. She'd written her a long letter and detailed all the steps she'd taken to try and save the business. The *marchesa* had responded with a note that said Arianna was not to blame herself.

"You have done all you possibly could," the old woman had assured her.

Arianna rose and walked slowly to the ornate indoor balcony just outside her office and looked down on the sales floor. Such a big, beautiful space. So handsomely designed, with lace and silk nightgowns and teddies and thongs artfully displayed.

And so empty.

Nobody was in the Butterfly except the one salesclerk she'd kept on until the closing.

Maybe the *marchesa* was right. Maybe she'd done all she could, but that didn't keep her from feeling guilty.

Almost five years ago, her grandmother had put three million dollars into the Butterfly. Without the money, they'd probably have gone under back then. Now, the business wouldn't just go under, it would be transformed from a place of tasteful intimacy to an unidentifiable cog in a giant money machine.

The Silk Butterfly was about to fall into the hands of a man named Dominic Borghese.

Arianna had never met him, but she knew all about him. Borghese was ruthless. Heartless. He flaunted his wealth and power. He'd come up from the mean streets of Rome and he never let anyone forget it.

The only bright spot in what was happening—if you could call it that—was that the loss of the business would not touch her grandmother's personal accounts. The *marchesa* would lose the Butterfly but not any of her own fortune.

She'd assured Arianna of that.

"They tell me it would not be prudent to invest my personal funds, Arianna," the old woman had explained. "That is why I've taken a loan."

And a good thing, too. Had her grandmother lost such a huge sum of money, the guilt would have been unbearable.

Arianna went back to her desk and took a small tin of aspirin from the top drawer.

Who could have dreamed things would end like this, when she'd first gone to work for the *marchesa* straight out of college?

"You are the future of *La Farfalla*," her grandmother had told her. "I want you to look ahead and recommend changes in how we do business."

Arianna had made recommendations but the *marchesa* vetoed them all. After six frustrating months, she'd left and gone to work for a fashion house. Sales at the Butterfly continued to fall while Arianna made a name for herself with her new employer.

A year passed. Then one morning the *marchesa* phoned. Arianna was to fly to Florence to meet with her at the *palazzo*. The matter was of some urgency. That was all she would say.

The meeting had been brief and to the point.

"I wish you to return to *La Farfalla di Seta,*" the *marchesa* had said. "I am getting old, child. No, don't waste my time or yours in denial. I was wrong not taking your advice before. We need a young woman's energy and vision to lead us."

"I'm flattered, *Nonna,*" Arianna had said with caution, "but the last time I was in charge of planning, you—"

"I'm not asking you to take charge of planning. I'm telling you that I am stepping aside. Don't look so surprised. Centuries of del Vecchio blood run in your veins."

"Cabot blood, too," Arianna had added. Despite having sent her to an American boarding school, her grandmother generally preferred to ignore that part of Arianna's lineage.

"That is another reason for you to take over. You understand the American market, and it generates the most profit. Clearly, you are the woman to lead us now."

And just look where she'd led it.

Arianna filled a Venetian glass tumbler with water from a carafe and gulped down three aspirin.

Maybe she shouldn't have made the move downtown. Maybe she should have made it sooner. Maybe she should have anticipated the economy's free fall.

Maybe she should give up second-guessing. What was done was done.

Hadn't she learned that lesson in a stranger's arms five years ago?

You couldn't travel the road ahead by looking back. She had to concentrate on what to do next, on how to support herself...

Herself, and her son.

Arianna drew a deep breath.

Her son.

She reached for the framed photo that was her desk's only ornamentation. A little boy looked out at the world from the silver frame, his eyes big and dark, his hair a tumble of black curls.

Jonathan del Vecchio Cabot. Her heart, her joy, her secret. Her child, fathered by a stranger.

It still seemed impossible.

One indiscretion. One night's passion in the arms of a man who didn't know her name any more than she knew his, and her life had changed forever.

She'd met him at a charity party at a hotel on Fifth Avenue. Met him? That wasn't what had happened. She hadn't "met" the man, she'd gone to bed with him.

How? How could she have done such a thing? Five long years had passed and she still had no answer.

She'd only gone to the party because she'd begun planning the Butterfly's expansion and high-powered parties were good places to make connections. Half an hour after stepping into the ballroom, she'd regretted the decision. The place was a sea of noise and glitter. Arianna was as adept at making small talk as anyone, but not that particular night.

She'd watched the expensively dressed women air-kissing the cheeks of other expensively dressed women, the men with them exchanging equally phony smiles and handshakes, and she'd longed for the simplicity and quiet of her apartment on Gramercy Park.

She'd been edging toward one of the terraces for a breath of fresh air when she saw the man. He was tall and dark-haired and almost dangerously beautiful. And he was watching her, his face taut with the hunger of a mountain lion as it watches its unwary prey.

Arianna felt her skin turn hot. She'd wanted to tear her eyes from his but she couldn't. Like a stricken doe, she'd stood absolutely still, half the length of the ballroom between them, while her heart pounded.

He knew what she was feeling, what he was doing to her. His eyes had narrowed and told her so. She'd felt her bones start to melt.

Go home, she'd told herself, *Arianna, for God's sake, get out of here while you can.*

Instead, she'd moved slowly toward him. When he held out his hand, she took it, felt the strength of him as his fingers claimed hers. She let him lead her out on the terrace and then she was in his arms, his mouth crushing hers, her arms winding around his neck, her body pressed shamelessly against his.

Arianna's hand shook. Carefully, she put down the picture.

She'd never felt anything like that excitement in her life. She'd had a couple of lovers. The relationships had been discreet. Pleasant. Dinner and the theater. A movie, a museum, walks in Central Park and, after a while, kisses and caresses and sex.

Nothing like that had happened with the stranger. There'd been no preliminaries. No pretense at anything more than hunger. They hadn't even exchanged names.

They hadn't said much of anything but what needed to be said.

"You're exquisite," he'd whispered, his voice deep and brushed with an accent. "My Princess of the Night. And I want you more than I've ever wanted another woman."

He'd touched her then. While they stood on the terrace, where anyone could have come out and seen them. He'd cupped her face, taken her mouth with his, run his hands down her body and slipped them under her short skirt and—and God, oh God, she'd come apart.

"Come with me," he'd said.

And she'd gone. To his penthouse suite high atop the hotel. To his bed, where he'd made love to her, with her, where he'd done things that had made her peak again and again in his arms.

A soft sound burst from Arianna's throat. She shut her eyes, trying to close out the memories, but she hadn't been able to do that in five long years. The images were crystal-clear. The feel of his body against hers. The taste of his mouth. How she'd responded to him, so wild and hot and hungry for everything he gave, everything he took.

She remembered the shock of awareness when it was over, how she'd stared into the darkness, waited until his breathing slowed, how she'd eased from his bed, dressed in the dark, taxied to her apartment where she'd showered and showered until her skin felt raw, trying to forget what she'd done.

But forgetting was impossible.

A month later, she missed her period. She'd been late before; that was what she'd told herself even as she bought a pregnancy test kit at the drugstore. And the man she'd gone to bed with had used a condom.

Condoms, she'd thought, her face heating as she remembered the night.

But condoms weren't one hundred percent reliable. And she wasn't late. She was pregnant. Pregnant, by a man whose name she didn't even know.

She'd handled it by pretending it wasn't happening, until she awoke one morning sick to her stomach. Forced to face reality, she'd made an appointment with her gynecologist.

"I can't have this baby," she'd told him.

But on the day of the scheduled procedure she'd looked at herself, naked, in her bathroom mirror. There was a life growing inside her still-flat belly.

Instead of keeping her appointment she'd driven to Connecticut and stopped at the first realtor's office she saw in a little town she'd passed through during a weekend in the country.

A month later, she'd signed the papers for a pretty little house three hours and a million lifetimes from Manhattan and anyone she knew. Step one, she'd thought, and girded herself for step two, telling the *marchesa* about her pregnancy—but her grandmother had suffered a heart attack before she had the chance. Her doctors were sure she'd recover fully but from now on, she'd have to take things a bit easier.

That had been the end of Arianna's news.

To this day, she'd never told the *marchesa* about her pregnancy, her baby's birth, her son's very existence.

Nobody knew.

Jonathan was Arianna's sweet secret. She spent weekdays at her city condo, weekends and vacations in the sunny country house where her child, and her heart, had taken up residence.

The stranger had stolen her self-respect, but he'd given her a son she adored.

Impulsively, she reached for the telephone and pressed a button. Jonathan's nanny answered. A moment later, Arianna heard her son's voice.

"Hello, Mommy."

"Hello, darling. Susan says you had a picnic under the big maple tree."

"Uh-huh. Susan made cupcakes with funny faces. An' she made hard-boiled eggs with faces, too. Olives for the eyes an' that red stuff for the mouths."

"Pimiento," Arianna said, and wished, as she did every day, that she could be in Connecticut instead of here. At least one good thing would come of the Butterfly's demise. She'd sell the condo, find a job closer to home, spend every day and night with her little boy.

"Mommy? Are you coming home tonight?"

Arianna swallowed hard. Her son always asked the same question.

"I can't, baby. But tomorrow is Friday, remember? I'll be home by supper time and we'll have the whole weekend together."

They talked for another few minutes. Arianna didn't want to end the call but Jonathan said, with childish innocence, that he had to go because Susan was going to take him on an adventure to find the lost wolf cave.

"Have fun," Arianna said cheerfully.

She hung up the phone, leaned her elbows on her desk and pressed her hands to her eyes. Ridiculous, this sting of tears. Susan loved Jonathan and he loved her. That was good, wasn't it? She didn't have to worry about him every day, she only had to miss him—

"Arianna?"

"Yes?" Arianna sat up straight and looked at her assistant, standing in the doorway. "What is it, Tom?"

"You okay?"

"I'm fine. Just a headache, that's all. What's happening?"

"Your grandmother's on line three. Your private line was busy, so—"

"Thanks." Arianna picked up the phone as Tom closed the door behind him. *"Nonna?"*

"Arianna," the voice at the other end said in familiar, imperious tones, "I have been trying to reach you for hours. How long can you possibly stay on the telephone?"

Arianna smiled. "It's nice to hear from you, grandmother. How are you feeling today?"

"Impatient. How else would I feel, waiting to talk with you, waiting for this dreadful Manhattan traffic to move?"

"I was on the phone, grand—" Arianna frowned. "Manhattan traffic?"

"Driver? How much longer until we reach SoNo?"

"SoHo," Arianna said automatically. "Are you in New York?"

"Certainly I'm in New York. Didn't you get my message? I telephoned your office yesterday"

Arianna riffled through the stack of papers on the side of her desk. "No. No, I didn't. Grandmother, you shouldn't have made this trip. You know what your doctors said."

"They said I'm fine and that I can do as I wish."

"I don't think—"

"Good. Don't think. Listen instead. We will be at your office in half an hour. That's what the driver says, though I suspect that will only be possible if this limousine sprouts wings."

"What limousine? And who is 'we?'"

Static crackled across the line. "I can't hear you, Arianna."

Arianna switched the telephone to her other ear. Was her grandmother on a cell phone? It didn't seem possible. The *marchesa* distrusted things like cell phones and computers, and couldn't be convinced to use them.

"*Nonna?* Can you hear me?"

"I—" Crackle. "...barely hear..." Crackle. "...tea for me..." Crackle. "...coffee for Signore..." Crackle. "...soon, Arianna."

"Grandmother? Grandmother!"

The line went dead.

Arianna hung up the phone, frowned and pressed the intercom button. "Tom? Did my grandmother call yesterday? No. I didn't think she— No. Never mind. No problem. Just—would you put up some tea, please? Coffee, too, and a plate of chocolate *biscotti* would be fine."

Why was the *marchesa* in New York? Perhaps she'd decided to be present at the closing of The Silk Butterfly. And who was with her? Her lawyer? Her accountant?

Arianna touched her hands to her temples. Of course. The man was bound to be a representative of Borghese International, come to audit the remaining assets of the Butterfly.

Quickly, she put Jonathan's picture into the desk drawer. Then she rose to her feet.

What did Dominic Borghese think? That she'd tiptoe out the door with a few bolts of lace under her arm? That she'd tuck a couple of dozen silk teddies under her coat? Perhaps he did business that way, but he had a nerve assuming she would behave like him.

"Tom!" Arianna strode from her office into the adjoining reception area where her assistant was pouring boiling water into a tea pot. "Tom, please print out the year's inventory records and bring them to me."

"The entire inventory? That's an awful lot of data."

"I want all of it, and the sales figures for the same period."

"You've got it."

"And forget the *biscotti*," Arianna said grimly. "Dominic Borghese's sending a flunky to check my integrity. I have to let him in, but I don't have to treat him with courtesy."

"Wrong on all counts, Miss Cabot. No one is questioning your integrity, and I would advise you to treat your guest with the utmost courtesy even if he were, as you say, a flunky."

Arianna's heart leaped. That voice. So deep. So soft. So—so filled with warning.

She took a breath and turned around. Her grandmother stood in the doorway. Beside her was the man Arianna had gone to bed with five years ago.

"Quite right," the *marchesa* said brusquely. "Arianna, where are your manners? No one is questioning anything and you will most assuredly treat our guest with courtesy. *Signore,* this is my granddaughter, Arianna del Vecchio Cabot. Arianna, this is our benefactor, Signore Dominic Borghese."

Arianna gaped. Say something, she told herself desperately. Say anything...

Instead, she dropped to the floor like a stone.

CHAPTER THREE

DOMINIC and the *marchesa* had flown to New York in his private plane.

The *marchesa* had slept most of the way. Dominic had spent the time thinking about the coming encounter with the woman who'd slipped from his bed.

For years, he'd been plagued with questions about her. What was her name? Why had she vanished?

The only thing he'd been sure of was that he'd never taken a woman as he'd taken her. No polite conversation. No pretense at civility. Just heat. Heat and hunger. And pleasure, *Dio,* pleasure beyond anything he'd ever experienced.

And she'd walked out while he slept.

At first, it had puzzled him. After a while, it had angered him. He supposed it was petty. They'd shared a couple of hours in bed. When it was over, after she'd cried out beneath him as he'd emptied himself into her, they'd owed each other nothing.

It was just that waking and finding her gone without leaving a note, a name, a telephone number, having her dismiss him as if he were a beggar in the streets...

Yes, that had made him angry.

Still, the night was history. He'd probably have gone on thinking about it once in a while, but when fate stepped in and the woman in his bed turned out to be the *marchesa's* granddaughter...

Only the gods could have scripted such a tale.

That the *marchesa* wanted him to marry her grand-daughter was a bonus. Of course, he had no intention of agreeing to the plan, though he'd yet to tell that to the *marchesa*. He would, when the time was right. Surely, there'd be a way to do it that would help even the score.

Petty? Perhaps, but revenge could be sweet.

As his jet flew through the clouds high over the Atlantic, he'd tried to imagine Arianna's reaction when she saw him. He'd expected her to be shocked, staggered, horrified...

What he hadn't imagined was that she'd take one look at him and pass out.

The *marchesa* screamed. Dominic cursed, rushed forward and caught Arianna before she fell. Her assistant came barreling through the door and added his cries to the old woman's.

Dominic shouldered past them both and laid Arianna on a tapestry-covered sofa. Her face was white and when he clasped her wrist, he felt her pulse racing beneath his fingertips.

The assistant was still making a fuss but the *marchesa* had fallen silent. Her face was pinched and as white as her granddaughter's.

Wonderful, Dominic thought grimly. One woman had fainted and the other was about to do the same, and if the damned fool assistant didn't shut up...

He swung toward him and barked out a single word. *"Silenzio!"*

It worked. The man clapped a hand to his mouth.

"What is your name?"

"T-Tom. Tom B-Bergman."

"Tom. Bring me some cool water."

"There—there's water in that carafe."

"Pour two glasses and give one to the *marchesa*." Dominic touched the old woman's shoulder. *"Per favore,"* he said gently, "sit down."

To his relief, she didn't argue.

"Is Arianna all right?" she whispered as she sank into a chair beside the sofa.

"Yes, she's fine. She fainted, that's all. Please, take that glass and drink some water."

The *marchesa* nodded again and brought the glass to her lips. Dominic turned to Tom. "Ice," he said crisply. "And a compress."

"A compress? We don't have—"

"Anything, for God's sake. A napkin. A scarf. Something I can fill with ice and hold to Signorina Cabot's forehead, *si?*"

"Si. I mean, yes. Yes, sir. Right away."

Arianna moaned softly. Dominic squatted beside the sofa and eased his arm beneath her shoulders. If it weren't for the presence of the old woman, he thought coldly, he'd let her lie there until she recovered consciousness on her own. But the *marchesa* was leaning forward, and the hand that held the glass was shaking.

Dominic smiled reassuringly. "You see? She's coming around already."

Tom bustled into the room with a bowl of ice and a silk teddy. "Will this do? It's the first thing I found."

"It's fine."

Dominic scooped some ice into the teddy and held it to Arianna's forehead. She moaned again and her lashes fluttered. Her eyes opened and met his. The color of her eyes was unusual, like the sky on a soft June morning. An innocent blue, he'd thought that night he'd taken her in his arms.

His mouth twisted. He put down the ice, took the glass

of water and held it to her lips as he raised her shoulders from the sofa.

"Drink," he said curtly.

"What—what happened?"

"You passed out. Drink some water."

She took a sip. As she did, she looked at him again and he knew the exact second the pieces fell into place. Her eyes widened. Color rushed to her cheeks.

"You," she whispered.

Dominic smiled tightly. "What a surprise."

Arianna pushed the glass aside and jerked away from his encircling arm.

"Sit up too quickly and you'll faint again."

"Let go of me."

He shrugged indifferently and did as she'd asked. What did he give a damn if she passed out a second time?

"As you wish."

Arianna sat up. Something wet and cold fell into her lap. She picked it up, looked at it and wished she hadn't.

"We had to improvise," Dominic said wryly.

She swung her feet to the floor. The room tilted and she took a deep breath and willed herself not to pass out again. Once was enough. More than enough. To faint at the feet of Dominic Borghese was bad. To do it in front of her grandmother, who looked as if she'd aged a dozen years, was horrendous.

"*Nonna.*" Arianna reached for the *marchesa's* hand. "Are you all right?"

"Never mind me, child. I'm fine. It's you I'm concerned about. What happened? Why did you faint?"

Why, indeed? Arianna hesitated. She could hardly tell her grandmother she'd collapsed because she'd looked up to see the father of her child standing in the doorway.

"Perhaps the signorina saw something that upset her."

Arianna shot a glance at Dominic. He was smiling as if he found the situation amusing. Amusing? To discover that the woman he'd seduced was the same woman he was going to put out of business?

"She didn't have anything to eat today."

Everyone looked at Tom.

"Not a mouthful," he said accusingly. "She's been so busy, preparing for tomorrow's closing... Arianna, won't you let me send out for something?"

"Just bring the coffee and tea for my grandmother and our—our guest. I'm not hungry. Unless... "Grandmother?" Arianna said, deliberately ignoring Dominic. "Would you like something to eat?"

"We just had lunch on Signore Borghese's jet." The *marchesa* smiled. "Such a lovely plane, Arianna. Tooled leather seats, low tables..."

"I'm sure it's wonderful," Arianna said politely, "but I'm also sure the *signore* didn't come all this distance so we can talk about his airplane."

"No." The *marchesa* sighed. "He did not. He came to see the Butterfly, now that he owns it."

"He doesn't," Arianna said quickly. "Not quite yet."

"Ah, but I shall by this time tomorrow." Dominic flashed another quick smile. "Does that trouble you, Signorina Cabot? That your beloved Butterfly will belong to me?"

Oh, he was definitely enjoying this. Why? Because she'd left his bed before she could embarrass herself again? It didn't matter. Whatever he thought, whatever she said, she'd lost the Butterfly anyway.

"Yes," she said coolly, "it does."

"Arianna," the *marchesa* said, "for heaven's sake—"

"No, no," Dominic said, "that's all right. I like a woman who speaks her mind." He tucked his hands into his trouser pockets and rocked back a little on his heels. "I'm curious, *signorina*. What bothers you the most about this transaction? That you will lose the Butterfly, or that I will gain it?"

She didn't hesitate. "Both."

"Arianna," the *marchesa* said sharply, "watch your tongue!"

"Signore Borghese might as well hear the truth, grandmother. It won't change the final outcome." Arianna turned to Dominic. "The Butterfly dates back centuries. From what I know of Borghese International, that won't mean a damn to you."

"You mean, from what you know of me," Dominic said smoothly. "Come now, *signorina,* don't be shy. All of Rome knows that I haven't a history as honorable as yours."

"I'm interested in the Butterfly's honor, not yours. I can't imagine you giving it the individual attention it deserves. All of this—*all* of it," Arianna said, spreading her arms, "will be just another cog in a corporate wheel."

"Meaning I won't run it as you did."

"Exactly."

"Well then, at least it won't go bankrupt and end up in the hands of your creditors."

It was a low blow, but Arianna knew she deserved it. "Believe me, I'd give anything to go back and change what happened."

"Unfortunately, it's impossible to change what we do once we've done it. Surely, even a princess knows that."

Dominic's voice was soft, his words clearly meant to have special meaning for her. A princess. That was what he'd called her that night. She wanted to slap his face, to tell him not to play this game, but her grandmother was watching them with rapt attention.

"That's true, *signore*," Arianna said politely. "But there are those of us who learn from our mistakes."

"Indeed. But…perhaps you can enlighten me about something, *signorina*."

Arianna looked at Dominic again. His eyes had narrowed to dark green slits.

"If I can."

"We've met before, haven't we?"

"No." Did she sound calm? How could she, when her heart was racing? "No, we haven't."

"Are you certain? You look so familiar. Perhaps we met in Rome."

"Rome? I don't think so."

"Florence? You do spend time in Florence, don't you?"

"No."

"Arianna, don't be silly." The *marchesa* gave a little laugh. "Of course she spends time in *Firenze*, Signore Borghese. Perhaps…" She looked from Dominic to Arianna. "Is it possible you two met there?"

"We've never met anywhere," Arianna said decisively.

"I never forget a face, *signorina*, especially one so lovely." Dominic frowned. "Wait. It's coming to me. A party. Here, in New York. Five years ago." His smile was smooth as silk. "Do you recall it now? Or shall I tweak your memory a little?"

The room seemed to tilt again. The bastard. Why was he toying with her?

"That won't be necessary, *signore*."

"We don't need such formality, Arianna. Call me Dominic, please."

"Dominic," she said, though the name seemed to stick in her throat. "I suppose it's possible we met a long time ago."

"We did. I knew it as soon as I saw your photo at your grandmother's *palazzo*."

"But you never said a word!" The *marchesa* laughed girlishly. "Dominic, how naughty. You should have told me you knew my granddaughter when I asked you— when we discussed business."

"I wanted to surprise you, *marchesa,*" Dominic said, lazily enough that it made Arianna's belly knot.

So, he'd known who she was all along. *That* was why he'd come here, so he could have the pleasure of taking the Butterfly from her in person. Apparently, she'd insulted him by slipping from his bed without a word.

Oh, if she'd only known his identity that night. She'd heard of Dominic Borghese. Who hadn't? And if half the things people whispered about him were true, she'd never have slept with him. The man was a savage...

A savage whose touch she'd never forgotten.

Heat rose in her face.

He was also an arrogant son of a bitch who'd come all this distance to rub her nose in the fact that he was the man taking the Butterfly from her. He wanted to play games? Fine. She'd accommodate him.

Arianna smiled and tucked her hands into the pockets of her silk slacks.

"You know, now that I think about it... Perhaps I do recall meeting you before."

"Really."

"Mmm." She was tempted to bat her lashes, but why

push a good thing too far? Instead, she gave him a big, bright smile.

"Unfortunately, I can't be certain. I meet so many people. You understand. Sometimes it's difficult to remember them all."

"Unfortunate, indeed."

"On the other hand, if our meeting was memorable, I wouldn't need reminding, would I?"

A muscle ticked in his jaw. "In that case," he said softly, "perhaps I can find ways to refresh your memory."

The warning was clear. *Don't underestimate me,* he was saying, *or you'll regret it.*

He was right. What was the matter with her? You didn't play dangerous games with a man like this, especially if you had a secret to protect. Twenty-four hours, that was all, and the Butterfly would belong to him. She could handle things for one day.

"For heaven's sake!" The *marchesa* looked from Arianna to Dominic. "What is all this? Do you two know each other or not?"

Arianna held her breath and waited. The next move had to be Dominic's. Seconds crept past and then he smiled at her grandmother, took her hand and brought it to his lips.

"We did meet once, a long time ago. I'm afraid your granddaughter has forgotten me, but I haven't forgotten her. What man could forget a woman who is the image of you, *marchesa?*"

The *marchesa* blushed. Arianna had never seen her grandmother blush in her entire life. Without question, the man had a way with women.

"What charm you have, Dominic. No wonder one hears such naughty whispers about you."

"What you hear is usually the product of someone's imagination." He grinned. "It's what you *don't* hear that's really interesting."

The *marchesa* giggled. Arianna tried not to roll her eyes but he must have known what she was thinking because he flashed her the kind of smile that made her want to slap it off his face.

"Coffee," Tom sang out as he breezed in with a silver tray in his hands. "And tea." He glanced at Arianna. "And some wonderful *biscotti*."

Saved by the bell, Arianna thought, and busied herself by playing hostess.

Dominic left the women in late afternoon.

He said his goodbyes politely, bending over the *marchesa's* hand, then Arianna's, though that involved a determined, if invisible, tug of war as she tried to jerk her fingers from his. Eventually, he applied just enough pressure so she finally gave up fighting.

Once on the street, he felt like a man let out of a cage.

No wonder the *marchesa* was trying to marry off her granddaughter. The old woman wanted more than his money. She wanted a man to tame a wildcat.

Dio, he'd be sorry for the fool who married her.

Some poor idiot would surely be taken in by that stunning face, that lush body, those innocent-seeming eyes. And what a shock that man would have when he realized he'd married a woman with a sharp tongue, a prickly disposition…and a taste for falling into bed with men she didn't know and had no interest in seeing again.

Dominic waved away his chauffeur. His head was full of questions. He needed to walk. To think. It had been, to put it mildly, one hell of an afternoon.

Traffic heading uptown was heavy. Cars and trucks

slipped past each other with inches to spare; pedestrians hurried along the narrow streets without concern for red lights or green. Dominic followed suit. He felt at home in New York. In many ways, the city reminded him of Rome. The impatient traffic. The energy and vitality of the streets.

Energy and vitality. Those words could also describe Arianna and what had drawn him to her five years ago. She'd been out of place at that party, stalking the room with impatience, her smile wooden, her eyes showing her boredom.

She hadn't been bored in his arms that night.

She hadn't been bored today, either. First she'd gone toe to toe with him in a verbal duel. Once she'd realized he wasn't to be trifled with, she'd done her best to act civilly, but he'd seen straight through the polite words and courteous smiles.

Arianna Cabot loathed him.

Dominic stepped off the curb. A horn honked angrily. He took a quick step back as a taxi whizzed past.

Amazing, that she'd gone to bed with him without checking his pedigree. Or maybe she had. Maybe she'd known who he was and wanted to see what it was like to sleep with a barbarian.

Either way, she'd made her point. He was good enough to sleep with but not good enough for anything else. She'd all but curled her lip each time she'd looked at him this afternoon. Not that she'd looked at him very often. Once her assistant brought in that tray she'd done her best to ignore him, even when the *marchesa* tried to include him in the conversation.

Arianna hadn't been able to hide her disdain.

In turn, he'd behaved as if he hadn't noticed…but he had. *Dio,* she infuriated him! Did she really think she could get away with treating him like that? She couldn't. He wouldn't permit it. He'd made that promise to himself the first time—the only time—a woman had made a fool of him.

How old had he been then? Seventeen? Eighteen? It had been summer then, too. He'd been working for a contractor, laying bricks at a rich man's villa just outside Rome. The owner of the villa had a daughter. She'd watched him working shirtless under the blazing sun for almost a week. Then she'd set out to seduce him.

It had taken no effort at all.

He was young and hot-blooded. She was sophisticated and beautiful. She'd welcomed him to her bed every night for two weeks until, with the foolishness of youth, he'd told her he'd fallen in love with her and asked if she loved him, too.

"Me?" she'd said incredulously. "In love with *you?*" And she'd laughed and laughed...

Dominic walked faster.

No way would he let history repeat itself. He'd tolerated Arianna's behavior for the *marchesa's* sake, but politeness only demanded so much of a man. That he should have endured her coldness, the icy glances meant to remind him that she was an aristocrat and he was a nobody...

A nobody who held the future of the del Vecchio family in his hands.

She had the bloodlines, but he had the money.

Dominic paused at the curb. His limousine glided to a stop alongside. His driver didn't get out. The man had been with him long enough to know that his boss didn't like shows of subservience in anyone.

Although right now, Dominic thought grimly, as he climbed into the car and it headed toward Fifth Avenue, right now, watching Arianna Cabot do a little bowing and scraping would be a pleasure.

The amazing thing was that he'd managed to control his temper today.

How many times had he almost shot from his chair, grabbed the ice princess by the shoulders and reminded her that she hadn't found him so distasteful the night she'd slept with him?

How many times had he come close to proving it by clasping that beautiful face in his hands and kissing her until her mouth lost its haughty stiffness and melted under his?

He'd kept his temper because it just wasn't worth losing it. He didn't want anything from Arianna. Not her uselessly old-fashioned business, not her body, not even a show of respect.

All he wanted was payback. Wasn't that what the Americans called it? And he'd have it tomorrow.

The car glided to a stop outside the hotel where Dominic kept a suite—the suite he'd taken Arianna to that night.

"Will you be wanting the car this evening, Mr. Borghese?"

Dominic shook his head. "No, George. Put it in the garage and take the night off."

"See you tomorrow morning, then. Seven o'clock, right?"

"Right."

Tomorrow morning, Dominic thought as he rode the private elevator to the penthouse, he would go back to the Butterfly and at the moment the place was supposed to become his, he'd tell the *marchesa* that he didn't want it and he didn't want her granddaughter, either.

He'd be damned if he'd take an old woman's sole

asset. As for marrying Arianna…did the *marchesa* really believe he'd give up his freedom, give up choosing his own wife, for the supposed benefit of joining his blood with the del Vecchios?

Dominic yanked off his suit jacket and tie and tossed them on a chair in the foyer. He walked into the living room as he unbuttoned his shirt collar and rolled back his cuffs.

The truth was, the *marchesa* wouldn't have looked at him twice if she still had money.

Dominic dumped ice into a glass, opened a bottle and poured himself a finger of Kentucky bourbon. It was a taste he'd acquired when he'd spent a couple of years in the States, though he hardly ever indulged it. It was important to have a clear head at all times.

Besides, he'd seen too much of what alcohol could do to people while he was growing up.

Still, a small celebration seemed called for, considering that tomorrow was going to be filled with surprises for Arianna.

Dominic stepped out onto the terrace and gazed down at Central Park sprawled far below him, a calm oasis of green in the concrete hurly-burly of the city. He lifted the whiskey to his lips and let the first sip warm his belly.

The bittersweet truth about the *marchesa's* "merger" suggestion was that *if* the del Vecchio fortune were intact, *if* he'd met Arianna the usual way, *if* they'd fallen in love—whatever that meant—*if* he'd asked her to marry him, the old woman would have moved heaven and earth to keep the marriage from taking place.

His blood would never be blue, but his bank account was fat. That was all that mattered to people like the del Vecchois.

Dominic lifted the glass to his lips and frowned when he realized it was empty. He went inside the living room, poured himself a second drink, then took the bottle outside to watch the sky darken and the lights in the park flicker on while he poured a third.

By the time he fell into bed, he didn't give a damn about anything but that moment tomorrow when he'd look Arianna in the eye and tell her his lawyers had already drawn up the necessary papers that would, in effect, cancel out the loan.

He didn't want the Butterfly. He certainly didn't want Arianna.

He'd tell her that. It was why he'd come all this distance, so that he could enjoy the look on her face when she learned that her grandmother had tried to sell her to him—and her reaction when he told her he'd sooner marry an alley cat than take her as a wife.

Dominic yawned, rolled over and fell soundly asleep.

CHAPTER FOUR

DOMINIC awoke to the insistent ringing of a bell.

He fumbled for the alarm clock and hit the off switch, but that didn't stop the noise. Neither did slamming the clock with his fist. Finally, he struggled up against the pillows, winced at the throbbing pain in his temples, and grabbed the telephone.

"What?" he barked.

"Buon giorno."

It was the *marchesa*. Dominic looked blearily at the clock. It was 4:55 in the morning.

"Marchesa." He cleared his throat. "I hate to sound unsociable, but—"

"Did I wake you, *signore?*"

Dominic closed his eyes. "As a matter of fact—"

"My apologies. I know it's early. I waited all night, as long as I could... Oh, Dominic. I made a mistake. I should not have done it, I know, but—"

"Marchesa." Gingerly, Dominic touched his hand to his head. Surely a man did not deserve such pain even if he'd been foolish enough to drink too much bourbon whiskey. *"Marchesa*, please, speak more slowly."

"Per favore, Dominic, address me by my name. I am Emilia."

Hell. All of a sudden, she wanted him to call her by her given name? The throbbing in his head got worse. What did the old woman want?

"Emilia," he said carefully, "perhaps you've forgotten the time difference here in New—"

"Listen to me, Dominic. I have created a problem."

The *marchesa*—Emilia—began talking, but she didn't slow down. If anything, her words took on added speed and urgency.

Half-listening, Dominic clutched the phone to his ear and made his way to the bathroom. He rummaged through the medicine cabinet for a bottle of aspirin, tapped three tablets—four, he thought, wincing—into the palm of his hand and gulped them down.

Why had he drunk so much last night? He wasn't a drinker and there was nothing to celebrate. He'd go to today's meeting, make his announcement about the immediate liquidation of the company, then fly home. Never mind mentioning her grandmother's absurd marriage plan to Arianna. He had no time for something as self-indulgent as revenge. When he could get a word in, he'd simply tell the *marchesa* he wasn't interested. Then he could go back to Rome and put this ridiculous episode behind him.

The *marchesa* was still talking. About what? Dominic thought wearily, and headed for the kitchen.

"Emilia," he said, interrupting the stream of words, "as a special favor to me, take a couple of breaths and start again, yes? Tell me what's wrong."

What was wrong, the old woman said, was that she, and she alone, had ruined everything.

"Everything!" Her voice shook. "And I am so terribly sorry."

Dominic turned on the kitchen lights. One-handed, he took down the coffee, spooned some into the filter, changed his mind and spooned in more, then filled the pot with water.

"You cannot imagine how I regret my error!"

Actually, he could. He regretted his errors, too. He should never have come to New York, never have let the *marchesa* spend a moment thinking he'd really collect on the loan or so much as consider her ludicrous suggestion that he marry Arianna.

"Dominic? Do you hear me?"

"I hear you, Emilia. What error?"

"I—how do you say it? I let the cat out of the bag. Last night, at dinner, I told Arianna of our plans."

Dominic sighed and sat down at the kitchen counter. Was he going to have to drag each word from her? "What plans?"

"Our merger plans," the *marchesa* said, with more than a touch of impatience. "I told Arianna you were going to propose to her."

"You told her…" Dominic shot to his feet, took the phone from his ear and scowled at it as if the instrument was actually the *marchesa*. "But we had no plans."

"Of course we did. You and Arianna…"

"There is no me and Arianna. I never said I would agree to your proposition!"

"You never said you would not."

"You overstepped yourself, madam," Dominic said sharply. "I have no intention of asking your granddaughter to marry me."

"Well, you should have spoken sooner," the *marchesa* said in icy tones. "Not that it matters now. Arianna laughed when I told her she was to become your wife."

A muscle knotted in Dominic's cheek. "Did she, indeed?"

"Yes. It was as if I had told her the world's best joke."

"I see." The pot was filling with coffee. Dominic shoved a mug under the black, almost viscous stream. "Your grand daughter finds the idea of marriage to me amusing?"

"More than that. She said... Never mind. It does not matter."

"No. It doesn't." Dominic paused. "But I'd like to hear it anyway."

"I don't think so."

His hand tightened on the cup. "Tell me what she said, Emilia."

"She said—she said that she would sooner marry a Martian."

"A charming image," Dominic said coldly.

"I am sorry, but you insisted on knowing."

"I did, yes." Hot coffee sloshed over the rim of the cup onto Dominic's fingers, but he didn't feel it. "And an interesting choice, since I doubt that your beloved granddaughter would be happy as the wife of a creature with alien anatomy."

"I do not understand."

"You don't have to."

"No," the old woman said, as if his rudeness was to be expected. "I suppose not. I should have left this to you, Dominic. Perhaps you would have been able to convince her."

"I just told you I was not going to propose marriage to Arianna. Do you understand?"

"What I understand is that I am going to lose *La Farfalla.*"

"We will discuss that," Dominic said coldly, "when we all meet this morning."

"You and I shall meet. Arianna will not be there."

"What do you mean, she won't be there? Your granddaughter is a part of this, *Marchesa*. I expect her to attend the meeting.''

"I would have assumed she would *want* to attend, but she refuses.''

Dominic gripped the phone more tightly. "And I insist. I'm not offering her a choice. Tell her that.''

"I cannot.''

"Then *I'll* tell her.''

"You can't, *signore*. My granddaughter and I had words. I said some harsh things. I accused her of having forgotten the importance of honor.''

"And you were right.''

"The point is, after our quarrel Arianna decided to leave.''

"Leave? *Leave?*''

"She went to her house in the country late last night.''

Dominic scraped his hand through his hair. This was impossible. How could a straightforward plan become so complicated?

"Give me her telephone number. I'll call and make it clear that she must return to the city.''

"I don't know it. I didn't even know she had a country house.'' The *marchesa's* words were touched with acid. "It would seem there's a great deal I did not know about my granddaughter. For instance, until yesterday I thought you and she were strangers.''

"Believe me,'' Dominic said brusquely, "we are.''

"That is not what Arianna says. She admitted that she remembers meeting you, but she won't discuss it because she says it was a brief, unpleasant encounter.''

"Indeed.'' Dominic's tone was silken. "What else did she say?''

"Only that she has no wish to see you again.'' The *marchesa's* sigh whispered through the telephone.

"Truly, I regret saying these things, but how else can I convince you that she would not change her mind about attending the meeting even if you could reach her... which you cannot."

"Your granddaughter has lived in America too long, Emilia. You're right. She needs a lesson in deportment and a reminder of her obligations." Dominic reached for a pad and pencil. "Where is this country house?"

"I don't know its precise location. Outside the city. That is all I can tell you."

Outside the city. That certainly narrowed things down. Arianna Cabot's house could be anywhere within three states and God only knew how many hundreds of miles.

"Is this a problem? Is there a reason my granddaughter must be present today?"

Dominic almost laughed. Could a man's battered pride be called a problem?

"Actually," he said calmly, glancing at the clock, "now that I think about it, neither of you has to be present."

"What a relief! My quarrel with Arianna exhausted me. I will be very happy to leave this place."

"I can arrange that right now, if you wish." Dominic spoke quickly, as if taking the time to consider what he was about to do might be a mistake. "My driver can pick you up and take you to the airport. My pilot will fly you home."

"I do not wish to inconvenience you, Dominic."

"It's not an inconvenience. I'm going to stay on for a few days. I have some business here, but that needn't affect you."

"Well, if you're certain..."

"I am."

"Thank you, Dominic. And again, my apologies for spoiling your plans."

"No, no. *My* apologies for my bad temper. You had no way of knowing I didn't intend to ask your granddaughter to marry me."

"To be honest, I'm not surprised. I thought it was too much to hope for."

Dominic nodded. He was calmer, as was the *marchesa*. Now was the time to tell her he wasn't going to call in the loan, either....

But he didn't.

"My driver will contact you, Emilia. You can tell him when to come for you."

"*Mille grazie.*"

"You're welcome."

Dominic hung up the phone. He drank more coffee, black as sludge and with the same consistency. Why hadn't he told the *marchesa* that she didn't have to worry about the loan? The Butterfly was all the old woman had. He wasn't going to take it from her, he simply wanted to give Arianna a scare. Just a settling of scores to make up for the endless nights he'd spent thinking about her.

His hand tightened around the coffee cup.

She'd laughed at the idea of marrying him. But she hadn't laughed when he made love to her. She'd made the soft, breathless sounds of a woman being pleasured by a man, sounds that still drove him half out of his mind when he remembered them.

The message was clear. He was beneath the princess's notice, except in bed. She'd sooner marry a creature with three eyes and eight tentacles, marry *anybody,* than him.

Dominic dumped his coffee in the sink.

Arianna needed another lesson in humility. And he had time for that before heading home.

Back in his bedroom, Dominic stripped off his shorts and stepped into an icy shower. It didn't cool his anger but he hadn't expected it to. What he wanted was to get himself under control so that he could hone his rage and use it efficiently.

There was always a way to defeat an enemy. You just had to calm down enough to determine what it was.

Dominic got out of the shower and wrapped a towel around his hips. What was the name of Arianna's assistant? Tim. No. Tom. Tom what? Berg. Berger. Bergman, he thought, snapping his fingers. That was it. Bergman.

The number was easy to find in the directory. The phone rang half a dozen times before Bergman answered.

No sir, he didn't know a thing about his employer's country place. Yes sir, he had an emergency phone number for her, but he couldn't—

A few well-chosen words and it turned out that he could. Dominic could almost see the man jump to attention, and this was one of those times jumping to attention was exactly what he wanted.

Bergman gave him a number, Dominic scribbled it down and made a call to a private detective in Manhattan that Borghese International sometimes employed.

It took slightly more than an hour to get the necessary information, more than enough time to put on jeans, a blue short-sleeved soccer shirt and moccasins, and to arrange for the delivery of a car.

Finally, he called his pilot and told him to ready the plane, and his driver to tell him he'd be taking the *marchesa* to the airport.

"By the way, George..." Dominic frowned at the address he'd written down during his conversation with the detective. "Do you happen to know the quickest route to Stanton, Connecticut? Yes? Great. Uh-huh. I don't suppose you'd know where Wildflower Road is… No, that's fine. I'll find it."

Dominic hung up the phone and headed for the door.

Moments later, he was in a rented black SUV, racing toward a small town in the rolling Connecticut hills.

Arianna loved her house.

It dated back to the 1930s, which made it completely unfashionable. The celebrities who bought property in this part of New England preferred authentic colonials, even if they were falling down.

Her house was sturdily built. It had wooden floors and a brick fireplace, and was tucked against a stand of pine trees at the end of a long, unpaved road. Hardly anybody ever drove up that road except for Jonathan's nanny and an occasional delivery van.

This was a world far removed from the hustle and bustle of Manhattan, and Arianna loved it. She hadn't expected to: she'd only bought the place so she could raise her son in privacy, but after a couple of months the house felt more like home than anyplace she'd lived since she was a little girl.

The quiet of the woods always soothed her soul.

But not today, Arianna thought as she tore leaves of Bibb lettuce into a wooden bowl. Jonathan wasn't here. He'd gone fishing with a friend and the friend's father. A good thing, too, because her little boy could read her like a book. She didn't want him to see the anger she'd suppressed…anger at the man he would never know was his father.

Arianna tore a leaf in smaller pieces with more force than necessary.

She was almost as furious now as she'd been driving here. Except for the hour she'd sat beside her sleeping son last night and the time they'd spent together at breakfast this morning, the blood still pumped hot and fast through her veins.

Had Dominic really thought she'd marry him? Had her grandmother thought it, too?

Incredibly, the answer seemed to be yes. Bad enough Dominic imagined she'd trade herself for the Butterfly, but that the *marchesa* should have thought she'd do it…

"I'm an innocent bystander, Arianna," her grandmother had insisted. "I am simply transmitting a proposition. Surely, you do not think this was my idea."

Arianna plunged a paring knife into a tomato.

Maybe not. But the *marchesa* didn't seem all that offended by the message she'd brought from Dominic.

"What message?" Arianna had asked. "Has he decided that taking the Butterfly from us isn't enough? Does he want a pound of flesh, too?"

Her grandmother had ignored the outburst. "Signore Borghese says to tell you he will forgive the loan under certain conditions."

The shock of those words, the hope they'd offered, had made her heart skip a beat. Maybe Dominic Borghese wasn't quite the rat she'd thought.

"What conditions?"

"He wants you to agree to become his wife," her grandmother had said bluntly.

Arianna's mouth had dropped open. "He wants what?"

"Dominic wishes to marry you."

"What kind of joke is this, *Nonna?*"

"I thought it was a joke, too. But the *signore* is quite serious."

"I should marry him? That—that walking collection of conceits? A man I don't know, don't like, don't want to see again in this lifetime?"

She'd said a few more things, most even less polite, and only stopped when she realized it wasn't fair to blame the message on the messenger. But when her grandmother used the pause to drop in some words explaining why it might be a smart idea rather than a foolish one, Arianna had exploded.

"Foolish doesn't even come close! It's idiotic, insane and impossible."

"Signore Borghese could give you a comfortable life," her grandmother had said quietly.

"I am quite comfortable in my life already, thank you very much. How could you even think—"

"And you are the last of our line. We need an heir."

That hurt. There was a del Vecchio heir, but the *marchesa* didn't know it. Not yet.

"I'm sure there will be," Arianna said stiffly. "Someday."

"Someday," the *marchesa* scoffed. "When? A woman your age should have a husband."

"A woman *my...*? For God's sake, *Nonna,* I'm only twenty-nine!"

"Having a man in your life and in your bed would be good for you."

A picture flashed in Arianna's mind of Dominic, taking her in his arms. Moving over her, kneeling between her thighs, his body naked and strong and breathtakingly beautiful...

"I don't need a man in either place," she'd said coldly. "I'm doing fine as I am."

"Think of the Butterfly. You would keep it."

"Do you really imagine I want the Butterfly so badly I'd sell my soul to the devil or my body to his emissary? I'm sorry you're losing the Butterfly, *Nonna,* of course, but—"

"In times past," the *marchesa* had said with a regal lift of her chin, "a merger between powerful families was desirable. Our name is old and our lineage proud. Dominic may not carry the blood of the ancient Borgheses but he is dynamic and powerful. Can't you see the benefits of merging the two?"

"Are you saying you'd be happy if I accepted this ridiculous proposition?"

"Certainly not. I am simply reminding you that there are things one does for reasons that go beyond one's own desires."

"I won't trade our name for his bank account."

"The combining of the Borghese and del Vecchio houses would not be as crass as you make it sound."

"You *do* want me to do this! Well, I won't. I'd sooner rot. I'd sooner—I'd sooner marry a creature from Mars!"

"As you wish, child. I'll give Dominic your answer, but more diplomatically."

"You tell it to him exactly as I phrased it," Arianna had said furiously. She'd gone on for a few more seconds before she'd suddenly remembered her grandmother's fragile health and advanced age. *"Nonna,"* she'd said, "I love you with all my heart and I don't want to argue with you or upset you. Perhaps it would be best if I didn't come to tomorrow's meeting. Actually, there's no reason for me to be there."

Her grandmother had sighed. "You're right. Perhaps you should stay away."

Arianna sliced a scored cucumber into the bowl.

That was when she'd slipped up and said she'd go to her country house for the weekend. For the first time, the *marchesa* had seemed surprised.

"You never mentioned a country house before."

"Didn't I?" Arianna had said, as casually as she could. "I guess the subject never came up."

They'd chatted about inconsequential things long enough to heal the breach in their relationship. Then Arianna had left her grandmother's hotel, phoned Susan and begun the long drive to the country, which she'd hoped would calm her.

It hadn't.

One way or another, she had to get the anger out of her system by midafternoon. Jeff Gooding had promised he'd have the boys back by then.

"With lots of big fish for supper," Jonathan had said.

"*Real* big fish," Jeff's son had echoed.

Jeff had winked over the boys' heads. "You might want to figure on something for standby, just in case the fish don't cooperate."

Arianna smiled. What he'd meant was that the kids never caught anything at the pond. Jeff did, sometimes, but he'd told her the boys always made him release his catch. Fishing was an excuse to dangle lines in the water and talk man-talk. It had nothing to do with anything as awful as actually hauling fish out of the water and killing them.

Jeff Gooding was a widower, a nice guy who was generous with his time and often included Jonathan in his plans.

He's got a thing for you, Susan always teased.

But Arianna didn't have a "thing" for him. He wasn't

complex, like Dominic, or strong, like Dominic, or exciting, like...

Dammit! Arianna scowled as she quartered a tomato. She had Dominic on the brain. Jeff wasn't cold, selfish and egotistical like Dominic, either. He was a pillar of the community and a good role model for Jonathan. If there was one thing her little boy lacked, it was a male role model.

If she married Dominic Borghese, her son would have a role model. He'd have the man who was his very own father.

"Arianna."

Arianna's head snapped toward the screen door. Dominic stood on the porch, his tall figure limned by the sun.

The forgotten paring knife sliced into her finger. Bright red blood splattered over the white marble cutting board. She stared blankly at the blood, at the knife...

"Il mio Dio!"

Dimly, like the background noise of a radio turned low, Arianna heard the splinter of wood as Dominic put his shoulder against the frame. The door flew open.

"Do you make a habit of fainting?" he said gruffly, as his arms closed around her.

No, she wanted to tell him, only when I'm with you. But she wasn't foolish enough to say that as he carried her from the kitchen to the parlor, where he eased her onto the old-fashioned love seat near the fireplace.

"I'm fine," she said in a thready voice. "Just let me sit here for a minute."

"Apply pressure against the cut and put your head down." She felt his hand guide her fingers to the wound. "Like that. And don't move," he added as he left her.

He sounded like a man accustomed to giving commands and having them obeyed. Arianna was a woman who never took commands, but she did now. Following a sensible order was better than falling on her face, especially since she'd already done that once in his presence.

She heard his footsteps returning. He tied a strip of cloth around her finger.

"Thank you. That's—"

"Sit still."

"I'm trying to tell you, I'm okay."

"Of course. That's the reason your face is as white as paper." He took her hand, examined it and muttered something in an Italian dialect she didn't understand. "The cut looks deep. It might need stitches, and you might need a tetanus shot."

"I don't need a shot, and the cut isn't deep."

"How do you know how deep it is until you see it? Why must you argue with everything I say?"

"I'm not arguing. I'm simply telling you..." She took a breath. She *was* arguing, and there was no reason for it. She didn't have to explain herself to him. "Let go of my hand so I can see the cut."

"Will you pass out if you do?"

"No. I don't know why..." She did know. She'd been thinking about her son, about Dominic, and then she'd looked up and he was there, so big, so masculine, so real. "You surprised me, that's all."

His mouth twisted, just the way Jonathan's had when she'd told him she didn't think that Godzilla could really, truly destroy Tokyo.

"If you faint again, I'm taking you to the nearest hospital."

"I didn't faint. I *won't* faint." Arianna jerked her hand free of Dominic's. The cut was small, as she'd thought, and not very deep. The blood had already changed from a flow to a slow ooze. "It's fine," she said briskly. "Now, please leave my house."

"You need a proper bandage."

"I don't."

"Where are they?"

"I said—"

"I heard you. Where are the bandages?"

Unbelievable! He really thought he could boss her around in her own home. She opened her mouth to tell him that, then thought better of it. What mattered was getting him out the door, and fast.

"In the medicine cabinet in the bathroom," she snapped. "Down the hall, first door on the left."

She sat tapping her foot until he returned with a small packet, tore it open and put the bandage over the cut.

"That's better."

Insolent bastard, she thought, but just then his fingers brushed hers and a rush of electricity sizzled through her. She snatched back her hand, as annoyed at herself as she already was at him.

"I'm glad you think so. Now go away."

"Such a generous display of gratitude," he said, his sarcastic tone a match for hers. "I'll go when we've finished our business."

"Didn't the *marchesa* tell you? I'm not going to participate in whatever little victory ceremony you planned for today."

"Victory ceremony?"

Dominic got to his feet and folded his arms. Arianna tried not to notice how he towered over her. He was wearing jeans and a short-sleeved shirt that revealed muscled, tanned forearms lightly dusted with black hair. Manhattan overflowed with men who wore outfits like this on weekends. She supposed it was to make them look young and fit, but she'd always thought such styles just made men accustomed to custom-tailored suits look slightly foolish.

Dominic didn't look foolish. Not that it mattered. How he looked was what had gotten her in trouble in the first place.

"Yes," she said, "victory ceremony. That's the reason you came to New York, isn't it? To enjoy seeing my face as you took the Butterfly from me?"

It was too close to the truth to deny. Dominic narrowed his gaze on those innocent-looking blue eyes.

"Your grandmother offered it as collateral."

"Yes, well, that was her mistake."

"It would seem she made another mistake." His eyes glittered. "She tells me you found her merger suggestion amusing."

"Her merger sugg..." Arianna flushed. "The marriage thing, you mean. Come now, *signore*. Surely you don't expect me to think..." Her color deepened at the amused smile that curved his mouth. "She would never have come up with such an idea."

"And you think I would?" He laughed. "Trust me, Arianna. You're beautiful and I enjoyed the night we spent together, but I'd hardly give up my freedom to have you."

"Have me?" God, how despicable this man was! "Believe me, I'm not for sale." She shot to her feet, marched into the kitchen and picked up the salad bowl. "And I wouldn't marry you if my life depended on it."

"How about if your grandmother's future depended on it?"

She swung toward him, the bowl clutched in her hands. "What do you mean?"

"I lent your grandmother money. She was supposed to repay it in kind, not with the dubious honor of your hand in marriage."

"I don't believe that's what she tried to do. Besides, she *is* repaying the loan."

"She owes me three million dollars."

"You're getting the Butterfly."

"It's not worth three million dollars."

Arianna lifted her chin. "Don't blame me if you made a bad bargain, *signore.*"

"It seemed like the right thing to do at the time."

"Did it?" Arianna put down the bowl and slapped her hands on her hips. "Why did you lend her so much money in the first place? Did you find out who I was after that night? Was this all some sick scheme to get even with me for walking out on you?"

Dominic's eyes narrowed. "How about you? Did you know who I was when you came on to me at that party? Were you an appetizer, meant to sweeten the deal before the *marchesa* approached me with her request for money?"

"You bastard!" Arianna's eyes filled with angry tears. That she'd gone to bed with a man like this made her feel sick. "Do you really think I'd sell myself so cheaply?"

"No, probably not, or why would you have slunk away without telling me your name? Maybe you simply went slumming that night, and now you see that the price is higher than you expected."

The price she'd paid was an unplanned pregnancy, but he'd never know that. How right she'd been not to have tried to identify the man who'd fathered her son. Jonathan was hers. She loved him with all her heart—

loved him as fiercely, as intensely, as she despised Dominic Borghese.

And she had to get Dominic out of here, before their child returned.

"All right." She took a step back, as if putting some distance between them would help. "You came to New York to get even. Well, you've succeeded. I was wrong that night. That's what you wanted to hear, isn't it?"

Was it? How could he have known it wouldn't be that simple? That everything would change in this moment?

Five years ago, they'd been equals. A man and woman caught up in passion, wanting each other and not giving a damn about the rest of the world. Now, she was a del Vecchio princess who'd been offered for sale to a peasant.

The rules had changed.

The look on her face when she saw him at the door, that mix of fear and loathing, twisted inside him like a knife. Her desperation to get rid of him now, as if his very presence might contaminate her home, fueled his anger.

A man could let anger consume him, or he could use it. Dominic had learned that early.

"Say something," Arianna demanded. "Don't just stand there with that—that look on your face. I've apologized. What more do you want?"

Dominic didn't hesitate. "I want you to become my wife."

CHAPTER FIVE

IT WAS too much.

Arianna had endured almost twenty-four hours of lunacy and this was...

A bad joke? A madman's taunt? She looked at Dominic. He seemed cool, self-possessed, and entirely sane.

Maybe she was the one having the problem.

"You want me to..." She couldn't even say the words. "You want me to do what?"

"I want you to become my wife."

Become his wife? Well, of course. She should have known that he'd propose after everything he'd just said, that the idea was not his but her grandmother's, that he'd never give up his freedom to have her—as if she were an object that *could* be had—after all that, of course he'd propose.

They didn't know each other, didn't like each other, had nothing in common except a son he'd never know existed... Why wouldn't he want her to be his wife?

Arianna began to laugh. What else could you do when the whole world had gone mad?

Dominic's eyes narrowed to slits. "You find my proposition amusing, *signorina?*"

At least he hadn't dignified it by calling it a proposal, she thought, and laughed harder.

"*Basta,*" he growled. "There's nothing funny about this."

He was right. Actually, this was horrible. She took a couple of deep breaths.

"No, there isn't." The hysterical laughter drained away. Arianna folded her arms and looked up into that coldly set face. "Maybe you'd like to tell me what form of humiliation you expect me to endure next."

"Asking a woman for her hand is hardly asking her to endure humiliation."

Neither was being trapped in your own kitchen with the father of your child, when that child could be home at any minute. The timing of a trip to the pond was hard to predict. Jeff and the kids could be gone for hours, but if the boys got bored or the weather turned chilly…

Never mind trying to figure out what Dominic was up to. All that mattered was getting him out the door. He couldn't see Jonathan. For one thing, he'd tell the *marchesa*. For another…

For another, her son looked like his father.

Arianna had never realized it. Maybe she hadn't wanted to, but she could see the resemblance now. They had the same dark, slightly curling hair; the same full mouth; the same classic Roman nose.

But those things didn't make a man and a boy father and son.

She knew women who reached a certain age, gave up hoping to meet Mr. Right and turned to sperm banks to create the children they wanted.

As soon as she'd realized how much she wanted her baby, Arianna had thought of the child in her womb as having been conceived with the help of an anonymous donor. Now that she knew the identity of the man who'd impregnated her, knew that he was an unfeeling, inflexible egotist who took pleasure in wielding his power, she was more convinced than ever that the only parent her boy would ever know—or need—was her.

Dominic was playing head games because she'd nicked his ego.

Maybe he hoped she'd panic. Pass out at his feet again. Well, he'd wait forever. He was up to something and whatever it was, she could handle it.

"Still no answer?" He took a step toward her. "Perhaps you're waiting for me to say it again. I want you to marry me."

Arianna smiled, picked up a bunch of carrots and turned on the water in the sink.

"Nice try," she said politely, "but wasted."

"I beg your pardon?"

"Do you get your kicks trying to shock people? This 'I want you to be my wife' thing. That stroll into my office yesterday. 'Hi, I'm the man who seduced you and oh, by the way, I'm here to take your grandmother's company from her.'"

"Be careful what you say, Arianna."

"What didn't you like? Being reminded of how you got me into bed—or how you set up my grandmother?"

"I set up no one. I'm not a bank. I don't solicit borrowers. Your grandmother came to me for money, I took pity on her and we made a deal. As for seduction… If you need reminding of what happened that night, I'll oblige you."

He moved just enough so that she felt her heart hammer against her ribs. She swung toward him, brandishing the carrots like a weapon.

"Stay where you are!"

Dominic looked at the carrots and raised his eyebrows. Arianna flushed, tossed the carrots in the sink and shut off the water. The idea was to show him he couldn't rattle her. That meant holding her ground, no matter what.

"Let's not argue over semantics. What happened between us is old news. As for my grandmother... She handles her own affairs. If she was foolish enough to borrow three million dollars from you, that's that."

"Unfortunately for the del Vecchios, it isn't."

"What's that supposed to mean?"

"You heard my proposition. I'm still waiting for an answer."

"You mean, will I marry you?" She flashed a smile. "No, I will not. Is that clear enough or would you like me to say it in Italian?

"I know something that might change your mind."

"Nothing could possibly—"

"The *marchesa* is penniless."

She stared at him. "Don't be ridiculous. She can't be."

"She's as close to flat broke as one can be and still put food on the table."

"That's impossible."

"Because she's a del Vecchio?" He smiled in a way that made her breath catch.

"Because she has a fortune. A *palazzo*. Land. Paintings by old masters. Jewels. She has—"

"She has nothing. The *palazzo* is mortgaged to the hilt. The paintings and jewels have gone to the highest bidder. Think, Arianna. There have been signs. Did you choose not to see them?"

"What signs? Have you taken to reading tea leaves? If my grandmother had sold anything..." She stopped, stared at him in dawning horror. She thought of the Tintoretto that no longer hung in the great hall of the *palazzo,* the Rembrandt that was gone from the salon. The *marchesa* said she'd lent them to a museum. She thought of a ruby pendant, a diamond necklace, other jewels her grandmother no longer wore. Too expensive to insure, she'd said, when Arianna asked about them.

She stared into Dominic's eyes. By now, she knew that Dominic Borghese was a lot of things she didn't like, but instinct told her he wasn't a liar.

"Ohmygod," she whispered.

"Indeed," he said dryly. "But God didn't put her in this position."

"No. *You* did!"

"I had nothing to do with your grandmother's financial situation."

He was right. If anyone had done this to the *marchesa,* it was she. Did she say it aloud? Did Dominic read what he saw flash across her face? Either way, he spoke before she could.

"It wasn't anything you did."

"I talked her into all kinds of expenses." She swung away from him and clutched the edge of the counter. "New designers. More expensive fabrics."

"Listen to me." Dominic clasped Arianna's shoulders and turned her to him. "The del Vecchio fortune began draining away long ago. The *marchesa's* father lost an enormous amount of money on a foolish venture in Naples. Her brother lost almost as much at the gaming tables in Monaco. And the *marchesa* only made things worse. She made bad investments, refused to listen to her advisors, and she's lived a certain life style. I suspect she refused to believe she could run out of funds."

"But she did." Arianna's voice broke. "And I made it worse by demanding money for the Butterfly."

"You had no way of knowing the true situation. But

yes. She liquidated the last of her assets, took the loan from me and poured it all into the Butterfly.''

Arianna made a little sound of distress and sank into a chair. Dominic squatted before her and cupped her chin. She tried to brush his hand away but he ignored her. He slid his hand around her neck and urged her head forward and she gave in to the gentle pressure and rested her forehead against his shoulder. He smelled of sunlight and soap and man, and she felt as if she could stay in his arms forever.

All the more reason to lift her head and free herself of his embrace.

''When she loses the Butterfly, she'll have nothing left. How will she live?''

A muscle knotted in his jaw. ''She doesn't have to lose the Butterfly.'' He rose to his feet. ''I never wanted it in the first place.''

''You never...?'' Arianna shook her head. ''I don't understand. You accepted it as collateral.''

''Your grandmother is an unusual woman.'' His smile softened his face. It made her think back to the first time they'd made love, the way he'd smiled afterward and left her wondering how many other women he'd looked at that same way. ''Did she ever tell you how she managed to meet with me?''

''No. I mean, I assume she made an appointment.''

''She bluffed her way past two reception areas to my assistant's desk, and refused to leave until she saw me. She said she needed six billion *lire*. I said I wasn't a bank. She talked some more and I said I'd give her the money. She was too proud to accept it.''

Arianna laughed softly. ''Yes. That sounds like... You said you'd *give* her the money?''

Dominic shrugged, as if embarrassed to admit to such weakness. "She refused."

"She'd have seen it as charity."

"Yes. So we agreed on a loan. And on the interest rate, which was more than I wished her to pay."

"And you checked on her finances after the fact?" Arianna lifted an eyebrow. "Not a very clever way to do business, *signore*."

"I checked because I sensed she was a woman in distress. And if you're hoping it's all a mistake, *cara*, it isn't. My people were thorough."

"I should have suspected something was wrong. I asked her why she was borrowing money instead of investing her own, and she said it was on the recommendation of her advisors."

"If she'd paid attention to them years ago," Dominic said wryly, "all this could have been prevented."

Arianna nodded. She thought about her grandmother, living her final years in poverty. No. She wouldn't let that happen. There had to be a way.

"My *nonna* is an old woman," she said softly. "She's in poor health. Once you take the Butterfly, what will become of her?"

Dominic tucked his hands into the back pockets of his jeans and paced the kitchen.

"Dominic?" She rose and went toward him. "Let me pay back the money she owes you."

He shook his head.

"I can do it. Four hundred dollars a month."

He shook his head again.

"Five hundred."

He smiled. Arianna didn't blame him. Five hundred dollars a month on six billion *lire*… Doing the math was pointless. At that rate, she'd never pay off the loan.

"Two thousand," she said desperately. "Six."

The Butterfly wasn't making enough money for that but she'd find a way to meet the debt. Take another job. Sell the pearls she'd inherited from her mother, the lovely old china...

"Please, Dominic. There has to be a way."

She was looking at him through lashes that glittered with tears, her mouth trembling. She had looked at him the same way that night in his bed as he'd moved between her thighs and opened her to him. It had almost stopped him, that look on her face, as if she feared him and his possession, but then she'd lifted her arms to him, drawn him down to her, down, down, down...

"I can help you," he said, and heard the simple words buzz in his head like the soft whisper of bees drawn to the sweet nectar of an exotic flower.

"How?"

"Have you forgotten, *cara?* I made you an offer and I'm still waiting for your answer."

She stared at him. He could tell that she really didn't know what he was talking about. Then the color drained from her face.

"No," she said sharply. "I won't do it."

"You mean, you don't want my help."

"You bastard! You arrogant, insufferable—"

He pulled her close against him and kissed her. She fought him and he clasped her face between his hands, held her still, held her mouth to his until he felt her start to tremble.

"Marry me," he said in a husky whisper, "and your grandmother's life will go on as it always has."

"That's blackmail!"

"It's a simple statement of fact."

"I won't sell myself to you."

"Is that how you see an arranged marriage that will benefit two families? How many del Vecchio brides have been 'sold' over the centuries, do you think?"

"My grandmother wouldn't want me to marry for money."

"For money. For the del Vecchio name to remain powerful. For an infusion of new blood." His eyes grew hot. "She wants an heir. So do I."

He already had an heir. The words almost burst from Arianna's throat. God, what was she doing to do?

"The terms of the agreement are simple, Arianna. I'll forgive the loan. I'll sign the Butterfly over to you, to save the *marchesa's* precious pride, and you can do what you wish with it. Keep it, give it back to her…the choice will be yours."

"What's the matter, *signore?*" Arianna jerked free of his hands. "Are you such a bad catch you have to buy yourself a wife?"

Dominic made a sound that was almost a laugh. "I'm a good catch, *cara.* And that's problem."

"Such modesty."

"Such honesty, you mean. It isn't easy for a man like me to find the right woman."

"Oh, I'll just bet it isn't."

"I'm sure the *marchesa* realized that when she suggested we'd make a good match. And I'm sure she expected me to court you. Take you out a few times, send you flowers…"

"Do you really expect me to believe any of this? My grandmother told me how the subject of marriage came up. That you suggested it."

Dominic's eyes narrowed. He checked his watch, then reached into his pocket and took out a cell phone.

"Your grandmother is probably in my car right now,"

he said coldly, "on her way to the airport." He flipped the phone open and held it toward her. "Press the second button. When my driver answers, ask to speak with her."

Silence filled the room. Arianna stared into Dominic's eyes. Was it true? Could her grandmother have made such a bizarre suggestion?

She shook her head, backed away from his outstretched hand as if it held a venomous insect instead of a phone.

"Even if it were true, why would you consider it? It's crazy."

"I thought so, too." Dominic slid the phone into his pocket. "And then I began considering the possibilities."

"What possibilities? If you want a wife, why should it be me?"

Why, indeed? He thought about the way she felt in his arms, how she trembled when he touched her, how he'd dreamed of her the past five years...

"There are other women. You could have your pick."

A quick smile flashed across his face. "A compliment, *cara*. How nice."

"Don't patronize me, Dominic! You know what I mean."

"I could have my pick because I have a lot of money," he said bluntly, "and that's the problem. I don't want a woman professing undying love when all she really wants is my checkbook."

"You're losing me here. Isn't your checkbook what you're offering me? Three million dollars of it, anyway?"

Arianna put her hands on her hips. Her breasts lifted, straining against the thin cotton of her shirt. Dominic felt his body stir. Yes, he thought, this was one of the reasons he'd marry her…but not the only one.

He moved so quickly that she had no time to sidestep, his hands clasping her elbows, lifting her to her toes until her face was level with his. "That's why your grandmother's scheme has merit. Everything would be in the open. We'd both know why you married me. No undying declarations of love. No lies. You get to secure her future. I get—"

"A wife who would hate you." Arianna's voice shook. "Who would despise you. Who would—"

"Marriage isn't about sentiment."

"Not in your world, maybe, but it is in mine."

"You're behaving like a child, Arianna, wanting life to be a fairy tale. We all do what we must to survive."

"I'm not for sale!" Arianna slapped her palms against his chest. "Let go of me, Dominic. I'd do anything for my grandmother—"

"But not this." His mouth thinned. "I was good enough to scratch an itch, but not to be seen with in daylight and certainly not to marry."

The room became silent. The soft buzz of insects outside the screen door and the ominous tick tick tick of the wall clock belonged to another world. Time was running out, for the *marchesa,* for her, for Jonathan.

"Please," she said, "please, leave now."

"Why are you so eager to get rid of me?" He lowered his head and she saw herself mirrored in his eyes. "Is this your weekend hideaway? Do you have a lover who meets you here? Is he a better lover than me?"

He cupped her face, forced her head back. He could see what he was doing to her, that she'd gone from rage to defiance to something worse. Despair? Fear? Fear, yes. *What are you doing?* he asked himself, even as he tugged the pins from her hair until it tumbled around her shoulders.

"Admit the truth," he said roughly. "Say that you want me."

"I don't. I don't—"

He kissed her, crushing her mouth with his, nipping hard at her bottom lip. She gave a sharp little cry and he started to let go of her, hating himself for his loss of control, for taking what she didn't want to give, but then she whispered his name and kissed him back, wrapped her arms around him as she had that night, sobbed when he slipped his hand under her shirt and cupped her breast...

The shattered screen door slammed against the frame.

"Get your hands off the lady, you son of a bitch," a man yelled.

"Don't you hurt my mommy," a child cried and that, more than the man's fury or the pain of small, sharp teeth sinking into his leg, stopped Dominic cold.

CHAPTER SIX

THE entire world had gone crazy.

Dominic didn't know what to do first, peel the kid off his leg, defend himself against the man coming at him, or tell Arianna that shouting "No, don't! Stop!" wasn't having the desired effect on either the kid or the man.

If anything, it seemed to be encouraging the attack.

He acted on instinct, shaking the boy off just as the man threw a wild left. Dominic danced back, but the guy was persistent and came at him with the left again. His reaction was instinctive. He slipped the punch and countered with an uppercut to the chin.

Arianna's defender blinked, stiffened, and went down like a fallen tree.

"Jeff," Arianna screamed, and the boy threw himself at Dominic again.

"Dio!" Dominic roared as the kid's teeth found their mark a second time. He grabbed the child by the scruff of the neck and held the windmilling boy at arm's length.

"Arianna! Do something with your piranha!"

Arianna, kneeling beside her fallen lover with his head in her lap, looked at Dominic as if he were the devil incarnate.

"You—you—" She jumped to her feet, grabbed her son and held him tightly against her while she whispered words of comfort and stroked his hair.

She should be stroking *my* hair, Dominic thought grimly. *He* was the one who'd been mauled. His leg felt as if it had been chewed by a pack of Chihuahuas.

The man on the floor groaned and sat up.

The child in Arianna's arms buried his face in her shoulder and wept.

Without question, Dominic thought, he must have stumbled into an asylum for the insane.

He ran his hands through his hair, tugged down his shirt and slapped his hands on his hips. None of it helped him make sense of whatever in hell was happening here, but he was starting to think even an army of psychiatrists wouldn't be clever enough to do that.

A child who addressed Arianna as "Mommy"? A man who leaped to her defense? Was the child hers? Was the man her husband? Her lover? Was she leading a secret life in this little house in the country? Not that he gave a damn. Asking her to marry him had been a stupid, spur-of-the-moment mistake.

The world was filled with women who'd jump at the chance to be his wife, women who didn't come equipped with sharp-toothed children and lovers who thought you'd been poaching on their territory—except how could you trespass on a man's rights to a woman when you hadn't even known he existed?

"It would seem," Dominic said coldly, "that there are some things your grandmother forgot to mention."

The child jerked his head around. "Don't you yell at my mother!"

"Hush, sweetheart." Arianna's tone was soft but the look she gave Dominic was poisonous. "She doesn't know."

Dominic stared at her. "Excuse me? You have a child, a husband—"

"He isn't my mom's husband," the boy said firmly. "'Cause if he were, I'd have a father. And I don't."

Arianna blinked. This was the first time Jonathan had ever mentioned having—or not having—a father. His timing couldn't have been worse.

"You don't need a father," she said, and hugged him closer. "You have me."

"That's what I told Jeff," the boy said tearfully, "when he asked if I wanted him for a dad."

"Oh, hell." Jeff got to his feet. "I didn't think Jonathan would say anything. Arianna…"

"Did you actually discuss this with my son?" Arianna said in disbelief.

"I figured I'd see how he felt about it," Jeff said unhappily, "before I approached you."

"Well, you shouldn't have. Whatever were you thinking?"

Jeff winced as he waggled his jaw from side to side. "I think that son of a bitch broke my jaw!"

"Watch your mouth," Dominic said sharply.

"And who in hell are you, anyway? Coming in here, attacking Arianna—"

"He wasn't attacking me. And he's right. Don't use language like that in front of Jonathan."

"Lotsa people say sum of a bitch," the child said helpfully. "They say other stuff, too, like—"

"Jonathan. Honey." Arianna's voice was bright. "Is Billy outside? Why don't you go play with him?"

"He doesn't feel good. We caught a fish and he threw up. That's why we came home."

"Oh. Oh, well then…why don't you go into the living room and put on the Saturday cartoons?"

"You don't let me watch the Saturday cartoons."

"Today's different."

"It surely is," Dominic said coldly. "I suspect it isn't every day you play hostess to your lover and a—how do you say it?—a patsy at the same time."

"What's a patsy, Mommy?"

"Hush, sweetheart!" Arianna glared at Dominic. "Have you no sense of decency? There's a child present!"

Dominic didn't answer. It was becoming difficult to be civilized. The more time went by, the more he wondered what sort of woman would melt in one man's arms while she waited for another

"I was wondering when you'd get around to that."

"Not that it's any of your business, but Jeff isn't my... He's just a friend. And I don't know what you mean by a patsy."

"Oh, I think you do. At least now I understand the reason I was told none of this. You and the *marchesa* were afraid I wouldn't take the bait if I knew you had a child."

"Damn you, Dominic—"

"'Have you no sense of decency?'" he said, mimicking her. "'There's a child present'—a child I knew nothing about."

Arianna swallowed hard. "That isn't my fault. You came here thinking you knew everything about me. And—"

"And I didn't. As I pointed out, I was the perfect *pazzo*."

"I don't know what you mean!"

"It was clever, I admit." His mouth twisted. "You'd snag a husband and a fortune in one step. All you and the *marchesa* had to do was lure me in, make me think *I'd* been the one who'd maneuvered *you* into marriage...."

"Don't be crazy! It was nothing like that. Didn't I just tell you that the *marchesa* doesn't know about—about any of this? Maybe you should have asked me about my life instead of her!"

"What's he talking about?" Jeff put a hand against his jaw and winced again. "Who's the *marchesa?*"

"She's the matchmaker from hell," Dominic said coldly, his eyes never leaving Arianna's. "Do you really expect me to believe she knows nothing of this second life you lead?"

"You know what?" Fury made Arianna incautious. "I don't care what you believe. I just want you out of my house and my life."

"Finally, we agree."

Dominic started for the door. Arianna almost groaned with relief. Thank God! He was leaving, and he hadn't noticed Jonathan's resemblance to him. He'd go away and never come back. He'd be out of her life and her son's forever...

He'd go straight to her grandmother.

Of course he would. He didn't believe a word she'd said. He'd confront the *marchesa,* make these same accusations, talk about Jonathan...

Years of caution, of secrecy, of protecting her *nonna* from news she might not be well enough to handle, was all coming undone.

"Dominic!" She gave Jonathan a quick kiss and put him down. "Wait."

He turned to her. She saw the banked fury in his eyes and knew she had to be careful.

"We have to talk.

"We have nothing to talk about."

"Please. Just give me five minutes to take care of

things here. You can wait on the back porch. It's quiet and peaceful.''

Quiet and peaceful. As if he gave a damn about that. He'd been set up, used, manipulated…

''You'd be wasting your time.'' He folded his arms and glared at her. ''There's no point in talking about the Butterfly, Arianna. I'm going to do what I should have done all along.''

''I don't give a damn about the Butterfly! It's— it's—'' She shot a quick look over her shoulder at the child and the man. ''Please. Wait on the porch. Five minutes. Surely you can give me that.''

Dominic scowled. Why should he give her anything? This woman couldn't seem to take an honest breath.

He looked past her. The man she claimed was not her lover stood behind the child, one hand on the boy's head in a protective gesture. At least he had good instincts. If anyone needed protection, it was the boy.

He was a brave little kid who'd defended his mother against huge odds. From the looks of him, he was ready to do it again. He looked small but undeniably fierce, his posture matching Dominic's right down to the narrowed eyes and folded arms.

Dominic cocked his head. Such perfect mimicry…

''Dominic?'' Arianna put her hand on his arm. ''I'm begging you. Please.''

There was definite pleasure in hearing supplication in the voice of the princess.

''Five minutes,'' he said, as he moved past her. ''Not a second more.''

Half an hour later, Dominic was sitting on the porch steps, still waiting, still trying to figure out why he'd bothered to oblige Arianna by hanging around.

Whatever she had to say would only be more claptrap about her innocence in an unraveling scheme.

He didn't believe a word of it.

Twenty minutes ago he'd heard a door slam, a car engine start, a vehicle peel out of the driveway, its throaty roar a clear statement of dissatisfaction.

So much for Jeff of the glass jaw.

But Arianna hadn't appeared. He figured she was still soothing the boy.

And he was still hanging around. Well, why not? After all, it was a long time since anybody had tried to scam him.

Dominic leaned back on his elbows. Arianna was right. It was pleasant out here, as quiet as the countryside outside Rome. It was hot, too, the same as Rome, but flowering vines curled around the porch stanchions and offered patches of cooling shade.

A small bird with bright yellow feathers landed on the railing and scolded him for being there.

Dominic could hardly blame the bird. What *was* he doing here, except waiting to see just how far Arianna was prepared to go before she let the scam die a natural death?

He'd done a lot of scamming himself when he was a kid, conning tourists out of *lire* by claiming he was the best guide Rome had to offer, though half the time he'd passed off one old church or ruin by the name of another. Why not? he'd figured. Back then he had a righteous contempt for the rich.

Years later, he knew it hadn't been contempt at all. It had been envy.

Dominic sat up and let his hands dangle between his thighs.

A good sting called for a con artist with imagination.

Arianna and the *marchesa* had as much as he'd ever seen. They'd set up a close-to-perfect con. Dangle a beautiful woman in front of a man who'd already tasted her favors, let her put on a don't-touch-me act while he could think of nothing but the night she'd spent in his bed, then make him feel so sorry for her that he'd give her anything she wanted.

Perfect, all right.

Too bad for the del Vecchios that the wheels had come off their plan. Timing was everything, and the timing on this had gone bad. The kid was supposed to stay out of sight just a little longer, probably until Arianna let herself be seduced into bed again.

He was sure now that she'd known who he was the night they'd been together. Forget all that nonsense about electricity sizzling between them. What had been sizzling was Arianna's clever scheme on the back burner....

A scheme so clever it had taken five years to pull off?

Dominic frowned.

That didn't make sense. There wasn't a take in the world worth such a long build-up. Yes, the pay-off was big, but five years?

Okay. Maybe she hadn't set him up that night. That didn't mean that what was happening now hadn't been planned. The del Vecchio women saw their fortune gurgling down the drain, and he was their chance to get it back. The *marchesa* had dangled the bait. Arianna had set the hook with the marry a Martian routine...

Sighing, Dominic rose to his feet, tucked his hands in the back pockets of his khakis and went down the steps.

He could hardly wait to get home. What he'd told the *marchesa* about having business in New York wasn't true. The "business" had been Arianna. Now, he was eager to see Rome again.

Too bad he wasn't there right now, doing something simple like sitting at a café in the *piazza* near the Trevi fountain, drinking something tall and cool with Isabella or Antonia or any one of half a dozen other beautiful women who'd be happy to smile at him and say yes, without question they wanted the honor of being his wife.

At least he'd know, up front, if they had any surprises for him, like lovers tucked away in country houses no one knew existed...

Or children.

Saved by the skin of his teeth. Wasn't that what Americans said when you miraculously escaped a disaster? Imagine if Arianna had said yes, she'd marry him, and oh, by the way, had she mentioned she had a son?

Whose child was he? Dominic started down a narrow, foot worn path through the grass. Who had slept with Arianna and planted a seed in her womb?

Not that it mattered. After today, he'd never see her again. Anger, carnal desire, who knew what had been driving him? At least he'd come to his senses before it was too late.

What man would marry a woman he barely knew, business arrangement or not?

Dominic kicked a small stone out of the path.

The child was the final touch. A ready-made family, to start married life? He shook his head. No way.

Still, Arianna would make some man a good wife.

She was bright, she was beautiful, she was passionate. Not just in bed. In her work, too. He had to admit he liked that about her. If he'd married her, she'd have slipped seamlessly into his world, where money bought respect if not approbation, and if anyone had dared to look down on her because she was the wife of a man who'd come up from the streets, she'd have made short work of them.

Arianna was tough, like her grandmother. Maybe "strong" was a better word. It was an unusual quality in a woman who was beautiful. In his experience, beautiful women invariably acquiesced to men.

Not Arianna.

She'd apparently passed on that strength to the boy. Dominic laughed to himself. The way the kid had come at him, ready to take him... How old could the child be? Four? Five? He supposed he'd been pretty tough at that age, too, honed to steely resiliency by the streets.

If he ever had a son, he'd want him to be just like that. Confident. Sturdy. *If* he ever had a son...

Dominic caught his breath. The boy was just about the right age, but it couldn't be. He'd used condoms. He always did. He was always careful.

"Dominic?"

He turned and saw Arianna coming toward him. He met her halfway. She gasped with surprise as he grabbed her shoulders and hoisted her to her toes.

"Is he mine?"

Arianna's throat constricted, but she didn't bother pretending ignorance. She'd been preparing for this question while she'd dealt with Jeff, then put her son in for a nap and sat with him as he fell asleep. That was the only reason she could meet Dominic's hot gaze and lie through her teeth.

"No," she said calmly, "he's not."

Dominic's hands bit into her flesh. His expression was grim. Hers, she hoped, was neutral. When finally he let go of her and tucked his hands into his pockets, she breathed a silent "thank you" to the angel who'd surely been watching over her.

"Whose is he, then? Your friend with the bad left hook?"

Arianna shook her head. Was it cold out here, or was it her? She gave a little shudder and tucked her hands into the pockets of her shorts.

"I told you. Jeff is only a friend. Not even that. He's Jonathan's swimming coach. He has a son the same age and the boys like to spend time together."

"Were you widowed? Divorced? Who is the boy's father?"

"What is this, an interrogation?"

"It's a simple question."

"Here's a simple answer. I've never been married and Jonathan is mine. That's all you need to know."

"Jonathan. Quite a mouthful for a little kid. Don't you ever call him John or Johnny?"

"What I call him," Arianna said deliberately, "is none of your business."

"Be careful, *cara*." Dominic flashed a warning smile. "A little while ago, you were pleading with me to stay so you could ask me a favor."

"I didn't say that."

"You didn't have to. It was obvious. So I stayed, and now you think you can insult me. That's not a good way to get whatever it is you want."

He was right, it wasn't. She just didn't want him asking questions about Jonathan. There were too many questions and not enough answers.

"I'm sorry."

He laughed. "The words came out as if they'd been stuck in your throat."

"Really, I *am* sorry. You're right. I asked you to stay

and you did." Arianna glanced back at the house. Jonathan's room was upstairs. He probably wouldn't hear them, but she didn't want to risk it. "Let's walk a little further. The path leads into the pines."

Dominic shrugged. "As you wish."

She fell in beside him and they walked into the woods in silence. The tall pines shut out the sun, making the day seem suddenly cool, and she shuddered again.

"You're cold," Dominic said.

"I'm fine." She stopped walking and swung toward him. "I know you're—you're upset."

Dominic laughed and Arianna felt her cheeks redden.

"All right. You're more than upset. My grandmother made you think I'd be—that I'd be interested in marrying you. And now you seem to think she and I set you up."

"Go on." Dominic folded his arms. "Let's hear the rest of what you think."

"We didn't. I didn't, anyway. I didn't know who you were until yesterday, and I certainly have no wish to marry you." She paused. "Now you've stumbled across my—my hidden life."

"A truly bad title for a soap opera, *cara*."

"But accurate." Arianna took a deep breath. "How did you find out about this house? I've kept its existence a secret."

"There are no secrets from a man who can afford to buy them."

"You called this place a love nest." A breeze blew a strand of her hair across her face. She caught it and tucked it behind her ear. "It's never been that. I bought it after my son was born." She paused. "It was the only way I could think of to keep his existence a secret."

"Because he is illegitimate?"

"Of course not! He's my son. I'm proud of him. I love him with all my heart."

"But he has no father." Dominic's mouth thinned. "A child should not be held responsible for the errors of its parents. If his father didn't want to acknowledge him—"

"Jonathan's father doesn't know he exists. I wanted it that way. We had—we had only a brief relationship."

"A man is entitled to know he's sired a child, and a child is entitled to know his father."

"Dammit, don't preach to me, Dominic! That's easy for you to say, but you don't..." Arianna fought for composure. "The issue here is not my son's birth. It's the choices I made after it. There was no reason for the man involved ever to know about my child."

Arianna shuddered again. Dominic muttered an oath, ignored her protests as he wrapped his arm around her and drew her into the warmth of his body.

"And the *marchesa?* Surely she would be happy to know she has a grandson."

"The *marchesa* lives in a world that doesn't exist." Arianna looked up at him. "She still believes in white gloves, and servants, and calling cards, and—"

"And babies who are never born out of wedlock."

Arianna nodded as they turned and began walking out of the pine woods.

"Exactly. Still, I was going to tell her...but she had a heart attack. How could I give her such news when she was ill? So I waited. And waited. And the more time passed, the more difficult it became. I'd look at her and see the evidence of the years etched into her face, or she'd talk scornfully of some new medical test she'd had..."

"Time moves on."

"Yes."

"All the more reason for her to want to see you married. She wants to insure the future of the del Vecchios." Dominic paused. "As I wish to insure the future of the Borgheses."

He spoke softly, so softly that it was almost a whisper. Arianna was afraid to look at him, but he stopped walking and turned her to him. "I think your grandmother knows that, and hoped I'd find her suggestion not quite as outlandish as it might seem."

"You don't have to apologize for her. And I'm glad you admit it was outlandish."

Dominic lay his fingers lightly across Arianna's mouth.

"I did, at first. But then—I'm not sure when, but at some point, it began to make a strange kind of sense." His voice turned husky. "I would get a beautiful princess for my wife, she would keep her precious Butterfly, and someday there would be a Borghese-del Vecchio heir."

"Dominic—"

"But," he said, tilting her face to his, "I misjudged the beautiful princess. She doesn't want any of that badly enough to pawn her soul to the devil."

"You're not—"

"Hush." There were tears on Arianna's lashes. Gently, he wiped them away with his thumb. "It's all right, *cara*. There are better ways to find a wife than to fall into a game devised by a sly old woman." He slid his hands into her hair. "It could have worked, you know. Do you remember that night? You and I...we made the earth tremble."

Arianna met his eyes. She had lied to him about the

one thing that mattered more than anything else in the world. How could she lie to him about this, too?

"Yes. We did." Her voice shook. "I want you to know something, Dominic. I never—never in my entire life...what I felt that night, what you made me feel..."

He bent to her and kissed her, softly at first, then with growing hunger. She leaned into his embrace, her mouth open to his, her heart beating fast with the excitement of being in his arms again.

"Arianna." He pulled back enough so he could look into her eyes, forgot what he'd told himself about not wanting this woman, forgot even that he didn't want a child another man had given her. "*Bellisima* Arianna, let's start over. Let's pretend we only just met. We'll go to dinner. To the theater. We'll walk in the park. Whatever pleases you..."

"Mommy?"

They jumped apart, torn from each other's arms by the sound of that small, uncertain voice. Jonathan was standing on the porch steps, hair tousled, feet bare, a well-loved teddy bear clutched in his arms.

"Yes, sweetheart." Arianna tried to read her son's face. What had he seen? What had he heard? She went to him and held out her arms, but he took a step back. "Did you have a bad dream?"

"He's still here," her son said, staring at Dominic. "That man you said had to leave."

She looked back at Dominic. "He is leaving," she said quickly. "Right now."

Dominic shook his head. "Not yet." His tone was easy, his smile warm. He walked to the porch, squatted down when he reached the steps and held out his hand. "I think it's time we met properly, Jonathan. My name is Dominic."

Arianna held her breath. Her son stared steadfastly at this stranger. Then, slowly, he stuck out his hand and let it be engulfed by Dominic's.

"I never heard that name before."

"It's Italian."

"I know about Italy. They play soccer there."

Dominic nodded gravely. "Indeed they do, only we call it football."

"Jeff was gonna take me to a football game in the fall."

"Was he," Dominic said coolly.

"Do you have a little boy at home, like Jeff does?"

"I wish I did, but I don't."

"And do you want to marry my mommy, like Jeff does?"

"Jonathan," Arianna said quickly, but Dominic's voice cut across hers.

"What would you think if I did?"

"Dominic!" Arianna reached for her child and hoisted him into her arms. "Jonathan, you don't have to worry about me marrying anybody. I'd never—"

"I think you should marry somebody, Mommy. You don't know anything about stuff like football or soccer."

"Honey, we can talk about this another—"

"You could marry Dom—Dom—"

"Dominic," Dominic said helpfully.

"Dom'nic. 'Cause sometimes I think it would be nice to have a daddy, 'cept not one who gets knocked out so fast, like Jeff."

Dominic snorted. Arianna glared at him, then buried her face in her child's neck. "Jonathan," she whispered, "sweetheart, this isn't the time to—"

"That was a really good punch!"

Oh God. Her son sounded gleeful. "Jonathan," Arianna said firmly, "stop it right now."

"Just one kapow," Jonathan said, slapping his hands together so that the teddy bear swung in a wild arc, "and bam! Out ol' Jeff went."

Arianna put him down. "Listen to me, Jonathan."

"Gianni."

She stared at Dominic, who was exchanging man-to-man smiles with her son. "What did you call him?"

"Gianni. That's Italian for Johnny."

"I know what it means." The porch felt as if it were swaying under her feet. Arianna wrapped her hand around a stanchion. "But his name is Jonathan, not Johnny. Really, Dominic, don't you have an appointment back in the city?"

"He looks more like a Gianni than a Jonathan to me."

"Yeah, Mom. I look more like a Gianni than a Jonathan." The child made a face. "What do you call that? A nickname?"

Dominic smiled. *"Si."*

"That word's Italian, too. Right?"

"Right. It means yes."

"I always wanted a nickname, but my mom just calls me Jonathan." The child turned an innocent face to Arianna. "How come you never gave me a nickname?"

Arianna gave up. "You never asked," she said, and plopped down on the top step. She'd just have to ride out whatever was happening here.

"So, how come you were kissing my mother, Dom'nic?"

Arianna shook her head, then buried her face in her hands.

"Well, I like to kiss her." Dominic sat down, too, and pulled the boy into his lap. "Your mother is pretty."

"She's smart, too." Jonathan's voice filled with pride. "She runs a big store. In Manhattan. Do you know where Manhattan is?"

"Yes," Dominic said solemnly, "I do."

"I went to the park there once."

"Uh huh."

"An' to a museum."

"Jonathan." Arianna rose slowly to her feet. "That's enough. Say goodbye to Signore Borghese and go into the house."

"I thought his name was Dom'nic."

"It is," Dominic said. He stood up. "*Signore* means mister. And Borghese is my last name."

"Oh."

Oh, Arianna thought, while the hysteria mounted inside her, *oh?* Her son and his father were discussing names and sports and her—*her*—as if they were old pals.

This was a bad dream. It had to be. Maybe if she tried very hard, she'd wake up.

"Dominic." She took a deep breath. "Thank you for waiting. So we could talk, I mean. And thank you for being so understanding."

"You're welcome."

"I didn't expect..." Arianna put her hand on her son's head. "I thought it might take longer to convince you that, well, that... You know."

"Not to discuss today's events elsewhere?" He shrugged. "The timing of that matter is in your hands, not mine."

"Thank you. Let me just get Jonathan inside and I'll walk you to your—"

"Not that you have all that much time to deal with it."

"I know." She smiled as the tension inside her eased.

Dominic Borghese wasn't a beast after all. He'd given her a bad few minutes, well, a bad couple of hours, but obviously he understood that he couldn't tell the *marchesa* about her son any more than she could marry him. "I'm going to talk to the *marchesa* this week. I'll fly to Florence and—"

"Tomorrow," Dominic said.

Arianna blinked. "Sorry?"

"I said, you'll fly to Florence tomorrow." He frowned. "My plane's probably left already, but I'm sure my office can arrange for airline tickets on short notice." He looked down at Jonathan and smiled. "Have you ever been to Italy, Gianni?"

"His name is Jonathan," Arianna said sharply. She took a step back, tugging her son with her. "What are you talking about? He's not going to Italy. Neither am I."

Dominic's eyes met hers. He was still smiling, but the steel in that smile sent a chill down her spine.

"I've agreed to permit you your own timing with regard to telling your grandmother what must be told to her. As for the rest...I told you what I want of you, Arianna."

She was speechless. "You can't mean... You don't really think..."

"I do mean. I do think."

"No! I'd never—"

"Think before you speak, *cara*. There's a great deal at stake here. Your grandmother's finances. The future of the Butterfly." Dominic paused. "Your secret."

"But you said—you said you wouldn't—"

"Mommy?"

"Hush, Jonathan."

"Mommy!"

"Jonathan, please. This doesn't concern you. Why don't you go into the house? See if—if there's any popcorn. I'll be in and—"

"Mom-my," Jonathan said impatiently, "who's that lady?"

"What la…" Arianna looked across the yard. A moan burst from her throat. "Oh God," she whispered, "no. Please, no!"

Dominic's eyes followed hers. The *marchesa* was walking toward them, looking down at the uneven ground and leaning heavily on her walking stick as she picked her way through the grass. Dominic's driver was a couple of paces behind her, looking sheepish.

Dominic slid his arm around Arianna's waist and laid his hand on Jonathan's shoulder. He could feel Arianna trembling. He drew her closer, clasped the boy more tightly.

"*Marchesa*," he said politely, "what a surprise."

"Your plane was being serviced, Signore Borghese. Some nonsense about an engine, your pilot said. I had already given up my suite at the hotel and there I was, all alone. No host. No granddaughter. What was I to do? I phoned your apartment but there was no answer, and your driver was most reluctant to give me any information until I…" The old woman's eyes rounded. For the first time, she seemed to notice Jonathan. Her face turned a papery white.

"Arianna? Who is this child?"

"Mommy?" Jonathan looked up at Arianna. "Mommy, why is the lady such a funny color?"

The *marchesa's* mouth dropped open. "What did the boy call you?"

"*Nonna.*" Arianna broke away from Dominic and ran

down the steps. "*Nonna,* let me help you. Come and sit down."

"I want answers, Arianna! Who is this boy?"

"I'm Jonathan Cabot. Who are you?"

"*Dio.*" The *marchesa* whispered the word like a prayer. She put her hand to her throat just as Arianna's arm curled around her waist. "Arianna, tell me it isn't so."

"Please, grandmother..."

"Tell me the boy isn't yours."

"I *am,* too, hers! Tell her, Mommy."

Jonathan sounded brave but he leaned back against Dominic's legs and Dominic could feel him shake. He cursed under his breath and lifted the child into his arms, remembering all too clearly the pain of a childhood spent in the shadows.

"Signore Borghese?" The *marchesa* stamped her walking stick on the grass, but with far less force than usual. "Explain this immediately."

"I'll explain," Arianna said quickly. "I just don't know where to start."

"You don't have to, *cara.*"

Dominic spoke softly, but there was no mistaking the air of quiet command in his voice as he came down the steps, holding Jonathan in one arm, and stood close beside Arianna.

"Do you recall when your granddaughter and I confessed that we had known each other in the past?"

"A brief meeting, you said. At a party."

"It's true. We did meet at a party."

Dominic smiled at Arianna. At least, she thought, it would look like a smile to her grandmother but what she read in his eyes was a warning.

"The truth is that we had more of a relationship than

we admitted. And now we have some news that should please you."

"No," Arianna said breathlessly, "Dominic…"

It was too late. Dominic drew her into the curve of his arm.

"Your granddaughter and I are getting married."

CHAPTER SEVEN

THEY were married in the Manhattan chambers of a judge Dominic knew. The ceremony was brief and the only guests were the *marchesa* and Gianni.

Dominic had to keep reminding himself Arianna didn't want him to use that name. Her son's name was Jonathan, she said emphatically, just before the ceremony began. He was American, not Italian. She wanted Dominic to remember that.

The boy looked so crestfallen that Dominic came close to telling her he'd call the child by whatever name he wished, but he knew there were times it was best to let things ride.

"Let's not quarrel," he said pleasantly. "What's the importance of a name, anyway?"

Arianna didn't answer. She didn't have to. He knew that they were jockeying for position, establishing the rules for a marriage neither of them had planned. It was logical, though. For a man in his position and a woman in hers, an arranged marriage made sense.

That was what Dominic told himself, anyway. But when he stood beside Arianna as the judge spoke, when he felt her tremble, when he reached for her hand and she looked up at him as if he had the answers to all the questions in the universe, he found himself suddenly wondering if perhaps he was marrying her for some other reason.

There was no time to think about it.

"By the power vested in me by the State of New York…" the judge said and just that quickly, the ceremony—and the moment—were over.

The judge smiled. "Congratulations."

Dominic nodded. "Thank you."

"Well? Aren't you going to kiss the bride?"

Dominic turned to Arianna, prepared to offer nothing more than a *pro forma* brush of his lips against hers, but she turned her head to the side and his kiss landed on her cheek.

It made him angry.

Did she think the touch of his mouth would be some sort of contaminant? Was she too good to accept a kiss from a peasant? He wanted to grab her and force a real kiss on her, twist his hand in her hair and hold her still under the pressure of his mouth until she moaned and kissed him back.

But he controlled himself.

He was overreacting. This was difficult for Arianna. Everything had happened very quickly. Their arrangement, the ceremony, the *marchesa* learning about Jonathan—news the old woman had received with surprising good grace, just as he'd hoped, because she believed the boy was his—all of it had taken place in the blink of an eye.

He understood that his new wife needed time to adapt.

In fact, he decided to tell her that.

They had lunch at a restaurant in the east sixties. Dominic ordered vintage champagne and the *marchesa* offered a toast.

"To the future of our new *famiglia.*"

Dominic drank. So did the *marchesa*. Smiling, she

offered her glass to her newly found great-grandson and even Jonathan swallowed a drop of the pale golden wine.

Arianna raised her glass to her lips but that was all. She didn't drink, didn't smile, didn't acknowledge Dominic's presence.

"Are you okay, Mommy?" Jonathan asked, and she smiled then and said yes, she was fine, just a little tired, but Dominic knew it was a lie.

She was upset, that was all. There was still confusion in her eyes....

Or was it hate?

That evening, after they'd boarded his jet and both the *marchesa* and Jonathan were asleep, he slipped into the seat beside Arianna's and took her hand.

"I know this was very sudden," he said, "and that, perhaps, you have not yet adjusted to this change in your life...."

He got no further. She pulled her hand from his and looked at him through eyes so flat they might have been made of glass.

"Don't touch me!"

"Arianna..."

"You forced me into this marriage. Did you think I'd forgive you for that?"

"Your grandmother—"

"Don't blame it on her! And don't change the facts. You'd already announced that I was marrying you before my grandmother put a foot out of that car."

Stung, Dominic fired back.

"Excuse me, *cara,* but I don't see any chains on your wrists. You stood before the judge willingly this morning."

"Willingly? I was as trapped as—as a pawn in some medieval power play."

"You could have said no."

"And shatter my *nonna's* health and dreams?" Arianna shook her head. "You know better than that."

"Let me be sure I understand this. Because you wanted to protect the *marchesa* and because I provided a way out, because you chose to go along with the fiction I'd created right up to letting me put a wedding ring on your finger...because of those things, I'm the villain and you're the martyr. Is that it?"

Her face reddened. Seeing it gave him grim pleasure.

"You're twisting my words! That's not what I meant."

"No?" Dominic flashed a tight smile. "Then perhaps you'll tell me what you *did* mean."

"You were the one who wanted an arranged marriage. Now you have one. Don't blame me if you don't like what you got."

"That's not an answer."

"It's the only one you're going to get."

Dio, he wanted to... What? Slap her? Never. He wasn't a man who'd hit a woman, no matter how she treated him. He could shake her instead, or rave and rant...or haul her against him and kiss her until she had to acknowledge the truth, that they could make an arranged marriage work.

No, he wouldn't do that. He was angry, but he wasn't a fool.

"It's time we agreed to something, Arianna."

"What could we possibly agree to, except that this was a mistake?"

"One thing," he snapped, doing his best to hang on to his temper. "You will treat me with respect at all times."

"Fine. I can manage that, as long as you agree to the

one thing I require.'' She waited for him to give her his full attention. ''Don't even think of trying to sleep with me.''

Oh, the sheer pleasure of seeing the shock in his eyes. He looked at her as if she'd spoken in an unknown language.

''I beg your pardon?''

''I said, I won't share your bed. You want me to make it clearer? We're not going to have sex, Dominic.''

''We will.''

''We won't. It's not up for discussion.''

''You're right. It isn't.'' He leaned close, clasped her wrist and brought her hand up between them. She was putting his temper to an impossible test! ''We are man and wife.''

''Husband and wife.'' The tilt of her chin defied him not to recognize the difference. ''That doesn't give you the right to my body.''

''What are you hoping? That I'll tell you I'll divorce you if you demand a sexless marriage?'' His voice roughened. ''Or that I'll force you into my bed to do what we both know you want?''

''Are you threatening me?''

''You are my wife.'' He dropped her wrist and sat back, afraid of what he might do if she went on provoking him. ''I'll give you some time to begin behaving like one, but I warn you, I'm not a patient man.''

He got up and walked away. She plucked a magazine from a low table, snapped it open and buried her nose in its glossy pages as if she were actually reading it. As if she could. As if she could think of anything except what Dominic had referred to as this change in her life.

Change? He'd turned her world inside out. Did he

really think he could do such a thing and get away with it?

He damn well couldn't and the sooner he understood that, the better.

Arianna kept the magazine in front of her face until the plane touched down at Ciampino Airport. Then she reached for Jonathan.

"Say goodbye to your grandmother," Dominic said gruffly. "I'll get the boy."

"The *boy*," she said coldly, "is my son. I'll carry him."

"Do as you're told."

He brushed past her and carried the sleeping child to the chauffeured car that was waiting for them. *Dio,* he was furious! Did Arianna think she could treat him this way and get away with it? Did she think she could benefit by this marriage but go on pretending he'd forced her into it? By the time she joined him a few minutes later, Dominic was seething.

The car began moving and he pressed the button that raised the privacy partition.

Arianna reached for the child again. "I'll take him now."

"Gianni is exhausted. Let him sleep."

"His name is Jonathan. I keep telling you that. And he can sleep quite comfortably in my lap."

Dominic felt the anger inside him swelling until it seemed lodged in the middle of his chest.

"Find something else to argue over, Arianna. I'm not going to let you use the boy."

"*Use* him? Perhaps you've forgotten. He's my son."

She spoke the words quickly, almost defiantly, as if to establish her rights. And she did have rights, Dominic knew. Far better rights than his. She was Gianni's mother. He was, at best, a stepfather who'd only laid eyes on the boy a handful of days ago.

Still, he felt protective of the kid and determined not to let Arianna poison the boy's feelings for him.

After a moment, Arianna turned and stared out the window as the car swept through the dark streets of the city. When it began to slow as they approached the Spanish Steps, she swung toward him again.

"I assume you have a guest room. Be sure and tell your chauffeur to put my things there."

"Is that how it's done in the United States? Wives and husbands have their own rooms?"

"This is not the United States, and I am not, in any meaningful sense of the word, your wife. I expect—"

"I know what you expect," he said brusquely. "You've made it clear. And I've decided to accommodate you. I shall have my quarters. You'll have yours. In business, I take what I want. On a personal level, I never take what isn't offered to me."

The car pulled to the curb. In the headlights of an oncoming vehicle, he saw color climb into her face again.

"Remember that," she said, as if he were a street urchin who needed lessons in behavior, and he felt such rage that he'd have swept her into his arms, carried her into the house and to his bed if Gianni hadn't been present.

No. Dammit, no. He wasn't going to let her reduce him to that level.

Instead, he grabbed her wrist. She gasped and he knew he was hurting her, but at that moment, he didn't give a damn.

"You'll have to beg me to take you to my bed. Do you understand, Arianna? As far as I'm concerned..."

The door swung open. He looked up and saw the chauffeur standing outside the car, heels together, spine straight, looking like a soldier at attention.

"Signore?"

The only thing missing was a salute. Dominic recognized the driver as a new man and started to tell him that he could forget about all that obsequious nonsense, that he despised being treated as if he were an emperor, but Arianna made a sound that might have been a little snort of derision.

Damn her to hell, he thought, and stepped from the car.

Three days later, he decided to make a small gesture of peace. They were living under one roof, sharing mealtimes for the boy's sake, but otherwise behaving like strangers.

No one could go on living this way.

They'd both said some rough things that first night, but it was understandable. He'd been tired. So had Arianna. Add in the shock of the marriage and jet lag, and you had a situation primed for disaster.

So he came to breakfast Saturday morning dressed in light canvas trousers and a navy T-shirt. Arianna and Gianni were already there.

"Good morning."

Arianna didn't respond. The boy looked up and grinned.

"Good morning, Dom'nic."

He smiled back and ruffled the kid's hair.

"I've been thinking…how would you like to see Rome?"

Gianni's eyes lit. "Cool! Mom? Dom'nic says—"

"I heard him." Arianna took a roll from the bread

basket, broke it in pieces and began buttering it. She didn't look up. "I've seen Rome dozens of times."

"I haven't." Gianni had a hopeful expression on his face. "The only thing I saw was that big fountain the other day, when you and I went for a walk."

"Eat your eggs, please, Jonathan."

Dominic heard the edge in his wife's voice and decided to ignore it.

"Neither of you has seen *my* Rome," he said pleasantly. "There's a wonderful little church that's far off the tourist track, and a small garden with what's rumored to be a statue by Michelangelo inside. And I know a restaurant in the Jewish Quarter where they serve the most incredible fried artichokes."

"I don't like artichokes," Arianna replied, in a tone meant to end all discussion. "Jonathan, didn't I tell you to eat your eggs?"

"*I* like ardachopes," the boy said eagerly.

"You don't even know what they are. And you wouldn't like them."

"I bet he would." Dominic rose from the table, snatched Gianni up and swung him in the air. The kid liked that. It always made him giggle. "How about it, *compagno?* Want to go sightseeing with me today?" He held the boy at arm's length and dropped his voice to a whisper. "We'll go to the catacombs and see all the skulls and skeletons. How's that sound?"

"It's too hot for that," Arianna said quickly.

"Don't be silly. The catacombs are underground. It's probably 20 degrees cooler down there. Sound good to you, Gianni?"

"His name is—"

"Oh, yeah," Gianni said happily.

Dominic tucked him under his arm as if he were a football. The boy giggled even harder.

"We'll be home by dinnertime."

Arianna flashed him a look that could have frozen the Medusa, but he didn't care. He headed for the door without looking back. Maybe she didn't want to be his wife, but Gianni wanted to be his son.

His stepson.

This was his city. If his wife didn't want to share it with him, the boy did.

The day was filled with fun, but the smile on Gianni's face disappeared when they got back and found Arianna waiting. Dominic felt his own good mood fading. There was no mistaking her look of tightly banked rage.

"Go to your room," she told her son. The boy's lip trembled, and her expression softened. "I'm not angry at you, sweetheart."

"Don't be angry at Dom'nic, either. We had a really good time, Mom."

For a moment, Dominic thought she'd relent. Then she looked at him and her eyes hardened.

"Go to your room, please, Jonathan." As soon as he was gone, Arianna rounded on Dominic. "You will not undermine my authority again. I'm Jonathan's mother. I'll decide what he does and doesn't do."

Maybe if she'd suggested discussing things, Dominic would have reacted differently. But he was tired of her coldness, her rudeness, her dismissive attitude.

"You have it wrong. It is you who will not undermine *my* authority. This is my home. You are my wife. Gianni—Jonathan—may not be my natural son, but he is my responsibility now. I don't have to ask your permission for anything."

There was a quick flash of something in her eyes.

Despair? Pain? Whatever it was, he sensed that it cut much deeper than his words. She turned away from him and left the room.

Dominic listened to the tap of her heels against the marble floor, heard the snick of the door to the guest suite as it shut behind her.

For a moment, he regretted his angry words. Then he thought of how she'd treated him since they'd exchanged their vows and decided he didn't regret anything....

Except, perhaps, the marriage.

A month later, nothing had changed.

It was a blisteringly hot August afternoon. The air conditioning in Dominic's office was having trouble keeping up with the heat. Maybe that was why he put down his pen, stared blindly out the window and finally faced the truth.

His marriage wasn't working.

He'd really believed that a marriage based on expedience *would* work. There'd be no need for lies or fairy tales.

He was wrong.

Knowing your wife had married you for reasons that had nothing to do with her heart was no better than suspecting it. In fact, it was worse. Had he married a woman who professed to love him, he might have been able to delude himself into believing it.

He'd have laughed if anyone had told him he wanted to come home at night to a kiss, to look up from reading the paper after dinner and see a smile meant only for him. The truth was—and it was almost painful to acknowledge—he wanted the little signs of affection that went with marriage, even if they were phony.

Dominic leaned his elbows on his desk and put his head in his hands.

He'd lived alone almost his entire life, but he'd never felt lonely until now. Part of it came from little things, like hearing his wife's laughter as he came to the front door...and hearing it stop, once he put his key in the lock.

Part of it came from her treating him as if he were a barbarian at the gate. She jumped if he brushed her arm as he moved past her in a narrow space, and sometimes he caught her looking at him with an expression that suggested she expected the worst of him at any minute.

He wasn't a monster. He wasn't going to demand she spend her evenings talking to him, instead of going to her room after Gianni was tucked in. He wasn't going to order her to his bed, despite his earlier threats. Why did she look at him that way? Why did she catch her breath if he came too close?

She was driving him crazy.

Was it deliberate? Did she know what she was doing? Had she really only wanted him when he was a stranger?

Heaven knew she wanted no part of him now that he was her husband.

Especially because he was her husband.

Dominic sat up straight. His wife was right about one thing. He'd forced her into this marriage. He might not admit it to her, but why lie to himself? And he'd be damned if he'd let her force him to end it. Maybe that was her plan, to make him unhappy enough to tell her all right, he'd had enough, it was over.

He wasn't going to do it.

Frowning, he picked up his pen and looked at the stack of letters awaiting his signature.

''See if you can't manage to sign them before the day

ends,'' Celia had said, ''and before you snap at me and tell me to mind my own business the way you've been doing lately, Signore Borghese, kindly remember that getting your letters out *is* my business.''

It was a surprisingly blunt remark, even from his gorgon. Dominic had lifted his eyebrows, but he'd said nothing. He knew he deserved the chastisement.

He'd been staring at the letters for two days and the only thing that had changed was that the stack had grown higher.

He didn't actually have to read the mail. Celia was efficient. She typed his correspondence precisely as he dictated it, and in those instances where he told her to answer a letter herself, she always did so in ways he approved.

He wondered if she'd approve of the fact that he was married. He hadn't told anyone yet, except for his household staff. Why would you tell people you had a wife when, for all intents and purposes, you didn't?

Celia knew something was up, though. *Was he feeling all right?* she'd asked a couple of days ago. Certainly, he'd replied…but he suspected she hadn't bought the quick answer. He knew he wasn't behaving normally. Until a few weeks ago, he'd prided himself on being aware of everything that went on in his office.

He was the man in charge of what some called an empire.

How could you run an empire unless you had your head on your shoulders?

Dominic frowned.

It was a stupid metaphor and, lately, an even worse description of the job he was doing. His head wasn't on anything but his disastrous marriage.

His frown deepened. He plucked the first letter from the pile and stared at it.

Dear Carl, blah blah blah, as I explained when you telephoned, your plans for expanding Adrian International sound most promising, but unfortunately...

But, unfortunately, he really didn't give a damn about Adrian International.

Dominic cursed softly, dropped the letter and ran his hands over his face.

This had to stop.

He wasn't sleeping well at night, wasn't paying enough attention to work during the day, and he waffled when he made decisions. He'd always been a man who thought about what he was going to do and then did it, no regrets, no second-guessing, no time wasted on "what-if."

"Dominic Borghese runs his various enterprises with a firm hand and an enviable sense of conviction," a TV reporter in Milan had said of him recently. "Borghese researches an issue thoroughly before reaching a conclusion. As a result, he rarely needs to alter his position. If he does, you can count on something vital having changed in the equation."

Dominic tilted back his chair.

Really? What was the "something vital" that had changed his decision about marriage? He'd not only laughed at the idea of asking Arianna to be his wife, he'd laughed at the idea of asking anyone.

His long term plans had included a wife, but not now. And the wife he'd envisioned had been nothing like Arianna. What man would be foolish enough to choose a woman who was contrary? Who treated him with scorn?

Who'd borne another man a child?

That was another problem. He loved the boy more each day—who wouldn't? The kid was terrific. But he didn't like thinking about the faceless man who was Gianni's father. Arianna wouldn't talk about him at all, even though Dominic assured her he could accept that she had a sexual past. This wasn't the middle ages and trembling virgins weren't his style.

Then, why did it trouble him to know that some stranger had impregnated his wife? Why did he sometimes look at the boy and think how wonderful it would be if the kid could have been his?

The boy was the best thing, the only good thing, in this farce of a marriage.

Dominic went to a small refrigerator built into the wall, took out a bottle of mineral water and poured a glass.

Gianni was an amazing little boy. He was sweet-natured, he had a great sense of humor, and he showed an avid curiosity about everything...including the sleeping arrangements of his mother and stepfather.

"Aren't husbands and wives s'posed to sleep in the same room?" he'd asked Dominic as they walked to a *gelato* shop a couple of days ago.

"Not necessarily," Dominic had said calmly, lying through his teeth. Of course husbands and wives were supposed to sleep in the same room, but he wasn't about to tell that to a little boy.

He wasn't about to tell it to Arianna, either.

He would not order his wife to his bed, though he had to admit he thought about it.

Thought about it, a lot.

No. He wouldn't do that.

Dominic's hand tightened on the water glass.

Instead, he would let his work slip, snap at Celia,

drive his Ferrari so fast he'd been warned to slow down by a *politiziotto* that very morning—a thing virtually unheard of in a city where people drove as if they were on the course at Le Mans.

He'd do everything, including keep his promise about the Butterfly, which his attorneys were transferring to his wife's name.

Would she smile when he handed her the papers? Would she be happy to hear the amount of money he intended to put into the resurrection of the Butterfly?

Dominic lifted the glass to his lips and drank down the rest of the water, though he knew it would do nothing to cool his growing temper.

He knew the answers to his questions, too.

Arianna wouldn't show pleasure in anything, not if it involved him.

And that took him full circle, to the realization that since his wedding, he seemed willing to do anything...except deal with reality. He had a wife who was not a wife, and he was permitting it to happen.

The glass shattered under the pressure of his hand. He cursed, dumped the shards in the wastebasket and flung open the door to his office.

Celia looked up, clearly startled.

"Those letters on my desk?" he said as he strode past her. "Sign my name to all of them."

Celia stared at him as if she'd never seen him before. Was it because of what he'd said, or because he looked as furious as he felt? He didn't know. He didn't care. Nothing mattered except teaching his wife that she *was* his wife, and he was tired of pretending she wasn't.

Every man had his breaking point, and Dominic had reached his.

CHAPTER EIGHT

ARIANNA sat in a lounge chair on the terrace off the sitting room of Dominic's apartment, drinking an iced cappuccino as if she hadn't a care in the world.

One story below, in a flower-laced courtyard that looked as if it had come straight out of some glorious painting by Raphael, her little boy and his newfound best pal, Bruno, sprawled beneath a flowering tree, lying on their bellies as they played with a fleet of small wooden cars. On a terrace across the courtyard, a fat Persian cat basked contentedly in the sun.

It was a beautiful, peaceful scene in stark, almost brutal contrast to the despair in Arianna's heart.

A month had gone by since Dominic had forced her into marriage and brought her here, a month since she'd become his unwilling wife…and a month that she'd awakened each morning, terrified that it would be the day he looked at the child he called his stepson and realized that Jonathan was his, and all her lies had been for nothing.

Her life, which had seemed so complicated in the States, had taken on enough added twists and turns so that her former existence seemed simple by comparison.

In America, she'd run a business without capital and raised a child without anyone knowing it.

In Italy, she spent endless days doing nothing and raised her child in the home of the man who'd fathered him, living in fear of the day he stopped believing that child had been fathered by someone else.

Arianna put down her glass of coffee and touched her fingers to her forehead, where the beginnings of a headache threatened.

The situation was so ludicrous that she'd probably laugh if she clicked on the TV and saw the same story unfold in an afternoon soap, but this wasn't a soap. It was her life, it was real, and she sometimes felt as if she were dancing on the edge of a razor.

Maybe if she had something to do, something to fill the endless hours...

But she didn't.

She knew now that Dominic's talk about handing over the Butterfly had been meant to placate her, nothing more. He'd kept his promise to the *marchesa* and not foreclosed on the business, but all the rest had turned to dust. He hadn't given it to Arianna to run, hadn't put his people to work on finding ways to improve its financial health, hadn't even mentioned it again except to say once, in passing, that he'd sent in a team to inventory the stock.

Arianna hissed, closed her eyes and pressed her hand against her head.

The headache had arrived, as promised. No surprise there. The one thing she could count on, every day, was that her head would pound. Tension, stress... Sometimes, she felt like an advertisement for aspirin.

Had Dominic told her about the inventory just to bait her? Maybe he'd figured she'd say, *What happens when your people are finished? Will you keep your promise and let me take over again?*

If that's what he hoped, he was in for a disappointment. She'd never ask him for anything, never tell him she wanted anything, never let him see her beg.

God, how she hated her husband!

"Mommy? Hey, Mom!"

Arianna sat up straight and looked down into the courtyard. Jonathan smiled up at her and waved.

"Yes, sweetheart," she said with forced good humor, "what is it?"

"Can I go for ice cream with Bruno and his mom?"

"*Gelato,*" Bruno called, being helpful.

The boys grinned at each other. Jonathan was teaching his pal English; Bruno was reciprocating with lessons in Italian.

A happy arrangement, Bruno's mother called it. An unhappy arrangement, as far as Arianna was concerned. She knew it was foolish, but she didn't want her little boy turning into a Roman. He was American, not Italian. He wasn't Gianni, as even the *marchesa* now addressed him, he was Jonathan.

He wasn't Dominic's, he was hers.

"Mom? Can I go?"

"May I go," Arianna said automatically. She looked at the two boys and at Bruno's mother, Gina, who'd joined them and was smiling politely. The woman probably thought she was a terrible mother. "Yes. Yes, you may."

Jonathan and Bruno exchanged high fives.

"You could come, too, if you want."

Arianna knew the answer she should give; she could see the hopeful look on Jonathan's face, but even the thought of making the two block stroll while pretending to chatter happily with her pleasant neighbor made her stomach clench.

"I have a headache, sweetheart. I think I'll stay right here."

Gina clasped the children's hands. "It is the heat," she said politely. "It takes time to grow accustomed to it."

"Not for my mom," Jonathan said. "She grew up in Italy, right, Mommy?"

Worse and worse, Arianna thought, and answered the question with a question. "Would Bruno like to have supper with us tonight?"

Bruno bounced up and down with excitement. His mother laughed.

"I think that must be a 'yes.'"

"Good. Then I'll see you later."

Her neighbor waved, shooed the boys ahead of her through the gate that led from the cluster of elegant little houses and onto the *Via Giacomo.* Arianna watched the trio make their way along the narrow old street until they disappeared from view.

Then she sat back.

It would have been nice to go for ice cream with the boys and her new neighbor, who lived in the house next door. In fact, it would have been nice to become friends with her.

Jonathan and Bruno had discovered each other Jonathan's first day here, and Gina had gone out of her way to be welcoming, both to the little stranger from America and to Arianna.

Arianna sighed.

She'd been polite, but she hadn't been very gracious in return. *Thank you,* she said whenever Gina invited her for coffee, *but...*

After a while, Gina didn't bother asking. She said she understood.

"A newly married woman has much to do in her new home, *si?*"

She'd offered a woman-to-woman smile and Arianna had returned it, making them companionable conspirators in a world of happy brides and eager grooms.

What would her neighbor say if she knew the truth? That there were no happy brides or eager grooms in the Borghese household, that there were, instead, two people who maintained a polite front for the sake of a little boy…

That as far as Arianna was concerned, she had no new home.

She was imprisoned in a cage. Nobody could see the bars except her, but that didn't mean they weren't there. She was living in a city where she knew no one, with a man who'd all but bought her, and she had a secret so awful that it threatened to consume her.

She was depressed. Dominic was angry. Between them, they were miserable. That couldn't be anyone's definition of a marriage, not even his, though Arianna often wondered what, precisely, he'd thought he'd get for the purchase price he'd paid for her when he'd made his bargain back in the States.

A woman who loved him? Not that. Love hadn't been part of the deal. A woman who respected him? That hadn't been included, either.

Actually, she knew what he'd expected, that the passionate fuse they ignited would light again and make the arrangement acceptable, but she'd made it clear that she would not share his bed….

And he'd let her get away with it.

How come? Not that she'd change her mind, ever, but…but didn't it bother him, that he had a wife who wouldn't be his wife?

Arianna rose to her feet, picked up her empty glass and went into the house. The sitting room was dark and deliciously cool. She stood still for a moment, head lifted, eyes closed, and let the chill ease the pounding in her head.

He'd tried to make her play at being his wife in simpler ways, but she'd made her position clear on that, too.

"I have a housekeeper," he'd said the first morning, when he'd told her they'd eat breakfast together, for appearance's sake.

"I don't give a damn about appearances," Arianna had hissed, moments before Jonathan joined them, and Dominic had leaned toward her, his face dark.

"Do you give a damn about anything but yourself? Think of the boy. Use your head, Arianna. It will be better for him if he thinks we are happy together."

It was hard to argue with such logic and she hadn't even tried. There were other ways to make Dominic understand how she felt about the arrangement he'd forced her into.

The simplest was to ignore his suggestion that she make whatever changes she wished in the apartment, and in how his housekeeper did things.

The woman had approached her that same morning.

"I was going to purchase new towels to replace the old in the first floor lavatory this week," Rosa had said politely. "Perhaps the *signora* would like to do it herself, or tell me what colors she prefers."

"Buy whatever you wish," Arianna had said, just as politely. "It doesn't matter to me."

"Well, then, if there are any special foods you like, *signora,* you have only to tell me and I'll be happy to prepare them."

"Thank you, but that's not necessary. Cook as you normally do."

A tiny frown had appeared in Rosa's forehead. "The boy has no favorites, either?"

Arianna had relented. Jonathan didn't like broccoli or cooked carrots. He loved chocolate milk. There was no reason not to tell all that to Rosa, especially since Jonathan's view of this change in their lives was the exact opposite of Arianna's.

Her son was thrilled. He loved Italy, loved Rome, loved the vast, high-ceilinged apartment with its marble and hardwood floors, its views of the *Via Giacomo,* the crowds that gathered on the Spanish Steps.

"I *love* it here," Jonathan had told her, holding his arms out wide to encompass all the new treasures of his young life.

What he loved most was Dominic—and the feeling was obviously mutual.

Dominic treated Jonathan in a way that would make most women ecstatic. Your new husband and your child were crazy about each other? Well, that was wonderful, wasn't it? Weren't the TV talk shows, the magazines, the pop psychology bestsellers everywhere full of sad stories of stepfathers who didn't like their new children? Of children who couldn't tolerate their stepfathers?

It wasn't like that in this family.

Man and boy chatted about anything and everything. Baseball. Soccer. Movies. Whether it was truly gross to suck up strands of pasta from your fork, or were there even grosser things nobody had yet invented. A new video game Bruno had talked about—a game that Dominic would surely bring home the next evening, despite Arianna's objections that he was spoiling Jonathan.

"He's a great kid," Dominic countered. "And I'm not spoiling him. I like to play these games, too."

He played with Jonathan after supper, while she read in the sitting room. Tried to read. It was hard, with the sounds of Dominic's laughter and Jonathan's giggles coming right through the door.

Last night, she'd watched them as they talked about baseball, something about a pitcher and the New York Yankees, and suddenly her heart had swelled with joy.

My son, she'd thought, my little boy and his father.

She must have made a sound because they'd both looked at her.

"Mom?" her son had said uncertainly, and she'd smiled and said, whoops, she was sorry, she'd just smothered a sneeze…and she'd gone to her bedroom, shut the door, leaned back against it and shuddered.

Her husband was a ruthless man. He'd proved that already, when he'd forced her into this marriage. What would he do if he figured out that Jonathan was his?

Arianna took a deep breath.

What was that old saying about putting the cart before the horse? There was no reason to think ahead. So far, nothing had changed. Dominic hadn't noticed anything. Maybe he never would. Women were good at speculation about who babies took after; men weren't. Hadn't she been part of endless conversations about the offspring of women she knew?

He has Jack's chin, one would say.

Natalie's eyes, another would add.

And the discussion would go on and on while the men in the group just rolled their eyes and finally, if pressed, one of them would crack that yeah, the kid in question looked like his old man but, basically, he just looked like a kid.

No, nothing had changed. Dominic would not catch on. He would remain a sperm donor who'd given her her son but didn't know it. He'd remain the husband she didn't want, didn't love, didn't desire…

Arianna swallowed hard.

She didn't. Of course, she didn't.

She walked slowly through the apartment, noting that Rosa had left things ready for dinner as she did each evening. The dining room table was set. Platters and covered dishes would be stacked in the refrigerator and on the big table near the stove.

God only knew what the housekeeper thought of the Borghese marriage. She arrived each morning at seven, just in time to see Dominic emerge from his bedroom and Arianna emerge from the guest suite with Jonathan. She'd looked startled, the first time she saw their strange morning entrances. Arianna knew enough about upper-class Italian marriages to know that separate bedrooms weren't unusual, but for newlyweds?

Surely, brides here shared their husbands' beds just as they did in the States.

The housekeeper probably thought the new *signora* was crazy. Well, maybe she was.

Arianna turned on the water in the kitchen sink and washed out her glass.

A woman would have to be crazy, wouldn't she, to get trapped in an arrangement like this?

Dominic made it seem as if he was a knight in shining armor, marrying her to keep the *marchesa* from collapsing that day in the back yard of the little house in Connecticut.

Who was he kidding?

Arianna put the glass in the drainer.

He'd made his incredible announcement, that he intended to force her into marriage, before the *marchesa's* arrival. He didn't like being reminded of that little fact, either. Apparently, he liked thinking of himself as a martyr who'd taken a wife as an act of gallantry.

The truth was that he'd taken a wife because he wanted one. Because he wanted her…and he hadn't done a thing about it. Not a thing.

All these nights, she'd slept alone. Slept? Not really. Mostly, she lay awake, despising Dominic, despising herself for not finding a way out of this nightmare…

…despising herself for wanting him.

Arianna sank into a chair at the kitchen table and buried her face in her hands.

The truth was ugly. She didn't want to face it, but denying it was even worse. She hated Dominic—and wanted him. Wanted him, night after night while she lay alone in her bed, staring up at the dark ceiling and remembering how it had been to make love with him, remembering the feel of his hands, the taste of his skin.

Last night, she'd been sure he was coming to her. She'd heard the creak of the floorboards and her heart had climbed into her throat. She'd sat up, clutched the blanket to her chin, waited, oh yes, waited for the door to open, for Dominic to step into the room, to come to her bed and take her in his arms, put an end to this nonsense and make her his wife.

But the footsteps had hesitated only briefly, then continued past her door the same as they did all the other nights. And Arianna had awakened today as she did every day, detesting herself for wanting him.

The shame of it was a leaden weight lodged in her breast.

What kind of woman dreamed of possession by a man

who'd forced her into marriage? Who would probably tear her son from her if he ever learned the truth?

Suddenly, the walls of the enormous apartment seemed to be pressing in. Arianna got to her feet and hurried to the front door. Maybe she could catch up to Gina and the boys. Maybe...

She fell back as the door swung open. Dominic stood on the threshold, eyes dark, mouth narrowed. He looked wild and dangerous, and her heart slammed into her throat.

"Arianna," he said, and what he wanted, what he intended, what he was, at last, going to do, all resonated in that one word.

Arianna turned and fled down the hall. She heard the door bang shut, heard the sound of her husband's footsteps coming after her. His hands clamped, hard, on her shoulders and he spun her toward him.

"No," she cried, and swung her fist. She caught him in the shoulder. Pain shot up her arm. Dominic's body, his muscles, everything about him was unyielding. She swung again. He grunted, dodged the blow, hoisted her into his arms and strode down the hall to the guest suite.

"Dominic!" She was panting, weeping as he elbowed open her bedroom door. "You can't. I won't—"

He bent his head, took her mouth with his. He bit her lip; she cried out in shock and when she did, he plunged his tongue inside. His taste, his heat, filled her. He slid his hand over her, cupped her breast, and she felt her nipple pearl under his rough touch.

Heat shot through her, quick and sharp.

"No," she said against his lips, but her body refused to go along with the lie. She moaned, arched against him. This. This, yes. This was what she wanted.

Dominic fell onto the bed still holding her, still kissing

her. His heart thundered against hers as he slid his hand between them and began undoing the buttons on her blouse.

"Tell me," he growled. "Say it."

She couldn't. God, she couldn't, not even as she felt pleasure slipping along her skin like silk, even as she heard herself whispering his name.

Dominic cursed, gave up trying to open the buttons and tore the blouse open. Arianna lay exposed to him now. This was his, the lush curve of her breasts, the lightly perfumed cleft that dipped into a lacy white bra.

He kissed her mouth, kissed her throat, sucked at her nipples until she cried out in pleasure. She was clasping his shirt in her fists, writhing under him, against him, and he pushed up her skirt, slid his fingers inside her panties, watched her eyes blur with excitement.

She was hot. Wet. Ready. So ready. For him, only for him. The delicate scent of her arousal made him groan with desire.

"Say it," he urged, and she wound her hands around his biceps.

"Dominic," she whispered. "Dominic…"

Somewhere out on the hot Roman streets, a horn blared, then blared again. The commonplace sound jolted through Arianna, a sharp reminder of reality.

She froze, caught her breath.

What was she doing? Being taken in anger? Giving herself in anger? No. No…

"No!" The cry ripped from her throat.

She shoved against Dominic's shoulders. Pounded against them. He was blind, dumb, unaware of everything but his need. Sobbing, she hit him again. He caught her wrists and pinned her hands above her head.

"It's too late for that," he said roughly. "There's no turning back from what we both want."

"You forced me into marriage." Her voice trembled but she kept her eyes on his. "Are you going to force me into sex, too?"

She felt his whole body tense. She waited, feeling the bite of his fingers into her flesh, afraid he might not stop—afraid of how she might respond if he didn't. Then, after a million years seemed to have gone by, Dominic spat out a word in the same dialect she'd heard him use before, let go of her wrists and rolled off her.

"To hell with this," he snarled. "To hell with you, and me, and this farce of a marriage."

He got to his feet and hurried from the room. Arianna scrambled up against the pillows, wincing as she heard his bedroom door bang shut. Then she rose from the bed…and saw her reflection in the mirror.

Her hair was a tangle of wild curls, her cheeks were flushed, her mouth swollen from Dominic's kisses. Her blouse hung in tatters; beneath it, her breasts showed patches of red from the scrape of stubble on his jaw.

Her teeth began to chatter. To think that he would do such a thing…

To think that she would let him.

That was the truth, wasn't it? That she'd let him ravish her. That she'd wanted him to do it, yearned for him to do it…

Footsteps sounded outside her door. She stumbled back, eyes wide, but the footsteps kept going. The front door slammed, and Arianna let out her breath.

Dominic was gone, at least for a little while.

She swung away from the mirror, pulled off what remained of her blouse and flung it into a corner. She snatched another blouse from the closet and put it on.

No more. She had to leave him, face whatever he'd do in retaliation. This couldn't continue, not even to protect the *marchesa,* not even to protect her dark secret about Jonathan...

She laughed, though it came out more like a sob. How could she leave? Dominic held all the cards, and they both...

"Mah-mee. Hey, Mom."

Oh God. Jonathan was back, shouting to her from the courtyard.

"Mom? Where are you?"

She shot to her feet, ran her hands through her hair, hurried through the apartment and onto the terrace.

Jonathan and Bruno grinned up at her, then waved madly as they slurped at cups of *gelato.* Bruno's mother was there, too, eating hers with a spoon.

For reasons Arianna would never quite understand, this moment would be frozen in her memory. In all the years to come, she'd remember it with complete clarity. Gina's smile, and the little boys with ice cream dripping down their chins, and the oppressiveness of the hot Roman afternoon...

And the sudden squeal of brakes, the horrendous shriek of tearing metal, the unending scream of a woman crying out in horror...

Mostly, she would remember knowing that something terrible had happened to her husband.

"Dominic?" she whispered.

"Mommy?" Jonathan said, his face gone white.

Gina's cup of ice cream fell to the ground.

"Come," she said, grabbing both boys, anchoring them to her sides and dragging them into her house.

Arianna flew into the apartment, through the endless

expanse of rooms, down the stairs, out the front door, to the street...

And saw a woman, numb with shock, clutching a wailing infant in her arms.

Saw a charcoal-gray baby stroller lying overturned in the road, wheels spinning lazily.

Saw her husband's bright red car, its hood wrapped around a lamp post, its front tires up on the curb, the driver's door flown open.

But what she saw that made her heart almost stop beating was Dominic, lying in the road beside the car, his arm bent at an angle that made her stomach roll, his head turned to the side, blood oozing slowly from his temple.

"Dominic," she whispered, but her voice rose to a scream as she ran to him, dropped to her knees, took his hand in hers and brought it to her lips.

Did his fingers offer the faintest pressure in return, or was it only her desperation that made it seem that way?

"Dominic," Arianna sobbed. She kissed his bruised knuckles and never left him until the paramedics came and gently but forcibly shifted her aside, so they could move her husband onto a gurney and put him in the ambulance.

CHAPTER NINE

WHY did people speak in whispers in hospitals?

Hospitals weren't quiet places like libraries. Hospitals were filled with noise. Bells rang with frightening urgency. Carts rattled as aides rolled them down the hall. Down at this end of the building, in the emergency section, there was a seemingly constant whirr of wheels as ambulance attendants rushed gurneys into the building, while doctors shouted instructions at nurses.

The only quiet thing in the entire place, as far as Arianna could tell, was her. She sat on a wooden bench outside Treatment Room One, hands tightly clasped, heart in her throat as she waited for word about Dominic.

Half an hour had passed since he'd been rushed into the white-tiled treatment room. A team of green-clad doctors and nurses had brushed Arianna aside, engulfed Dominic and lifted him onto an examining table.

"What happened here?" someone had barked, even as hands began undressing him.

"Motor vehicle accident," one of the EMTs said. "Victim swerved to avoid a baby carriage, climbed the curb and wrapped his car around a traffic barrier."

"Speeding?"

"No. Would have been a lot worse if he had."

"Seat belt?"

"No. He was thrown from the car. Probable compound fracture of the left humerus, possible concussion.''

''Who's the orthopedist on duty? The neurosurgeon?''

''I'll find out,'' a nurse replied, and as she'd hurried to the door she'd noticed Arianna, pressed back against the wall. ''You can't stay here,'' she'd said briskly. She'd put a hand in the small of Arianna's back, pushed her into the hall, and drawn the curtains.

People had hurried in and out of the room ever since, but no one had paused to say anything to Arianna.

And she was going crazy, imagining what was happening beyond those curtains. What if Dominic didn't… What if he was seriously hurt? He'd been so white, so still. He might—he might—

Arianna shut her eyes. ''Please,'' she whispered, ''please, don't take him from me.''

Dominic was alive. He had to be. He couldn't die. He couldn't leave her.

The curtains snapped back. Arianna shot to her feet as a woman in a hospital coat stepped briskly from the room, holding a clipboard and a pen.

''Signora Borghese?''

''Yes.'' Arianna tried to step past her but the woman obviously had experience with desperate family members and easily blocked her way. ''How is my husband?''

''I must ask you some questions, *signora*. Is your husband allergic to any drugs?''

''I don't know. How is he?''

''Does he take any medications?''

''I don't know that either. Please, tell me—''

''Has he a history of heart disease? Diabetes? Stroke? Convulsions?''

Arianna stared at the woman. "Convulsions? Is he— oh God, please. Tell me what's happened."

The stern face softened, if only fractionally. "Nothing, *signora,* I promise. I'm simply trying to put together your husband's medical history. How about prior surgeries?"

Arianna shook her head.

"Hospitalizations? Broken bones? Concussions?"

"I don't know anything about his medical history! Please, is Dominic—how badly is he hurt?"

The woman capped her pen. "He has a break in the left humerus." Arianna shook her head again and the woman touched the upper portion of her arm. "Right here. It's a bad break, but there wasn't much tissue damage. Eight weeks, twelve at the most, in a cast and the arm will be fine."

Something had been left unsaid. Arianna searched the woman's face.

"What else? I know there's more. My husband's head was bleeding. He was unconscious."

"Yes. We believe he suffered a concussion. The doctor ordered a CAT scan. We'll know more once it's done."

"But isn't he awake yet? Surely, by now..."

A look of compassion flashed in the other woman's eyes. "No," she said gently, "not yet."

Arianna swayed unsteadily. The woman grasped her arm.

"You'll be no help to your husband if you fall apart, *signora.* Are you here alone? Shall I call someone to come and stay with you?"

Arianna shook her head again. There was no one to call. She had only an elderly grandmother and a small child. Dominic had never mentioned having a family and she had never asked. She'd never asked him anything about his life, she'd been too busy hating him, when all he was guilty of was wanting her—and wanting her son.

His son.

He'd tried to make the three of them into a family and she hadn't let him. Why hadn't she seen that until now?

"No," she said, "there's no one. Thank you. I'll be—"

The curtains parted again. An attendant wheeled out a gurney on which Dominic lay motionless.

"Dominic," Arianna whispered, her voice breaking. She reached for his hand, clasped it tightly in hers and hurried alongside the gurney as the attendant wheeled it down a corridor, into an elevator, and then to a door marked Radiology, where they stopped her again.

"You'll have to wait outside, *signora.*"

Arianna leaned over Dominic and brushed her mouth gently against his.

"I'll be right here, *mio marito,*" she murmured.

The door swung shut.

She stared at it, drew a shuddering breath and turned blindly toward a bank of telephones on the wall.

She didn't know Gina's phone number but the operator found it for her and put the call through. Gina answered immediately, as if she'd been hovering near the phone and waiting for it to ring.

Gianni was fine; Arianna was not to worry about him. He'd had supper, he and Bruno were playing trains.

"And how is your husband?" Gina asked carefully.

"I don't know. It's too soon."

"I'll get Gianni."

Arianna closed her eyes and took a deep breath. She had to be strong when she spoke with her son.

"Mommy?" Her son's voice trembled.

"Yes, sweetheart."

"Did Dom'nic die?"

The childlike bluntness of the question shook her. "No," she said quickly, "no, baby. Dominic didn't die."

"What happened to him?"

She told him some of the truth. Yes, there'd been an accident. After that, she lied. Dominic was fine, the doctors said, but he'd have to stay in the hospital for a bit.

"Why?"

"Well, he broke his arm. Remember last year, when Billy Gooding broke his?"

"He had to wear a cast."

"Right, sweetheart. Dominic will have to wear one, too."

Jonathan's tone grew hopeful. "And we'll all write on it an' draw pictures?"

Arianna made a sound that was almost a laugh. "Yes. We'll all decorate his cast, baby. Okay?"

"Okay. Maybe I'll draw a picture of a cat." There was a brief pause. "How come Dom'nic has to stay in the hospital? Billy didn't."

"Well, Dominic hit his head, too. He'll have to stay here until the bump goes away."

"Oh." Another pause. "Mommy?"

"Yes?"

"Could you tell Dom'nic that I miss him?"

Tears welled in Arianna's eyes and streamed down her cheeks. "I'll tell him," she whispered.

Gina took the phone again, assured Arianna that she and her husband were happy to have Gianni spend the night, even the next few days. Arianna wiped her eyes, choked out a "thank you," ended the call and then, for the very first time, phoned Dominic's office.

He'd given her his private number. She'd countered by telling him it wasn't necessary.

"I can't imagine any circumstance under which I'd want to call you," she remembered saying.

Her throat constricted. How foolish she'd been. How selfish.

The phone rang and rang. Why wouldn't it? Nobody would answer a private number except Dominic, and he was here, locked away from her in a room filled with lights and machines...

"Dominic Borghese's office. This is the *signore's* assistant speaking. How may I help you?"

The voice was cool and professional, but it lost those qualities when Arianna identified herself as Dominic's wife.

"His wife? But the *signore* never mentioned..."

Arianna interrupted and explained what had happened.

"*Dio!* I felt in my bones that something was wrong. It is why I answered the telephone. *Signora,* my name is Celia. What can I do to help you?"

"I wondered," Arianna said, "I wondered if you would know...if you would know if my husband has a personal physician. They're doing everything they can here, but I want to be sure—to be sure—"

Her voice broke. She was going to weep again and tears didn't change anything. She'd learned that early, sobbing against the fates that had snatched her mother and father from her.

"I understand, *signora.* Yes, your husband has a doctor. I'll call him and have him meet you at the hospital, *si?*"

SANDRA MARTON

315

"Thank you. Tell him— Oh. They're bringing Dominic out."

"If you need anything else—"

"Yes. *Grazie*. I'll call you when I know more."

Arianna jammed the phone back on the wall. The attendant was wheeling Dominic's gurney down the corridor and she ran after it, but a hand closed on her arm.

"Signora Borghese? I'm the radiologist who took your husband's CAT scan. They're taking your husband to surgery, to set his arm."

Arianna tore her eyes from the gurney. "What did the CAT scan show? Is my husband—will he be all right?"

The radiologist nodded. The scan, he said, confirmed a concussion. With luck, there would be no swelling of the brain.

Without luck... Arianna couldn't bring herself to ask.

A tall, white-haired man hurried in and introduced himself as Dominic's personal physician. Arianna began asking questions. He held up a hand and stopped her.

"Give me a few minutes, *signora,* so I can speak with the doctors who examined your husband. Then we'll talk."

Arianna waited. And waited. Finally, the doctor returned. The arm would heal cleanly. The head... He touched her shoulder gently. The sooner Dominic regained consciousness, the better. Meanwhile, they'd moved him to a private room. If the *signora* would please wait just a little while...

But it was dark before a nurse finally told Arianna she could see her husband, and led her to a darkened room. It was the first truly quiet place she'd been in since coming to the hospital hours before.

Dominic lay still, as he had all afternoon. An IV was

hooked to his arm; other tubes and lines snaked out from under the blanket.

Dominic, Arianna thought, *oh my husband.*

She took his hand and said his name. He didn't move, didn't so much as blink. Tears welled in her eyes. She leaned down and pressed her lips gently to his brow. Then she sat in a chair beside him, took his hand and waited.

She didn't really know what she was waiting for. A blip or a beep from one of the machines ranged alongside the bed? A word from a doctor?

She only knew that she would not leave this room until Dominic was with her again, until she could look into his eyes and tell him—and tell him—

Arianna's head fell back against the chair and she slept.

Hours passed. Then, just as the sun burnished the seven ancient hills of Rome with gold, Dominic began surfacing from unconsciousness to a sea of confused dreams.

He was alone in a vast room. Arianna was there, too, and he was hurrying toward her. He wanted to take his wife in his arms and tell her that she *was* his wife, by God, that he was tired of living like strangers, that he had married her because he wanted her in his bed.

In his life.

But no matter how many steps he took, he couldn't seem to close the distance between them. The room grew larger; Arianna's figure grew smaller. He called out her name and she spun away from him and began to run.

Dominic ran, too. Then he stopped. What was he doing, chasing after a woman who didn't want him?

A staircase yawned ahead. He ran down it to a shadowed street, jumped into his car, gunned the engine and started to drive away. He would leave Arianna, forget her...

He couldn't. Couldn't leave, couldn't forget. He put the car into a hard U-turn....

Il mio dio!

A woman pushing a stroller stepped out from between two parked cars. He swore, stood on the brakes. The woman jerked toward him, eyes widening with terror. Everything slowed, slowed—but not enough.

Dominic yanked the wheel to the right. The car, responsive as a thoroughbred, followed his command instantly. It spun, climbed the curb, shot ahead toward a concrete traffic barrier that blocked the *piazza*, and he knew he would never see his Arianna again.

Malleable metal struck unyielding concrete. Pain shot through his head, his body, and as a towering black wave of unconsciousness closed over him, he thought, with agonizing clarity, that it was too late. His pride had made him waste precious time. Arianna would never know— she would never know—

"Dominic?"

Dominic moaned and thrashed from side to side.

"Dominic," a soft voice pleaded urgently, "please, please open your eyes and come back to me."

Arianna's prayer was the strength he needed. Dominic opened his eyes and saw his wife leaning over him, smiling and crying at the same time.

"Arianna," he whispered, and when he did, she gave a sob and buried her face against his throat. He lifted the one arm that seemed to work, wrapped it around her and thought that he had never heard a woman weep as hard as his wife was weeping at this minute....

And that he had the world right here, in the curve of his arm.

"I have been in this prison a lifetime and I tell you all, I am not staying another day!"

Dominic sat up against the pillows, glaring at the little group assembled at the foot of his bed. The orthopedist who'd tended his arm, the neurologist who'd consulted on the concussion, the charge nurse all stood with their arms folded and stern expressions on their faces.

His personal physician and his wife stood off to the side. His doctor looked amused; his wife looked—Dominic scowled. Who could tell? Women were good at wearing masks.

"You've only been here three days," the nurse said sternly. "That's hardly a lifetime, Signore Borghese."

"Have you ever been a patient in this place?"

"Well, no, but this is an excellent hospital, and—"

"And, it is a hospital. A place for sick people." Dominic sat up straighter. "Do I look sick to you?"

"But your arm," the orthopedist began.

"I broke it," Dominic said sharply. "You set it. Is there some magic mumbo-jumbo still to be performed that I don't know about?"

The orthopedist scratched his ear. "I guess not."

"Your turn," Dominic said to the neurologist. "Or don't you have a comment to make?"

"You had a concussion," the neurologist said mildly. "A bad one."

"I can walk and talk and perform all your ridiculous little tests. I've stood on one foot so long I began to think I was a stork, and I've touched my index finger to the tip of my nose enough times to be sure it's still there.

Very scientific, that particular test.'' Dominic's jaw hardened. ''Shall I repeat it for you with my thumb?''

The doctor grinned. ''No, no, that's not necessary.''

''Good. Then we are agreed. I am leaving this morning.''

''But—''

''But, you have a choice. Sign me out, or I'll do it myself.''

Dominic's physician sighed and stepped forward.

''Send him home, gentlemen. I've already discussed matters with Signora Borghese. Between the two of us, we'll keep an eye on him.''

Dominic looked at Arianna. He still couldn't read her expression. He hadn't been able to, not for the past three days. He still remembered waking at dawn the day after the accident, struggling up from a dream and finding his wife beside him, hearing her soft voice and then feeling the dampness of her tears against his throat as she wept in his embrace....

Unless that, too, had been a dream.

The nurse had come in, alerted by the machines he'd been hooked to, followed by the doctors, and Arianna had stepped back from the bed. The next time he saw her, hours later, he'd waited for her to tell him that she'd cried as he held her, that she'd pleaded with him to come back to her....

She hadn't said anything. And he hadn't asked. The neurologist had told him it was not unusual for a man waking from a coma to imagine things.

That was the probable answer.

It was too much to hope that Arianna would feel— that she would want—

Dominic cleared his throat. ''Arianna?'' He knew his expression gave nothing away. He watched his wife impassively, as he would in a boardroom when an important deal was on the table....

Or as he had watched his mother, years and years ago, when she'd told him she was moving to Milan and leaving him with a friend in Rome. He'd been twelve then, terrified but determined not to show it.

Dominic felt a muscle jump in his cheek.

He was thirty-four now, and suddenly he knew he was just as terrified.

All the more reason to show nothing.

"Arianna?" he said again. "Will it be a problem for you, having an invalid at home?"

Arianna bit her lip. She wanted to throw her arms around Dominic and tell him that she'd been praying for this day, that she wanted him home, home with her, more than she'd ever wanted anything in her life.

But Dominic was studying her as impersonally as he might have studied a stock report. It was the same way he'd looked at her for the past three days: politely, but with no real interest.

Those few moments when she'd wept in his embrace, when he'd held her close and whispered her name, might have happened a thousand years ago.

She'd been a fool to think it had meant anything, that the way he'd held her, the feel of his lips against her hair, was anything but the reaction of a man who'd cheated death.

"Arianna?" he said again. "Do you have any objection to having me at home?"

"No," she said politely, "none at all."

Dominic nodded. "Fine."

"Fine," she repeated, showing nothing, because even though her heart was filled with joy at the thought of having her husband back, she could see, very clearly, that he didn't feel the same way.

CHAPTER TEN

THEY went home in Dominic's limousine, the big car moving slowly through the early-morning streets.

Too slowly, evidently. Dominic leaned forward and spoke to the driver.

"I am not made of glass," he said impatiently. "Faster, yes?"

The man nodded and picked up the pace. Dominic settled into the corner again, glowering. Glowering was all he'd done since leaving the hospital, but Arianna wasn't surprised.

Her husband's activities were going to be restricted for a while. No going to work. No eye strain. No stress. Doctor's orders, all of it, and she'd been charged with the responsibility of seeing to it that Dominic obeyed.

She had about as much chance of that as a sand castle had of withstanding the tide. Dominic was not cut out to be a docile invalid. More to the point, all those restrictions meant he'd be trapped in the apartment with her.

The night he'd come out of the coma and held her close to his heart had less substance than a dream. Yes, he'd held her. But it hadn't meant anything. He'd been seeking comfort. She'd just happened to be there.

Still, she was his wife. She would be conscientious about his recovery. To that end, she'd done what she could to guarantee a quiet week.

Celia would phone twice a day to assure her boss that all was well. Dominic had wanted hourly calls but Arianna and Celia had closed ranks and agreed that twice a day check-ins would be more than sufficient.

Rosa would not come in at all. No vacuum cleaner running, no banging of pots and pans in the kitchen, no cheery voice singing operatic arias off-key. The apartment would be quiet.

Jonathan would be away, spending the week with the *marchesa.* This visit to Florence had been planned before the accident. Arianna smiled to herself. Her son was as thrilled with his new great-grandmother as she was with him. He'd been excited about the visit, but ready to cancel it after the accident.

"I want to see Dom'nic," he'd said.

Dominic had solved the problem by talking with his stepson on the phone.

"Do you really want to disappoint your *nonna?* She's been planning this visit for weeks. When you return from *Firenze,* we'll do a bunch of things together."

So Jonathan had agreed to stick to the schedule just as long as he could welcome his stepfather home this morning.

"I'm so glad Dom'nic's okay," he'd kept saying, with a look in his eyes that made it clear how much he worshipped him.

Arianna shot a quick look at Dominic. He was sitting as far from her as possible, staring straight ahead.

Her husband felt nothing for her, but he loved the son he didn't know was his. All those hours in the hospital that first day, waiting to learn if Dominic was going to be all right, she'd been haunted by the realization of how unforgivable it would be if father and son lost each other before learning the truth.

The lie she was living was wrong, but what could she do about it? She'd dug herself in so deep that there was no way out. Telling the truth was far, far too dangerous. Who knew how Dominic would react? What he would do? He was a powerful, vengeful man.

She might lose her child.

She was already losing her husband.

Once, knowing he'd married her for all the wrong reasons had filled her with anger. Now, he didn't want her at all. Not for whatever warped sense of revenge he'd thought she deserved, not for passion...not for anything.

That should have pleased her.

Why didn't it? What did she want from the man who was her husband? Hate? Love? Emotion of some kind. Any kind...

Not true. He'd shown her emotion the day of his accident and she'd rejected it. What if she hadn't stopped him? If she'd let herself be pulled down into that sea of passion.

Arianna's eyes blurred. She turned her face to the window as the car pulled up to the house. The chauffeur got out, but Dominic was already moving, reaching clumsily for the handle, muttering under his breath at the indignity of being helpless, when the door flew open.

"Dom'nic! Oh Dom'nic, you're home!"

Jonathan flung himself into Dominic's lap.

"Jonathan! Be careful. Dominic's arm—"

Arianna caught her bottom lip between her teeth. Man and child were embracing, her little boy laughing, her husband joining in, though his eyes were suspiciously damp.

"Hello, Gianni. Did you miss me?"

"Somethin' fierce!" Jonathan pulled back, his brow

furrowed. "Mom told me you were all right, but I kept hearing the crash in my sleep, you know?"

Dominic nodded. "I know," he said gruffly.

"Even talking to you on the phone every day wasn't... I mean, sometimes I just thought, 'cause you were in a hospital and all..."

Dominic wrapped his good arm around the boy and drew him close. Arianna tried not to weep. Her child and his father loved each other so much.

What should she do?

Better still, what *could* she do, without bringing on disaster?

Jonathan left for the *marchesa's* an hour later and any pretense at polite conversation stopped.

Dominic went out on the main terrace, settled in a chaise longue and closed his eyes. Arianna stood beside him, waiting for him to acknowledge her presence. Was he going to ignore her for the entire week?

"Dominic? Shall I bring you something?"

"Nothing," he said politely. "Thank you."

"What about lunch? You must be hungry by—"

"Where is Rosa?"

"I gave her the week off."

Dominic opened his eyes. "You did what?"

"I gave her—"

"You should have consulted with me first."

"It's your home. She's your employee. I know that, but—"

"What *I* know is that I might need her assistance."

"For what?"

"How should I know for what? Making me lunch, for one thing. Finding me a shirt in the closet. I'm as helpless as an infant, in case you haven't noticed. How should I know what the hell I'll need her for until I do?''

"I'll be happy to help you," Arianna said calmly. "I've already made some sandwiches and some—"

"I don't need help from you."

The words snapped like a whip. Arianna stiffened under their lash, hating herself for the sudden tightness in her throat.

"Sorry. I forgot. You don't need anybody or anything. Not ever."

She whirled around, marched away from him and Dominic winced in expectation of a glass-rattling slam, but Arianna apparently controlled herself. The violent bang never came, though her body language had made it clear that was what she wanted to do.

Dominic sighed and laid his head back.

What was that all about? Had he even suggested he didn't need anybody or anything? No. He had not. Hadn't he just said he needed Rosa?

His wife was in a bad mood. That, at least, he understood. She hated him, hated Rome, hated the life he'd brought her to, and now she was trapped with him in this apartment for the next few weeks.

She probably figured the accident was all his fault, that he'd been angry and driving too fast, but that wasn't true. He'd just been coming back to take her in his arms and tell her he was sorry, that he hadn't meant to frighten her or hurt her, that he'd only wanted to make her see that—that—

What? That their marriage was a mistake?

Dominic closed his eyes. That's what it was, wasn't it? One hell of a mistake. How long could it go on? He couldn't share his space with Arianna much more, inhaling her scent, seeing her at breakfast and dinner and knowing she hated him, hated the existence he'd forced on her.

His head was pounding.

All right. This wasn't the time to make plans that stretched past tomorrow. He'd simply institute some changes so that she wasn't burdened with his care.

He'd call Rosa, tell her to resume her normal schedule even though the idea of pots rattling and the vacuum cleaner roaring made him shudder. And if Rosa launched into her ear-shattering rendition of Mimi in *La Bohème,* he'd have to threaten to murder her.

He'd call a temp agency, too, and hire a butler. A valet. *Dio,* just the idea of having someone wait on him made his belly churn, but he'd turned out to be damnably useless at simple things like buttoning his shirt or pulling on his trousers one-handed. He didn't even want to think about the intricacies of bathing.

Rosa couldn't help him with personal things like that and his wife surely couldn't. She wouldn't want to touch him. To undo the buttons on his shirt, slip her hands under it so that he felt the cool press of her fingers against his skin…

Dominic groaned.

Wonderful. His arm was in a cast, his head was pounding, his wife despised him and he was turning himself on, just remembering what it had been like that first time, when she hadn't hated him, and imagining what it could be like again if the way she'd curled into his embrace that night in the hospital hadn't been a drug-induced dream.

If she felt what he did at the sight of her, this combination of need and desire and something more, something tender and gentle and—and—

"I'm sorry."

He looked up. Arianna stood over him, a tray in her hands, her expression as emotionless as the apology.

"No." Dominic sat up. "I'm the one who should apologize."

"It's all right. You're ill."

"I'm not ill. I have a broken arm. That's not an illness."

"You have a concussion. I shouldn't have yelled at you."

"I *had* a concussion. And you didn't yell."

"You're supposed to take it easy. And I did yell."

"No. You..." He paused and his lips turned up at the corners. "If we're not careful, we're going to end up fighting over who owes who an apology."

Arianna didn't answer. Then, slowly, she smiled.

"You're right. Okay, how's this? We were both wrong."

"That's perfect." Dominic looked at the tray and raised his eyebrows. "Are those tuna salad sandwiches?"

"Uh-huh." Arianna put the tray on the table beside him. "Rosa said you liked tuna."

"Did she shudder when she said it?" Dominic grinned as he reached for a sandwich. "She thinks anything made without garlic and proscuitto is fit only for *stranieri*."

"For foreigners. She told me."

"Ah. Then the good news is that she doesn't think of you as a foreigner."

"Don't be too sure. She said she could understand my liking tuna but the *signore*, after all, was Italian."

Dominic laughed. "She thinks I pick up bad habits when I visit the States."

"Yes. Well..." Arianna cleared her throat. "There's lemonade. Cookies, too. If you want anything else..."

She started to turn away. Dominic reached out and caught her wrist.

"Don't go."

"I don't want to bother you, Dominic. The doctor said—"

"Stay and have lunch with me. Please. It's my first day home. Keep me company."

He waited, his heart racing. How could it be so hard to wait for an answer to such a simple question?

"All right," she said slowly. "Thank you. I will."

It was, Arianna knew, a flag of peace. Dominic was envisioning the endless weeks ahead and making the best of the situation that he could.

Well, so could she.

They managed polite conversation during lunch and then during what remained of the afternoon. At seven, Arianna fled to the kitchen, grateful for the chance to make dinner.

She was exhausted from the strain of pretending she and Dominic were friends. Perhaps not even that. More like acquaintances. Surely not husband and wife. Not a man and woman who'd once come together in passion...

And created a child.

They ate in the dining room, Arianna at one end of the table, Dominic at the other. It was a beautiful room with white marble floors and pale, pale rose silk wallpaper. She'd thought about lighting candles and using them as a centerpiece, but dinner by candlelight was for lovers, not for them.

As at lunch, they made polite conversation. It didn't go as well as it had before. After a while, they fell silent.

Dominic paid rapt attention to his plate, stabbing his fork
into the pieces of meat Arianna had cut for him, poking
at the potatoes and asparagus.

He didn't seem to eat much of anything.

"If you'd rather have something else..." Arianna finally said.

"What?" He looked up, his eyes met hers and then
his gaze slid away. "Oh. No, this is fine."

"Is the meat too rare? I asked Rosa and she said—"

"It's fine."

"Rosa also said you like asparagus, but—"

"For God's sake, Arianna! Rosa isn't an expert on
what I like and don't like. Why you would think..." He
stopped, put down his fork and let out a long breath.
"I'm sorry."

"No. No, that's all right. You must be—"

"Grumpy."

"Tired." Arianna pushed back her chair and stood up.
"After all, your first day home..."

"Yes. Exactly." Dominic pushed back his chair, too.
"I'll help you clean up."

"No!"

The word shot from her throat. The last thing she
wanted was to spend more time with him and be reminded of how little he had to say to her, how uncomfortable he was just looking up and seeing her across the
table. It was different when Jonathan was here. Alone—
alone, she had to face the truth. She had no place in
Dominic's life.

"I mean..." She forced a smile. "You should get
some rest."

Rest? It was barely nine in the evening. Dominic suspected he would get no rest this night whatever the hour.
He'd lie awake instead, seeing his wife's stiff smile as

she pretended that spending almost an entire twelve hours alone with him wasn't a chore.

"Yes," he said quickly, "I think that's what I need. A good night's sleep." Was his smile as forced as hers? "That was an excellent meal. Thank you."

"I'm glad you enjoyed it."

"You're sure you don't mind if—"

"Of course not. Good night, Dominic."

"Good night." She turned away, then swung toward him. "Unless…?"

"Yes?"

Unless you want to have some coffee. Unless you don't want to leave me just yet. Unless you want to reach out, as I do, and bridge this chasm between us…

Arianna swallowed dryly. "Unless you, uh, you have objections, I thought I'd make a roast chicken tomorrow night."

A roast chicken. That was why she'd called him back. To discuss tomorrow's menu. Was that all they'd talk about in the endless days ahead? His taste in food and Rosa's knowledge of what he liked and didn't like? Maybe. What else could they discuss? What could Arianna say to him? Surely not the words he ached to hear, that she was happy he was home, that she was happy she'd married him, that—that—

"Roast chicken is fine," Dominic said, and fled to the safety of his bedroom.

Arianna stood staring after him. After a long moment, she began clearing the table. The day had been hot and muggy. Now, as darkness embraced the city, thunder rumbled far in the distance.

Wonderful. Just what this night needed. The drama of a thunderstorm, as if there wasn't enough drama hanging over this house already.

"Arianna?"

She turned and saw Dominic in the entry to the dining room, his hair mussed, his shirt partly unbuttoned, and she knew with fearful clarity that the passion she'd felt for him the first time they'd met had never changed, would never change.

Thunder rolled through the sky again, an unwitting counterpoint to the sudden pounding of her blood.

"Yes?"

She saw his Adam's apple move up and down as he swallowed. "I'm—I'm sorry to bother you, Arianna, but—"

It was the first time she'd ever heard uncertainty in his voice.

"Are you in pain?" she said quickly. "I'll get the tablets the nurse—"

"I'm fine. It's just…I can't get these damn buttons undone."

Her eyes flew to the buttons that marched with military precision down the front of his pale blue shirt. Two were open. Two, just enough to form a vee that showed his tanned skin. The remaining buttons were still closed, all the way down to the black leather belt that circled his waist.

Arianna felt her face heat. Her eyes swept up and met his. He looked as miserable as a man could look. Well, why wouldn't he? He didn't like asking anyone for help, especially her.

"Oh. Of course. I should have offered…" She took a breath so deep she felt it all the way down to her toes. Then she smiled pleasantly and tried to ignore the way her hands had begun to tremble. "I'll get them for you."

He stood unmoving as she came to him, his eyes locked to her face.

"I sprained my wrist a couple of years ago," she said, reaching for the first closed button. "I couldn't believe how useless it made me feel."

One button undone. Why didn't he say anything?

"It was my left wrist and I'm right-handed, like you, so I thought, well, this isn't going to be a problem."

Two buttons. More of his chest was visible. Tanned skin, muscled pectorals, dark whorls of hair. Wasn't he going to say anything? Was he just going to let her chatter like an idiot?

"But it was. A problem, I mean. I had an awful time with the silliest things. Like—like putting up my hair. It was longer then, and—"

"You have beautiful hair, Arianna."

Her fingers stilled on the button. His voice was so low. So rough. The sound of it sent a tremor of electricity dancing down her spine.

"Thank you. That won't be a problem for you, at least. I mean, your hair is short. Not that I won't help with it, if you ask. Wash it. Comb it. Or..." She clamped her lips together. *Stop babbling!* "There! Just one last—"

"Take it down."

Her eyes flew to his. "What?"

"Your hair. Take it down."

"Dominic." Arianna swallowed hard. "I don't think—"

"Please. Take out those clips and let your hair loose."

She didn't have to make the decision. He'd made it for them both. His hand was in her hair; the clips at her temples dropped to the floor and he combed his fingers through the pale strands.

"I never forgot the feel of your hair against my mouth, Arianna. Against my skin."

"Dominic." God, she could hardly breathe. The way he was stroking her cheek, his hand warm against her face... She looked up. "Dominic," she whispered, "what—what are you..."

He kissed her. Gently, tenderly, the brush of his lips like silk, as soft as the whisper of his fingers against her cheek. She stood trembling, breath stilled, and then she made an almost imperceptible sound and he kissed her again, his mouth searing hers with its heat, holding her only that way, with a kiss, until she felt as if she would melt.

Lightning sizzled outside the window.

A moment later, a lifetime later, Dominic lifted his head. Arianna swayed unsteadily. Her eyes met his as he cupped her jaw, slid his thumb over her bottom lip.

"Say it," he whispered. "Arianna. Tell me what you want."

I want you to love me.

The truth, so long concealed within her heart, was stunning and as dangerous as the lightning bolt that slashed the black sky. She knew he waited to hear her say that she wanted to make love with him...but now she knew that would never be enough.

She loved Dominic.

And what was worse, she wanted him to love her.

How many secrets could a woman live with before she broke?

Something must have shown in her face. Dominic dropped his hand to his side and took a step back.

"It's all right." His voice was thick; she could tell what letting go of her had cost him. "I shouldn't have asked." She shook her head, put her hand on his arm and he stepped away again, as if her touch burned him. "Really, it's all right, *cara.* It's been a very long day."

"Dominic, wait…"

He walked away and she stood in the center of the room, feeling numb as she watched him go.

She heard his door shut. The storm, growing nearer, sent a gust of wind howling through the trees in the courtyard.

Arianna wanted to howl, too. Howl, and weep, and beat her fists against the wall, but she wouldn't. Feeling sorry for herself had never helped, not when her parents died, not when she'd learned she was pregnant. What had gotten her through, each time, was facing the truth.

That was what she had to do now.

She had to find a way to end this sham of a marriage, fall out of love with a man who didn't love her, and tell him he had a son. Nothing to it, she thought, and gave a choked, painful laugh.

She slept fitfully, tumbling in and out of an endless dream in which she walked a long, narrow path beneath a sky where thunder rolled endlessly and lightning lit the somber clouds.

She was alone. So terribly alone.

A roll of real thunder from the storm outside the house rattled the windows. Arianna shot up in bed, shaking from the dream.

Lightning lit the room. There was a distant hiss, as if a giant cat were showing its displeasure, and the illuminated face of the bedside clock went dark. So did the world. Not even a glimmer of light shone through the windows from the street.

Her heart thudded. She'd been terrified of storms like this when she was little. Her parents had understood. Her grandmother hadn't.

"Don't be a coward, Arianna," the *marchesa* would say when she found her hiding in a corner as a storm pounded the sky above the *palazzo*. "Del Vecchios are never afraid."

She'd stopped being afraid. Of life, of loss, of violent storms, but tonight she might as well have been a little girl again, frightened of the roar of thunder, of the jagged streaks of lightning, of the thick, black darkness...

Of the emptiness in her heart.

"Dominic," she whispered brokenly, "oh Dominic."

The door swung open. A bright beam of light pierced the darkness, found her huddled against the pillows. Arianna threw up a hand against the glare—against the risk of letting Dominic see her tear-streaked face.

"Arianna?" He swung the flashlight away from her. "Are you all right?"

"Fine," she said brightly.

"It's a bad storm. I thought it might have awakened you, and then when the lights went out..."

"Really. I'm—" another roar of thunder "—fine."

Dominic didn't believe it. She didn't sound as if she were fine. She sounded terrified.

"Arianna," he said gently, "it's all right to admit you're afraid."

"I'm not."

"*Cara,* everyone is afraid of something. It's not a sign of weakness to admit it."

"I'm not a child, Dominic. I know that."

"All right. In that case, I'll leave you the flashlight. If you need me—"

"I won't. I keep telling you, I'm—"

Thunder roared directly overhead. Lightning slashed through the darkness, and Arianna almost jumped from the bed.

The hell with this, Dominic thought. She was frightened, she was his wife, and it didn't matter that she'd been making it clear for more than a month that she didn't need him. He wouldn't be much of a man if he turned his back and walked away.

He was beside her a second later, curving his one good arm around her, drawing her close against his naked chest.

"I'll take care of you, *cara*," he whispered. "Just lean against me."

It was the second time he'd offered her his strength, but she didn't need it. Didn't need anything. Didn't need him...

He slid his fingers into her hair and slowly raised her face to his. For one endless moment, Arianna held back. Dominic whispered her name again, his voice so tender, so filled with need, that she felt her fear give way.

"Dominic," she whispered.

She clasped the back of her husband's head, drew his face down to hers and kissed him.

CHAPTER ELEVEN

DOMINIC groaned as their lips met.

The years spent without Arianna faded away. All that mattered was the taste, the touch, the sweet pleasure of holding her close again.

He'd tried to put memories of a nameless woman and the one night they'd shared behind him but he'd never managed to do it. Now, he'd found her and made her his wife.

And this—this was their wedding night.

His kisses deepened. Was he moving too fast, asking too much? No. He wasn't. Arianna was returning kiss for kiss; she was touching him, moving her cool hands over his face, his shoulders, his chest. He murmured her name, cupped her breast through her thin nightgown and she shuddered with pleasure.

"Dominic," she sighed, and his body tightened like a fist.

He told himself to slow down. This wasn't a hurried coupling of strangers. This was Arianna, his wife, holding him as if she never wanted to let him go.

He could linger over the flicker of her tongue against his. The little moans humming in her throat. The way she arched toward him as he bit lightly at her nipples through the cotton gown. There was time for all that and more. He could take her to the edge of eternity and keep her there until she was wild for his possession.

But she was wild already, writhing in his arms, sobbing his name, and he was on fire, so hard and swollen that his erection throbbed against her belly.

Still, he needed her to tell him she wanted him, longed for him, that she'd spent the last years remembering, just as he had.

She was saying it with every kiss. Why wasn't it enough?

"Dominic."

Had his name ever sounded so sweet on a woman's lips? Soft. Tender. As if she spoke it from her heart. The storm had stopped; a quarter moon had risen and in its watery light he looked at Arianna's face and saw something in her eyes, something that filled him with joy.

"Arianna. *Come sei bella.*" He drew her closer, kissed her, fell back on the bed with her and a sharp pain lanced through his arm. The breath hissed between his teeth and Arianna reared back.

"What? Oh. Oh, your arm! Dominic, I should have thought—"

Pain still shimmered through him but he caught her wrist, brought her hand to his mouth.

"Don't pull away."

"But your arm…"

"I'm all right."

"You aren't. I don't want to hurt you."

He pressed a kiss into her palm, nipped gently at the soft flesh at the base of her thumb.

"You could only hurt me by leaving me now."

It was true. The pain was subsiding. All he needed was the soft feel of his wife as she sank down against him.

He tangled his fingers in her hair and brought her mouth to his for a slow, deep kiss. *Dio,* the sweetness of her mouth. The way she sighed as their lips met, so that the soft whisper of sound became part of the kiss.

"Arianna." His voice was husky with need. "I want to see you, but I can't undress you, not with one hand. Do it for me. Take off your gown, *mia principessa*."

She wanted to, wanted his hands on her skin. It was five years since she'd been with a man. There'd been no one since Dominic.

Now, he was her lover again.

And he was her husband.

The realization excited her. To bare herself to her husband. To have, at last, the wedding night she had denied them both.

"Undress for me, Arianna."

Nerves warred with anticipation. Her body had changed since he'd last seen it. She was rounder. Fuller. Would he notice? Would he find her beautiful still?

"Cara." He ran his hand down her back, stroking, caressing. "Let me see you."

Arianna slicked the tip of her tongue over her lips. Then she got to her knees beside him and slowly drew her nightgown over her head.

Moonlight scattered wisps of ivory light over her skin.

Dominic looked at her, his eyes moving slowly from her face to her breasts to the gentle curve of her belly.

"I—I've changed," she said unsteadily.

She had. Time and the birth of a child had turned her from a beautiful girl to an exquisite woman. For a heartbeat, he felt a pain that had nothing to do with his broken arm. If only he were the man who'd given her that child...

Arianna crossed her arms over her breasts. "Maybe this—maybe this wasn't such a good idea."

Dominic smiled. "It's the best idea I've ever had,"

he said gently. He kissed the curves of her breasts. "You're more beautiful than before, *cara,* so beautiful you take my breath away." Eyes locked to hers, he eased her arms to her sides. "My only wish is that we hadn't spent all these years apart."

Tears rose in Arianna's eyes. "Mine, too."

He reached out, touched the tip of his finger lightly to the dusty rose center of one breast.

"But we're together again. That's all that matters."

He moved his thumb, his hand, and she moaned.

"You have beautiful breasts, *cara.*" His hand drifted down the valley between them, glided over her stomach, cupped the feminine delta between her thighs.

"And this part of you, this place I remember because it is where the taste of you was the sweetest…"

"Dominic." Arianna caught his hand. "If you do that—if you do that—"

"What?" His voice became thick. "What will happen if I do that, Arianna?"

She closed her eyes as he slipped his hand between her thighs and found her. It was too much. It was too much…

And it wasn't enough. She needed more. Needed—

"Please," she whispered, "please."

"Tell me."

"Make love to me. Come inside me. Oh God, Dominic, I need you, need you—"

Her cries made his blood pound. Between them, they tugged off his sweatpants. His erection sprang free. Arianna caught her breath, touched him, felt the velvet-encased hardness of him pulse against her hand, and instinct took over.

"Dominic," she whispered, "my husband."

Eyes on his face, she lowered herself on him, took

him slowly inside her, deep inside her, her cry of pleasure a sweet counterpoint to his husky groan of satisfaction.

This, oh this was everything. Dominic, filling her. Dominic, his eyes dark with passion. Dominic, his hand curved around her hip, his breathing quickening as she began to move.

His touch, his whispers, urged her on. Her head fell back; she rode him hard, no inhibitions, no shame. Love had driven her past those barriers to a place she'd never believed existed.

Dominic watched his wife moving above him. Her body glistened with sweat; her hair fell in a tumble down her back. She was the most beautiful woman who had ever lived and she was his.

He groaned, felt the tightening in his groin, but he forced himself to hold back. He wanted to watch his Arianna as she flew toward the stars. When she cried out his name and convulsed around him, he pulled her down to him, rolled above her and let go of everything, his heart, his soul, his dreams, everything he was or ever would be.

He felt her come again as the power of his orgasm shuddered through him. Their cries of release mingled and when he bent his head, kissed Arianna and tasted the salt of tears, he didn't know if they were hers or his.

"Dominic." His wife's voice broke. "Dominic, *nonlo lasci mai.*"

"I won't," he whispered, "I'll never leave you, *cara mia.* Never."

Still joined, he stirred inside her, kissed her, and as they began the journey to the stars again, Dominic finally faced the truth.

He'd married Arianna for only one reason.
He loved her.

Time passed. Moments, hours—what did it matter?

Arianna sighed and stroked her hand lightly down Dominic's back. His skin was warm and supple, the muscles beneath it hard and well-defined.

"Are you all right, sweetheart?" he murmured.

She smiled. "I am very all right."

Dominic smiled, too. He rolled to his side, still holding Arianna against him. "Yes. You most certainly are," he said, brushing his mouth softly over hers. "It was enough, then? The way we made love?"

"It was wonderful." A blush colored her cheeks. "Was it all right for you? Having me on top?"

"Well," he said thoughtfully, "I'm not sure."

"Oh. I thought—I mean, I never—"

"Arianna." Dominic caught a handful of her hair and gently tugged her face up to his. "I'm teasing you, *cara.* It was incredible. I was just hoping to convince you we'd have to try it a couple of dozen more times. Strictly so I could give you an opinion, of course."

"Ah. Well, I suppose, in that case..."

Her lips curved in a smile. He smiled, too, and then he kissed her, lay back and drew her head to his chest. "I was a fool, five years ago, Arianna."

"No. It was me. I should never have sneaked off but it all seemed so—so wrong. What we did. What *I* did. I'd never—"

"Neither had I, *cara,* but then, I'd never wanted a woman as I wanted you...as I want you still."

Another kiss, longer and deeper than the last. Dominic sighed. "I thought about hiring someone to find you." He stroked his hand over her hair, toying with the soft curls that wound lightly around his fingers. "Then I thought, but if she didn't care enough to leave me her name…''

''I was embarrassed.''

''*Si*. I know that now, but then…'' He sighed again. ''A man can make a fool of himself, *cara*, trying to protect his precious pride. I convinced myself it was best to forget you.'' His voice roughened. ''But I never did.''

''I never forgot you, either,'' Arianna admitted softly. ''I dreamed about you, fantasized about walking into a room and finding you waiting for me.''

Dominic drew her closer. ''I'm here now, *cara*, and we'll never lose each other again.''

There was a sudden tightness in Arianna's throat. She loved this man so much! How could she have lied to herself for so long?

And how could she go on lying to him?

Honesty was important in any relationship but especially in this one. Dominic had made that clear. He'd taken her as his wife because he hadn't wanted a marriage built on lies.

And theirs was built on the worst possible kind of lie. He had a son, and he had the right to know it.

Now, Arianna thought. Right now, before her courage failed.

But Dominic was whispering to her, caressing her…

And she was lost to everything but his touch.

He said he would make breakfast, if she would tell him how to do it.

Arianna gave a dramatic sigh, told him to sit at the kitchen counter and drink his orange juice and she would make breakfast for them both.

He sat down and watched his wife bustle back and forth. It was a wonderful sight, he thought, and grinned.

Arianna caught the grin out of the corner of her eye. "What?"

"Nothing."

"Nothing, the man says." She turned the bacon in the skillet, then reached for the eggs. "I saw that smirk, *signore* You can't tell me it was nothing."

Dominic raised his glass to his lips. "I was just thinking that you're a definite improvement over Rosa."

She laughed. "Wait until you taste your bacon. You might not agree."

"No, I don't think I'll change my mind, not even if you burn the bacon." He cupped his chin in his hand, rested his elbow on the countertop and regarded her thoughtfully. "For one thing, you're easier on the eyes."

Rosa probably weighed 250 pounds. Arianna tried not to smile.

"That's nice to hear."

"And you don't harbor a burning desire to sing at La Scala."

"You haven't heard me in the shower, or you wouldn't even joke about the possibility."

Dominic raised his eyebrows. "You didn't sing a note when we shared the tub a little while ago." A smile tugged at the corner of his mouth. "Of course, I suppose, even one-armed, I did a pretty good job of keeping your mind off everything, but—"

Arianna leaned over the counter and silenced him with a kiss.

"Stop boasting," she said softly, "and tell me how you like your eggs."

"Cooked."

"Oh, you're funny today, *signore.*"

"I'm happy," he said simply. "Aren't you, *signora?*"

She looked at him. "Yes. Oh yes, I am."

They smiled at each other and then Arianna sighed and reached for the eggs.

"The bacon really will burn if I don't make the eggs soon. How do you want them?"

"Scrambled, wife."

He said the word teasingly but it sent a tremor of pleasure through her. She looked at him, her lips curving in a smile. He smiled back. She cleared her throat. If she didn't make those eggs soon, they'd both forget all about breakfast.

And they couldn't do that because after breakfast, if she didn't lose her courage completely...

"Scrambled," he said, "with cream, not milk."

"Cream's bad for you."

"Maybe. But it makes the eggs cook up softer," he said with the authority of a man who'd washed dishes in a Roman *trattoria* for three months when he was seventeen.

"It makes your arteries scream with terror."

He grinned. "I'm too young to have talking arteries."

Arianna leaned over and kissed him again. He cupped the back of her head and deepened the kiss. After a moment, she sighed and drew back.

"I think I'd better make those eggs," she whispered. She touched her finger to his mouth. "To keep up your strength."

They smiled at each other. She turned away and he watched her whip the eggs. Well, not really. What he was really watching was the way her delectable bottom wiggled from side to side.

She was wearing a T-shirt and panties. He'd wanted her naked; she'd looked at him as if he'd lost his sanity so they'd compromised. Jeans for him, the panties and T-shirt for her.

And what a fine compromise it was.

Dio, he was a lucky man. A beautiful wife who loved him, for surely she did, even if she hadn't yet said the words. And a child he adored almost as if the boy were his own.

Untrue. He loved the boy *exactly* as if he were his own. What if he adopted Gianni? That would make them father and son. A real family.

The thought filled him with happiness. He rose from the stool, grabbed two plates and brought them to the stove just as Arianna turned off the burner.

"Let's eat on the terrace."

She blinked. "I can't go outside like this!"

"The terrace off my bedroom is private. Nobody can see us."

"Dominic…"

"Outside," he said firmly, and scooped the eggs and bacon onto the plates.

Arianna rolled her eyes, grabbed napkins and silverware and followed him.

He was right. The terrace was heavily screened with pots of tall flowering plants. Arianna sank into a chair, felt the warm kiss of the sun on her face and the soft pressure of her husband's mouth on the nape of her neck and wondered if any woman had ever been as happy as she was today.

Without warning, a coldness stole into her bones. She'd never been superstitious, but the *marchesa* had once employed a housekeeper who'd believed in evil eyes and all the rest.

Never let the gods know you're happy, the woman

would mutter darkly, *or they'll go out of their way to make you suffer.*

Arianna shuddered.

"What is it, *cara?* Are you cool? We'll go back inside."

"No," she said quickly, "I'm fine. I'm just—I'm just so…"

Dominic leaned closer. "Happy," he whispered.

She nodded, so filled with emotion she was afraid to speak.

"*Si.* I understand. It's almost too much. For me, too."

Their eyes met. The expression on Dominic's face made her breathing quicken.

"Breakfast can wait," he said gruffly, and he drew her down onto a chaise longue hidden like a secret island within a bower of flowers and made love to her until she could think of nothing but him.

This time, when Dominic asked if she wanted to see his Rome, Arianna said yes.

He phoned for his driver who took them to the Forum, to the Capitoline Hill, to the Coliseum and to all the places she'd visited a hundred times as a child but never really seen until now.

Then he said he wanted to show her something outside the city.

"I wish my arm weren't in this damned cast and sling. We could go by ourselves, without a chauffeur."

"I can drive."

"But my car is a Ferrari. A brand-new one."

She knew it was. The dealership had delivered the car to the house the day after Dominic's return from the hospital.

"How nice," she said politely, pretending she didn't

hear the unease in his voice. "And how convenient, that I can drive a stick shift."

She almost laughed at the look on his face, but he surprised her.

"Well," he said, and cleared his throat, "that's fine. We'll go back to the apartment, get the car and take a drive. There's something I want you to see."

Tension radiated from his body in almost palpable waves for the first twenty minutes of the journey. Arianna bit her lip as he offered helpful advice.

That's a turn up ahead.

Must you really pass that car?

And her favorite, delivered with admirable wariness: *Maybe you're driving too fast,* cara, *what do you think?*

What she thought was that she'd yet to go above fifty and she knew, from things Celia had said, that Dominic probably never drove below that speed, especially on a road like this. But she held her tongue and after a while, when she saw him begin to relax, she glanced at him and smiled.

"It's a lovely car, Dominic."

"And you drive it well."

"Thank you. I love to drive. I only learned how a few years ago." She shot him another smile. "The *marchesa* thought women who drove were, you know, kind of fast."

He laughed. "I'm not surprised." They drove in silence for another few minutes. "Did you learn to drive after you bought the house in Connecticut?"

"Before that. I liked the idea of getting out of the city for an occasional weekend."

"Ah. I thought perhaps, after you had Gianni—Jonathan—"

"Gianni." Arianna moistened her lips. "It's a good

name, perfect for—for my son. I'm sorry I was so stupid about using it.''

''You weren't stupid, *cara*,'' Dominic said softly. ''He is, as you said, your son. I was wrong to insist on using something other than his given name.''

''Well, let's agree that we were both wrong and that, from now on, his name is Gianni.''

Dominic smiled. ''Good.'' He waited a minute. ''The man who is his father… You said he doesn't know.''

Arianna felt as if a hand had reached into her chest and wrapped around her heart.

''That's right.''

''You didn't think he'd want to know he had a child, you said.''

''Uh huh.''

''Because, God knows, if I had a son—''

''When I made it, it was the right decision.''

''I'm sure. I'm not second-guessing, *cara,* I'm just trying to imagine what it must have been like for you, finding yourself pregnant and having nobody to turn to.''

Her hands tightened on the steering wheel. ''It was like everything else in life,'' she said lightly. ''Things happen, you live through them. Besides, it was an easy pregnancy. I was fine.''

''For which I shall be eternally grateful,'' he said, and smiled. ''As for Gianni—you're done a wonderful job of raising him.''

''Thank you.''

''He is a son any man would be proud of.''

''Thank you again.'' *Where was this conversation heading?* She wanted to tell him about Gianni, but not while they raced along a road in the middle of nowhere.

''That's what I want to talk to you about, Arianna… Oh. Do you see that turn ahead? Take it, please.''

She made the turn onto a road even more dusty and narrow than the one they'd been driving. Tall pines rose up on either side, filtering the sun and offering welcome relief from the heat.

"Where are we going?"

"Another minute or two… There. Up ahead. See it?"

What she saw was a white villa, rising as if in a dream against a backdrop of dark green hills. She slowed the car as they entered a circular driveway, drove past a white marble Diana, her hunting dogs at her heels, pouring water from a brass ewer into a travertine marble fountain.

"Pull over," Dominic said, his voice a little rough.

"Are we visiting someone?" Arianna put her hand to her hair. "If I'd known…"

"No one lives here. No one has, for a long time."

Dominic stepped from the car, came around to the driver's side and pulled open the door. His cheeks were strangely flushed. For a moment, she worried that he might have a fever, but when she gave him her hand his fingers were icy cold.

"I first saw this house many years ago," he said softly.

He led her up the wide marble steps to the front door. He pulled a key from his pocket, opened the door and motioned her ahead of him.

Arianna gasped with delight. The house was unfurnished but it was easy to see its timeless beauty.

"Oh, Dominic, it's beautiful."

"I think so, too." Pride edged his voice. "I helped restore it."

She swung toward him. "You?"

"I wasn't always a rich man, *cara*. Surely you've heard the stories about me. About my background."

''I never listen to gossip,'' she said softly, ''and whatever I did hear doesn't matter.''

''Still, you have the right to know the truth about the man you married.'' Dominic drew her forward, walking slowly through the graceful, empty rooms. ''I was born a bastard,'' he said simply, ''and grew up on the streets of Rome. I have no idea who sired me, and my mother walked out of my life when I was still a kid.''

''Dominic.'' She turned toward him and put her hands on his shoulders. ''It doesn't matter.''

''But it does.'' He clasped one of her hands and brought it to his lips. ''You see, I'm not foolish, *cara*. All the jokes people make about men not being in touch with their feelings…'' He smiled. ''It's not true. We're in touch. We just choose to ignore them.'' His smile faded. ''I know, for instance, that the reason I never wanted to trust a woman with my heart was because my mother broke it.''

Arianna's throat constricted. ''Please. You don't—''

''Let me finish, *cara*. It wasn't easy, working up to this, but I owe it to you.''

''You don't owe me any—''

He bent to her, kissed her mouth gently, then put his arm around her shoulders. They began walking again, down airy corridors, through silent rooms.

''As a boy, I did things I'm not proud of. I lied to tourists, I picked pockets, I did whatever I had to do to survive and I told myself it was nothing even close to what the world owed me. Then, one day, I got caught with my hand in a tourist's pocket. I was arrested, jailed… I was out in thirty days, but I vowed I'd never lose my freedom again. So I looked for work. One place I found it was here, as a laborer.'' His mouth twisted. ''I laid bricks, pounded nails, and learned for the second time that it was foolish to trust my heart to a woman. It was the final lesson, *cara.* I knew I wouldn't make the same mistake again. So I went out into the world, worked my way across Italy doing construction, landed in Sicily, and ended up working for a man most of Italy feared.''

''Dominic. Please. You don't have to—''

''Arianna.'' He laughed, cupped her chin and kissed her. ''Are you afraid I'm going to tell you I'm part of some dangerous *famiglia?* No, sweetheart, I'm not. The work I did was very simple. I helped him build a house. This man had a good heart, even if he kept it well hidden. He liked me. I liked him. He came to treat me almost as a son. And when he died two years later—peacefully,'' he said, with a quick smile, ''he left me a legacy.''

''And that was the start of Borghese International?''

Dominic shook his head. ''It was a very small legacy, *cara,* though it was a lot to me back then. I was amazed and grateful, and used the money as a stepping stone.'' He drew her closer. ''I'd heard about emeralds in the jungles of Brazil…and I got lucky. Eventually, I was no longer Dominic Borghese, construction worker. I was Borghese International. I had wealth, power, everything…but I didn't have the only thing a man really needs.'' He paused, and his voice softened. ''I didn't have a family. Now, thanks to you, I do.''

Tears had risen in Arianna's eyes. ''Dominic. My darling Dominic. I'm so sorry. So very sorry you lived such a hard life.''

''Don't be. I didn't tell you this story to make you weep but to make you see what you—and Gianni—mean to me.'' Dominic cleared his throat. ''And to see, too, why it was so hard for me to trust you. To let you inside here," he said, tapping his heart, "where I vowed never to be hurt again." Dominic took an unsteady breath. "I want us to marry again, *cara*. A real wedding this time, you in a white gown, me in one of those silly suits men wear on such days."

He paused, drew himself together. "And if you will permit it, I want to do one other thing to make us a real family. I want to adopt Gianni and make him truly my son."

A sob burst from Arianna's throat. Dominic felt his heart turn heavy. She didn't want these things. It was her right, he knew that, but—

"Dominic." She put out her hand, touched his face. "All the things you said about trust. About never letting anyone hurt you again…" Her voice cracked. "I love you," she whispered. "Think of that, remember it, believe in it."

Those were the words he'd waited to hear. Then, why was a coldness wrapping around him?

"What are you trying to tell me, Arianna?"

She took a steadying breath. "I lied to you about Gianni's father. He isn't someone in the past."

His face went blank. "What does that mean?"

"It means there's no need for you to adopt Gianni because—because Gianni is your son."

CHAPTER TWELVE

DOMINIC rocked back on his heels. Arianna remembered when he'd fought with Jeff Gooding, how none of Jeff's blows had hurt him.

What she'd just told him made him reel.

"Dominic, please…"

He stepped back from the hand she held out. "Am I supposed to believe this? That Gianni is my son?"

"It's true. He's yours. That night we made love…"

"One night, Arianna. That was all. Just one night."

"That was enough. I got pregnant."

"You got pregnant." His voice was as flat as his eyes. "I used condoms."

"I know. I don't know what happened. An accident…"

A muscle began to tic in his jaw. "How are you so certain the boy is mine?"

She didn't flinch. It was a brutal question, but she supposed she deserved it.

"Because I wasn't with anyone else. Not for months before. And not after. You were the only one. I didn't sleep with anybody else."

"There are tests," he said coldly.

"Do them. They'll all prove the same thing. You're Gianni's—Jonathan's—father."

Dominic stared at her. "I thought," he said slowly, "when I first saw him, I thought…"

"Yes. I was afraid you would."

"His coloring. His eyes. The way he smiles..." He thrust his hand into his hair, swung away from her and paced across the room. "Mine. The boy is mine?"

Arianna nodded. "He's your son. There were so many times I thought you'd realize it, but—"

"But," he said, turning to her, his voice sharp, "when I asked you, is the child mine, you said he wasn't."

"No. I mean, yes, that's what I said, but—"

"Another 'but.' You are filled with 'buts,' Arianna. But it must have been an accident. But you slept with no one else. But Gianni is mine." He balled his hands into fists. "But you lied to me when I asked if he was."

Arianna was trembling. She'd seen Dominic angry, but never like this. His face was white, his voice cold, the look in his eyes terrifying. She took a step toward him, held out a hand in supplication but he brushed it aside.

"Try and understand," she pleaded. "I hardly knew you when you asked me if Gianni was yours. I didn't know what you'd do if I admitted that you'd fathered him."

"If I'd *fathered* him?" He came at her quickly; she backed up and he caught her wrist, his fingers pressing hard into her flesh. "You make it sound as if I were a stud horse."

"I didn't mean—"

"You carried my child for nine months, gave birth to him, and never once thought of finding me and telling me I had a son?"

"What for? We were strangers. I didn't think you'd want to know."

"I see. You didn't think I'd want to know, so—"

"Stop repeating everything I say! And let go of my wrist. You're hurting me!"

He looked at his hand, wrapped around hers, as if he'd never seen it before, gave a snort of disgust and flung it from him.

"Four years," he said quietly. "Four long years, during which my son had no father. And now, even though we're married, you still said nothing." His voice rose with barely tempered fury. "Have you an explanation for that, too?"

He saw the muscles in her throat move as she swallowed.

"I—I thought about it on our wedding day."

"You thought about it." Dominic folded his arms. "And you decided…?"

"You know I married you against my will. What did you expect me to do? I was unhappy. I thought I hated you. And—"

"And your unhappiness was more important than the truth."

"No. I didn't say that."

"Oh. Sorry." He smiled politely. "Go on, Arianna. I won't interrupt. This is such a touching story that I'm eager to hear the rest."

"I was angry, and frightened. I didn't know how you'd react." Her eyes brimmed with tears again. "I was afraid you'd try to take my son from me."

"I see. First, I was a stranger who would deny paternity of the child in your womb. Next, I was a crazed monster who'd try and take that child from you. Amazing that I can be both, don't you think?"

Temper flared under Arianna's despair. "Don't talk to me as if I were a fool, Dominic! You're taking two different sets of circumstances and mixing them together."

"In that case, let's skip ahead. Forget our wedding day. Let's consider the weeks that came after it." His mouth thinned. "Six weeks, to be exact. Six weeks during which you could have said at any time, Dominic, I have something to tell you."

"By then, things had grown more complicated." Arianna moistened her lips. "I saw that my son—"

"Our son," Dominic snapped.

"I saw that he'd come to love you. And that you— that you seemed to love him."

"And those are certainly two perfect reasons for not telling the boy and me the truth."

"Our marriage wasn't going well," Arianna said, rushing past the sarcastic words. "I thought it might not last, and—"

"You mean, you hoped it wouldn't last. And if it didn't, why would you ever want me to learn the truth?"

"No," she said quickly, "it wasn't like that. I knew I'd have to tell you, but I thought—I thought—"

"You thought?"

The room was warm with midsummer heat, but Arianna began to shake.

"I thought," she said in a whisper, "more than ever, that you might try and take Jonathan from me. And then you were hurt in the accident, and I knew how I really felt about you, and I knew I had to tell you, but the time was never—was never right."

"That's because you'd gone long past the right time, Arianna. The day you learned you carried my child was the day you should have started searching for me."

"Try to see this from my vantage point," she pleaded. "I thought—"

"I know what you thought. That you could play God. Make my decisions for me. Make my child's decisions for him. Keep us from knowing we were father and son."

Arianna glared at him, eyes bright with defiance. "You make it sound so easy, but what was I supposed to do? Hire a private detective? Ring your doorbell, introduce myself and say, hi, remember me? We spent a couple of hours in bed a couple of months ago and oh, by the way, I'm pregnant."

"That would have been a good start."

"Stop being so damned sanctimonious! Think about how you'd have reacted to that kind of announcement. All those women, eager to marry you for your money, remember what you said? Are you going to tell me you mightn't have thought that's what I was after, too?" She stepped forward, her eyes locked to his. "Be honest, Dominic. What would you have done if I'd come to you five years ago?"

Dominic tried to get past the anger burning hot in his belly while he considered what she'd said.

What *would* he have done? Welcomed her into his life? Rejoiced in the fact that a night of anonymous sex was going to saddle him with at least an eighteen year commitment?

Probably not.

He'd have been upset, angry, disbelieving. He'd have questioned her motives, demanded a DNA test…but, in the end, he'd have done the right thing. Financial support. Visitation rights. A man who grew up without a father wouldn't ignore his own offspring.

But would he have felt the same burst of joy at the news he'd impregnated a woman he'd met at a party as he felt knowing a little boy named Gianni was his? Because he did feel joy, tucked away under all his anger.

The answer was simple.

He would not.

Loving a child you knew was one thing. Loving a handful of cells in the womb of a stranger was another. He was willing to admit that.

The part he couldn't forgive was what had happened in the last six weeks. Arianna wasn't a mystery woman anymore, she was his wife. His wife! She'd had all this time to tell him about Gianni and she hadn't. Was it fear that had kept her quiet…or was it his desire to adopt the boy that had forced her to admit everything?

Her secret would have been uncovered once his lawyers began asking for birth certificates, hospital records, who in hell knew what.

Was that why she'd suddenly told him the truth?

And those words, that declaration of love. False. As false as she was.

He swung away from her, his heart filled with pain.

To think he'd imagined himself in love with her. That he'd prayed she loved him, too. *Dio,* he was pitiful! As easy a mark as the tourists he'd played for suckers when he was a boy.

But he wasn't a boy anymore. He was a man who'd been taken in by a clever woman, and he wasn't helpless. He'd built his fortune on an ability to make quick, intelligent decisions.

It was time to make one now.

His wife was the mother of his son. She was also extraordinary in bed. Two admirable qualities, he thought coldly, and knew what he had to do.

He turned and faced her, watched her search his eyes to discover her fate.

"You're right," he said. "I can take Gianni from you."

"If you try, I'll fight you with everything I have!"

He had to admire her courage. She was white-faced, she was trembling, she had to know he held all the cards…but she was still as fierce as a mother bear guarding her cub.

"We're in Italy. My country. My laws." His smile was razor-sharp. "My connections, and my money. What do you think would be the odds that you'd win?" He let that sink in. When he saw the shadow of fear in her eyes, he spoke again. "But taking you from Gianni would hurt him, and I love my son too much to do that."

Arianna sagged with relief. "I love him too much to hurt him, too," she said quietly. "I know it will be hard, but we can get past this."

"Get past what? The fact that I'm Gianni's father? That you're a liar?" Dominic shook his head. "I don't think so."

"I only lied because I had to. Can't you see that?"

"Oh, I see many things." He came toward her, enjoying the way she edged away. "For instance, I see how wrong I was to think our marriage was based on honesty. But that's all right, *cara*. Without taking you as my wife, I'd never have known I had a son. Gianni would have grown up thinking his father had abandoned him—and I could have passed him on the street someday and not have known he was mine."

Arianna was weeping openly, the tears streaming down her face. For a heartbeat, Dominic wanted to take her in his arms and tell her—tell her—

Tell her what? She'd lied to him, not just about Gianni but about loving him.

The moment of weakness passed. He'd been a fool before. He damned well would never be one again.

"Never mind, *cara*. I've always been a pragmatist. Maybe that's the reason I have to admit that this has all worked out. I have Gianni. He has me. And he has you, a mother he loves." He smiled thinly. "And, there's something to sweeten the package. Your performance in bed last night." Dominic raised his hand to his forehead in a mocking salute. "My compliments, Arianna. It was as memorable as it was the first time we met."

Fury replaced the anguish in her eyes. This was the real Dominic Borghese, and she hated him with a passion.

"You're despicable," she said, her voice shaking with emotion. "I don't know why I ever thought anything else."

"*Cara,* you're not paying attention. I'm trying to tell you that I'm going to keep you."

"Damn you, don't call me..." Arianna's mouth dropped open. "What did you say? You're going to *keep* me?"

Dominic gave a lazy shrug. "It's the most sensible thing to do. I won't divorce you and take sole custody of my son—and please, don't bother telling me I couldn't do it. I can do anything I set my mind to." He spoke softly, but there was no mistaking the steel behind the words. "Surely you've learned that by now."

Oh, she had learned everything she needed to know. That he was cruel and vindictive, that he'd stop at nothing to get revenge. It sickened her to think of how she'd lain in his arms last night, how she'd let him use her body, her heart.

"I despise you," she whispered. "You *are* a monster, just as you said. Do you hear me? You're a—"

"I'm a man who sees right through you." His expression hardened. "And I'm warning you, Arianna. Behave yourself, be a good mother to my son and a gifted courtesan in my bed, and I won't throw you out. I'd hate to lose a woman with such assets."

She swung at him and her fist found its mark. It was a good, clean shot to the jaw. He had to admire her for it, and for the defiance shining in her eyes.

"A woman of many talents," he said, and he cupped her nape, dragged her to him and kissed her.

Arianna fought, but even with one arm in a cast, Dominic was far too strong. After a few seconds, she gave up and stood unmoving in his rough embrace.

At last, he raised his head.

"You can hate me all you like," he said thickly, "but when I take you to bed, you'll spread your legs and moan, just as you did last night, or I'm liable to reconsider. Do you understand? Your gifts are varied, but there's a limit to my patience. Gianni can learn to live without you, if he must, and I can always find another playmate."

He let go of her and she stared at him, wondering how she could ever have thought she loved him.

"I hate you. I truly, truly hate you!" Her voice trembled, then rose as he walked away from her. "Do you hear me, Dominic? I hate you!"

She heard his footsteps echoing through the empty rooms, then the sound of the front door slamming shut. After a long time, she wiped her eyes and made her way through the house and down the steps.

The Ferrari was where she'd left it. Dominic was striding along the narrow, tree-lined road. He had his cell phone to his ear and she knew he must be calling his driver to come and pick him up.

She climbed into the car, turned the key and shifted into gear as soon as the engine roared to life. Foot pressed to the floor, she zoomed past him, shooting a glance in the mirror as she did, smiling with satisfaction when she saw the gray dust blow into his face.

But her smile was only a memory by the next day, after she'd telephoned virtually every attorney in Rome, identified herself as the wife of Dominic Borghese and asked for information on divorce and child custody.

Their advice was always the same.

She could stay in the marriage and keep her son.

Or she could leave it…and lose him.

CHAPTER THIRTEEN

FALL came to Rome and though everyone said the city's climate was milder than New York's, Arianna felt chilled all the time.

She needed to eat more pasta, Rosa said, to warm her bones. She needed to drink more *vino,* Gina said, to thicken her blood. Arianna smiled at each of them and said she was sure she'd get used to the colder weather.

It wasn't true.

It wasn't the weather that chilled her, or a lack of nourishing food or earthy red wine. Her heart was frozen, that was the reason, and nothing would ever thaw it.

She was living with a stranger who despised her. She told herself that was all right. After all, she felt the same way about him.

Gianni, at least, was happy.

"We have to talk about my son," Dominic had said brusquely the day the boy was due back from his visit to the *marchesa.*

"*Our* son," Arianna had said, and he'd acknowledged the correction with a curt nod.

He'd done most of the talking. That was all right, too. Arianna had no wish to drag their child into the mess they'd made. They'd agreed to go on as before, sharing meals, keeping up the pretence that they were a married couple the same as anybody else.

They'd sat Gianni down that same evening and carefully told him Dominic was his father.

Her little boy's eyes had grown wide with wonder.

"My father? You mean, I've got a daddy? Like Bruno?"

"Yes," Dominic had said, taking the boy into his lap. "Just like Bruno."

"Did you 'dopt me?" Gianni asked, looping an arm around Dominic's neck.

Dominic cleared his throat. "I didn't have to. You're my son."

"For real?"

"For real," Dominic replied, with a little smile.

"How come you didn't live with us before? How come nobody told me? How come—"

"It's a long story and we'll tell it to you someday. For now all that matters is that we're together—and we always will be."

Gianni thought that over. "So, you and Mommy made me together?"

"Yes."

"But you only just got married. How could I have been borned before then?"

"Your mother and I knew each other a long time ago, Gianni. Then we—we lost each other."

"Bruno lost a kitten once," Gianni had replied solemnly. "He didn't know where it went, but then his dad found it in the house next door. Did you and Mom lose each other like that?"

"Something like that," Dominic had said, and changed the subject.

Arianna knew Dominic was right. They'd have to tell the boy more someday. For now, the explanation her husband had offered was enough.

Her husband, she thought, as she sat on the terrace wrapped in a heavy sweater. The man she loathed.

Her son worshipped him.

Why wouldn't he? Not a night went by that Dominic didn't come home with some special treat. He was buying the child's affection, stealing it from her....

Except, he wasn't.

Gianni offered his love freely, and how could she blame him? Dominic hated her, but he loved his son. And he was a great father, warm and loving, consistent in setting down simple but meaningful rules. He played with Gianni every evening after dinner, took him places on the weekends.

Her husband was the best father a child could have.

And she—she was turning into the kind of mother a child didn't deserve.

She was listless. Unenthusiastic. Dull. Worst of all, she was weepy. Oh, she never broke down in front of Gianni. As bad as things might be, she'd never let that happen. She saved her tears for the darkness of night, when she lay alone in the guest room bed, waiting—as she had in the past—for her husband to come and claim her.

"Signora?"

Arianna turned toward the door. "Yes, Rosa?"

"I wondered...do you prefer chicken or fish this evening?"

Rosa had taken to asking her questions she'd never bothered asking before. Arianna suspected it was deliberate, an act of kindness meant to draw her into some kind of participation in life. What must the woman think of a bride who spent her days moping?

"Signora?"

"Fish," Arianna said, for the housekeeper's sake. "Fish sounds fine."

"And for a vegetable? I bought some—"

"You decide."

Rosa's face fell. "As you wish," she said, and her sigh seemed to linger even after she stepped back inside.

Arianna rose from her chair and walked slowly to the terrace railing.

Even Gina sensed something was wrong. She'd gone back to issuing polite invitations to coffee. Arianna had accepted a couple of them, hoping they'd cheer her up, but it hadn't worked.

She moped by day and hated herself for it.

And she waited by night, and hated herself even more.

Dominic had made such ugly threats that day at the villa. She'd been steeled for his appearance in her room that same night.

She should have known better.

Her husband wouldn't take her by force. She'd called him a monster, but he wasn't. He was just a man, as vulnerable as any other. More vulnerable, maybe. Life had scarred him and without intending to, she'd managed to open the old wounds.

She'd hurt him deeply, and he'd retaliated. He'd been in a blind rage when he'd told her what he'd do to her. She should have known it was an empty threat.

Dominic wouldn't force himself on her. In her heart, she'd know that all along. But if he did come to her as she lay dreaming of how it could have been if he'd loved her, if he drew back the blankets, touched her with his gentle hands, kissed her with tenderness and then with passion, whispered the words she longed, oh longed to hear...

Arianna blinked back her tears.

He wouldn't. His pride wouldn't permit it. He would never forgive her.

She'd never forgive him, either. Never. She had feelings, too, and he'd trampled them to dust. She would hate him for the rest of her life.

A cold wind moaned through the denuded garden in the courtyard below. Arianna felt the wind's bitter touch, bowed her head and wept.

Dominic scanned the last page of the document lying on his desk, picked up his pen and scrawled his signature at the bottom.

Done, at last. The Silk Butterfly belonged to Arianna.

He'd meant to sign it over weeks before, but first there'd been the car accident and then…

And then, he'd been too blind with fury to think straight.

He was much calmer now. All his anger had drained away. What was the sense in it? He had gained a son. It wasn't as if he'd lost a wife.

He'd never had one in the first place.

Dominic pushed back his chair, swiveled it around and stared out the window at the ruins of the Coliseum. It was one hell of a view and more than a couple of major hotel chains had tried to buy it from him, but he always refused to sell.

There was something about the sight of that ancient building that reached right inside him. He used to imagine it as it had once been, filled with noise and energy, gladiators facing whatever life tossed at them with courage and pride.

His perspective had changed. Lately, the sight was a constant reminder that no matter how hard a man tried, life could always find a way to defeat him.

Almost always, Dominic thought, and turned his chair around.

"Celia?" he said, stabbing the button on his intercom. "Celia? Dammit, don't you hear me?"

"The entire city can hear you," his assistant said calmly, "without the intercom."

Dominic jerked his head up. Celia stood in the doorway, the usual portrait of efficiency, pen and notebook in hand. He glowered but decided to ignore the comment.

"Did you make those phone calls?"

"I did."

"And? Must I pull each word from you?"

"And, only one of the shops has heard of the new toy."

"I don't care how many have or haven't heard of it. What I want to know is—"

"If I found one in stock. Yes. Felici's had a Kitty Kat Robot. It will be wrapped and ready for you to pick up."

"Good." Dominic got to his feet. "I'm leaving."

"So I see." Celia watched her boss walk past her toward the reception desk, her expression as dispassionate as ever. Her boss was not a happy man. She couldn't understand it. He had a beautiful wife and a child he obviously loved, but it wasn't enough. There were times she wanted to shake him...but there were certain liberties even she would not take.

She sighed, stepped behind his desk to straighten it for the next day, spotted the document lying there and scanned it so she could file it away...

"Signore Borghese? *Signore!*" He turned as she hurried after him. "You forgot this."

"Ah. *Grazie.* I'm glad you noticed."

"Oh, I am, too. A man who brings gifts to his wife and child may be able to buy happiness, sooner or later."

Dominic's face reddened. "What did you say?"

Celia stood tall. "Go ahead. Fire me. What you do with your life isn't my business."

"No," he said coldly, "it is not. Watch yourself, Celia. Some day, you'll go too far."

"Your son worships you. Your wife adores you. And still you march around here with a face that terrifies your employees and drives away your clients."

"That's nonsense. And I know my son loves me. You don't have to point it out."

"Your wife does, too."

"That's it. Get your things together. You're fired."

"Fire me. It won't change the facts."

"Dammit," Dominic roared, punching his fist against the wall, "how dare you tell me what my wife feels?"

"She lived in that hospital when you were hurt. She never left your side. She thought you were dying, *signore,* and if that had happened, I think she would have died, too."

"You don't know what you're talking about."

"Don't I?" Celia smiled sadly. "*Buona notte, signore.* I'll pack my things."

"Don't pack anything," Dominic growled. "Who would employ you, except me? Keep your job, keep your tongue and trust me when I tell you that you don't know everything."

"Trust has to be earned, Signore Borghese. It isn't a commodity you can demand of a person."

"Riddles. Just what I need. What in hell is that supposed to mean?"

"Only that *you* don't know everything, either, especially when it comes to the feelings of women. Good night, *signore*."

Dominic opened his mouth, then shut it. Could a man ever win an argument like this? How could you discuss feelings? It was as he'd explained to Arianna, that day at the villa. Men knew feelings existed, but facts were what mattered.

Only facts.

Grim-faced, he left the building, climbed into his car and set off for the toy store, Kitty Kat Robot, and another evening of trying to figure out why he should give a damn about his dead marriage when he didn't love his wife.

When she, heaven knew, didn't love him.

Gianni climbed into his bed with his Kitty Kat clutched to his chest.

"Thank you again for my present, Daddy."

Dominic's heart still swelled at that word on his son's lips.

"You're welcome, Gianni." He bent down and kissed the boy's forehead. "Sleep well, son."

"I will, unless I hear Mommy crying."

"Unless... What do you mean?"

"Mommy cries sometimes. Late at night. It's just a tiny little sound, like Kitty Kat made when we turned the switch on and she went 'meow,' remember?"

Dominic swallowed hard. "Maybe it isn't your mommy. It could be a sound from outside."

"Mommy said the same thing when I asked her about it, but I know it's her." Gianni hesitated. "Daddy? 'Member when I asked you why you and Mom didn't sleep in the same room? An' you said husbands and wives didn't always do that?"

Dominic nodded. "I remember."

"Mommies and daddies do. I asked Bruno. He told me."

Bruno. A four-year-old boy supplying answers to questions a thirty-four-year-old man couldn't answer.

"Not always."

"Maybe if you and Mom were in the same room, she wouldn't cry."

Dio, Dominic thought, and pulled the blanket to his son's chin.

"Go to sleep, Gianni."

"Buona notte, Papa."

Dominic smiled. "Good night, *mio figlio.*"

He shut off the light, closed the door and stood silently in the hall. Now what? His wife wept because he wouldn't let her leave him, his secretary was convinced that he was a fool, and his son thought the answer to everything was sharing a room.

Maybe it was.

Maybe what he needed, what they both needed, was to go to bed together. That was what he'd warned her would happen. He could still do it. Walk into Arianna's bedroom tonight, pull down the blankets, strip off her nightgown...

Dominic leaned his forehead against the wall.

Making love to a woman who hated him wasn't the answer. Perhaps giving her the Butterfly was. Then she'd have the son she adored and the shop she loved.

Maybe that would be enough to make her smile again.

He took a deep breath and walked into the sitting room. It was empty. Of course. Arianna left it as soon as Gianni went to bed. He paused, inhaling the light fragrance of her perfume, remembering how it had scented her skin the night they'd made love. No. He wouldn't think about that. Love had nothing to do with what they'd shared.

Why sentimentalize sex?

The paper giving her the Butterfly was in the pocket of his suit jacket. He retrieved it, smoothed out the creases, went down the hall to her room and knocked.

"Yes?"

"It's me." *Brilliant, Borghese. Who else would it be?* "I, uh, I need to talk to you."

"Can't it wait until morning?"

"No," he said tightly, "it cannot."

There was silence. He thought he heard the faint rustle of fabric. Then the lock turned. He tried not to focus on the fact that her door was locked against him. It would only spark his anger, and he wasn't going to lose control like that again.

The door opened a couple of inches. Arianna peered out at him. Her face was shiny, her hair was brushed out so it hung loose to her shoulders, she was wearing a simple white terry cloth robe, and he knew, in that instant, that he wasn't just a fool, he was a deceitful fool because he'd never stopped loving his wife.

"May I come in?"

She moved back. He stepped inside the room.

"What do you want, Dominic? It's late, and—"

"It's eight o'clock. *Dio,* don't look at me like that. I'm not going to—"

Never stopped loving her, and never would stop loving her.

"—not going to touch you."

"Tell me what you want, please."

He thrust the paper at her. "Here."

She looked at it, her hair falling forward against her

cheeks. How he longed to smooth back the soft curls, slide his fingers into it and raise her face to his.

She looked up, frowning in puzzlement. "What is this?"

"It's what I promised you. Ownership of the Butterfly."

"Oh. Thank you."

She tossed the paper aside. He looked at it, then at her.

"Oh? That's it?"

"What did you expect me to say? Good night, Dominic."

She opened the door wider so that he'd get the idea. Well, he got it. But he wasn't going anywhere until she explained herself.

"Did you actually read that document? Do you know what it is? I said that I've turned over the—"

"I heard what you said. Good night."

"Wait a minute." A muscle jumped in his jaw. "That's what this was all about, remember? The Butterfly. I said I'd give it to you if you married me."

"My grandmother will be happy. Thank you again. And good—"

"Dammit, Arianna, what do you want from me? I kept our bargain and all you can say is—"

"What do you want me to say?" Her eyes flashed; he looked at her in surprise as it occurred to him that he hadn't seen that look, that anger and vitality, on her face in a very long time. "I thanked you. End of story."

"The hell it is!"

"Keep your voice down. You'll wake Gianni."

Dominic kicked the door shut behind him. "You'll wake him anyway. He says he hears you crying during the night."

Color flooded her face. ''I do not cry! Whatever Gianni hears, it's not me weeping.''

''Of course not. Why would you weep?''

''Indeed.'' She folded her arms, lifted her chin. ''Why would I?''

''I don't know.'' Dominic moved toward her. She retreated. He was angry already and that made him angrier. What was she afraid of? Had he ever hurt her? Had he ever stormed in here and taken her, as he'd threatened to do? As he'd ached to do, all these weeks—except he didn't want to take her in anger. He wanted her to come to him willingly, to sigh his name as she had once done, to kiss him and tell him, with each kiss, that she loved him as much as he loved her.

''Do you weep because you think you must tolerate my presence in your life?'' He clasped her shoulders. ''Because you have to look at my face each morning and know that I am your husband? Is that the reason you cry, Arianna?''

She shook her head. Tears glittered on her lashes, then spilled down her cheeks.

''Answer me, dammit.'' He shook her. ''Do you weep because you hate me?''

''I weep because I love you!'' The words burst from her throat. She knew she was making a mistake, that he'd never believe her, that she was making herself even more vulnerable, but she couldn't hide what she felt anymore, not from him, not from herself. ''I love you, Dominic. I know you don't want to hear it, but—''

She cried out as his mouth crushed hers in a kiss so filled with passion it made her dizzy.

''*Cara mia. Il mio cuore,*'' he whispered, ''you are my heart. My soul.''

''Dominic. Dominic, my love…''

He kissed her again, cupped her face, scattered more kisses on her eyelids, her nose, her cheeks.

"I've been so cruel, *cara*. But when I thought you'd deceived me…"

"I know it was wrong. I should have told you about Gianni as soon as we were married, but I was afraid. I didn't know you, didn't know what you'd do—"

"*Si.* I understand. You were cautious, and you were right to be. You had a child you were determined to protect at all costs." Dominic took a deep breath and lifted her face to his. "I let the ghosts of my past rule my heart, Arianna. I wanted you to love me and when I thought you didn't… I was wrong to lash out at you, *cara.* Can you forgive me?"

"There's nothing to forgive. I hurt you. I didn't meant to, but I did." Arianna framed his face with her hands, brought his lips to hers and kissed him. "I'll never hurt you again, *il mio amore.* I swear it."

Dominic gathered her tightly in his arms. "*Ti amo, mia moglie.*"

Such glorious words. Arianna's lips curved in a smile. "And I love you, my husband. I always will."

Dominic lifted his wife in his arms. She linked her hands behind his neck.

"Where are we going?" she said softly.

"To our bedroom. I'm going to make love to my wife." He grinned. "And tomorrow—"

"Just like a man, already planning ahead." She kissed his mouth tenderly. "What about tomorrow?"

"Tomorrow, we'll take Gianni and drive to the villa. It's time our son had a real cat. And a dog. And a pony. And—"

"And a mother and father who love each other," Arianna whispered.

"And who always will," Dominic whispered back, as he carried the woman he loved into his room, and into his life.

Gianni took all the credit for his parents' wedding in the spring.

He and Bruno—"the font of knowledge," Dominic said, laughing—had been discussing things. Bruno said brides always wore white gowns and grooms always wore funny black suits.

Gianni said it wasn't true. He'd been at his parents' wedding and they hadn't dressed that way.

"Well," said Bruno, "they should have."

Gianni mentioned it to his mother. His mother smiled and mentioned it to his father who laughed, hoisted him into the air and said he thought that was a great idea.

Next thing he knew, there was a thing called a bower set up in the garden behind the big house they all lived in now, and it was covered with pink and white roses.

There was a guy playing a violin. A couple of guys, actually. There were guests smiling at each other, and there was good stuff to eat and bubbly stuff to drink and, just like that first time, he even got to taste some.

But this wedding was lots better.

His mom looked like a princess in a long white dress with a big skirt and a neckline that showed her shoulders. She said the dress was made of lace. She had flowers in her hair, like the ones on the bower.

His dad wore a funny black suit, just like Bruno had said, but it didn't look funny on his dad. It looked sort of cool.

He stood next to his dad, under the bower, in a suit that was kind of the same, holding his dad's hand tight as his great-grandma came down the aisle with his mom.

"Mia bambina," he heard his *nonna* whisper, which was silly 'cause his mom wasn't a little girl anymore.

His mom took a step toward his dad, who was looking at her, and—wow! Were those tears in his dad's eyes? There were definitely tears in his mom's.

"Mia principessa," his dad said to his mom, *"come sei bella."* That was okay because it was true. She really did look like a beautiful princess.

All of a sudden, his *nonna* tapped that black stick of hers against the ground. Everybody seemed surprised. Not him. His great-grandma was always doing stuff nobody expected. It was one of the bestest things about her.

"You will excuse me, *per favore,*" she said, "but I have something of importance to say. Today, the del Vecchios and the Borgheses become one." Then she smiled, in the way that meant she was feeling pretty pleased with herself. "And I am delighted to tell you all that it is good to know an old woman like me can still devise a clever plan that works well, from start to finish."

His mom blinked. So did his dad. Then they began to laugh. Things got quiet after that and the ceremony began, and his great-grandma took his hand and the two of them got a little teary-eyed together.

And when the ceremony was over, and he squeezed between his parents and they lifted him in their arms and they all kissed and hugged each other, Gianni Cabot del Vecchio Borghese figured he was absolutely the luckiest, happiest kid in Italy, in America, in the whole, wide world.

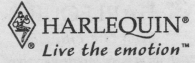

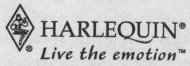

FROM *THE SICILIAN SURRENDER* BY

Sandra Marton

Quickly he scooped her into his arms. She kissed his throat as he carried her up the stairs. When he reached his bedroom, he shouldered the door open, kicked it shut behind him and took her to the bed, settling her down beside it, letting her slide down his body until her feet touched the floor.

"I don't want to hurt you. If it's too much, if you want me to stop—"

She put her hand over his mouth. "I'm not made of glass."

"I know. But—"

She kissed him, her mouth soft and warm. Then she stepped back, her eyes never leaving his, and reached behind her for the zipper that went down the back of her gown.

"Let me do that," he said in a thick voice.

She lifted her hair and turned her back to him. Slowly he drew down the zipper, kissing every inch of her spine as he uncovered it. Then he slid down the thin shoulder straps and, in a whisper of silken sibilance, the green silk floated to the floor.

He drew her back against him. She was almost naked now.

"Fallon," he said, and turned her toward him.

COOPER'S CORNER

The intimacy of
Cooper's Corner...
The high stakes of
Wall Street...

Trade
Secrets

Containing two
full-length novels
based on the bestselling
Cooper's Corner continuity!

Jill Shalvis

C.J. Carmichael

Many years ago, a group of
MBA students at Harvard made
a pact—each to become a CEO
of a Fortune 500 company
before reaching age forty.
Now their friendships,
their loves and even their
lives are at stake....

HARLEQUIN®
Live the emotion™

Visit us at www.eHarlequin.com

PHTS